BLACKFEET SEASON

By Vella Munn from Tom Doherty Associates

Daughter of the Forest

Daughter of the Mountain

The River's Daughter

Seminole Song

Spirit of the Eagle

Wind Warrior

Blackfeet Season

VELLA MUNN

BLACKFEET SEASON

FORGE®

A TOM DOHERTY ASSOCIATES BOOK
NEW YORK

BLACKFEET SEASON

Copyright © 1999 by Vella Munn

A Forge Book
Published by Tom Doherty Associates, Inc.
175 Fifth Avenue
New York, NY 10010

Forge® is a registered trademark of Tom Doherty Associates, Inc.

Library of Congress Cataloging-in-Publication Data

Munn, Vella C.
    Blackfeet season / Vella Munn. — 1st ed.
        p.   cm.
    "A Tom Doherty Associates book."
    ISBN 0-312-86734-4 (acid-free paper)
        1. Indians   of   North   America—Fiction.
2. Siksika   Indians—Wars—Fiction.   3. Crow
Indians—Wars—Fiction.   I. Title.
PS3563.U48B57   1999
813'.54—dc21   98-33241
                                        CIP

First Edition: March 1999

Printed in the United States of America

0   9   8   7   6   5   4   3   2

BLACKFEET
SEASON

Prologue

In a time hidden by the mist of years, the Blackfeet had nothing but their legs to carry them over endless prairies as they hunted buffalo, the beast vital to their existence. Stories of a spirit tribe living in the bottom of a distant lake spoke of strange, swift animals called *pono-kamita* or Elk Dogs, but although many braves went in search of the magical creatures, none of those men were ever seen again.

Then came Long Arrow. Chief Good Running had taken the orphan into his tepee and raised him as his own, but Long Arrow still believed himself an outsider. A handsome, courageous hunter, Long Arrow decided he would try to find the Elk Dogs. If he succeeded, he could rightfully take his place within the tribe. And if he failed . . .

The journey took four times four days and then another four times four days, but finally he reached a massive lake surrounded by snow-capped mountains. Awakening from an exhausted sleep, he saw a small boy standing over him. The boy told Long Arrow to follow him to the bottom of the lake, which Long Arrow did, discovering he could breathe underwater.

After Long Arrow shared a pipe with the boy's grandfather, the boy took him to the Elk Dogs and showed him how to ride. Long Arrow wanted nothing more than to take a few of the animals back with him, but he wasn't a thief and was afraid to ask for such a wondrous gift.

Several days later Long Arrow spotted the grandfather's feet, which were hooves, and despite his shock, asked about them. Pulling his black robe around him, the grandfather told Long Arrow that because he was the only outsider to have ever seen the hooves, he could have three wishes.

Long Arrow requested the old man's multicolored belt, his medicine robe, and the Elk Dogs. After promising to give Long Arrow half of his herd, the old man explained that the medicine robe would make it possible for Long Arrow to sneak up on wild Elk Dogs and the belt would allow him to hear their songs and prayers, thus allowing him to learn more about them. As a final gesture, the old man gave Long Arrow a magic rope so he could take the herd back with him.

When Long Arrow returned home astride one of the Elk Dogs, the rest following behind, the tribe hailed him as a hero, and the lives of the Blackfeet were forever changed.

1

Fall, a short span of peace before the cold and danger of winter, had touched the vast plains. The wind lived here with the Blackfeet and was a changeling, alive with energy and promise in spring, hot and drying throughout summer, sometimes an angry force driving snow and sleet across the sprawling land. Now while grasses turned brittle and sparse trees gave up their color, the breezes played with what was left of summer's heat, sometimes cherishing it, sometimes throwing it carelessly about. Mornings were cold and a threat of what was to come, but as the sun warmed the land, the wind laughed.

This moment is all there is, it seemed to say. *Today is enough.*

But those who'd lived through the winters fashioned by Creator Sun knew different.

Darkness closed in around the young Blackfoot known as Night Thunder, but although the sounds the rest of the raiding party made as they went about setting up their sleeping places called to him, he wouldn't leave his solitude until he'd given thanks to Old Man for safely bringing him and the others this far, until he'd listened to the wind and learned at least a little of its wisdom.

Before light today, he'd made a sacrifice of an arrow to Sun by tying it to the branch of a bush and praying for courage. Then he'd joined the others in the sweat lodge where Middle River, who'd just become a Sun priest, passed around his smoke pipe and prayed to the Above Ones and Earth Mother. Following that, the party of six had bathed in Beaver Creek, braided their hair and fastened their war bonnets in place, put on clean shirts, leggings, and new embroidered moccasins. Then, with bow-and-arrow cases slung over their shoulders and shields suspended from their elbows, they'd mounted their horses.

Knowing they had a great distance to cover before catching up to their enemy the thieving Snakes, they'd ridden hard all day. Conversations were easy and boastful because there was as of yet no need for caution, and a warrior who speaks boldly about his past accomplishments will continue to succeed, to go on living. Although Night Thunder was no stranger to the land they traveled, he'd let his thoughts tangle in the hills and valleys, then tried to lose those thoughts in the hazy horizon. He was untested as a warrior. How could he boast?

Kneeling in front of his horse now, he hobbled the animal's front legs, leaving enough slack so it could feed but wouldn't be able to run. Then he stood, his fingers sliding absently over Deep Scar's shoulder until he found the hairless groove that had given the animal its name. For a moment, no more than two breaths surely, resentment flooded him, but because it did no good to question his father's decisions, he turned his thoughts to prayer.

"Old Man, hear this warrior's words," he whispered into the night. "You may say I have no right to call myself a warrior because I am young and have yet to prove myself. But my heart beats strong within my chest; hear its song and believe. Strength flows through me and I know—know I am ready."

Pausing, he pressed his hand over his left breast and the knot of scar tissue that had finally stopped throbbing. "My flesh has healed but the mark remains for you to see. That is why I do not cover myself tonight, so you will see the truth of me. I stood with the others throughout the Sun Dance, stood proud and strong and unafraid throughout the ordeal because I held thoughts of you close to me."

A memory came to him like a charging buffalo; he couldn't escape it or the admission that he *had* been afraid. As had been done since the beginning of time, *O-Kan'*, the Sun Dance ceremony had taken place during the first full moon of summer. Weak from fasting and purification, he'd put on a bone bead necklace and the soft garment that hung from waist to ankles. Then, when his time came, he'd stood trembling but resolved before his father Bunch of Lodges as the older man ran a wooden skewer through his chest flesh and attached the skewer to the center lodge pole.

Pain had lashed at him, but he'd fought it by focusing on the sacred medicine bundle tied to the top of the pole, by going back in time to the four days and nights he'd spent in search of a vision, and because he would *not* fail before his father's eyes. Teeth clenched over the eagle bone whistle he'd held in his mouth, he'd fought the skewer's thongs like a speared fish until he'd broken free. His blood had stained his body and the ground around him, but unlike some of the other young man, he'd remained on his feet, hadn't fainted. When his vision had cleared, he'd looked around until he found his father, but Bunch of Lodges had done nothing to acknowledge his journey to manhood.

Somewhere in the distance a wolf howled. Tilting his head to one side, Night Thunder waited for an answering cry but there was none, causing him to wonder if it was possible for a wolf to be lonely—as lonely as he felt tonight.

"Old Man, creator of all things, I thank you for your hand in bringing me here. When we reach the Snakes tomorrow, I will carry you on my shoulder, and you will give me an eagle's sight, a wolf's intelligence, the keen hearing of an owl, a bear's invincibility."

The autumn wind caught his words and threw them at him, forcing him to hear them again. He hadn't meant to sound boastful; that would never be his way. But perhaps Old Man would listen only to the words and not the emotion behind them and punish him for his arrogance.

"Look down on me, Old Man," he continued. "See me for who I am, a youth stepping into manhood. A youth who knows his place in this world that you have made and wants only to follow your guidance. To learn from your wisdom. To—to gain the courage needed for battle."

Should he say more, perhaps try to bury his admission of fear? It seemed such a short prayer, nothing like the lengthy ceremony that had taken place before he and five others had ridden off after the Snakes, but he hadn't eaten since last night and felt lightheaded. Maybe after he'd filled his belly, he would come back out here and be capable of exploring the emotion that had added weight to his heart and stripped strength from his legs.

Maybe.

"Ha! You think she would so much as look at you? If you do, you have never seen your reflection in the water. Only a woman whose eyes have been clouded by years and cares not whether she is warmed by buffalo hide or a fat, soft belly would welcome you into her bed."

"What are you saying, Middle River? That White Calf has allowed *your* horses to mingle with her father's herd? Tell us, how many have you taken to stand before her tepee? Surely hundreds, for White Calf is worth that many."

Good-natured laughter followed Raven's Cry's question and stopped Night Thunder from reaching for the parfleche, which held the pemmican he'd brought to eat during the long, swift journey. Although they were so deep in Snake country that they couldn't take a chance on building a campfire, the silvery moon was full, making it possible for Night Thunder to make out his brother's solid form as Raven's Cry stood facing Middle River. Naked except for a loincloth, Raven's Cry made a lie out of what Middle River had said about his being fat because his brother—his half-brother—was made up of hard muscle and strong bone, nothing else.

Middle River, who was leading the raiding party because being a Sun priest gave him the right and responsibility, folded his arms over his chest and stared up at Raven's Cry, reminding Night Thunder of a dog protecting a bone he has just snatched from a cooking pot. Then, shrugging, the older warrior turned to face the others.

"Perhaps it will take all of us to steal enough horses to satisfy White Calf's father," Middle River said. "What say you? Do you think she will share herself with six men?"

"It is good that Sleeps Too Long is not with us," Raven's Cry retorted in his deep-throated way. The moon's light seemed to have centered around him, painting him in stark detail like an eagle floating in a cloudless sky. "If he was, he would call us fools for even thinking such a thing."

"True." Middle River made a show of sighing and pressing his palm against his forehead. "Who but our chief is worthy of her?"

"Chief Sleeps Too Long already has a wife," someone else pointed out. "If he is so determined to find another woman to bear living children and help prepare his feasts, let him choose a widow, not White Calf."

"Our chief is no longer married," Middle River pointed out. "Have you forgotten? And even if he was, who would bring him greater glory than White Calf? That is why I have not approached her father, but if White Calf is not taken with Sleeps Too Long's angry ways, then I will step forward."

Although the discussion about White Calf and her marriage prospects continued, Night Thunder didn't try to keep up with it. The maiden was blessed in ways he barely understood, ways which left him in awe of her. Not only was her spirit so powerful that even distant tribes had heard of her, but no other girl had a straighter back, sleeker hair, longer arms and legs, stronger hands. It did him no good to dream of taking her into his tepee—even if he'd had one. When the time for her to marry came, her father would choose a powerful war chief, not him.

But if he proved himself during this raid . . .

Three days ago Middle River had announced his intention to set out after the Snakes who had stolen several Blackfeet horses from the elderly man who'd taken them to feed a short distance from the summer village at Prairie Dog. As word of the proposed revenge-making spread, the tribe's women had set about preparing food for Middle River and his followers to take with them. If his mother had still been alive, Night Thunder told himself, she would have supplied him with more pemmican than he could comfortably carry, but she had died many years ago and he was beholden to his two aunts who had given him several handfuls of the lightweight food made from buffalo jerky, berries, and fat.

This wasn't his first journey into the land of their enemy; there was no reason for him to ask himself whether he was ready to sneak into a hostile camp and take back what had been snatched from them. Hadn't he been allowed to accompany Middle River two moons ago and help cut the ropes holding several Kalispell horses? But then one of the Kalispells had shouted a warning and the horses had run off and the Blackfeet had had nothing to show for the five-day expedition.

It was going to be different this time—it was! And when it was over, he would be invited to join the men's Pigeon society, leave behind the Little Birds with their foolish ways.

The sound of approaching footsteps pulled him out of the past and dreams of the future. Glancing up, he saw Raven's Cry coming toward him. He sensed himself begin to draw away from the larger man's looming presence but stopped himself in time.

"Why are you sitting here alone?" Raven's Cry asked. "Tell me, *Nis-Kun'*, did you bring your prayers into camp with you?"

"Does it matter?"

Night Thunder sensed more than saw his brother's frown. "You make me think of a coyote snapping at his wounded flank, *Nis-Kun'*," Raven's Cry said. "Be careful or your wound will fester."

"If it does, it is my concern, not yours," he retorted, determined not to acknowledge Raven's Cry's insistence on calling him "younger brother." "Do you not have better things to do than disturb me?"

"Disturb? We are blood; there should be no secrets between us."

"No. There should not be." *But there are.*

"All this talk about White Calf has made me weary," Raven's

Cry said as he dropped to his knees near Night Thunder. Despite the hours of watchful travel, Raven's Cry's body had lost none of its alert carriage. "A wise man does not dream of being able to fly," he continued. "Middle River may fool himself into believing he may be chosen to marry her, but I know better. So does everyone else."

Not bothering to say anything, Night Thunder bit into the last piece of pemmican he would allow himself tonight. Having his brother so near made him feel like a rabbit or prairie dog, small. If only Mother Earth had seen fit to create him in Raven's Cry's image. But no. She had fashioned him like most Blackfeet, sturdy and long legged but not from the rib of a grizzly like Raven's Cry.

"What do you think?" Raven's Cry asked. The moon remained on him, shadowing and yet warming his outline. "Does any man here have a chance of making White Calf his wife?"

You, maybe. Somebody. Instead of giving voice to his thought, Night Thunder shook his head. "Not unless we capture a hundred horses and count more coup than there are fingers on both hands. Then perhaps her father will set us one against the other and have her marry the survivor."

"And if no one lives, perhaps Grass Eater will keep the horses for himself."

"He would have to fight our father first," Night Thunder pointed out unnecessarily. "Bunch of Lodges is not a man to surrender anything he believes is his. And he will claim any horses you and I seize."

Raven's Cry grunted in that grizzly way of his. "You say that because you and our father have never walked the same path."

"Is it my doing?" Night Thunder demanded. "You think I could have done something to make him smile at me?"

"No. Nothing will change him. Nothing. He has only been harder since Red Mountain's death." After stretching out on the ground, Raven's Cry propped himself up on one elbow. "I wish I had not agreed to come on this journey," he said softly.

"What? Why not?"

Instead of immediately answering, Raven's Cry stared at the

space between them, reminding Night Thunder of the times—many times—when his brother became lost inside himself. When he was like that, Night Thunder didn't know him and in ways he would never admit, feared him.

"It is my time to lead," Raven's Cry said after a lengthy silence.

"You have had a dream? Proof that the gods walk beside you and guide your feet and those who accompany you?"

"No." Raven's Cry spat the word. "No. Not yet!"

Night cradled the Blackfeet village at Prairie Dog, isolating one tepee from another so that a stranger might think there were only one or two lodges in the *Siks-in'-o-kaks* or Black Elks clan instead of more than twenty. The location had been chosen because of its proximity to a meandering creek that drew animals from miles around and made hunting easy. But although the clan had spent the summer there, winter brought fierce winds to Prairie Dog, chasing away all but a few buffalo. Before long, the clan would take down their tepees, load them onto horses and dogs, and head south.

Tonight, however, was for playing "hands." Every brave who hadn't gone with Middle River was involved in the game, and even those who weren't playing joined in the ancient song that accompanied the wagering, teasing, and elaborate hiding of bones.

From where she stood outside the crowded tepee, White Calf listened to the men's deep voices and the high-pitched laughter of children. She tried to concentrate on the song's rhythm, to absorb the gradually increasing chant that would eventually become so loud that even a buffalo stampede might not be heard above it, but her thoughts wouldn't leave her alone.

No, not just thoughts, she admitted to herself. She was once again restless and uneasy in ways she'd never be able to explain. There'd been no danger to her people since the Snakes had snuck in and made off with the horses. No one had reported that a coyote had barked at him, a sign that something bad was going to happen. There hadn't been any geese around, wise birds who often foretold of inclimate weather. Thunder, whose great power even the smallest child feared, had long been silent.

What then was making it impossible for her to relax tonight?

Why had he exposed himself to his brother that way, Raven's Cry wondered as he struggled for the nothingness that would become sleep. The wind had quieted as they talked and prepared for tomorrow, but now it was awake again with hints of winter in its teeth. Maybe the approaching snowstorms were responsible for his mood tonight. The land around them was giving up the struggle that had begun in spring, seeming to die but merely going into hibernation. But he wasn't grass or a mouse. Like *eye-i-in-nawhw*, buffalo, he had to face the killing season with his eyes and ears and muscle. Only, he wanted more.

Had prayed for more since leaving Prairie Dog with his father's bag of sacred eagle bones and feathers tied around his neck.

Other men, even foolish ones like Middle River, were visited by the night thoughts that foretold the future. Surely it wasn't so hard to do, especially not for a man who could outwrestle an arrogant Brave Dog or Bull. He had endured not just four days and nights of fasting but six and after endless prayers had seen his spirit as a large black raven perched in a tree over him, screeching and calling until the noise had half deafened him.

He had been so proud when he returned to camp, almost as boastful as his father. Bunch of Lodges had embraced him when he'd told him about the raven, had even smiled, something that came rarely to the shaman with the grief-scarred calves.

Maybe, Raven's Cry thought, if his father didn't greet him every morning by asking about his dreams—if he'd had any, whether he remembered them clearly, whether they had meaning . . .

But Bunch of Lodges was a man with ways like stone. The shaman wanted only one thing of his second-born and first-living son, for Raven's Cry to become a mighty chief. Maybe that's why he'd approached Night Thunder tonight, because by being with someone younger, he could become a child himself.

No! Not a child! He was a man, a warrior!

Far from his father's haunting gaze and insistence that he carry the sacred war pouch he'd put together and prayed over.

His lips pressed tight against the groan no one would ever hear, Raven's Cry turned onto his back, pulled his hide blanket over his shoulders, and looked up at the sky until he could make out the stars known as the Seven Persons or Great Bear. It was time to leave the day behind and cease his tangled thoughts of the man without whom he and Night Thunder wouldn't exist.

In the age of Old Man, he knew, the Blood society camp had been led by the brave Heavy Collar who carried the bones of his dead wife with him. One spring, it was said, Heavy Collar had killed a bear but the bear returned as a ghost and, startled, Heavy Collar had thrown the bones at it. This had angered the ghost bear who chased Heavy Collar back to camp. Heavy Collar had hurried into the tepee where the others were but the ghost bear, the ghost bear . . .

The dream began as mist or perhaps the thick fog that sometimes rises from frozen earth in winter. Raven's Cry stood at the edge of the mist trying to warm himself by rubbing his arms, but his moccasins were worn through and cold seeped into his feet until his naked body ached.

As he looked around for a blanket, the mist began to fade. Surprised, he stepped forward, suddenly finding himself caught in the grip of a powerful storm-wind. Although no longer cold on his flesh, the wind made his ears and eyes and teeth ache but he couldn't fight it, could only go where it pushed him.

On and on he went, sometimes struggling to remain upright, sometimes grizzly-strong. His moccasins had repaired themselves and the robe he now wore over his shoulder was no longer brown but white.

White. Sacred.

Shivering, he dug his feet into the hard soil hoping to stop and think about what had happened, but the wind grew teeth that clamped onto him, propelling him on.

A prayer pounded through him, but it was gone before he could give voice to the words. Something fastened itself around his throat and he thought he might choke, yet he couldn't concentrate on that. Couldn't concentrate on anything except the need to continue moving.

A sound now, like a hundred distant drums.

No. Not drums but . . .

Floating, he spread his arms so the wind could more easily support him and lifted his head so he could see where he was being propelled. His weight, which could break through an iced pond, had evaporated and yet he didn't feel vulnerable or helpless. The prairie stretched around him without end and the dry grasses that fed the buffalo were so long that he might become lost in them if he fell; but he had no fear that the wind would stop carrying him— he trusted, listened, saw.

He'd become a bird, had been given the gift of flight even though he had arms and not wings and those arms were taking him closer and closer to . . .

Horses. Tens upon tens of them.

With strong legs and bright eyes.

Waiting for him.

2

The breeze nipped and snapped on the third morning the Blackfeet had been out, and Night Thunder thought about wrapping his buffalo hide coat around his shoulders, but he needed to harden himself for winter. Deep Scar responded to the wind by throwing his head as high as he could as if biting back. Smiling, Night Thunder buried his free hand in his stallion's mane.

"Soon," he crooned. "Soon you will pit your speed against that of the buffalo. Your legs are long, your chest broad. That is what matters, not how you look. And your heart beats with the strength of a wolf. Together we will bring down many buffalo and . . ."

He'd been about to brag that his arrows would find more of the beasts than any other brave, but unlike Raven's Cry, he had yet to kill his first buffalo. Still, he continued to talk to Deep Scar about the hunts that must take place before Cold Maker's grip brought prairie movement to a halt and protected the buffalo from all but the most desperate hunter. Deep Scar's ears frequently flicked back, which made Night Thunder believe the horse was curious about the upcoming expeditions that would involve all but the tribe's most infirm.

Six men—he refused to think of himself as a youth—were on the move this morning, but because it was difficult to isolate the tracks the Snakes and stolen horses made from the wandering trails left by the area's wildlife, the men had once more spread out through glistening bluestem, prairie smoke with its plumes of seeds, and cordgrass so tall it could swallow both horse and rider. As a consequence, he had no one to talk to except Deep Scar, not that he'd want to carry on a conversation with his brother. Usually Raven's Cry dominated the space around him simply by being, but this morning he hadn't said so much as a word, which made Night Thunder wonder if Raven's Cry was displeased with him. Then again, maybe his brother was silent because his spirit was speaking to him.

"Ah, you have taken the wind into you, haven't you," he observed as Deep Scar pranced. "Do you know of Wind Maker, the Under Water Person who makes the waves of White Lake roll, thus causing the wind? Perhaps not. Perhaps your soul speaks of things known only to animals."

Frowning, he straightened and looked around as he pondered the thought processes of horses. Their sudden fears, along with their tendency to tangle themselves in ropes and eat poisonous plants, put him in mind of small children. When he'd first been given a mount by his reluctant father, he'd brought his face close to Deep Scar's nostrils so they could breathe in each other's essence and now Deep Scar knew they were one, but perhaps that was all the horse understood.

There might be buffalo nearby. The prairie was deceptive that way, gently rolling ground and long grasses hiding whatever was at any distance. Because the others were intent on tracking their enemy, they might pay scant attention to what else the earth spirits chose to reveal. Perhaps Ground Man had left his below place and walked upon the earth today; a warrior who had tuned his senses to the earth might hear Ground Man's message and learn many truths.

A meadowlark sang as it flew overhead. As he turned to watch it, he caught sight of his and Deep Scar's shadows, which were their souls. His mother had still been alive when he'd first heard of *Sta-au'* the ghost of wicked people whose souls were compelled to spend eternity where they'd died instead of being accepted at Sweet Grass Hills. If an evil, unhappy *Sta-au'* was about this morning—

Ahead, Middle River stopped, lifting his arm in a signal that he wanted the others to cease movement. Although he strained to see, Night Thunder was too far behind his leader to determine what had caught his attention. Middle River, although keen of ear, didn't have the best sight and someday another brave would challenge his right to lead raiding parties, but today no one questioned what he was doing.

By alternatingly urging Deep Scar on and drawing lightly on the rope around the horse's lower jaw, Night Thunder slowly worked his way to within a few feet of Middle River. Then, balancing easily, he kneeled on Deep Scar's back and shaded his eyes, straining to make sense of his surroundings. The dawn sky had been a dull gray and although the sun had pushed aside some of that, there was no blue, nothing to serve as a line between earth and heaven. Still, something was different about the land ahead of them, not the land itself really but the air just above the grasses.

"They walk in a single line," Middle River explained although that was obvious. "See. The dust they kick up is like a thin creek, not a wide stream."

Another quick movement was all it took for Night Thunder to go from kneeling to standing, his toes digging into Deep Scar's backbone. Now that he was looking down on the dust hovering over the grass-blanketed prairie, he was able to make out the dark dots responsible for the disturbance.

"Eight," he said.

"You are sure?"

"My eyes tell me the truth, Middle River." Deep Scar hadn't so much as twitched, which made it possible for him to concentrate, not on his balance, but on what was ahead of them. *Sometimes,* he thought, *it is better not to have taken on the weight of a man or woman who has seen many winters, winters that rob the eyes of their strength.*

"Eight Snakes?" Middle River asked.

"I do not know, they are too far away. What I see are the horses.

I cannot tell how many have riders."

"Five horses were taken from us. Perhaps that means there are three Snakes, all on their own mounts."

Three of the enemy. The enemy. His throat suddenly and unexpectedly and foolishly dry, Night Thunder struggled to swallow. By the time he'd recovered the ability to speak, Middle River was telling the others that they should follow the fleeing Snakes, gradually decreasing the distance between them, but not attempting to overtake them until their enemies stopped to let the horses feed.

Deep Scar grunted but didn't move when Night Thunder dropped to a sitting position. Although his father would never acknowledge it, he had trained his disfigured horse well. "What if they see us?" he asked.

"Then we chase them." Excitement glittered in Middle River's small, deep-set eyes. "Perhaps they will be so frightened that they will let go of the horses and run."

"I hope not." Raven's Cry spoke for the first time, his voice dense and slow. "My knife is ready to do battle. I want to count coup."

The others loudly agreed and Night Thunder did the same, his words fearless. Inside, however, something he didn't want and struggled to deny simmered to cold life.

By the time the Blackfeet had gotten close enough to the fleeing Snakes that they could tell there were indeed three enemy warriors, the sun had completed most of its march across the sky. There were clouds in it now, and night would come like a leaf fluttering to the ground, silent and slow. Because he'd been on horseback before he was able to walk, Night Thunder's legs felt no discomfort and he continued to sit straight-backed. He was both hungry and thirsty, but he'd long ago learned to accept those conditions. After switching Deep Scar's rope from one hand to the other, he glanced back at his brother. Raven's Cry had been alive nearly six moons by the time he was born, and by right Raven's Cry should be riding closer to the lead, but his brother didn't seem to care. In truth,

Raven's Cry appeared unaware of where he was or what they were doing.

Not sure why he was reaching out to his brother, Night Thunder signaled confidence by clasping his fist over his chest. After a moment, Raven's Cry did the same

"What are your thoughts?" Night Thunder asked.

"Thoughts?"

"Do you doubt what we are doing? Perhaps you believe Middle River is wrong to delay attacking? If you were leading us, what would be different?"

"I do not know."

"Not know?" He nearly pointed out that long before he'd been old enough to carry a warrior's spear, Raven's Cry had painted his body black to signify success in battle and had run around camp boasting of his prowess, but although he might think such things, he knew better. "Your thoughts are elsewhere today," he said instead.

"Yes." Raven's Cry drew out the word. "They are."

"Then what—"

"There!"

Startled, Night Thunder struggled to make sense of what had happened. After a moment, his gaze settled on Quail Legs who was pointing excitedly.

"Ha! Yes. They have stopped!" Quail Legs announced. Without waiting to see what the others were going to do, the skinny brave with long, sticklike legs dug his heels into his horse's flanks. His war bonnet was nearly dislodged, and he hung onto it with one hand.

For a moment, Night Thunder stared at him. Then, because everyone else had begun galloping after Quail Legs, he did the same. Deep yells sparked around him, causing something that surely must be excitement to flow through him. Beside him, Raven's Cry bellowed like a charging grizzly. Night Thunder found it hard to breathe, told himself that the promise of battle, of counting coup, of becoming a warrior was responsible for this—this hot weakness. All too aware of what he was doing, he fingered the small medicine bundle he carried around his neck.

Quail Legs was right. As he came over a slight rise, Night Thunder saw that the Snakes were running as fast as the roped horses trailing behind them would allow. How foolish the Snakes were! Didn't they know that a man alone might escape while any burden would hold him back? But the Snakes had traveled so far and risked so much. They wouldn't easily give up their bounty.

"Catch them! Kill them!" Middle River bellowed.

"Kill!"

"Count coup!"

Whether he said anything or not, Night Thunder didn't know. He clung to his sweating, heaving mount; he reached into his leather belt and pulled out his stone knife, held it so tight that his knuckles threatened to cramp.

And he didn't allow himself to think, to acknowledge his weakness.

Quail Legs was the first to overtake the Snakes. Leaning down, the too-thin brave sliced at the rope that held two of the riderless horses together, the cut clean and efficient. Then as he attempted to straighten, Quail Legs lost his grip on his horse's belly and nearly fell off. He managed to save himself by wrapping his arms around the animal's neck, but his knife slipped to the ground.

Propelled forward like an ant in a swollen creek, Night Thunder raced past Quail Legs. A quick prayer—a plea—to the gods for giving him healthy muscles was all he had time for.

Now free of his burden, his bounty, the Snake warrior who'd been leading the horses turned to meet those who were almost upon him. He wore a heavy bear claw necklace and had painted his face black as proof that he'd counted coup many times.

The world around Night Thunder became movement and noise, lights and dark, screams and curses, but all he could see was that black face and the necklace beneath it. His heart a mad drumbeat, he tried to stop Deep Scar, but although the stallion dug his hooves into the ground and dropped his haunch, forward movement propelled them into the Snake's mount. Both horses squealed but whether from pain or surprise Night Thunder couldn't say, had no time to consider.

It wasn't supposed to be like this! A warrior plans his battles, prays in advance, makes sure all his weapons are within easy reach, studies his foe for weakness, knows—

—knows what he is doing.

Even as those thoughts raced through him, Night Thunder felt Deep Scar lose his balance. Commanding himself not to drop his knife, he catapulted away from flailing legs and deadly hoofs. By some miracle he landed on his feet. For a heartbeat, he knew and accepted that he was going to run, not toward the Snake, but away from battle.

Then—maybe because he'd been born Blackfoot and knew what a Blackfoot must do—he faced his enemy.

The midnight-painted Snake's horse was larger than Deep Scar with the result that although the animal had been knocked to one side, it hadn't fallen. The Snake, looking huge and deadly from where he perched on his mount's back, smiled, yellowing teeth standing out from their dark surroundings.

"Die," the Snake said.

No!

Gripped by something that was both fire and ice, Night Thunder struggled to keep from collapsing in a useless heap. He had become a deer, a rabbit, a creature who knows nothing except to run from danger, but his legs had forgotten how.

"Your time has come, child," the Snake taunted. "The Blackfeet are such fools that they send children to do their fighting."

"I am a man!" *A man.*

"Ha! Have you counted coup? How many buffalo died with your arrows in them?"

His knife held in front of him like a bull buffalo with a single deadly horn, the Snake jerked his horse first to the left and then the right in a dancing motion. He hadn't stopped smiling and his eyes had become so large that Night Thunder wondered if he might drown in them.

Despite himself, he gave way, his feet moving without control.

"An infant!" the Snake laughed as several of the Blackfeet took off after the Snakes who were trying to flee with the horses that hadn't been cut free. "Ha! At least your chest is scarred. Did you cry when they pierced your flesh, little one? Blubber for your mother?"

He could bury his knife in the Snake horse's chest and release the life-giving blood there. Maybe the animal would fall with his master under him. Maybe—

But a warrior doesn't kill a horse if there is any other way and he wanted, needed, to be a warrior.

"Speak!" the Snake ordered. "Or perhaps terror has stolen your tongue."

Yes. No! If he uttered a word, his voice would be high and sharp like a child's and the Snake would know the truth about him. Now his legs begged to be allowed to run, and it took every ounce of strength in him not to let them do what they needed to. He smelled his own fear, felt his bladder demand to release itself.

"I weary of this game," the Snake said. "The others have left us alone. They know it is between you and me. What shall it be? Perhaps you want me to kill you so you do not have to face your people. Ah, but why should I make it easy for you?"

"Yes!" His grin now dominated his features. "Yes! I shall count coup on you and cut off your hair and you will spend what remains of your life dressed in women's clothing, unable to marry."

Run! Run!

The Snake warrior urged his horse even closer. As he did, Night Thunder took a backward step, then yet another. His belly cramped and his arm barely had enough strength to support his knife. Although he hadn't taken his eyes off the Snake—hadn't dared—he wondered if Middle River and Quail Legs and the others, mostly his brother, were aware of what was happening.

Raven's Cry, their father's favorite since Red Mountain's death, only living son of Bunch of Lodges' sit-beside-him wife, older, already a member of the Pigeon society.

If he ran, Raven's Cry would force him into an untanned buffalo hide dress taken from the village's oldest woman, and he would have to wear it all his life.

Death was better.

A sound, both illusive and clean came to him. The faint wolf howl wrapped itself around him, entered him. Became him.

As his bladder gave way, Night Thunder gathered himself and sprang forward and up, his weight grinding into the Snake's thigh, his knife first finding only air and then—

The Snake bellowed and Night Thunder's fingers became coated with blood. He tried to clamber onto the horse's back by gripping the Snake around the waist, but the animal bucked, and he lost his desperate hold and fell back.

Landing, not on his hands and knees as he feared he might be, but on his feet, he shook his pounding head and begged his vision to clear.

The Snake, who was trying to control his horse, clamped his hand over his wounded side, but that didn't stop the dark bloody rivulet from flowing.

"Kill him!"

"Yes, kill him!"

Barely aware of the unexpected cries of encouragement, Night Thunder spread his legs and locked his knees into place to keep from collapsing. He could still see the Snake's teeth but the man was no longer smiling.

As he'd done before, he tried to form words, but his throat still felt as if a giant had clamped its hand around it. He prayed no one knew the reason behind his silence.

"Take him, Night Thunder!"

Kill. Kill?

His knife could split flesh; the blood on his fingers was proof of that. He was capable of movement; surely he was. Without taking any more time to test his ability to speak, he reached out, thinking to make the animal and thus its rider his prisoner. His fingertips touched the buffalo-hair rope, and then it was gone.

The enemy was forcing his horse to wheel around; in a moment he would be galloping away.

But not before—

Springing forward, Night Thunder slapped the Snake's ankle.

White Calf's fingers froze in midmovement. She'd been helping her mother stretch a buffalo hide and listening to her mother's chatter about her first grandchild's attempts at walking, but suddenly she could no longer hear.

Knowing her mother would understand and wait her out, White Calf "left" the hard ground she'd been kneeling on and let her spirit rise and begin to float. She didn't know what she was looking for, couldn't guess what she might find and yet the journey was vital.

A sound.

Yes, a sound.

Like . . .

A wolf howled.

"You have counted coup," Raven's Cry said.

Night Thunder lifted his water bag to his lips and drank deeply. He still felt as if he might shatter into a thousand pieces like crushed ice, and he had to grip the bag with both hands to keep it from trembling, but at least his voice had come back to him.

"I did," he said, struggling to keep awe and disbelief to himself.

"Our father will be proud."

He started to agree, but he had forgotten how that path was walked. Or maybe the truth was, he couldn't bring himself to talk about what he'd done and experienced, emotions not understood, or maybe understood too well.

"What I do does not matter to him," he told Raven's Cry. At least it was night and his eyes safe from probing gazes. "His questions will be to you; you know that. Did *you* count coup? Was it *you* who found the horses and brought them back into our possession?"

It hadn't taken long to retrieve the string of horses and because that was more important than trying to overtake the fleeing Snakes, no one had done more than brag about what they would have done to their outnumbered foes if they'd captured them. Taking advantage of the remaining daylight, they'd started back toward Blackfeet country. Only now that it was too dark to see where they were going had they stopped.

By then Night Thunder had been able to put much of his muscle-stripping fear behind him; at least he'd tried to convince himself that it wasn't him who had forgotten everything the clan's men had taught him about being a warrior. The others had congratulated him repeatedly since he'd been the only one to wound and count coup, their praise fueling his slowly returning self-confidence. Still, he couldn't stop asking himself why he'd been so terrified of the Snake warrior.

His brother had been the last to speak, perhaps deliberately waiting until they were alone.

"What passes between Bunch of Lodges and myself is not your concern," Raven's Cry said in a tone that aged him. "It is not my doing that our father smiles more at me."

"He barely acknowledges my existence," Night Thunder whispered. If he wasn't careful, his voice would waver. "But our horses are ours again; that should satisfy everyone, even him."

Raven's Cry sucked in the corners of his mouth, then pressed his fingers against the bridge of his nose as if trying to force something back inside him. After a moment, he turned so that he was facing the unseen wind and drank deeply of it.

"What was it like?" he asked. "To bury my knife in an enemy—I pray the time will come when my spirit allows me to do that thing."

Had he turned to his spirit? Night Thunder forced his thoughts back to that time of desperate fear and unthinking action, but although he all too clearly remembered how his urine had run down his legs, too much remained hidden in mist. Now he prayed that the mist would follow him to sleep.

"You *will* become a member of the Pigeon clan," Raven's Cry said. "Maybe even a Mosquito."

"A Mosquito? I have never been to war."

"But your bravery—"

"Do not speak to me of bravery!" he snapped, too late realizing he'd voiced something better kept to himself. Had Deep Scar or Middle River or Quail Legs been afraid? Had his brother? No, only him. "It—it will never be my way to brag."

That, as he expected, caused his brother to grunt in disbelief because being a Blackfoot brave gave one the right to proclaim loudly and frequently of his accomplishments. More than that, it was expected because sharing stories of glory showed young boys what their paths should be.

"Let others talk of what happened today," he said as he got to his feet and stepped into the night. "I do not wish to."

Despite the hunger that threatened to consume him, Raven's Cry continued to sit unmoving long after his brother had left. Bunch of Lodges would all too soon learn that Night Thunder and not he had counted coup. More than that, Night Thunder had wounded the enemy while all he'd done was watch.

It should have been him! He needed it to be him!

Muttering under his breath, he started to get to his feet but wound up settling back down because if he joined the others, they would tease him about Night Thunder's accomplishments.

His brother hadn't been biding his time until the Snake brave exposed his vulnerability to him; he was convinced of that. The way Night Thunder had backed away just before his sudden attack wasn't the way of a warrior, not that anyone would remember that. No! When the band returned to the village, all talk would be about Night Thunder's bravery, his speed, and the accuracy of his knife. He could never call him *Nis-Kun'* again.

Disgusted, Raven's Cry freed his food bag from the belt his mother had made for him and pulled out a piece of dried meat. He chewed, concentrating on what he was doing, but finally he'd eaten as much as he should tonight and again asked himself if he was ready to join the others.

No.

After feeling all around to make sure there were no large rocks hidden under the prairie grass, he stretched out on his back and stared up at the stars as he'd done last night. He was tired, his legs and shoulders a little stiff. If he succeeded in emptying his mind, perhaps he could fall asleep.

Would he dream?

Would the dream be the same as last night's?

Closing his eyes, he searched behind his lids for what remained of the images, but there was nothing. He remembered enough to be convinced that he'd seen a large, hidden herd of horses, something he'd never done before.

It was said that last winter, some of the hated Crees had lost nearly half of their herd when the animals panicked and then ran during a fierce thunderstorm. Since then, the Crees had searched and searched for their lost wealth, but they'd found nothing, probably because the horses had perished during the stampede that had taken them into the cliffs and deep gullies of the Blue Mountains.

But if there'd been truth behind his dream and the runaways were alive and out there somewhere . . .

Sleep hadn't come easily to Bunch of Lodges since his firstborn son's death, and an old woman had counseled him to think of himself as a butterfly, weightless, tossed to and fro by any breeze, not caring what happened to him.

Raven's Cry did that now by imagining himself a small, white butterfly with feelers thinner than the finest hair. This butterfly didn't need to concern itself with filling its tiny belly. Instead it endlessly played with a spring wind, first allowing Wind Maker to take him where Wind Maker pleased, then sitting on Wind Maker's back and guiding the spirit over the prairie. It mattered not at all where the butterfly went, what it saw, heard, did . . .

The dream began. As before, Raven's Cry felt himself being drawn forward by an unseen force. His surroundings were unfamiliar and

yet he sensed he'd been here before. He was alone, sometimes naked, sometimes draped in a heavy winter coat that made him look
like a plodding buffalo.

There was a cliff, not a cliff really but a sudden drop in the
landscape and below that—

He saw a mare. Instead of feeding, she had her head up and
her ears pulled forward to listen. Another horse appeared, larger,
darker. A stallion.

The stallion moved around behind the mare, reared and came
down, penetrated.

Both animals squealed. Screamed.

3

As the hawk pushed into the sky, dawn touched the dark bird with golden fingers. For a long time it tailed this way and that, reminding Raven's Cry of a small child trying to put sleep behind it by toddling from mother to cooking pot to tepee entrance and then back to its mother, but finally the distant and momentarily brilliantly colored bird's head dipped down, its wings outspread and yet not relaxed and Raven's Cry knew it had found what it needed to sustain itself.

From where he sat on a slight rise, he studied his surroundings, alert for any movement, but the great plains was covered by tall grass and had uncounted little valleys he couldn't see into. If he had the hawk's sight or the sight of his namesake, he would know whether the bird of prey had found a mouse, rabbit, or maybe a snake.

But he was only a man with a man's eyes and nose and ears.

As the hawk folded its wings against itself and began its killing dive, in his mind, Raven's Cry sensed the predator's confidence and determination and took those things into him. The hawk had no doubt of its ability to sink its talons into yielding flesh and fill its belly for all the days of its life. As if in answer to that powerful confidence, a small sound like the squeak of careless moccasins on wet grass came to him on the wind as the hawk reached the earth. He waited for the bird to rise into the air again, but it didn't, and he guessed it was feeding where it had made its kill. A hawk killed and ate, killed and ate, and never once did it question why that was so or whether its claws and beak would always be equal to the task.

Sighing, Raven's Cry turned and faced the raiding party's camp. He'd awakened when daylight was just a promise, and he'd hoped the others would remain asleep for awhile so he'd have the silence he needed for thinking, but although two warriors were still stretched out on their blankets, the others were talking and moving about, and he decided to return.

Middle River, wise in the way of tracking but not so swift of foot because his round belly slowed him, was cleaning the wax from his ears. Just the same, his ability to hear must be impaired because he spoke so loudly that the distant hawk surely heard. Night Thunder sat blanket-draped and cross-legged near Middle River, his head bobbing just a little in response to what Middle River was saying.

"It is good that you counted coup while so young," Middle River told Night Thunder in that sure way of his. "You will have many nights to think about what you did and thus learn from the act. The memories will make you wise and the next time you will show yourself to be a great warrior."

Night Thunder a great warrior? Raven's Cry tried to imagine his younger brother leading others into battle, but he remembered a fat-legged boy who'd cried when one of the camp dogs bit him and had been heartbroken when his mother died. Night Thunder had been slow to grow to the height of a man and even now was barely as tall as their father. Even when he, Night Thunder, and Red Mountain were children, it was he, Raven's Cry, who'd been the strongest because the gods had seen fit to fashion him from boulders and great handfuls of mud. Red Mountain had hated that his younger brother could pin him to the earth, but it no longer mattered because Red Mountain was dead.

Bringing last night's dream with him, Raven's Cry joined the others. Both Night Thunder and Middle River glanced at him but did nothing else to acknowledge him as was the Blackfeet way when one returned from solitary prayer. He settled himself on the ground and stared at a tiny hole from which ants occasionally left or entered. Ants, like all creatures, were sacred and shouldn't be disturbed although as a child, he'd sometimes poked a stick into their homes, not because he wished to harm them, but because he'd been curious—and still was—about how they lived.

When he'd caught him doing that or studying the movement of snakes or looking for messages in the constantly changing cloud-shapes, his father had insisted he put his mind to training for battle and war as befitted a future chief, but although he'd concentrated as the braves showed him how to string bows, track game, ride, and fight, his mind had remained on ants and clouds and he'd longed to sit at Bunch of Lodges' side and learn the shaman's prayers or how to turn certain herbs, roots, leaves, and the gifts from animals, birds, and fish into healing medicine. But it had been Red Mountain who would have walked in their father's footsteps.

"You are quiet this morning," Middle River said as he squatted and placed a twig in front of a couple of ants. "Is it because you envy Night Thunder? Perhaps you are angry at your spirit for not showing you how to count coup before your younger brother did."

"A man does not question his spirit's wisdom," he retorted. "Be careful, Middle River. If you speak thus of the spirits, perhaps River will take you into its depths and never release you."

Although the older warrior laughed, Raven's Cry noted that a worried expression had crept into his eyes. "I meant no disrespect," Middle River said. "But you have not yet congratulated your brother."

"Yes he did," Night Thunder quickly insisted. "When it was just the two of us."

Raven's Cry remembered telling his brother that their father would be proud of him, but he hadn't slapped his brother on his back or called him a man as the others had.

"Did you?" Middle River asked. The two young men who'd still been in bed got up. Although one walked to the edge of the encampment to relieve himself, the other obviously considered this conversation more important.

"What passed between my brother and myself is for our ears," Raven's Cry pointed out. "A wise man does not proclaim his every thought."

"Hm. Perhaps," Middle River muttered. "And perhaps the truth is, you wish Night Thunder had no hand so you could have been the one to slap the enemy."

Once—they'd been no more than five or six winters old—he'd held a sharp rock to Night Thunder's fat little wrist and tried to cut through his flesh, but when his brother began to cry and bleed, he'd come to his senses and still regretted what he'd done. Although a sobbing Night Thunder had threatened to tell his mother, he hadn't and Raven's Cry had never forgotten that. Since then, although there'd been times when his younger brother had tried his patience and stepped on his temper, he'd never again touched him in anger.

"I wish Night Thunder no ill," he said as he got back to his feet. For the first time since awakening, he became aware of how cold it was and regretted not having covered himself with his sleeping blanket. Only a man whose mind is too full walks about half naked when frost touches the ground. Shivering, he folded his arms across his chest. "I am weary of this childish talk. My mind seeks more important matters."

One of the ants had climbed over the twig, but the other was trying to move it. The creature was so small and yet his strength was as great as Night Thunder's courage, and Raven's Cry envied both of them. "Answers to my dream," he finished.

"You dreamed? A dream that walks you into the future?"

"Perhaps."

The brave who'd just sent a stream of urine to the ground joined them. "Sleep released me several times during the night," Long Axe said, yawning. "Once when I awoke, I heard sounds from where you lay."

"What sounds?" Raven's Cry asked.

Long Axe frowned. "Words but not ones with meaning, the

kind of muttering one makes when his thoughts are beyond his control."

That's the way it had felt, as if he'd been a discarded feather caught in an errant breeze, and yet he couldn't make himself believe that what he'd experienced had been without purpose. A moment ago he'd been certain he'd tell the others about his dream, but now he knew he wasn't ready to do that.

"Perhaps," he said. Turning away, he started, not toward his belongings, but toward his horse. His white-maned mare wasn't as tall or powerfully muscled as his brother's stallion, but New Snow's lungs were strong and her heart beat with a courage he could feel through the flesh on the inside of his thighs when he sat astride her. Not only that but her hide was unblemished, her hair sleek although she'd begun to put on her winter's coat.

"Wait," Night Thunder called out. "I too sensed your restlessness during the night. If there was meaning in what came to you—"

Feeling vulnerable, he whirled back around. "If there was," he said. "I will reveal it, but a wise man listens in solitude to his own wisdom before placing it in front of others."

Night Thunder scratched the inside of his right ankle but didn't take his gaze off his brother so he could see whether he'd been bitten by some insect. Raven's Cry had wanted to say more; he was certain of that. And yet something had silenced his brother's tongue. Raven's Cry had never been a man to brag, but he had a responsibility to share his dream visions. It was possible—the thought stopped Night Thunder's thumb in midscratch—that Raven's Cry had been given a glimpse of danger or even death. If that was so, it would make it difficult for him to speak, but sooner or later he would and when that happened . . .

This morning was the first time White Calf had worn the long-fringed elk skin dress. Yesterday as she'd sewn the last of the rattlesnake buttons and porcupine quills into the yoke, her thoughts had gone no further than how she would look with her hair caught in a braid down her back so everyone could see the triangle-within-a-triangle design she'd worked into the hide over her shoulders, but then she'd been nothing more than a girl aware of her new woman's body because the sun had been on her face and the song-birds' voices had filled her ears and made her feel alive.

There was no sun today because the clouds were stacked layer upon layer and the urgent wind that threw leaves and dirt about made it impossible for her to hear the birds, and she was no longer simply a Blackfoot.

Behind her, the village stretched out along the now nearly dry creek bed, but although White Calf might have taken comfort from the familiar tepees with their colorful and boastful designs or been disturbed by the children who were already about, she didn't turn from her study of the horizon. Because she was who she was, the others walked and whispered in awe of what went on inside her, and she would be left alone for as long as she needed.

Shivering, she drew her legs close to her body and pulled the soft elk hide down around her ankles. Then she leaned forward and ordered her mind to empty itself of everything except what had to be. From where she sat, she could see to what a child might believe was the end of the world; but she could run all day without reaching the most distant point because she was one of the People who spent their lives in search of new horizons, and she knew how vast their world really was. Today she felt lost in it, trapped by it.

Still, despite the sense of unease that clawed at her the way the wind clawed her exposed cheeks and throat, she wouldn't rush this time of contemplating Mother Earth. This great expanse had come into being when a lonely Creator Sun had spat on space dust and fashioned it into a ball of mud that became Earth. The ground all around her and what grew from that earth meant life to the Black-feet, and she began by giving thanks.

Life moved around her, a skittish dance of leaves and grasses, dust and insects. As that happened, her body became less and less until she could no longer feel her cheeks, her fingers, or strong legs. She imagined herself a tiny white butterfly flitting among flowers even smaller than itself. A butterfly knew the cycle of its life and the joy of flying and brought sleep. A new Blackfoot mother some-times fashioned a small piece of hide into the shape of a butterfly, which she tied to her infant's hair so the child would get a good night's rest. White Calf would be happy as a winged insect because she had always longed for the gift of flight and loved the sweetness of honey. Butterflies lived only a few days but that was all right because it was foolish to ask the gods how many winters anyone would be given in which to live. Yes, a butterfly in a world without hungry-beaked birds.

Shaking her head at her whimsy, she stood and started walking in the direction of the weak morning sun that struggled to show itself. She wasn't foolish enough to believe she could travel clear to Sun's resting place, but movement had always made it easier for her to think. Something waited at the edge of her consciousness these days, making it impossible for her to concentrate fully on the tribe's talk about the need for a great buffalo hunt before winter. Whatever disturbed her had something to do with the coming cold time, but she knew better than to try to force the vision. It would come, like all the visions that had come before it, when it was ready.

The Snakes, Arapaho, Assiniboine, Cree, and Crow called her people Blackfeet because the soles of her ancestors' moccasins had turned black from walking over burnt prairie grasses, but to her, those who made up her world would always be the People. She would have been content simply to be one of them, a maiden an-ticipating courtship and marriage. But something wondrous had happened to her when she was still a child and from then on she'd been different. Perhaps, she thought as she walked, the difference had begun even before she'd touched the sacred white calf, but if her thoughts and dreams had gone in ways other children's hadn't, she'd been too young to know and now couldn't remember.

Her mind wanted to drift into yesterday, and she let it because sometimes she had to make her peace with the past before the future made itself known to her. She felt gentled and quieted as she remembered the long ago day when she'd been compelled to leave her playing companions and had wandered aimlessly toward some low foothills.

The warriors had spoken of a small herd of buffalo far enough away that no one had felt compelled to overtake them while their food supply remained plentiful, but her childish mind had proclaimed the warriors lazy. Even then her legs had been strong and energy had flowed through her, demanding to be used. At least she'd thought the simple need for exercise had ruled her as she skipped farther and farther from the village. She'd traveled far enough that she'd grown thirsty when she first heard the sounds.

Those sounds returned to her this morning, as clear and deadly as they'd been on that distant day. She'd easily recognized the yips and snarls of wolves as they spoke to each other. Although her father had never taken her hunting with him and her brothers, she knew the difference between a playful barking and the urgent call to hunt. The wolves weren't after her; they had more than enough food this time of the year and no starving need to ignore their usual reluctance to approach humans. It shouldn't bother her that the creatures were hunting and yet she felt drawn, not by the possibility that she'd see a pack bring down their prey and tear it apart, but by something—something else.

Her trot became a run, and in a dim and unimportant way she believed she was running faster than she ever had. The howls became more excited, more intense, so close now that she guessed they were just over the next rise. Her heart pounding in her small chest, she hurried to the top of the hill and stood with her hand shading her eyes. At first it had been impossible to make out anything except dark movement, then she realized that a trio of wolves had circled something and were closing in on it, their teeth bared in anticipation, ears pricked forward so they could catch the sounds their soon-to-be-kill made.

In her mind she saw, no longer wolves, but her tribe's warriors as they surrounded a wounded and trapped buffalo. It was right that warriors and wolves killed, it was the way of things. As long as the killer took no more than necessary to sustain life, Mother

Earth was pleased and no one—certainly not a girl—should try to interfere. Instead, she would study the drama and learn from it. Pleased and a little awestruck because she was privy to something that usually took place far from the eyes of man, she started to crouch.

It was then that she noted what the wolves had trapped. The buffalo calf couldn't be more than a few days old, its legs still unsure under it, its mouth open as it bleated for its mother. Its head seemed too large for its body, ugly and precious at the same time. Despite its tender age, it knew its life was in danger as witness by the way it tried to back away from one wolf after another, but it was surrounded. Its death would come soon—hopefully mercifully quick—and then she would no longer have to listen to its terrified—

White. The calf was white!

She hadn't noticed its color before because it had angled itself so its body had been hidden from her behind the oversized head, but now the sun glinted off its heaving side.

White buffalo were sacred, fashioned by Creator Sun and Mother Earth and given to the People to worship and revere. She'd never seen a white buffalo and only the oldest men and women spoke of the time one had been spotted in the midst of a herd being driven to their deaths over a cliff at Blue Haze. The chief had immediately ordered the others to guide the herd away from the cliff, thus saving the sacred animal and those it lived with. Although the entire hunting party had prayed that the white buffalo would return to them, it had disappeared. In truth, some of the younger warriors questioned whether their fathers and grandfathers had actually seen it.

Trembling so violently that she could barely stand, White Calf—she'd been called Long Legged One then—had struggled to find her way from awe and disbelief to what she needed to do. If she remained where she was, the wolves would kill the newborn and maybe not even a scrap of flesh would be left as proof of its existence.

It was easier that way; how could she, a mere child, stop the wolves from doing what Mother Earth had created them to do? But the calf had come from Mother Earth's belly. Surely She would not allow this most precious of her children to be killed.

Was that why she was here? To save the sacred creature?

Screaming in an attempt to distract the wolves, White Calf charged down the hill. Startled, the wolves whirled toward her, fangs bared. Terror slammed into her at the sight but died an instant death when she heard the newborn buffalo cry out. She stopped only long enough to reach down for a handful of rocks. Although the ground under her was littered with loose gravel, her feet were sure, and she had no fear of falling. When she was close enough that she could see into the nearest wolf's yellow eyes to their milky center, she cocked her arm and heaved the rocks at it with all the strength in her girlish body. The rocks hit the wolf square in the face, the sound of stone hitting flesh and bone loud and sharp.

In a dim way she knew she didn't have the strength to throw that far or with enough force to inflict pain and yet the wolf jumped back. A small cut opened below its right eye and began to bleed.

"Please forgive me, Wolf," she prayed aloud because wolves, like all creatures, were sacred. "I do not mean to injure you, but I cannot let you kill Mother Earth's child."

The wolf shook its head and curled back its mouth so its powerful teeth were exposed from tip to gums, but she only continued to advance on it while yelling that Mother Earth would strike it dead if it ripped into the calf's soft white throat. Yipping like excited children, the wolves briefly touched each others muzzles, and she would always wonder what they'd said to each other although it didn't matter because, howling now, they loped away.

The calf could have, should have run. As far as she could tell, it hadn't been injured and it was the way of buffalo to flee. Instead, when she approached it, it lowered its head and then extended it toward her. She giggled when the soft tongue wrapped itself around her outstretched fingers and when she dropped to her knees in thanksgiving, the calf took her tangled hair into its mouth. They'd still been together, touching and being touched, when her searching father and his brother had come upon them.

White Calf's vision blurred and she could no longer make out the details of her world. She pressed her fingers against the sides of her head in an effort to push her thoughts back into the past and the start of the journey that had set her apart from all others, but this morning wouldn't leave her alone.

Sighing, she gave into what was now taking place within her mind, the journey both familiar and new—sometimes frightening. The white-coated vision that had sent her out here had come to her daily for the better part of a moon now, and she'd stopped asking herself if it meant that the white calf no one had ever seen again was sending her a message that it would soon return because whiteness meant one thing. Winter.

Uneasy, she ran her hand over her shoulder, but although she was aware of the fine detail of her handiwork, it didn't distract her from what she'd come here to accomplish. Her people depended on her to look into the future. Hadn't it been she who'd told them where to find two yearling elks last winter when food supplies had fallen short, she who knew where eagle feathers had fallen so the shaman Bunch of Lodges could use them in his ceremonies and medicine, she who could count the number of fish a stream contained, she who'd told Middle River which direction the Snakes had gone with the People's horses?

She sometimes knew without knowing how she did when a baby would be born and if it would be healthy or whether a hunter would succeed. Searching for those answers exhausted her, and she insisted that she be consulted only when knowing what the future might bring was vital. Because everyone was in awe of her, they respected her wishes.

She was grateful for that. She was also lonely.

The white blanket vision, cold and wind-sharpened came over her again, and she no longer thought about being lonely. Instead, hesitant and afraid and yet resigned, she stared into the image's depths. It swirled like a river's whirlpool, like snow during a blizzard and made her dizzy. Nothing seemed to exist beyond the pulsing waves, and she pondered whether all animals, birds, and fish had been frightened away. Maybe nothing living had ever existed in the place her mind was taking her to, but if that was true, then she was "seeing" neither earth or sky but what existed beneath her feet.

Ground Man lived within the earth and when he was angry, the world shook and sometimes the land itself cracked open and fire burst forth. No one had ever seen Ground Man so she didn't know what color he was, but the old people told of melted rocks so deeply red and orange it hurt the eyes, it seemed impossible that anything white could exist down there.

So, not buried deep in rocks and dirt, but where?

Concern once again nipped at her with sharp teeth. She was disturbed by her inability to lay her fear to rest when usually what revealed itself in her mind gave her a sense of peace even when it foretold danger because at least then she knew. This time was different, as if the future—if that's what she was looking into—had not yet chosen the direction it would walk.

Pain, unexpected and so sharp that it made her gasp, caused her to press her hands to her stomach. She'd had a hearty dinner of boiled buffalo meat last night and yet she felt as if she hadn't had anything to eat in weeks. The eye-tearing cramp spread quickly through her, making her weak and although she hated doing so, she thought about how a starving deer looked with its bones pushing against its taut flesh. The storytellers told of the time before horses came into the People's world when the braves couldn't bring down enough meat to see the tribe through winter, but she'd never known anything except reliance on swift mares and stallions and the wealth and success that came with them.

Legend said that Long Arrow was the one who had enriched her ancestors' lives by bringing horses back from the underwater land he'd gone to. She believed in the legend just as she believed that Mother Earth would never take back her gift, and yet her mind and body might be warning of a time when the People would be without food.

Was that it? Was that what she had to tell the shaman and Chief Sleeps Too Long?

No. The word or whisper or thought or whatever it was held her rooted in place. Confused, she forced herself to mentally step into the twisting and turning whiteness. Cold stripped the warmth from her nose and cheeks and numbed her fingers, but she couldn't stop. Her earthly body remained where she'd left it and yet the rest of her continued to move. A sound roared through her and something slammed into her with such force that she was nearly knocked to the ground. Eyes closed to slits, she strained to see and as one heartbeat turned into another, she slowly made sense of what was happening.

Ai'-so-yim-stan. Cold Maker was here with her. He was a man and yet not a man, white-clothed with white hair, his skin as pale as his hair. He sat upon a snow white horse with colorless eyes, his arms outstretched so she could see that he held a massive cloud in each hand. Wind Maker was there too, standing at the edge of Whisper Lake while he blew on the water and made the waves roll, thus causing the wind to gust. In summer Whisper Lake was a beautiful and peaceful place, but it could become a monster if Wind Maker so desired and today he did.

No, not today but soon. This winter. A winter of freezing storms and perhaps death.

The sun had broken through the clouds and begun to dry the dew-dampened grass by the time White Calf returned to the village. She took comfort in counting the tepees, relieved to find that there were still as many as she had both fingers and toes and that smoke spiraled up from the openings at the top.

Hoping for a few minutes in which to turn back into nothing more than a Blackfoot maiden, she slipped around the far side of the chief's tent, but before she could reach the one she shared with her parents and youngest brother, she heard her name being called.

Bunch of Lodges was walking toward her. Although nothing of importance was going to happen today, the stocky shaman had painted his cheeks with black dots and wore his two-feathered headdress with its fox tail hanging down his back. A miniature shield decorated to resemble a bear was fastened around his neck by a rawhide cord and covered the upper part of his chest. She was careful not to look down at his legs because he wasn't wearing leggings and she didn't want the scars he'd put there to remind her of the son he'd lost so few moons ago.

"I have been looking for you, White Calf," Bunch of Lodges whispered. "You have been quiet and distracted for too long; it is time for you to reveal your thoughts—to me. Do not forget, it is *I* who am shaman. *I* who knows what must be done with your gift."

He was right; he'd always been right about that. But what would she say, that she feared a winter unlike any she'd ever known, fierce and perhaps deadly? If she did, the shaman would insist on being told every detail when she still didn't know enough.

"Must I ask again?" he demanded. "You have a gift; I have never said otherwise. But although all stand in awe of what you are capable of, you are not a medicine man. It is I—I"—he slapped his chest for emphasis—"who has trained and sacrificed. *I* the others come to for healing."

You couldn't heal Red Mountain. Your firstborn son died in your arms. Shaking off the words she or anyone else would never utter, she nodded agreement.

"You had a calling and you heeded that calling," she told him. He was half a head taller than her and carried enough fat within his belly that he seemed even larger. Still, she refused to allow him to take advantage of his greater size. "What happened to me was not what I wished; it simply is."

Apparently that was what Bunch of Lodges wanted to hear because he nodded so energetically that his headdress threatened to dislodge. Settling it back in place, he took a sideways step as if to let her pass, but before she could, he captured her wrist. As his fingers first pressed and then began to caress her flesh, she fought the urge to pull free. Like all maidens, she dreamed of the day when a brave would make her his bride and she would settle her willing body under his blanket. There wasn't a man among the People who didn't want her; she knew that in the same way she knew she needed to learn more about her cold, white vision. Her father valued her as other men valued a large herd and wouldn't pass her off to the first suitor to approach him. She would go to the highest bidder in both wealth and position and that man was Bunch of Lodges.

Why then hadn't he gone to her father? True, he already had a sits-beside-him wife but she was an ugly crone and his second wife had died when their only child, Night Thunder, had been no more than seven winters old. Her father would be happy and the entire tribe would be strengthened if she lived in Bunch of Lodges' tepee, but she couldn't make herself think about spreading her legs for someone as old as her father, a man who still drank from the pool of grief and sometimes studied her as if she were a wolverine he feared might attack—

"I do not want to speak of what your spirit-eyes see after all," he said abruptly. "Instead, I ask you to look to where Raven's Cry is and tell me what you know of my son."

Bunch of Lodges had two living sons but he so seldom spoke of Night Thunder that she suspected the young man didn't exist in his heart. "You fear for *their* safety, do you?" she asked.

"Not fear," he insisted. "Raven's Cry is like a stag among fawns, but my father's heart needs to know when he will return."

She was willing to do what she could to supply him with the answer, but as long as he held onto her, she couldn't concentrate. Twisting her wrist first one way and then the other, she stared at him until he released her. Fighting the need to rub her flesh clean of his feel, she looked into his small eyes. He smelled of the fat he'd rubbed over his chest and the pipe she'd seen him and the chief smoking last night, and in his eyes she found what remained of Red Mountain. Pushing aside the memory of the dead young brave took effort but at length she found Raven's Cry.

Bunch of Lodges was right. Raven's Cry was a large brave, healthy and strong. The truth she kept deep inside her was that during those times when she imagined giving herself to a man, it had been Raven's Cry who waited for her.

Where was he today? That's what she needed to learn so Bunch of Lodges would have no more use for her.

"He—" Straining, she struggled to "see" past the mist that came before any vision revealed itself. "He and the others have retaken the horses the Snakes stole from us," she said at length.

"Ah! I knew it!"

"Now they—they are riding in the direction of the rising sun."

"What? That cannot be!"

"It is," she said slowly. "They ride with purpose, pushing their horses when the animals want to stop and eat."

"Why?"

She seldom comprehended what went on inside the minds of those her visions revealed and could only guess where they were going. What she knew and told Bunch of Lodges was that Raven's Cry rode in front. She didn't tell the father about his son's somber expression or about what tailed the men.

A wolf.

4

The Cree, like the Tetons, were scalpers. True, they considered it more honorable to kill while exposed than by ambushing their enemy, but Raven's Cry would spit on any Cree he came across. No, he would do more than spit!

Straightening, he stretched his spine and looked around. He and the five other Blackfeet were much closer to the barren, flat-topped hills he'd "seen" in his dreams than he'd realized, forcing him to ask himself how long he'd been lost in his thoughts and making him wonder what he would do if he learned that the horses of his dreams weren't wild after all but under Cree control. He didn't dare forget that their enemies had claimed this land.

Even now more than a day after he'd told the others of his visions, he only half believed they were following him, only half believed in the visions himself.

"Are you certain you wish to search for horses here?" Middle River had questioned not long ago. "Look at the ground. So little grass grows that not even deer or antelope have left their signs. It is useless earth; you must know that. Or could it be that the need for revenge which consumes your father has become yours and nothing else matters?"

The Cree had murdered and scalped his brother Red Mountain. Of course he hated them, but he'd dreamed of wild horses, hadn't he? Why couldn't Middle River accept that? Maybe, Raven's Cry admitted not for the first time, Middle River questioned his insistence that they ride deep into Cree land because he himself was filled with the same questions and his doubts had made themselves known even though he hadn't said anything.

Enough! Thoughts that bounced about like rocks kicked by careless children were impossible to contain or understand. He needed to lose himself in images of mares and stallions and the rich-growing land they'd been in, not question why those images had come to him. Not ask if he would be called a fool for the rest of his life.

"Raven's Cry, it will soon be dark. Our horses need to rest."

Irritated, he swiveled so he could look back at his brother. "I am not mindless," he retorted. "I know enough to pace our mounts."

"I did not say that. I simply wish to pull you into this moment," Night Thunder pointed out in that patient way of his that sometimes made him sound much older than his years.

"My thoughts go where they will," he replied. "It is not for you to attempt to guide them."

Just the same, he drew on New Snow's rope, stopping her. New Snow's head immediately went down as she began feeding. His fingers tightened on the rope, but he forced himself not to jerk because she wasn't defying him, simply fortifying herself. The other warriors had been walking in a wide circle around him, but although Night Thunder had done the same earlier, his brother now remained close by.

"What do you want?" he demanded. "Do you doubt the truth of what I have spread before you and the others?"

"No," Night Thunder said slowly. Instead of meeting his eyes, he scanned his surroundings, his mouth taut. "But we have never been here before, and it is possible we are near some lake, a lake that is home to underwater spirits. We must avoid those monsters. I—"

"Ha! You fear this place because you have just left our father's tepee and taken the first step into the world of warriors. You may have counted coup but that one thing does not make you a man."

Night Thunder didn't say anything and Raven's Cry was instantly sorry he'd spoken so sharply because his brother was right to remind them of danger. However, his own emotions stood behind his words and if he'd known how to express himself or been sure enough of himself, he might have revealed more, but he couldn't because . . . because . . .

Somewhere in the distance might be more horses than a single man could lead, tens upon tens of them. He felt their presence deep inside him, heard and smelled them although he'd never seen them. That was what he'd told the others and what, because he'd spoken softly and yet surely, they'd believed—at least none had said they hadn't. It had been both a simple and brave thing to point toward where winter lacked the strength to bury its teeth in the earth and tell the others that was where they would find a fine herd, and it would be foolish to stop and rest and smoke their pipes as travelers often did, but that had been before he'd had time to think and wonder and doubt, before he'd asked himself whether envy of his brother's accomplishments had been behind his claim.

He was doing it again, letting his thoughts whirl in maddening circles!

When Night Thunder grunted and pointed, he followed the line of his brother's arm. Middle River had been complaining that his horse's backbone was so sharp he couldn't ride without a blanket between him and the animal, but instead of dismounting, the warrior had continued to plod forward until he was now far enough away that dusk had begun to claim him. Someone called out to him. In response, Middle River held up his hand for silence.

Shutting out the sound of his mare's chewing, Raven's Cry concentrated. Sometimes when the wind stilled, he could hear insects as they went about their lives, but there was too much of a breeze for that today. Just the same, he heard something.

Vaulting to the ground, he sprinted to where Middle River waited. The older warrior frowned down at him, and Raven's Cry wondered if he was expected to supply the answer, but how could he when he had Blackfeet eyes and ears, not White Calf's mystical senses?

Ignoring Middle River and Night Thunder, who'd overtaken him, he imagined himself pushing past the wind to what was important. Was that a snort, a hoof slapping the ground?

It wasn't yet dark, the sunset red-hot and brilliant, by the time Raven's Cry had his answer. In a small and hidden valley beyond a flat-topped hill with rich black soil nurturing buffalo-grass, they discovered thirty-one sleek horses. The animals were nervous and alert in the way of creatures who knew better than to let their surroundings lull them but not so wild that they ran.

Horses! Unclaimed and valuable! The land exactly as it had been in his dreams! Although he strained to see if they bore the notched right ears that proclaimed them as belonging to the Crees, there wasn't enough light to determine that.

Insisting that this was his time and his discovery, he'd ordered the others to remain behind. Middle River had grumbled that as leader, it was his right to accompany Raven's Cry, if not go in his stead, but to his surprise, Night Thunder had spoken up saying that only those visited by telling dreams should walk into the truth of those dreams. Raven's Cry had been about to thank his brother when he'd seen something in Night Thunder's eyes that had silenced his tongue.

Now as blackness enveloped him and the intoxicating sounds of horses filled his ears, he thought back to what might have lurked inside his brother. He still thought of Night Thunder as a youth although his face had become more angular in recent moons and his muscles more clearly defined. A boy cares little for the future and thinks little of the past, yet Night Thunder had been caught somewhere other than today, either that or his thoughts had been ones he hadn't wanted and fighting them explained why he'd had no interest in sneaking into the unknown.

A familiar bellow distracted him. When it was repeated, he

recognized it as the sound of an aroused stallion—the sound he'd heard in his dream.

It was easier to smile now that he no longer questioned himself, and because he was alone, he allowed his grin of thanksgiving to spread as wide as his lips allowed. He *had* had a vision and that vision had become the truth!

He couldn't say how long he remained out there listening, accepting, giving thanks, but if his companions hadn't been talking among themselves when he returned, he might have never found them in the dark. He told them everything and then repeated himself twice more when they demanded details. His dream had been of horses peacefully grazing, and he had no fear that they would escape during the night. Tonight, he said, they would rest, tell the story of Long Arrow and the first Elk Dogs, and prepare their ropes; in the morning they would make the herd theirs.

"The stories are true," Quail Legs exclaimed the next morning as the raiding party stared down at the grazing horses. "True after all."

"Cree horses, all of them," another warrior laughed. "And such fine ones."

"Surely the Cree must be foolish and clumsy to allow so many to escape and then not be able to find them."

The excited but softly spoken exclamations turned Night Thunder's attention first one way and then the other, but he didn't take his eyes off the herd. Most of them were mares, at least half with foals by their sides. Two of the stallions were of mating age but the rest were yet to see their second summer. Although the question should have been how he and the others were going to successfully round up so many, he was still too much in awe of the animals' existence to concentrate on that.

"I did not believe before," he admitted. "I have told myself that the tale passed from Crow to Hidatsa to Pawnee could not be and there was no herd running wild and hidden, but it is them."

Although the others had already pointed out that except for the foals, the horses indeed had notched ears, he now did the same. "I laugh at the Cree and would count coup on all of them if they were here," he proclaimed.

"You?" Quail Legs snorted. "Do not forget, it was you who begged your brother not to venture into Cree country."

He hadn't begged, he hadn't! "My thought was that we did not dare forget that the Snakes might follow us."

"Ha! Your thought was also that your brother is not a shaman," Quail Legs insisted. "Admit it. You doubted his vision."

"So did you." He opened his mouth to say something else to silence Quail Legs but suddenly it no longer mattered. He'd caught a glimpse of Raven's Cry's profile and was struck by how much wiser his brother looked this morning, at peace for the first time since he'd told them about his dream.

"What do you want us to do?" he asked Raven's Cry. "Tell us, how do we make the horses ours?"

For a long time no one spoke and although everyone was looking at Raven's Cry, he didn't seem aware of their scrutiny. Finally though, he uncoiled the rope he'd wrapped over his shoulder and shook it out.

"The mares will not leave their children," he said. "And the stallions will not run from the mares."

It had been as simple as that, Night Thunder admitted, as the day began its journey into night. Although they'd initially roped the foals, the little ones were now free to tail after their tethered mothers because first their mothers and then the stallions and finally those who were neither adult nor child had come under Blackfeet control. The stallions had been the hardest to handle, but the braves had tied them to the two oldest mares they'd retrieved from the Snakes and the quiet mares had calmed the stallions.

Exhausted but content, he pulled off his moccasins and began massaging his feet. He and the others had been like excited children as they raced from one prize to another. Laughter had coated the air and warmed him and kept him on the move even when his arms and legs had demanded rest, but now he felt as winded as Deep

Scar looked and was glad that silence had overtaken everyone. Still, when he spotted his brother absently rubbing his mare's neck, he walked barefoot over to him.

"I am ready for it to be dark," he admitted. "Sleep will be an easy thing tonight."

Raven's Cry nodded, but his attention remained on New Snow. "It is right that the Cree horses are now ours," he said.

"I have had the same thought, but is it enough?"

"Enough?"

Had he made a mistake by broaching the subject? No matter, he had. "They killed Red Mountain, took the elk he'd slain, and left him bleeding, alone. Is his life worth no more than thirty horses?"

"That is not for us to answer. Only our father can say."

"He will." Reaching out, he wrapped his hand around New Snow's ear but the slack-lipped mare barely reacted. "He will be proud of you, will sing your praises at the feast to celebrate your success."

"Yes, he will."

"You say little. It is what you want, isn't it?"

Night Thunder half expected his brother to order him to leave him alone. Instead, Raven's Cry sighed and leaned against his mare's side. His gaze drifted to the horizon, but his eyes remained focused and Night Thunder wondered if his brother saw anything beyond what was going on inside him.

"I do not know what I want," Raven's Cry said at last.

"But—"

"I do not want visions! If they had begun when I was a boy, if my vision quest had been a simple thing and Raven spoke to me frequently, I would feel different. But I do not have our father's years of learning the ways of the spirits; neither of us do." He finished with a slight laugh.

"True," Night Thunder admitted. Now that his sweat had dried, he was beginning to chill and in a few minutes would have to go in search of his shirt. "Red Mountain was the one to walk in his footsteps."

"Maybe . . . Today I think I would rather be a horse and not care about anything except filling my belly."

"But then you would have to carry your owner wherever he ordered."

"Ah, yes, unfortunately." Raven's Cry laughed again and for a heartbeat Night Thunder believed that he and his older brother were thinking with the same mind.

"This thing—" Raven's Cry tapped his forehead. "This thing inside me which makes me different from animals is beyond my understanding."

"It is not like you to say such words," he said although he agreed. "You are always so sure."

"Sure of what my body can do, not so certain of other things."

If the dream had come to me, I would embrace it, not fear it. Even before the thought had finished itself, Night Thunder shook it away. Raven's Cry feared nothing. If Raven's Cry had been the one to battle a Snake warrior, he'd have done so with courage riding at his side. He wouldn't have felt terror—or have no understanding of what had compelled him to attack at the last moment.

Raven's Cry sighed and straightened, distracting Night Thunder. He gave New Snow a final pat before turning from her. The far-away look had left his eyes and in their place Night Thunder found the brother he'd never quite understood, or wanted.

"I will not have my words go beyond you," Raven's Cry said softly. "Do you understand? I spoke in weariness and because this journey is new to me. You will not share my doubts with anyone. Anyone."

Before Night Thunder could respond, a distant movement caught his attention. For a moment he feared it was the Cree come to reclaim their lost herd, but then he realized he was looking at a wolf. Pointing, he waited until Raven's Cry nodded.

While he stood on muscleless legs, Raven's Cry started toward the creature, then stopped. Neither aggressive nor afraid, the wolf seemed to be studying them. He looked healthy, full-grown with fur thick enough to keep him warm through the fiercest winter. He was beautiful in a way that held Night Thunder spellbound, the yellow eyes placid and intelligent, the sunset's red lights framing the creature so that it seemed part of the day's ending.

"He is not hunting," Raven's Cry whispered. "The way he—he has not come here to kill."

"I know."

"Then what . . ."

If the wolf sprang at him, Raven's Cry might not have time to draw his knife to defend himself. Night Thunder was about to warn his brother of that when he realized something that stole the breath from his lungs. None of the horses had taken note of the wolf's presence. True, the foals were large enough that they were no longer an easy kill, but their mothers should have been issuing whistling alarms. Instead the mares continued to graze or doze.

"Be careful," he hissed because he lacked the words to point out what couldn't be. "What—what are you doing?"

Instead of answering, Raven's Cry started walking again. Not once did he drop his gaze from the wolf, but his steps were sure. Fascinated, Night Thunder felt his own legs begin to move but when a rock bit into the bottom of his foot, he stopped, shocked that he'd considered exposing himself to a creature capable of tearing out his throat.

The wolf had stretched out its muzzle as if trying to capture Raven's Cry's scent. Its mouth opened, lips drawn back in warning. The sound of Raven's Cry's sucked in breath came to Night Thunder and he did the same.

The sun, red and brilliant as if it was bleeding, had changed the world from grays and brown. The wolf was beautiful, still deadly, still a creature of awe but now magnificent and Night Thunder sent out a formless prayer of thanksgiving. They were in Cree country and should have already started home, but that no longer mattered. Only the fact of the wolf's presence did.

That and the way the creature stared at his brother and him.

*   *   *

Last year the Cree maiden Little Rain had spent four days and nights in a tepee, alone except for the old woman who'd been her guardian as she passed from childhood into puberty. During that time she'd chopped wood, sewn, dressed hides, and listened at night as the old woman told her ancient Cree tales. She'd been given little to eat and when she'd grown lightheaded, she'd closed her eyes and cried while scratching her head with a pointed stick.

Her prayers for a vision had been answered on the third night when she'd "heard" soft raindrops and "felt" moisture on her upturned face. When she told the old woman that, the old woman had announced the vision to her waiting family, and on the fourth night four women who controlled spirit power had prayed for her, piled the wood she'd chopped, and then pushed it over before carrying it off. Finally Little Rain, as she was now called, had been led to her home and prayed for. A feast had followed and while her parents distributed presents among the guests, she'd eaten until her belly ached.

Today was different. Although her mother had set out enough food to feed the entire Cree village, Little Rain had no interest in eating. Instead she stood alone in her parents' tepee with the smells and possessions that went back as far as her earliest memories, as the weight of her red-and-yellow dyed calfskin wedding dress settled around her.

She should be happy. She was happy. And scared.

No, not scared. She loved Takes-Knife-at-Night and could hardly wait to leave her father and live in a place of laughter, but she'd never known any man's words and ways except her father's and it seemed strange to know that would end today. Things would happen to her tonight that would turn her into a woman, and if her prayers were answered, her husband's child would begin to grow inside her.

Along with that prayer, she'd also asked her spirit to touch Takes-Knife-at-Night with gentleness so that she would want to spend all the days of her life with him. Tomorrow her thoughts would turn to how she might pray for his safety during hunting and battle but today—

The blanket covering the door lifted and her father hobbled inside. Weasel Tail's eyes opened wide as he became accustomed to the dim light, and when his attention settled on her, she prayed that once, just this once, he would smile and tell her she looked like a bride with eagle feathers braided into her hair and a small sun painted on her cheek. Instead, his features remained grim. Perhaps grief had turned him into stone.

"He waits," Weasel Tail said. He lifted his walking stick and pointed it at her, then rested against it again. "Your husband-to-be is ready for you to join him. It is not wise to keep him waiting."

"I know. I was—I simply wanted a few moments to myself."

"Do you? Your mother said she would come for you, but if she did, the two of you would speak of women's things and I do not want that today. She has had years in which to show you the way of a wife; nothing more needs to be said. Nothing."

Her father wore fringed leggings that hid the never-healed wounds that had stolen his ability to run or even walk without pain, and he would make an effort to keep his disability to himself as long as their guests were around, but she knew, hurt for him, and wished she possessed a magic knife that would cut that pain, that bitterness out of him.

"I will not disappoint you," she told him. Laughter along with the music of excited and happy voices slipped past the tepee's hide and she pulled their guests' joyful mood into her. If only she could show her father the way to do the same. "Please, be glad for me."

"I am."

"Then show me your gladness." Nervous but determined, she stepped closer and covered the hand that gripped his stick. "Smile for me, for my husband, for your wife."

"You want me to forget what the Blackfeet did to me?" he snapped. "Ha! How little you know about the ways of a warrior."

He was no longer a warrior because a Blackfoot had stolen that from him, and although he was right and it was time for her to become a wife, she couldn't walk away from her father without trying to reach him one last time. The blanket-door had slid back in place and almost no daylight made its way down from the smoke-hole above them. As a result she spoke to a shadow-man.

"I remember a father whose greatest joy came from showing his children how to ride," she began. "I remember sitting behind you on a horse and holding onto you as we galloped and thinking there was nothing I would rather do. Please—" She increased her grip to keep him from pulling free. "This is the last time I will stand here with you like this. Do not rush its end."

He didn't speak, but she thought she heard his breath catch.

"You were a loving father. I was happy with you, at peace. I thank you for being what I needed, but I fear—I have not seen that man for a long time."

"The Blackfoot destroyed him."

"No. No he did not! Father, you killed the warrior who injured you. His scalp hangs from your lance."

"A lance I will never again carry into battle."

He was right when she would give anything for him not to be. "What do you want me to—You live. He does not. But I fear he destroyed more than what you needed to run. In his last moments of life, his spirit-knife found your heart. I do not want to walk into tomorrow believing your heart is dead."

His breathing became louder and harsher, but he hadn't cried when he'd seen his grievously wounded leg and she knew he wouldn't cry now. "I want revenge!" he hissed. "To do to the Black-feet what was done to me."

"You killed him! Please, let it be enough!"

"I cannot!" he shot back. This time when he lurched away, she didn't try to hold onto him. "Little Rain, you do not know what it is to be a warrior. A woman cannot possibly understand that without revenge there can be no pride."

But she *did* understand. Only, revenge ruled more than Cree men. Her father had ended the life of a Blackfoot warrior and that warrior's people would not allow his death to go unavenged. The dead Blackfoot had been far from his tribe when he and her father claimed possession of a just-killed elk, but that had been in the spring and since then the Blackfeet had come closer and closer until it was said that they were no more than a two days' hard ride from here. The knowledge frightened her and made it impossible for her to concentrate on the joy of becoming Takes-Knife-at-Night's wife.

"Go," Weasel Tail ordered as if he'd been reading her thoughts. "Step inside your husband's tepee. Think of nothing except pleasing him."

But that was impossible.

5

When the men who'd found Red Mountain's mutilated body brought him home to Bunch of Lodges, the shaman had carried his beloved son into his tepee, spread a ceremonial blanket over him, and ordered his family to gather in a prayerful circle. Bunch of Lodges, dressed in his buffalo horn headdress and bear cape, had burned sweet herbs, danced, sung, shaken rattles, and placed a new sacred pipe bundle on Red Mountain's unmoving chest. He'd prayed to Bear because Bear was sometimes able to heal himself and Bunch of Lodges had wanted a miracle, needed a miracle.

He'd questioned everyone about their behavior; had someone walked completely around his lodge or passed between his sacred pipe stem and the campfire or committed the unforgivable sin of unwrapping the pipe and accompanying sacred rattles, whistles, blessed sweet grass, and pine needle? No one had confessed to any of those things that would have explained why the magic he'd made to protect Red Mountain hadn't worked.

Ignoring her incessant wailing, he'd ordered his wife to paint her son's body red and cover the bloody scalping wound with woodpecker feathers. He'd sung for hours while various female relatives beat drums, dipped an eagle's feather in medicine water, bit off the tip of the feather and chewed it before spitting at the body. Despite those things and others, Red Mountain hadn't come back to life and at length, a heart-broken Bunch of Lodges had placed his son's body on a platform made of poles secured in the fork of a large tree. He visited his son's resting place daily to mourn and kept the young man's bow and arrows as well as the moccasins he'd worn on the last day of his life.

This morning, too many days after his two living sons had ridden off with Middle River, Bunch of Lodges sat outside his tepee while his wife made a stew by adding dried prickly pear cactus, rosehips, and milkweed buds to simmering chunks of buffalo meat. Like him, Dirty Knee Sits had scarred her legs at Red Mountain's death and wailed over his bones daily, but the two of them never spoke of what they'd lost. In truth, they seldom said anything to each other, and if he hadn't been hungry, he wouldn't have remained near her now.

After pointing his pipe at the sky, earth, north, south, east, and west, he lit it and inhaled *kinnikinnick,* a mixture of dried barks, herbs, and tobacco deep into his lungs. Doing so protected him from evil and evoked a spiritual blessing, but this morning he also smoked to calm himself.

"You use too much rosehip," he told his wife. "I will not be able to taste anything else."

"If you do not like it, you do not have to eat it," Dirty Knee Sits retorted without looking at him.

"Maybe I will take another wife, one who can cook."

"Do then. I do not care."

This was madness; he had no wish to argue with the old woman, particularly not over something they'd argued about so many times before. Sighing, he let his thoughts wander back to when he had taken a second wife, the maiden who'd borne him Night Thunder but had died before Night Thunder had seen his eighth winter, and without giving him another child although he'd evoked every magic at his command in attempts to fill her belly with more of his seed. Morning Willow had had skin soft as a butterfly's wing and he'd strutted like a buck in rut after being with her. Unlike his sun-shriveled, sits-beside-him wife, Morning Willow had seen lovemaking as a game and a joy, not simply a duty, but she was dead and only Dirty Knee Sits, with her heavy-handed way with rosehips, remained—Dirty Knee Sits and Night Thunder, whose birth had weakened and eventually killed Morning Willow.

Dirty Knee Sits left her cooking pot and walked over to but didn't sit down beside her husband. Instead, she planted her hands on her ample hips and loudly cleared her throat. Bunch of Lodges remembered when she had been afraid of her shaman husband, but, unfortunately, that had been long ago. Now there were times when he almost feared her.

"What have you seen?" she demanded. "What images have the spirits revealed to you? Surely after so much smoking and magic making, you know whether Raven's Cry returns with our stolen horses."

His dreams had revealed nothing, not that he was going to tell her that. "A wise man does not shout his wisdom," he retorted. "Instead he holds it safe and secure against him." His impulse was to get to his feet and walk away, but if he did, he'd have to listen to his growling stomach all day.

"I did not ask you to shout, did I?" she snapped. Then she dropped her voice, something she did only rarely. "Husband, I have no other son anymore. You could not protect him for me. My mother's heart needs to know if Raven's Cry is well. Surely you will not deprive me of that?"

"You must learn patience, woman." Why did she insist on blaming him? Surely she knew that someone else had displeased the spirits, thus harming Red Mountain. "Creator Sun does not smile at one who questions his ways."

"Are you patient?" she demanded. "I do not believe your prayers have not been for him."

No, he couldn't tell her that because nothing mattered more than feasting his eyes on Raven's Cry, and if Dirty Knee Sits knew nothing else about him, she knew that. "I made much magic before he left," he told her. "Untainted magic that will see him safely back to me."

"And to me too."

Although Bunch of Lodges had been staring at the ground, he now looked up at his wife, looked deep into her milky eyes for the answer to why he'd wanted to take her into his tepee all those years ago, back to the time when they'd had more in common than a single son. She had been a good mother to Red Mountain and Raven's Cry, but she'd resented the fact that he'd taken a second wife and resented Night Thunder from the moment of his birth, and maybe that was when they'd drawn apart.

No, it had begun earlier, in bed. Her cold ways had caused him to turn to Morning Willow and were why his manhood had hung limp and useless between his legs for so long. This loss of his prowess was her fault, hers!

"A woman should have the wisdom to let her child walk his own way so he becomes a man," he snapped. "Raven's Cry is no longer a boy; do not try to make him one."

"He is all I have!"

"I care not what beats inside your heart," he told her. "It is not for a man to know everything a woman thinks and feels."

"Ha! You know nothing about me, husband."

He should divorce her, order her out of his tepee and life. A thousand times the words had rested on his tongue, but they'd always remained buried and they would today. His decision had a little to do with his fear that she would seek revenge by loudly proclaiming that he was no longer a man but a "faint heart" and no other woman would accept his marriage offerings, a little because he feared Raven's Cry would choose her over him, a little because he didn't want to live alone in an empty tepee with no one to acknowledge his wisdom and skills once his sons had taken wives and moved to their own homes, and too much because she reminded him of a *Sta-au'*, a wicked ghost.

As for why she remained with him—a glance at her supplied the answer. What man would want the dried-up old creature? Without her position as the shaman's wife, she would have nothing.

Feeling old, he got to his feet and looked beyond Dirty Knee

Sits to the horizon. The day had come to life with a fine layer of mist draped over the earth that made him think of a placid lake, but he didn't feel placid and wouldn't until Raven's Cry had returned.

It shouldn't be like this! He should trust his magic's ability to protect Raven's Cry but how could he when Red Mountain—

"I must collect buffalo chips today," his wife said in that droning tone of hers as if the bitter things they'd just said to each other no longer existed. "My supply is low and we need more heat these mornings. I hate—"

A sharp cry quickly repeated silenced her. Eyes hopeful, she looked around. While Bunch of Lodges was still trying to make sense of what, if anything he'd spotted in the distance, she called out, "Raven's Cry! Please let it be . . ." She began lumbering toward the movement.

Unwanted fear gripped him and he felt cold, but then he told himself that there'd been joy in his wife's voice. Thus he could hurry after her and ready his arms, his body, his heart for an embrace.

Everyone was talking at once as he made his way toward those who were now gathering to welcome the approaching warriors. He strode into the group of villagers and smelled but did not truly smell the smoke and pipe tobacco clinging to their bodies, sweat, and the buffalo fat some had smeared over their hands and faces. His eyes, not as strong as they'd once been, were slow to tell him the entire story but the others supplied the answers.

"So many horses!"

"A great herd!"

"They are wealthy men now! Ah, watch, one of them will take all glory for himself and want to become a chief!"

"So many horses!"

The waiting took so long that he felt half sick from it but finally the surrounding fog gave up the last of its secrets. Six men had gone out to regain the horses the Snakes had stolen from the Blackfeet and six men had returned but the horses—the horses! On this morning, the tribe's supply had nearly doubled!

Raven's Cry and Night Thunder dismounted at the same time. One, slighter of stature with hands and feet that looked too large for the rest of him stood where he was, staring at Bunch of Lodges. The other, the fine and powerful brave with Morning Willow's beautiful eyes, hurried forward and enveloped his father. Crying a prayer of thankfulness to Old Man, Bunch of Lodges allowed himself to be lost in health and strength and life and became young again.

"You are safe! Safe!"

"Of course, Father. So, what do you think of what I have accomplished?"

"You—you are responsible for all these horses?"

"Yes."

Yes! His heart felt as if it might explode with happiness.

That night Chief Sleeps Too Long threw the feast of all feasts to celebrate the warriors' success. Everyone, from toddler to oldest man, gorged themselves on smoked buffalo, venison, antelope, and rabbit. In addition, the women had filled a large pot with the wild peas and prairie turnips they'd collected on the plains along with beans, corn, pumpkin, and squash bartered from the Pawnee. By then the story of Raven's Cry's dream and the truth of that dream had been told a hundred times. Those who'd remained in the village now also knew that first the warriors had attacked the Snakes and wrestled back their stolen mounts—and that Night Thunder had counted coup.

His father had looked long and hard at him when he'd heard that, Night Thunder remembered, and had even nodded approval, but tonight the old man's words were about Raven's Cry, always about Raven's Cry.

As was the way of children, the villager's youngsters had run about naming and renaming the new horses and climbing onto the backs of the skittish foals. Because a Blackfeet child learned to ride from the moment he was old enough to sit up, no one had tried to stop them from clamoring around the animals that had once been in Cree hands, but even the youngest children knew enough to wait until the half-wild creatures had been taught Blackfeet ways before engaging in races or skillful maneuvers.

Now it was dark and the air was cold enough that everyone had gathered around the warmth of the great fire Chief Sleeps Too Long's mother had built. Middle River had been the first to regale the assembled tribe with their adventures and then the others on the raiding party had given their own versions.

Night Thunder had spoken just before his brother, his voice strong and brave as he'd given exacting details of how he'd been attacked by the war-painted Snake brave. As he did, the children listened with their mouths slack and eyes intent, and he was aware that several maidens studied him with open interest. Unaccustomed to speaking in front of so many, he'd avoided meeting the adults' eyes, but because the others would wonder why if he didn't, he'd addressed his father several times. Bunch of Lodges had nodded solemnly and tapped his chest self-importantly but had said nothing.

"How brave you were!" a youth barely a year younger than him had exclaimed once he'd finished.

"He was indeed," Raven's Cry had agreed. "I bow before my brother's courage."

Those words of praise had flushed his cheeks and strengthened his resolve to say nothing about how frightened he'd been, but his moment in the firelight was done and then Raven's Cry had told everyone about his dreams and the journey into Cree land and his thankfulness to the gods for having gifted the Blackfeet with so many fine horses. Now Bunch of Lodges was getting to his feet.

"Tonight I feel alive again," the shaman began. "For too long I have been as one dead, but once again my heart beats like that of a young man. Raven's Cry, my son, my magic is powerful!"

Night Thunder frowned but before he could so much as form a mental question, his father went on.

"Every dawn since the death of my first son I have smoked my sacred pipe and prayed to the spirits that my wisdom, my gift that has made me medicine man would enter Raven's Cry. I told no one this because I wanted my thoughts and prayers to be clean."

He also hadn't wanted anyone to know in case he failed the way he'd failed when he tried to bring Red Mountain back to life, Night Thunder thought.

"It has happened!" Bunch of Lodges exclaimed. "My magic is once again powerful. Whatever sin led to Red Mountain's death is behind me. Mother Earth and Creator Sun have heard my prayers. Raven's Cry will walk in my footsteps. He too will be a shaman, a shaman like none other."

"How can that be?" Chief Sleeps Too Long asked, then scratched at his belly which was greatly swollen by the amount of food he'd consumed. "Raven's Cry did not grow up walking by your side so that your skills are now his. He is a warrior, not a shaman."

Uncomfortable, Night Thunder divided his attention between his father and the chief as did many others who obviously sensed that the feast was no longer simply a celebration but had taken on deeper meaning, perhaps a battle of words between the tribe's most powerful men.

"I am the shaman!" Bunch of Lodges retorted. "You are chief. Do not question my magic."

"I simply say what others are thinking. Red Mountain was to have taken your skills for his. It was he you—"

"Do not speak his name tonight," Bunch of Lodges interrupted. "Tonight I speak of my son Raven's Cry."

I am your son too, old man. Weary and yet tense, Night Thunder accepted the pipe the man to his left handed him and inhaled. Pipes were sacred, the stem symbolizing backbone, the bowl the head, the color as red as blood. He should be glad he was considered man enough to partake of the ceremonial sharing of tobacco, but what did it matter if Bunch of Lodges had words only for Raven's Cry?

The chief, his chest now thrust out nearly as far as his belly, gave a short nod. Then he belched. "As you wish, Shaman. But I ask all of you to listen to my words and take them into you. I say that a man must walk in one way from the time he takes his first steps if he is to reach the end of his journey. Raven's Cry is a warrior. As a child he played warrior games. He did not fashion sacred medicine bundles and learn prayers."

Bunch of Lodges' face darkened beneath its painted circles and stripes and firelight snaked across his features, turning him into something dark that might invade the children's dreams. "You say he simply had a dream like any other dream? Ha! You are wrong! Wrong!"

Movement out of the corner of his eye distracted Night Thunder both from the argument and the unholy thing that was happening to his father. He saw Raven's Cry get to his feet, but although everyone's attention was now on focused Raven's Cry, his brother didn't say anything. Instead, he turned his back on the group and walked into the night.

He was wise, Night Thunder thought as darkness settled around the tribe, isolating and uniting them against the wilderness. Either that or foolish beyond belief. Although all sang his praises now, Raven's Cry wasn't yet a member of the warrior societies and thus shouldn't speak out against either his chief or father. And yet he'd left a ceremony in his honor. Why?

An uncomfortable silence followed Raven's Cry's departure, the silence forcing Night Thunder to again ask why a Blackfeet shaman and a war chief were throwing angry words at each other on a night when all should be happy. His people laughed and played, sang and had ceremonies. They didn't fight among themselves because united the Blackfeet were strong, but if anger divided them, their enemies might conquer them.

"A vision." Bunch of Lodges whispered and yet with nothing except the snap and crack of the fire to attack it, his words carried. "My son had a vision. White Calf? White Calf, tell us. My son saw with his spirit and not his eyes, did he not?"

Because she'd been addressed during a ceremony, White Calf knew to stand in order to properly respond. As she rose, Night Thunder was struck by how graceful she made the simple movement. Earlier, the raiding party had joked about who would win the maiden's hand, but none of them laughed now. If he'd done more than count one coup, perhaps she would smile at him but . . .

Chief Sleeps Too Long stared unblinking at White Calf. Firelight glittered in his eyes and made Night Thunder ask himself if ghosts' eyes held that same intensity. Wondering if anyone else had noticed the hungry way the chief was looking at the maiden, he studied the assembled men. Taking in his father, he suddenly felt as if he'd been touched by lightning. Bunch of Lodges' eyes too were bathed in red but not just from the fire. His nose had flared and his lips were slightly parted.

They want her. They both want her.

Not fully believing what he'd just observed, he turned his attention to White Calf. She was dressed in a short dress that followed her body's curves and was speaking in that low-throated and soft way of hers as she explained that she hadn't yet spoken privately to Raven's Cry about what had happened inside him, and until she had she couldn't say whether he'd had a vision-dream. Surely both chief and shaman heard her words, and yet it seemed that their attention was on her, her form, her shining hair and large eyes, the way her arms rested easy at her sides, and the length of leg her dress didn't cover.

It had been no secret that Sleeps Too Long coveted White Calf. In truth, the chief would have taken her as his sits-beside-him wife while she was still a child if White Calf's father had accepted his proposal gifts of horses and robes, but although many believed the tribe would have been strengthened by the union, there had been no marriage and Sleeps Too Long had taken a woman renown for her skill in tepee making—a woman who'd recently left him. White Calf was no longer a young girl and many men, Sleeps Too Long among them, had asked her to step inside their blankets and speak of matters of the heart. Night Thunder had wondered if she might chose the chief. Tonight, for the first time, he asked himself if his father, the shaman, might be the one to win her hand.

"But you will speak to my son," Bunch of Lodges was saying to

White Calf. "And when you have, all will know that your gift lives in him as well."

"I—perhaps."

Chief Sleeps Too Long started to say something, but although it was considered rude to do so, Bunch of Lodges interrupted him. "Not perhaps, White Calf. He will tell you everything and you will know that your heart and his share the same rhythm."

"That will never be!" Chief Sleeps Too Long snapped. "You ask the impossible, Shaman."

"Do I? Ha! Look at my son's herd. Think of his courage in leading the way into the land of our enemies. It was his wisdom that made it possible for six men to bring back so many. His alone."

"If I had been there, you would be singing my praises, not his," the chief retorted.

"Yours! You who has yet to father his first child?"

"Stop it! Stop it!" Dirty Knee Sits sprang to her feet and started toward her husband. "You will anger the spirits!"

Because night shadows still claimed her, Night Thunder couldn't make out Dirty Knee Sit's expression and although everyone else was looking at her, he turned his attention to White Calf. The young woman hadn't moved except to clench her fists and was staring into the fire. The flames painted her with their richness and it seemed to him that she'd become part of the welcome heat, that if she wanted, she could float up into the smoke and leave earth behind.

He didn't love her; he wasn't sure he knew what it meant to love or be loved, but he understood why his father and the chief were fighting over her. Yes, fighting over her because as prized as the wild Cree herd was, White Calf was the greatest prize of all.

"I will not have these words thrown about," Dirty Knee Sits said once she'd planted herself in front of her husband. "I want to sing my son's praises. I will not have tonight ruined."

Several guests began muttering among themselves and more than one head nodded in agreement. Bunch of Lodges glared at his wife and his jaw clenched. He breathed deeply, then slowly extended the pipe he'd been holding, handing it to Sleeps Too Long.

"My wife speaks with wisdom," he said, reluctantly it seemed. "If we have more to say to each other, it will be done in private."

The chief stared at the pipe for so long that Night Thunder thought he might refuse it, but he finally took it and placed the end in his mouth because if he didn't smoke, no one would believe him and he would be seen as a liar.

"Hm," Sleeps Too Long said. "But when we are done, all will hear our thoughts and decide which of us speaks with the greatest wisdom."

"Not us," the shaman returned. "A new generation of men has stepped forward today. We, all of us, must prepare for them."

Night Thunder had folded back his buffalo-skin bedding and was thinking longingly of how wonderful it would feel to fall asleep, but because his father was kneeling beside the small stone alter next to the family's heating fire, he knew that would have to wait.

When Bunch of Lodges lit the pile of sweet grass and waved his hand over it, the just-released aroma of incense spread throughout the large tepee. Dirty Knee Sits sat cross-legged on the bed she'd never shared with her husband, her mouth pinched in disapproval but silent.

Raven's Cry, who hadn't said a word to their father since leaving the feast, had run his hand over the shield Red Mountain had carried on the last day of his life. It wasn't a battle shield because as an apprentice shaman, Red Mountain wouldn't have gone to war. Instead of depicting acts of bravery, it showed a buffalo standing within the sun. Neither the buffalo nor the sun had protected Red Mountain and kept him alive and Night Thunder could never look at it without questioning the why of that.

"I will speak of things now that will not be mentioned outside these walls," Bunch of Lodges began. He was still wearing his ceremonial head covering and hadn't removed his face painting. "I was unwise to say something before the chief."

"Not just the chief," Dirty Knee Sits said. "The others—"

"Silence! For once, silence! When I am done, you may say what is on your mind but not until then. Raven's Cry, my heart swells with pride when I look at you. I only wish I had been by your side when the dream came to you and you led the others to the horses. There is not one among the tribe who does not sing in praise of you."

"Father, that is not all that happened while we were gone." Raven's Cry's voice sounded as if it was trapped by the tautly stretched hide walls that made up the tepee's walls, needing freedom and yet unable to find it. "We found and attacked the thieving Snakes. Brave things were done then. My brother counted coup while I did not. There must be a feast to celebrate that deed."

Bunch of Lodges waved off the suggestion. "There is no time for foolish feasts," he said. "I have prayed often for this day, dared to dream that my grieving heart would find peace."

The conversation was going to be about Red Mountain, but why should he be surprised because everything was always about him? Resigned, Night Thunder watched as his father lifted Red Mountain's shield from where it hung on the wall and carried it to the still smoldering sacred grass. Bunch of Lodges held the shield over the smoke and chanted a prayer to Creator Sun because it was He who had fashioned the mountains.

"You are powerful, my son," Bunch of Lodges said, his gaze back on Raven's Cry. "And you will grow more powerful with each day. Tomorrow you will go with me as we seek proof of bear, raven, kit-fox, and wolf who all have great power."

Night Thunder wondered if his brother would mention that a wolf had remained in view most of the time they were returning to camp, perhaps ask his father about the meaning behind that, but Raven's Cry remained silent.

"When we have seen them," Bunch of Lodges continued. "Then I will know that what I believe is true."

"What do you believe?" Night Thunder asked, not because he cared, but he needed to determine if his father was even aware of his presence.

"What?" Bunch of Lodges blinked at him, then turned his attention back to Red Mountain's shield. "My firstborn died, not because my magic was imperfect, but because someone did not know the way to walk. I know that! My father's heart wants to punish those responsible for such carelessness, but the Blackfeet do not fight among themselves. Thus, the time has come, finally, for revenge."

"Revenge?" Raven's Cry asked.

"Find the Cree who murdered your brother! Find and kill him!"

"Hush. Quiet, my little one."

"I cannot help myself. My husband, if I do not speak of such things, my fears will remain inside me and my heart will not hear yours."

Sighing, Takes-Knife-at-Night sat up, but because his hand remained on her breast, Little Rain didn't feel a sense of loss. Tonight was their second as husband and wife and despite the soreness between her legs, she'd almost feverishly been looking forward to more lovemaking. However, this afternoon two braves had ridden into camp with news that a band of Blackfeet had found and claimed the missing Cree herd. This could not be, every Cree warrior had insisted. The horses bore *their* marks and belonged to*them*! No one had spoken of how it had been possible for the Blackfeet to find what the Cree had all but given up searching for. Instead the talk had grown and grown again about what the tribe must and would do in order to recapture the herd.

"Our braves speak with such anger," she began with darkness sheltering her words. "Their rage frightens me. We must prepare for winter, not war."

"Little Rain, your woman's heart rules you, and I love you for that." Bending down, he kissed the tip of her breast. "It is not the way of a woman to think first of battle and war, but a warrior must."

She'd been told that her entire life, but although she'd given up arguing, she would never understand why a man believed he couldn't hold his head high if he didn't risk his life and attempt to avenge every wrong.

"I know what you must do," she told him, her tone resigned. "That is why I am afraid."

"My wife," he chuckled. "I do not fear death; it is not the way of a warrior to run from the risk of dying. Would you sing my name in praise if I fled the enemy?"

"No, of course not. But our time as one has just begun. I want us to raise our children together, to hold hands and laugh through the years of our lives, not speak of a man who is no more." She wanted to tell him that the thought of waking up alone terrified her, but emotion filled her and she couldn't utter a world.

"We share the same dream," he whispered. "But I do not embrace old age when my eyes and ears and strength have failed me and I am useless. It is much better to die bravely now. Besides—" He drew out the word, teasing her with it until she blinked and focused on what she could see of the features that had become precious in the short time since he'd declared his love for her. "Surely you have not forgotten how my name was given to me."

Without releasing her, he boastfully tapped his chest. "Your husband is a man who bravely snuck into a Snake hunting camp at night and took one of their weapons as proof of my courage when others said it could not be done. Do you believe I fear the cowardly Blackfeet?"

"No, of course not," she said because it was expected of her. Besides, she didn't know what he felt down in those quiet places no one else could touch. "But my husband, my father—"

"I know. I know." Sighing, he flopped back on their new bed and stared up at the smoke hole. "Your father always fought bravely. His bow and arrows were among the finest made and the strength in his arms—I have thought of that and believe there is only one answer for what happened to him."

What had happened was that her father had snuck up on a lone Blackfoot who'd just killed an elk and in the ensuing fight, her father and the Blackfoot had attacked each other.

She didn't know how long the battle had lasted and had never asked. What mattered was that her father had finally run a knife through his enemy's chest but not before he'd taken several crippling wounds in his thigh, wounds that had pierced his own heart and left him bitter even though his vanquished foe's scalp now hung on a pole outside his tepee.

"Little Rain," Takes-Knife-at-Night whispered. "Did you hear me?"

"What?" she asked, trying to pull herself out of the past.

"Your father was wounded that day because he had not properly prepared himself for battle."

"No! He always purified himself!"

"Yes, yes, I know. But he had done so for so many years that this time his thoughts were on what was to come, not on waiting until his spirit had given its blessing. It was carelessness, only carelessness, but he must live with that for the rest of his life."

"No!" she insisted although she'd privately wondered the same thing. "My father—"

"Hush," Takes-Knife-at-Night soothed as he pulled her down on top of him. "I do not want our talk to be of that tonight."

A wise woman kept her thoughts to herself when her husband needed her at night and if he and the other warriors decided to attack the Blackfeet, he wouldn't touch her again until he'd returned from battle because lovemaking sapped a warrior's strength and left him weak for the enemy, but even as she ran her fingers through his hair and touched her tongue to his chin, tension continued to hold her in its grip.

No. Not tension. Hatred of the Blackfeet had consumed her while she'd ministered to her father's wounds and remained full and rich in part because it fed off her father's hatred. She might not speak of it again tonight, but that didn't stop her thoughts; nothing ever would.

She hated the Blackfeet!

Would hate them for all the days and nights of her life!

6

"Thunder is everywhere. He roars in the mountains, shouts far out on the prairie. He strikes the high rocks, and they fall to pieces. He hits a tree and it is broken into slivers. He smashes the people, and they die. He is bad. He hates the towering cliff, the tree, all living men. He loves to crush them to the ground. Yes! Yes! Of all, he is most powerful; he is the most strong."

Bunch of Lodges paused but although Night Thunder knew the legend of the ancient man who'd sought Raven's strength and then used that strength to free his wife from Thunder, he knew better than to let his thoughts drift. The tale of how Thunder, when defeated, had given the first medicine pipe to the ancient man might simply be Bunch of Lodges's way of entertaining his guests, but he couldn't make himself believe that because little of what his father did was without meaning.

"Everyone feared Thunder," Bunch of Lodges went on. "But if a man with a raven's feather and an arrow with an elk-horn shaft can cause Thunder to tremble, then surely the Blackfeet are strong enough to revenge Red Mountain's murder."

So this was what the tribewide gathering was about. He glanced first at Chief Sleeps Too Long who seemed more interested in smoking his pipe than what was being said and then at Raven's Cry, but his brother didn't acknowledge him. Instead, Raven's Cry stood tall and still as a mountain pine with his eyes on his father and the fire—smaller than the great one that had burned during the feast—in front of him.

"My oldest son has been truly named," Bunch of Lodges continued. He'd angled his body so it was turned away from the chief. "It was Raven who gave ancient man the courage to conquer Thunder and now Raven's Cry whose dreams have turned him into a wealthy man with a great herd of horses unlike any other. More than just wealthy. He has now proven himself worthy of avenging his brother's murder."

Bunch of Lodges had become like a dog with a buffalo rib to gnaw, and gnaw, and gnaw. Nothing except revenge mattered to the shaman these days, certainly not the fact that because his youngest son had counted coup, he had just been made a member of the Pigeon clan for men.

"I have made magic and sent prayers to the spirits and know that this thing I say is so." Bunch of Lodges touched the right side of his face, which he'd painted black to symbolize courage. "In two nights, the moon will be full. In two nights, Raven's Cry and those he chooses will strike out toward the Cree."

"No!" Middle River insisted as he scrambled to his feet. A swirl of smoke encircled the brave and made him cough. "I am leader, a Sun priest! It is I who said we must take back the horses the Snakes stole from us and first spotted the cowardly thieves, I who led Raven's Cry into Cree land. I will lead again. I!"

Despite his dyed skin, Bunch of Lodges anger was evident. Stalking toward the young warrior, he lifted his spear with its decoration of eagle feathers and a bear's ear.

"No." His voice was like a rock dropped on more rock from a great height. "My magic will protect those who go with Raven's Cry and his dreams will make it possible for him to find Red Mountain's killer and make revenge. It is *his* time, not yours."

The solidly built Middle River puffed out his chest, making Night Thunder think of a courting grouse. But Middle River had led only two raiding parties since becoming a warrior and was still unmarried. He might boast and call himself mighty, but his features and body lacked the imprint of the years, and he still had much to learn about fighting and surviving.

"Your sons are still untested, old man," he said. His blanket began to slide off his shoulders, and he yanked it back in place with an impatient gesture. "First let them learn from me and the other warriors and then—"

"Learn from you? If there is a child here, it is you. I am weary of tears and mourning and rubbing dirt into my scars so they will not fade. The time has come for Red Mountain's soul to find peace. In two nights when the moon—"

"No, please."

White Calf had stepped into the firelight without his having been aware of her. She seemed small tonight, but maybe that was only because night had so recently sheltered her. He wanted to study her, only her, but his unwilling eyes were drawn to his brother, and he realized he'd never seen that expression on Raven's Cry before. Raven's Cry seemed to be looking at something not of this world, as if he'd come over a hill and discovered a ghost doe drinking from a clear pond in land alive and rich with rain.

"I do not want to be here," White Calf said once she had everyone's attention. "I hear you speaking in anger and I want to walk away from it, but that is not possible." One hand went to her seed necklace. The other indicated the knot of women sitting nearby. "I know what is in their hearts because mine hears the same thing and I must speak for all of us."

Bunch of Lodges sucked in a loud breath and Middle River's jaw clenched but neither of them spoke.

"Winter comes," she said. "Its promise is in the morning wind and at night all reach for their blankets. "Look at our store of meat. It is not enough to feed us until spring. We must hunt, all of us, as the Blackfeet have always done. The women have sharpened their knives and hide scrapers and sewing awls, but these tools remain unused because no buffalo have been killed in too many moons."

"The warriors have always provided," Chief Sleeps Too Long

snapped from where he sat. Although he held his pipe near his mouth, he was no longer smoking. "Do not speak against us, woman."

Night Thunder couldn't suppress a gasp. It was one thing for the chief to treat his wife like a dog in the privacy of their tepee—which all knew he did—it was quite another to say that to White Calf.

Although White Calf had started at the harsh words, she now turned her attention back on the chief, and her voice was so calm that it was almost as if she hadn't heard his outburst.

"Revenge is for men. It fills their time and thoughts and I understand that, but I . . ." She paused. "I have 'seen' a great herd where the winter wind lives, a place I do not want to go. But the buffalo wait for us there—this I believe. They are fat and lazy because no warriors have disturbed them for so long that they do not remember a time of danger and the wolves take only a few, but if Blackfeet men first go in search of Cree, the snows will have arrived to shelter and hide the buffalo from us. Our children will cry from hunger. Some will die."

That, more than anything else, seemed to have made an impact on Chief Sleeps Too Long and Middle River because nothing mattered more than caring for the little ones who would become women and warriors and thus ensure the Blackfeet's future.

"Bunch of Lodges." Now she addressed the shaman. "I hear the pain and rage in your voice and I hurt for you. I understand. Because I am Blackfoot, I understand. But I beg you, from my woman's heart I beg you to put aside your hatred and grief for now and order your sons to bring down buffalo instead."

Bunch of Lodges slipped out of his moccasins and then removed the rest of his clothing before joining his sons in the sweat lodge. Usually when he painted himself, he first applied a layer of fat, but he hadn't taken time for that tonight with the result that his cheeks and nose and forehead felt tight and drawn. It didn't matter because soon sweat would cleanse him.

Although the willow-branch frame with its buffalo-skin covering was tall enough to allow him to move about freely on hands and knees, he felt trapped by it tonight. Everyone knew he and his sons were having a sweat tonight, but he didn't care what they might think or say. The only thing that mattered was that White Calf had spoken out against him earlier and he'd told her he would consult the spirits before responding to her concerns. He'd saved face by respectfully acknowledging her vision and had assured everyone that he too would seek a vision that he was certain would serve as proof that the tribe would grow fat this winter, but now he had to sit across from his sons and show them the way into his heart.

Only not all of his heart.

Raven's Cry and Night Thunder were waiting for him, their naked bodies already slick with their own moisture. Even in the dim light, they looked nothing like brothers, one of them lean with long and slender legs, the other so powerful that he sometimes wondered if the day would come when that coiled strength broke free. How he loved that power, that strength! Without acknowledging the young men, he knelt before the hot rocks and sprinkled water from an elk water bag onto the rocks. Steam immediately enveloped him, making it difficult to breathe. The only illumination came from the rocks' faint glow, and he hoped his sons would be so intent on what he had to say that they wouldn't notice how withered his manhood had become.

"The Elk Dogs are everything to the Blackfeet," he began once he'd seated himself cross-legged on the ground, one hand hiding what shamed him. "They are ours because Long Arrow had the courage to journey under the great lake to where the ancient Elk Dogs lived. Although Long Arrow was an orphan, he brought those we now call horses back to the tribe and Chief Good Running made him his son."

Raven's Cry nodded in response to the ancient tale. Bunch of Lodges thought Night Thunder did the same, not that it mattered.

"There is truth in the stories of our ancestors." He sprinkled on more water and then scooted away as the moist heat became too intense. He'd always preferred spreading his wisdom in the sweat lodge because only those who'd been invited in could hear, and in the darkness he didn't have to concern himself with what his expressions might reveal.

"It is my duty to bring yesterday's truth into today. Before tonight's meeting, I walked among the horses that now wait behind my tepee. What I saw filled my heart with pride. Pride because Raven's Cry is my son."

His sons' breathing had become more labored, and he fought to bring enough oxygen into his own lungs. "White Calf spoke eloquently of our need to prepare for winter. None will say she did not speak the truth, least of all me, but although she is blessed, hers is a woman's wisdom."

Although his sons wouldn't interrupt, he wished Raven's Cry would say something so he'd know his reaction to White Calf's warning, and to the maiden herself.

"I have not been turned from the path I walk," he continued. "I looked into the horses' eyes and saw Red Mountain's eyes. Even as I sit here with the living, I feel his presence. I hear him crying."

He waited for his words to sink in and then continued by repeating his conviction that the time had come to put the sin against Red Mountain to rest and the spirits had shown him that Raven's Cry was the one to do that. Then, driven by the energy that never failed to consume him when he spoke with a shaman's tongue, he said what only the three of them would ever hear.

"I speak of Raven's Cry, but I have two sons. Together they went out and together they returned. Both have brought me much pride."

A sharp sound that might have simply been the cracking of a red-hot rock momentarily distracted him. "No greater pride can come to this father than to have both sons ride out together to bring peace to Red Mountain's soul. This is why we are here tonight, so I can tell you that you will link your arms and hearts and do what must be done."

He felt exhausted, but if he fell silent now, the rest would fester inside him.

"And when you return, I will lead twenty head of horses to the tepee where White Calf and Grass Eater live and they will see that Raven's Cry is a fit husband for her." *Raven's Cry, not me, because he is youth and spirit while I can no longer spill my seed inside a woman.*

"What are you saying?" Raven's Cry gasped. "She will not—"

"Yes, she will!" He had long dreamed of ways of making White Calf want him for her husband, but although her father had hinted he would not be opposed to the union, pride and shame had held him back. Now, however, now! Yes, her power would flow through his son to him!

"Listen to me," he continued. "Why would she agree to marry a cruel-voiced, sharp-handed man like Chief Sleeps Too Long when she can have a handsome young husband like you?"

"I am untested. I—"

"You are not untested," he interrupted. Sweat rolled from him as if he was a horse galloping after a fleeing deer, and he felt less human, more animal for it. "You have done what has never been done before. Your dream sets you apart from and above all others. I see the way you look at her; I know your heart beats strong for her."

"It was only a foolish man's thought that made me look at her," Raven's Cry admitted. "A child does not believe he can outrun the finest stallion."

"You did more than match a stallion step for step, my son. You journeyed toward the Blue Mountains where you found and brought home a fine herd. Do not think of yourself as a child any more. Do not! You are a man, a warrior! A warrior worthy of bedding White Calf. When you have done what you must so Red Mountain can have everlasting peace, we will present the herd to her father and she will understand."

A man doesn't leave the sweat lodge until the one who invited him in so wishes, but it was all Raven's Cry could do to remain where he was. His father now called him a warrior and he wanted to believe him. Nothing mattered more! But only a few days ago he had still been learning what it meant to hunt and raid and battle. Was it possible all that had changed because of a dream?

A dream?

Sleep had been like a hawk, swift and beyond his reach, but finally Night Thunder managed to pull the blanket of nothingness close around him. Still, he remained aware of how easily the blanket might be snatched away, and when the sound came, he believed it was the first time.

Jerking upright, he stared into the night to where Raven's Cry, his father, and Dirty Knee Sits slept. Embers still glowed from the warming fire and reminded him of what his father had said during their time in the sweat lodge, but the unexpected sound was repeated before he could lay those memories around him and they evaporated.

He reached around for his moccasins and after grabbing his bow and three arrows, he slipped his sleeping robe over him, then stepped outside. A nearby camp dog whimpered and another some distance away yipped, but they and their companions remained in camp instead of walking into the darkness to seek the answer to what had awakened them and him. He'd just begun to strain to hear when the spine-tingling sound was repeated.

A wolf was nearby, not out on the prairie but in the direction the horses had been tethered. Wolves were a problem in the spring when foals were so small and unsure that they could easily be brought down, but it had been several moons since guards had been posted to stay with the herd at night. Besides, he'd only heard solitary howls and not the companionable chatter that signaled a pack. Still, if the lone wolf frightened the horses, they might stampede and injure themselves. Cursing the nervous way of horses and the inconsiderate wolf responsible for his having to stomp about in the middle of the night, he struck out. It was hardly the first time he'd protected horses from their enemy and the thought that he might be in danger barely crossed his mind because only a starving wolf was desperate enough to attack a human; yet he felt uneasy in a way that defied words.

The day had been gray and overcast, but the clouds had crept away during the night, leaving the heavens brilliant with stars and a half moon and the prairie softly alive. The stars and moon had been there since the beginning of time and would continue to send their cool light over the earth for eternity. From earliest childhood, he'd heard of how the Blackfeet would live forever with one generation nurturing the next and although it was difficult to think about what might take place once he was dead, the stars gave him a sense of peace that coexisted with his unease. He was only a speck upon the earth just as each star was a speck in the heavens, important unto themselves but mattering little in the vastness.

A whistle halfway between alarm and panic stopped his musings. At least one horse was on the verge of terror and if the others absorbed the foolish one's emotions—

Another whistle and then a bellow like that of a stallion proclaiming his rights gave new voice to the night. Although he'd been asleep a few moments ago, Night Thunder now felt as if he could walk forever, wanted to. Still, he'd long ago given up a child's foolish thoughts and knew better than to lose hold of reality. If the wolf hadn't been out there, he would have broken into a trot and then started running for the sheer joy of feeling his muscles work, the sound of his moccasins slapping on hard earth, the taste of the prairie in his mouth and nostrils, but that would have to wait.

Moonlight found the wolf and bathed it in white silver. The creature stood proud and defiant on a slight rise above the now nervously milling horses and yet it seemed to Night Thunder that the wolf took no more notice of the animals than a man might take of an insect. Rather—no! The wolf couldn't possibly have been waiting for him!

Shaking when a moment before he'd been calm, Night Thunder stopped and regarded the creature as intently as he was being regarded. A wolf had followed them home from Cree land, but that animal had been so far away that he and his brother had joked about it and then turned to other matters while this one couldn't be dismissed.

Because there was no need to tether the foals, they were free to move about and one of them, either more curious or more stupid than the others, had left the shelter of its kind and was walking in that stiff-legged way of the young toward the waiting wolf. Night Thunder could have hurried after the foal and chased it back where it belonged, but something made him wait and watch. The foal walked and stopped, walked and stopped. Occasionally it turned to look back at its mother and the others and when one of them nickered, it nickered back.

The foal had been a late birth. Smaller than most of the others with a stubby face and doelike eyes, it had just begun to grow its thick winter coat. The Blackfeet revered and valued and loved their horses and tonight with the moon and stars providing the only light, Night Thunder loved this little one. It knew no fear, and if he told it how he'd felt while fighting the Snake warrior, it wouldn't understand, but that was all right because he needed to unburden himself and not be criticized.

Shifting his weight, he stepped on the stub of a bush, which nearly punctured his moccasin. He winced and hopped to one side, which only took a second, but that was all it took for the wolf to begin slinking toward its prey.

Alarm smashed into him, and he quickly fitted an arrow into his bow and aimed it at the thick chest. Stalking had pulled the wolf's head low and placed its predator's eyes in shadow so that it seemed to have begun to sink into the earth. A snake moved with muscleless ease as if it were floating, and now the wolf was doing the same, deceptive in its deadliness. The foal issued a small squeak.

Even as he readied himself, Night Thunder imagined he was standing with his arms outstretched, the horse secured with one hand, the wolf with another while he fought to decide which would live tonight and which would die. He'd grown up around horses and knew their ways while wolves were mystery and the subject of many of the tales told around night-fires. He'd been taught not to

kill unless he had a need for a creature's gift, and he had no need
for this wolf's pelt, but if his arrow didn't find its heart, the foal's
might stop beating.

Forgive me Mother Earth. I do what I must, not what I want.

His prayer was still on his lips when he let the arrow fly. Straight
and deadly, it sped toward the wolf, and he saw it part the pale
chest fur, sensed the killing impact and yet—

Nothing.

Breathless, he clutched the bow so tightly that his fingers
screamed a silent protest, but his concentration was so fixed on the
wolf that he couldn't heed the discomfort. The horses stomped and
whinnied and back in camp a baby cried, and now it seemed as if
all of the dogs were growling. He felt wedded to the ground as if
Winter had frozen him to this spot and with his chilled blood came
a numbness of the mind. His arrow had reached its target; he knew
that in the deepest regions of him, and yet the creature's magnificent
fur remained unspoiled by blood. Instead of nipping at where the
arrow had gone in, the wolf lifted its head to the moon and howled,
the sound long and hollow.

Pain bit at him, belatedly forcing his mind from what couldn't
be and yet was. By concentrating on each small movement, he managed to relax his grip on the bow and prepare another arrow for
flight. Still not breathing, he lifted it and sighted down the arrow's
length. The muscles in his forearms, elbows, and shoulders tensed
in preparation for something he'd done countless times, and as the
stars flirted with the moon, he sent out the second deadly shaft.

This one too found the wolf's chest, and, like the first, made
no impact. Behind him, the dogs changed from baying to sharp,
loud yips and in front of him, the wolf continued to howl. That
sound, separate from all the others, sliced into him the way a plunge
in a cold creek did after a sweat bath, turned him weak, terrified him.

He whimpered, the sound like a baby's cry except lower because the years had aged his throat and lungs even though at this
moment he had no more control over his body and world then he'd

had at the moment of his birth. The whimper surrounded him, yet didn't penetrate because although he could no longer hear the wolf, the primitive howl remained inside him. He shook and shivered and his legs screamed to be allowed to run and the moon answered the stars' seductive message by spreading its warmthless light over the prairie and the wolf's fur captured some of the icy glow and became beautiful.

The wolf started toward him, deadly and magnificent, head still low with its muzzle outstretched as if determined to capture an enemy's scent. Still whimpering, Night Thunder began to back away, but if the wolf charged, he couldn't outrun it. He bent his ash wood bow around his last arrow and shot straight and true. By now the wolf was so close that he clearly saw the arrow bury itself up to the last feather in powerful muscle. This time surely he would succeed!

Without so much as acknowledging that he'd been wounded— if he had—the wolf continued its slow but certain advance, and Night Thunder screamed.

He was still screaming when the first warrior reached him. Feeling as if he was floating above both himself and the creature with the small, yellow eyes and black-tipped ears, he could only point before his legs gave out and he sank to the ground. After that, everything happened in a blur. More warriors joined the first. A few of the dogs slunk forward to stand in a restless group near the men. The horses continued their nervous dance and the curious foal cantered back to its mother and suffered her punishing nip on its rump.

He continued to point, first unable to believe that the others couldn't see the wolf, then numbed by the realization that the beast existed only for him.

It stood now, no longer moving, unblinking, an almost peaceful expression in its eyes. Its sides remained motionless and Night Thunder fought to convince himself that its fur hid its lungs' working.

Finally his father stalked up to him and demanded an explanation. As he struggled for words, the wolf became less and less distinct, a weightless form folding itself into the fog when there was no fog. At length the beast no longer existed.

"You saw a wolf and were so frightened by it that you bellowed like a small child?" Bunch of Lodges insisted. His long, gray hair jutted this way and that like a wind-tossed bird's nest.

"I didn't mean—I didn't mean to make a sound."

"All heard you." Bunch of Lodges indicated the disgruntled braves and near-naked children who stood around them. "A cry like that can mean only one thing, great danger. We all ran to your side but where is the danger? Where is this wolf you babbled about?"

"Gone," he whispered.

"Gone? You frightened him off?" Sarcasm tinged every word.

"No," he insisted even though he should remain silent. "I shot him three times."

"Ha! Where is his body, Night Thunder?"

"My arrows penetrated and yet they did not."

"You missed," his father insisted. "You say the wolf came so close that you could see into its eyes and yet your arrows did not draw blood? This from someone who has just counted coup? Perhaps you did not strike the Snake warrior after all."

"No! I—"

"Silence! I see before me a coward. Not a warrior but a coward."

It was then he realized that White Calf had come with the men but was standing apart from them, her expression somber.

When he'd gone out alone to seek his spirit, Night Thunder had given more thought to how much his empty belly would pain him during his time alone than whether his prayers would be answered, but he shouldn't have because Thunder had come to him before he'd weakened. This morning, as he stood alone on the spot where he'd last seen the wolf, he forced his thoughts backward to his time of leaving childhood behind. It had been summer, the grasses dark with tiny insects, as he'd walked and prayed and sang. His daylight prayers for a vision had gone unanswered but then he'd fallen asleep near an old buffalo trail and had no longer felt the insects crawling over him. There'd been nothing, no dream, no awareness of any kind up until the moment Thunder beat upon his drums and he'd found himself sitting upright staring into blackness.

Again and again Thunder pounded his great drums, and lightning had slashed at the heavens, but it hadn't rained and he'd taken that as proof that Thunder had come to him. When he returned home and explained what had happened, Bunch of Lodges had nodded agreement. Chief Sleeps Too Long had questioned his quest's success because everyone had heard the thunder, but Bunch of Lodges had insisted there would have been no sounds if Night Thunder hadn't been on his quest, and because no one dared question the shaman it was so.

In his heart, Night Thunder had sometimes wondered if Sleeps Too Long had been right, but he no longer did because he *had* seen a wolf last night, not an earthly wolf but a ghost Wolf.

The creature had been there, he repeated endlessly to himself as he paced along the path his memory told him the Wolf had taken. He knew how to track and his eyes were keen enough that even without bending over, he could tell whether a single grass blade had been crushed. There was no sign that even a small bird had recently passed this way.

"Thunder," he whispered. "My spirit, hear my plea and gift me with your answer. This thing that happened in the night cannot be and yet it was. My brother spoke of his dream and when we followed it, it led us to a great herd. Such a thing has never happened to him, yet he accepts it without question. I want to understand why I saw a wolf when no one else did, but I lack the wisdom. Please, I need your guidance. Your wisdom."

He waited with his hands rigid at his side and his eyes closed to slits against the morning's sharp breeze but heard only birds and horses and behind him his people beginning their day. His father was there with his anger and embarrassment and he knew the older man wasn't done with him, but that didn't matter now. Only awakening his spirit did.

"Hear me, Thunder. I am your child, named for you. You came to me during my spirit quest and I embraced you. Surely you will reach out for me now and I will understand. Surely."

Although the wind beat itself against the grasses and sent the horses' tails and manes flying, Thunder didn't speak.

7

When Raven's Cry spotted his brother, Night Thunder was standing where they'd found him babbling about a ghost wolf last night, but although he wondered what had prompted Night Thunder to go back there when he'd acted and sounded as if that was the last place on earth he wanted to be, he didn't join him. Instead, dressed in breech-clout, leggings, and a light buckskin robe, Raven's Cry ambled away from camp.

As he passed the others, he realized that all conversation was on what Night Thunder had done and said and what the reasons for his behavior might be. Twice he was asked his opinion, but he'd simply shrugged and gone on his way, and because everyone looked at him in a new way these days, no one had pressed him. For all they knew, he was being visited by a spirit or dream. Even though no spirit rode on his shoulders, he was grateful for the solitude.

The land was less flat out this way than where the tepees had been erected, and although he knew everything about the earth beneath his feet, at first he filled his mind with idle thoughts about what he might find over the next rise or under the nearest clump of grass; but except for startling a covey of quail and causing a small, gray mouse to dart back into its home he didn't see anything that held his attention for more than a moment.

He would be expected to lead the warriors his father chose as they ventured back into Cree land and sought out whoever had been responsible for Red Mountain's death—he who had never done such a thing before.

"I have bided my time long enough," Bunch of Lodges had insisted last night. "I waited for my sons to become men and told myself that Red Mountain would be patient. But now I no longer have to wait. Both of you have proven yourselves."

He'd said more than that, as was his way, repeating his insistence that the long overdue revenge must be exacted and that no one except those who carried Red Mountain's blood in their own veins should do what needed to be done. Raven's Cry had no argument with his father's belief and had always known the time would come for him to arm himself and seek out the enemy, had wanted it from the moment he'd seen what the Cree had done to Red Mountain, but he'd thought he'd be given more time, that he'd be more sure of himself.

Perhaps Night Thunder was seeking his own spirit's wisdom and strength this morning and that was why he'd gone back to where he'd seen the ghost Wolf—if that's what it had been. If he was successful, he would return to the tribe and offer an explanation for his earlier actions and the explanation would be accepted and he would no longer be thought a fool.

His brother wasn't important. Whatever burdens Night Thunder carried were his own. Sucking in air, Raven's Cry tried to decide what messages might be in the world this morning. There was no doubt that summer was over. Heat no longer had a taste, a pressure, and wouldn't return for a long time. Everyone would see to it that they had new winter blanket-coats, yet how could he think about what he needed to sustain him through the bitter winter when he was being asked—pressured—to prove himself as a warrior and a man?

The hill he'd been climbing fell off sharply on the far side, and he paused as he considered whether he should attempt a direct descent or walk down at an angle. If he had this much trouble deciding how to master a hill, he was not yet ready to bury a knife in his brother's murderer. The question added yet more unwanted weight to his pounding head so he cast it off. Instead, he tested the sturdiness of what was under his feet and stared at the sky until he was certain that what he'd spotted above him was a red-tailed hawk. Pleased with himself, he half-walked, half-scrambled down the hill and listened to the sound the rocks he'd disturbed made as they tumbled to a new resting place.

Belatedly shamed because he knew how to walk silently and should have done so even though there was no danger here, he stood on tiptoe and looked around. At first nothing except prairie made an impact, but then he realized he was staring at a crouching figure on the top of the next hill. From what he could tell at this distance, it was either a child or a woman, and when he came a little closer, he saw that whoever it was wore a heavy, dark necklace that stood out in contrast from a sun-bleached dress. Then the figure stood and turned to regard him, and he knew it was White Calf. Thinking to leave her alone with whatever was on her mind, he started to back away, but she motioned him to come closer.

"I did not mean to disturb you," he said when he was certain she could hear him. "If you seek solitude, I can—"

"No, it is all right." Although she ducked her head in that shy way of maidens in the presence of a man, he could tell she was smiling. "I am weary of my own thoughts."

"You too?" he couldn't help admitting. "I thought it was only me."

"No," she whispered, chuckling with him. "My thoughts often exhaust me. It is the same with my dreams, my visions."

She spoke so easily of what was mysterious and frightening to him that his impulse to distance himself from her and her magical ways evaporated. Not sure what he could and should say to her, he told her about the hawk he'd been watching and she said she'd seen it too and he realized this was the first time they'd been alone together. Her father would disapprove of him being so forward around her before Bunch of Lodges had had time to present the marriage-offer horses to her father, but her voice was like the soft music of a morning bird, and he hadn't yet heard enough of it.

"I am glad you are here," she said. "I need to talk to you and . . ."

"Talk to me?" he prompted. Her dress was so soft that it faithfully followed the lines of her body, revealing full breasts made for suckling babies and hips that could easily bring those babies into the world, slender arms with strength in them, legs that could ran effortlessly and would one day spread and invite a man in.

She was saying something. With an effort, he forced away the heat-making thought and concentrated. Still, he remained acutely aware of his body and needs and desires he hadn't had as a child. She'd been there when Night Thunder pointed at nothing last night and babbled that he'd seen a wolf.

"I say this because there is something you must know," she told him. "If the time comes when you wish to share my words with others, that is your right, your wisdom, but I leave them with you."

"Me? But my brother saw what didn't exist."

"Not just him. I did as well."

Sometimes Creator Sun allowed Moon to share the skies with him. This was one of those mornings, and although the moon was but a faint shadow compared to the sun, both provided backdrops for White Calf. If it hadn't been so, maybe he could have simply heard her soft words, but she stood there at peace with the two heavenly bodies and her words spread over him, and he accepted them.

"Tell me," he whispered. "What did you see?"

"Wolf. Not a flesh and blood wolf but a spirit that exists in a place beyond the reach of humans and reveals itself only when it has wisdom to impart—or danger to warn of."

"Danger?"

She'd tamed her thick hair into two braids that draped over her shoulders, the ends kissing the top of her breasts. Now she ran a hand over one of the braids, lifting and then dropping it. "I know what your father wishes you to do."

"You heard him?"

"Not heard. What Bunch of Lodges says to his sons is for their ears alone, and despite what others might think, my senses are only human, but I know."

Was he truly standing here with White Calf, talking to her as if they were the closest of friends? "And this is what you want to talk to me about?"

"That and Wolf."

"Wolf?" he breathed. After giving himself a moment in which to compose his thoughts, he asked what, for now, was the greater question. "I must be told something," he said. "Did you call me out here so we could be together? I thought my feet had no direction, but if you have the power to compel me—"

"No, no," she said with a little laugh. Then she shook her head and gave him a shy smile. "How little my people understand of my gift. Raven's Cry, please believe me. I have no power to cast a spell over anyone. I cannot take someone's will from them or touch their souls. I am not a shaman. I do not—"

"My father says you were born with the knowledge of the ancient shamen, but that you refuse to share that wisdom with him."

She looked a little taken aback by that, and he was momentarily afraid of her and her unknown powers, then her gentle eyes touched him and he relaxed.

"Your father and I do not walk the same path," she said. "I have told him this and I tell it to you now. He has spent his life learning the skills of healing and magic making. I was nothing more than a foolish child playing in the grass when I found the white calf. In many ways, I am still that child because I have no control over what comes to me in my thoughts."

She touched the side of her head. "In my dreams, if they are dreams. Sometimes people have need for knowledge of the future and I try to give it to them, but I cannot always walk that way. When that happens, I must accept."

He wasn't sure what she was talking about, but it was difficult to concentrate on her words with her youth and small but strong body so close to his. For many moons now he'd been aware of how maidens' bodies spoke to his in ways he couldn't control and yet excited him. As was the way of his people, he'd been careful to remain a respectful distance from an unmarried woman and would never force an unwanted contact, but he wanted to take White Calf in his arms and explore her, do what his father had once done to his and Night Thunder's mothers.

"Raven's Cry, perhaps you do not want to hear this from me."

With a start he realized he hadn't responded to what she'd just said. "No," he assured her. "That is not it. But it is not right for us to be out here alone. Your father—"

"I know." She sighed. "My father would not approve. But he does not treat me the way other men treat their daughters because I am not like other women and my journey confuses him." Once again she laid her hand along the side of her head, unconsciously stroking it. "It is hard for him because he believes our family has been blessed by my gift and he nurtures that gift. Still, he wants me to be like others. So . . ." She glanced down at the ground, then met his eyes again. "So do I."

That was the way he felt, and he told her so without giving himself time to weigh the wisdom of his words. "My telling dream has changed me," he admitted. "I look at the new herd and I want to proclaim my powers and yet I have never had a dream like that before and I may never have one again."

"I know."

Something in her tone pulled him out of himself and he looked, really looked at her. From the moment she'd touched the white calf, she had been different from everyone else. He'd accepted that, but now he truly understood that it had not been of her making and had, in fact, left her lonely.

"Do you wish it had been otherwise?" he asked. "That you did not have the gift to look into the future?"

"Maybe. But what is, is. I cannot change that." She'd spoken slowly, dully, but now she lifted her head and her next words came faster. "Perhaps you are right and you will never have another telling dream. But if you are like me and this is the beginning for you, I want you to hear my words and learn from them."

His father's greatest wish now was that one dream would follow another and that he'd walk in a shaman's path and call White Calf his wife, but he didn't tell her that. "What words?" he asked.

"They are few. And simple." Her breasts rose and fell as she sucked in a deep breath. "So many times I fought myself and what came to me on the wind. Sometimes I prayed and fasted and went on spirit searches while I begged to be nothing except a Blackfoot girl, but those efforts changed nothing. I now know to simply accept what comes. When it comes."

"I do not understand."

She didn't seem to have heard him. "My dreams have always been the truth and sometimes—sometimes that brings me great pain," she said. "I have no control; I simply must believe."

"Pain?" he asked, even though he could feel it in her, bleeding like a wound.

"There is one dream I have told no one about. It touches me and then touches me again. I cry. I drop to my knees and sob and deny that it exists, but I know—I know I am looking into the future of our people."

He didn't want this, not with her eyes deep and anguished and her body looking as if it might shatter like thin ice, and yet he couldn't turn from her. "Tell me."

"You?" she whispered and he believed she'd been pulled so deep inside herself that she'd forgotten he was there.

"Yes," he encouraged. The prairie had been here since Creator Sun fashioned it and would always exist and this morning he was part of that, strong. Wise. "It is time for that dream to leave your heart. Give it to me."

"Leave my heart?" she asked with a small sob. "I wish it could be so."

He had been on a raid against the Snakes and had captured many fine Cree horses but those things hadn't made him a man. Standing here with her, helping her, would. "Fear trapped inside a person becomes like a wound. It festers and consumes the body. Let it out, White Calf. Release it."

Crying, she started to reach for him. Then her hand dropped to her side and he knew she needed to remain within herself until the words were done. "I see into tomorrow's tomorrow to a time when the buffalo are no more."

"That cannot be! I am sorry," he amended. "I do not mean to speak against you."

"It is all right. I too speak against myself, tell myself I am wrong. But I am not."

A playful whirlwind chased through the grasses and tossed them first one way then that like a spring creek playing with what has fallen into it. "Why are the buffalo gone?" he asked.

"Strangers, not the People, have killed them." The strength must have gone out of her because she sank to the ground and her head sagged. He joined her, sitting so close that their knees nearly touched.

"Strangers?" he prompted.

"Men with pale skins and weapons that shoot fire and kill without thought of tomorrow. When they come, everything will change. We—the Blackfeet—everything will be different. Our children and our children's children will not know what it is to live with the seasons, to follow the buffalo, to race our horses with the wind."

Hating her every word, he wanted to smash them to the ground, to tell her she lied and such a thing could not be, but ice had touched his heart. "When?" he asked.

"I do not know. I do not want to know. Our children will kill some of the early pale skins but more will come. There is no end to them, no end. They will build stout wooden tepees called forts and hide in them with their weapons—their rifles."

"Rifles?" The word tasted like bitter acorn meat.

"Long sticks that shoot fire and tear apart flesh." She sounded exhausted. "More will come in things like travois that they call wagons and the pale skins will spread over the land. They will bring creatures like buffalo only smaller which are called cattle and those cattle will eat what is meant for the buffalo."

"This cannot be. It cannot!"

She didn't react to his outburst, and he guessed she must have said the same thing to herself time and time again. "Our lands will be taken from us," she whispered. "The pale skins will force us into the land of the winter wind. Sickness—I, I cannot speak of the sickness and death."

He'd taken her hand without knowing he was going to. It felt cold, almost as cold as his heart, and he began rubbing it.

"The worst—it will be called Starvation Winter and many, so many, of our children and children's children will die that . . ."

Despite her anguish, she wasn't crying, making him wonder if her grief went beyond tears. He now remembered times when she seemed distant and everyone had left her alone and he'd wanted nothing to do with her, but if she'd been swamped by those images, how lonely and scared she must have been!

"Why are you telling me this?" he asked.

"I do not know."

"Because you believe we are alike?" he prompted. He still wanted to run from her, but she hurt and her heart bled and he couldn't leave her after all.

"Maybe. Yes. Raven's Cry, I am sorry. I should not have—"

"Hush," he whispered around his frozen and yet frantically beating heart. "Yes, you should have."

White Calf remembered almost nothing of their return to the village. Her fingertips still held the memory of when Raven's Cry took hold of them and warmed them, and she recalled that they'd walked together like old friends. Still, looking at him now, she knew he wasn't a friend but something—something more.

"Look," he said, then pointed. Following his direction, she spotted Chief Sleeps Too Long's sister's youngest child trying to sit astride one of the largest dogs. Every time the dog moved, the little one fell off but, undaunted, crawled back on again. White Calf couldn't help laughing.

"I like the sound of your laughter," Raven's Cry said. "It is much better than tears."

"Yes. It is. But—what I said earlier, do you believe me?" she had to ask.

Stopping, he looked down at her. "I cannot think about it more today. Maybe tomorrow."

That's what she'd done over the years but in the end all her running and hiding had been for nothing and she'd been forced to accept. Still, there was wisdom in his words, and she was grateful for them.

"I remember trying to ride a dog," she said as they stood, now a respectful distance from each other, yet closer than strangers. "My grandfather said that dogs were only for guarding and that before horses came to us, they pulled travois but had grown lazy and I should not waste my time with them, but he laughed and clapped when I didn't fall off, and then he hugged me and we laughed together."

"Memories of laughter are good. We should all have that."

She started to ask how he'd become so wise when she spotted Chief Sleeps Too Long coming out of the sweat lodge. After looking around, he stalked over to the child and swatted her on her small bottom, his tone sharp. When the child began to whimper, she took an involuntary step forward, but Raven's Cry stopped her.

"That is not for you to concern yourself with," he said. "Our chief's sister must speak to him."

"She will not. She is afraid of his temper." She wanted to admit to Raven's Cry that the way of men was foreign to her, and she did not understand why Sleeps Too Long had been made chief, but he would tell her about the chief's fierce courage in battle and his leading ways and she would say that a gentle, loving heart was more important and maybe what she and Raven's Cry had begun to share would be forgotten. She didn't want that.

"Our chief wants to marry you," Raven's Cry said.

His simple words were all it took for her body to turn into a tightly drawn bowstring and she began rocking back and forth in an attempt to release the tension. "I know."

"Will you accept his proposal gifts?"

"What gifts? I have seen nothing. Besides, he has a sits-beside-him wife and I do not . . ." This wasn't right. She and Raven's Cry shouldn't go on speaking to each other here where everyone could see and certainly not about who she would or wouldn't marry.

"If you did, he would make you his sits-beside-him wife."

"Yes. He would."

"And then all eyes would be on the two of you and no other man and wife would be more powerful or more respected."

She couldn't imagine ever respecting Sleeps Too Long's ways but said yes anyway.

"Then you might smile at him."

"His sits-beside-him wife fears him, and I do not want to share my—my bed with a man like that. Besides . . ."

"Besides what?" he pressured. The chief had spotted them and was glaring at them, but Raven's Cry boldly returned his gaze.

"I am different from all others. Only a man who understands that will understand me."

"Perhaps that man does not exist."

"Perhaps."

"Would you be content to live alone then?"

He'd pushed her too far, and she was both unwilling and unable to take the next step, which would reveal too much of her heart. "That is for my heart to know, only mine. It is time for you to return to your father and plan attacks and killing."

"Not just attacks and killing. We will be bringing peace to my brother's spirit."

"So you say."

He grunted. "You do not approve."

"It is not for me to speak of men's ways," she told him. Chief Sleeps Too Long was coming toward them, looking like a dog who has discovered that another has taken meat he'd intended for himself.

"But I want to hear your thoughts on this; they are important to me."

Surprised, she took her gaze off the chief and stared up at Raven's Cry. His size had long set him apart just as she walked a singular path, but that wasn't the reason she felt close to him this morning, not the only one. "Why?" she asked quickly because Sleeps Too Long would soon reach them.

"Because you speak with wisdom that goes beyond yourself."

"I do not always want that wisdom, just as I have grown weary of the never-ending hatred between us and the Cree. The killing, the fighting, will exist for all time unless someone says that is enough."

"And you want me to be that man? My father would never allow it."

"I know." Sleeps Too Long was only a few strides away; what they said to each other might not remain between them. Still, this was too important. "You will do what you must, but before you ride out after the Cree, I want you to heed last night's warning."

"What warning?" Sleeps Too Long demanded.

How she hated his sharp tongue with its hot ways, but this was her people's chief, a man who'd kept them safe from Snake, Cree, Flathead, and Crow attack and she was grateful to him for that. "The wolf," she said.

"There was no wolf," he insisted. "Either that or Night Thunder had been so frightened by the creature that his arrows missed what should have been an easy kill."

"No," she retorted. "He did not miss. The wolf was there and yet it was not."

"How can that be?" Sleeps Too Long demanded. Then his lips parted and his mouth hung slack. "A spirit wolf?" he finally asked.

"Yes." She wanted to turn to Raven's Cry because she felt free and open around him, because she knew he would listen.

"When I joined the others last night, I looked where Night Thunder was pointing. Everyone said they saw nothing, but it was different for me."

"Different?"

"Wolf left his shadow behind so I would understand."

"Understand what?" Raven's Cry asked softly.

"That sometimes wolves bring death."

8

In ancient times, it was said, four Blackfeet had gone to war against the Cree. Led by *E-kus'-kimi*, they'd traveled until they came to the Sand Hills where they spotted a fresh travois's trail. The trail led them to the sounds of a camp, but although they heard young men shouting war cries and women chopping wood, the four Blackfeet saw nothing.

Still, they crept forward. When E-kus'-kimi spotted a stone-pointed arrow lying on the ground, he picked it up because he recognized it as having belonged to his dead father. A little while later they saw a man on horseback racing after buffalo. The man stabbed one through the heart with his spear and jumped off his horse to start butchering the beast. Wondering if the man could be his father, E-kus'-kimi rode closer, but the man scrambled back onto his horse and galloped away.

The buffalo became a dead mouse and next to it rested an arrow painted red. This arrow, like the first one, had belonged to E-kus'-kimi's father and so he took that, too. Although the other Blackfeet were killed the next day during a battle with the Cree, E-kus'-kimi survived and lived for years beyond counting. The arrows, everyone understood, had been his medicine.

Sitting alone in the dark with only a wisp of smoke from the dying campfire to keep him company, Raven's Cry pondered why the tale filled his thoughts tonight. The warriors who'd accompanied him on this journey to avenge his brother's murder were all asleep, heaped together like exhausted puppies, but he'd given up seeking nothingness. Instead, he repeated the tale word for word to the end. Then, free of it, he recalled the time he'd recently spent with White Calf.

She'd reminded him and Chief Sleeps Too Long that a ghost wolf sometimes warned of death, and he believed her, but if a warrior allowed himself to be trapped by fear-making predictions, he might lose heart. Instead, he fastened his mind on the things he and White Calf had shared while they were alone. Her visions of a time when pale skins would put an end to the Blackfeet way of life turned his blood cold, and if it was within his power and he could change the future, he would have thrown her words against boulders or taken his knife and slashed them to pieces, but he couldn't. What coiled around him was the realization that she'd opened her heart to him, allowed him to see her tears, and when she had, he'd held her hand.

Like his dreams of the horses, White Calf was beyond comprehension, but if he could find a well-hidden band of horses and easily capture them and White Calf walked beside him, surely he was more than a young warrior. Maybe he was the same as E-kus'-kimi.

Yes! E-kus'-kimi had been protected in battle because of his vision and what he'd carried of his father. He, Raven's Cry, would be protected because of his dreams, and because White Calf had sought him out! They'd touched and looked into each other's eyes and spoken of things no one else knew about and thus were no longer strangers. Perhaps—perhaps the day would come when—

"It is cold."

Startled, he swiveled around to discover Night Thunder standing behind him, a blanket held tight around his shoulders. "Yes," he said although the truth was, until his brother mentioned it, he hadn't been aware of the world beyond his mind. If it had been the enemy instead of his brother, he might be dying.

"I think—" Night Thunder placed a couple of dry buffalo chips on the embers and then held out his hands to warm himself. "I believe White Calf was right and we should be hunting buffalo."

"Our father will not listen," he reminded him. "There is no use in trying to make him walk in a direction other than the one he has chosen."

"I know. Still . . ."

He'd thought Night Thunder was about to sit down. Instead, his brother backed away from the fire and placed his hand to the side of his face to shield his eyes from the glow. He stared out at the horizon, his body arrow-straight and taut as if waiting to be attacked. Frowning, Raven's Cry wondered if his brother was remembering the day he'd counted coup. Middle River and the others had sung his praises, but Night Thunder had remained silent, his face pale.

"We are not yet near the Cree," Raven's Cry said. "Are you afraid?"

"Do not speak to me of fear!" Night Thunder hissed. "Do not speak with our father's tongue! I look—I look for Wolf."

Grunting, Raven's Cry got to his feet and came to stand near his brother. Clouds had covered the moon tonight, making it impossible to see beyond the campfire's light. Still, he slowly swept his eyes over his black world, listening intently until he'd convinced himself that nothing was out there. Then he mentally reached for Night Thunder, and found, not a boastful young warrior, but an unproven youth.

"You speak of a wolf," he said, choosing his words deliberately. "Tell me, did White Calf's warning frighten you?"

To his surprise, Night Thunder's temper didn't flare again. Still, his body grew even more tense. "Our chief laughed at her just as he laughed at the other women when they begged him to send hunters after buffalo instead of here," his brother said, his tone sober. "If I was chief, I would not have done so."

"You believe we are wrong to be doing this? Perhaps you believe I lack the skill to keep us safe."

"You are not a shaman. A single dream does not protect you from danger or give you wisdom."

Not long ago, his brother wouldn't have dared disagree with him, but perhaps, despite his reservations, Night Thunder truly was no longer a child. Just the same, he didn't know what to call someone who cried out in terror when his arrows failed to penetrate a wolf's heart.

Only if White Calf was right and it had been no ordinary wolf—

"Everyone here has prepared themselves for battle," he pointed out. "We will ride and look and listen until we find a band of Cree and do what must be done."

Night Thunder sighed, looked around again, and then returned to the fire. "I hope you are right."

"Listen to me," he said. "I am awake tonight because I wish to pray to my spirit and strengthen myself for another wisdom-making dream. Your presence stands in the way of that."

"You'd rather I follow you in silence tomorrow to what might be danger and death?"

"A warrior does speak of such things."

Night Thunder started to reply, but his words fell away. His head snapped up and he looked quickly around. Alarmed, Raven's Cry did the same.

For a heartbeat, he thought he'd spotted movement in the distance, but when he blinked and strained to see, he realized he was looking at twin points of cool, red light that stood out in sharp contrast to the night.

"What is it?" Night Thunder demanded.

"I do not . . ."

A breeze gentle as spring mist touched his exposed flesh and warmed him. At the same time, his heart pounded as if determined to break through his chest and he couldn't draw a breath. That unseen creatures regarded him and other Blackfeet from the safety of night was something he'd never doubted, but none of those deer, bears, antelope, even cougars had fire-eyes. Magic eyes.

Wordless, he pointed.

The small but intense lights became larger and larger by degree. They challenged and tested his sanity and the night became foreign. His brother's quick intake of breath told him he'd seen the same thing and that, like him, he had no explanation.

"Eyes," Night Thunder whispered at length.

"Yes," he said with a certainty that defied explanation.

"Wolf eyes."

"Yes."

Despite the fur blanket he'd thrown down to protect himself, the ground chilled Raven's Cry. Attempting distraction, he stared up at the stars and looked for the first people, all of whom had gone to live in the sky after they'd died. There was the outline of Bear and another of First Eagle but the ancient people had made themselves a home so low in the horizon that sometimes it was impossible to see them.

He wondered if it was cold up there or whether the stars and moon gave off enough heat to see his ancestors through the longest winter, but not even the village's oldest man had been able to answer that question. After repositioning himself so that a sharp rock no longer dug into his back, he struggled to put his mind on the question of where he and the others should look for the Cree.

He'd lost count of the number of times the others had pressed him about that. His answer had always been the same; the spirits would gift him with the truth when they were ready. In the meantime, he said, he would keep his thoughts clean and simple and pray for dreams like the two that had led him to the horses.

Night Thunder, a still-grumbling Middle River, Quail Legs, Long Axe, and the others had believed his words, or if they hadn't, only his brother had spoken of his doubts around him. Their silence should have made it easier for him, but it hadn't because how could he hope to capture a dream if he couldn't sleep?

A horse snorted and then one of the warriors began to snore, and he gave himself up to the ragged cadence of indrawn and expelled breath. Breathing in time with the sleeper relaxed him, and he realized he was no longer cold. The horses had stopped moving about, and he could imagine their lower lips sagging as they fell asleep. Perhaps the stars slept when the sun took over the sky; either that or they went somewhere to feed and grow strong again. He wished he knew it was because—because . . .

Wolves were flesh-eating creatures, brave and fierce predators who loved and depended on one another. In many ways they were like the Blackfeet because they had leaders and followers and communicated in the way they acted and carried themselves and all knew their place within the group. Blackfeet and wolves understood that the lives of their children came before all else and no sacrifice was too great as long as the next generation survived and thrived.

But what he and Night Thunder had seen tonight hadn't belonged to a mortal pack. Rather, it had stood alone, maybe hunting and maybe not because if it was a spirit . . .

Why would a sacred Wolf approach not just one Blackfoot warrior but two?

He and Night Thunder didn't speak with the same heart and mind. They had different mothers and sometimes regarded each other as if they were strangers. It did not . . .

A wolf was out there tonight, waiting. And not just an ordinary wolf, but one capable of leaving one place and entering another without having to travel there. Eyes closed, Raven's Cry called up the wolf's image. Once he'd accomplished that, he took in his surroundings and bit by bit the image became clearer until he knew where Wolf stood and what the spirit creature was looking at.

In the morning, Raven's Cry told his companions that he'd dreamed and in that dream he'd seen a small band of Cree men and women trailing half a hundred buffalo. The Cree were near Clear Valley, which was just beyond Black Earth Hills, and were so intent on overtaking the herd that they thought of nothing else. It would be a simple matter for the Blackfeet to overtake them.

Neither he nor Night Thunder said anything about what they'd witnessed as they stood around a small fire.

Tomorrow, Takes-Knife-at-Night would ride away with four other Cree hunters so they could kill the buffalo they'd been trailing. Although Little Rain wished she could accompany him instead of waiting behind with the handful of women, she didn't have the skill necessary to thrust a spear or arrow into a running buffalo while on horseback and would only be in the way. It was better that she wait and rest at the temporary camp they'd set up until the killing had been done and then turn her energy into helping provide for the tribe.

She was eager to see how many buffalo her husband's arrows and spears would bring down and certain she'd have much to boast about because he'd spent the day preparing his weapons and planning the design he intended to paint on his horse. After taking a sweat bath with the other hunters, he'd join her, and as they'd done every night since becoming man and wife, they'd make love.

Now he was snoring softly while the sound of his breathing waited to show her the way to the same place.

She hadn't spoken to her father since before the buffalo tracking had begun, which was good because her heart felt lighter when Weasel Tail didn't fill the air with his hatred and the pain he endured didn't become hers.

Marriage was good. Loving Takes-Knife-at-Night was right. As she'd told her mother, she was happy, and the only thing that could make her happier was if her husband had planted his seed inside her.

Humming softly, she turned on her side so she could snuggle up to his back. The nights were cold enough that she'd brought a second blanket for them to sleep under, but when she was close to him like this, it seemed as if she would never need anything except him.

Sleep. Yes, she would sleep against him and in the morning she—she would . . .

Nothingness touched her briefly, danced away, came back again and she reached out with her thoughts to embrace it. All but surrounded by emptiness now, she listened to her husband's heartbeat.

She was still listening when the other sound came. At first she told herself it was nothing, but it became louder and louder and she knew it was many hoofbeats thudding on packed earth. Then someone screamed.

Uttering an oath, Takes-Knife-at-Night sprang upright, knocking her away from him. "Attack!" he bellowed. "We are being attacked!"

"No!" Alarmed, she reached out and grabbed his ankle, held on desperately. "My husband, stay with me!"

"I cannot. My wife, my life, I cannot!"

He was right, and because in her heart of hearts she'd known that even as she begged him to remain with her, she released him. She'd fallen asleep naked but wasn't aware of that until she stood and scraped her side against one of the traveling tepee poles. As her husband, also naked, snatched up his knife and bow and arrows, she yanked a dress over her but didn't take time to belt it or slip into her moccasins. Without so much as a glance at her, Takes-Knife-at-Night pushed aside the opening flap and disappeared.

"No!" she whimpered. "No."

Unable to remain where she was, she too stepped outside but not before picking up her stone scraping knife. A campfire had burned all evening with the result that a large bed of hot coals remained, the red light issuing from them enough that she instantly understood what was happening. The hunting camp was under attack by enemy warriors both on horseback and afoot. Her husband was already in the midst of the turmoil, but she had to find him, stand beside him, fight and maybe die with him.

The attackers could be Snake or Crow or Blackfeet or maybe Flathead. Who didn't matter. She didn't waste time questioning why a peaceful buffalo-hunting band of Cree were being attacked because various tribes had been at war since the beginning of time and would do so forever. Instead, crying out her husband's name, she darted here and there.

Out of the corner of her eye, she spotted a horse pounding toward her and threw herself to one side, just missing being hit. With no conscious thought of what she was doing, she slashed at the horse's side as it passed. When the animal squealed in pain, she sent up a quick prayer that its soul would forgive her, but there was no time to learn whether she'd inflicted a fatal blow.

Ahead of her, two men were locked in combat. From what she could tell, neither was wounded and they might struggle forever, not that it mattered because neither was Takes-Knife-at-Night. Sounds assaulted her, grunts and curses, hooves pounding the earth. No children had been brought along, and she was spared the awful sound of youthful screams. The air smelled of sweat and smoke, lathered horses and men and maybe fear.

Someone grabbed her arm with talonlike fingers, her capture happening before she'd been aware of the danger. She tried to pull away, but her enemy's grip tightened and she was yanked against him. Terror whipped through her but was gone so quickly that maybe she'd only imagined it.

She was Cree! To be Cree sometimes meant fighting and the body dying; that was the way of things. Her soul would live forever.

The hand she held her knife in remained free, and she suffered her captor's presence, waited her time. He wrenched her first one way and then the other, and she realized he was trying to turn her so that he could see her face in the firelight. Although she fought only a little and prayed for the instant when she could strike, he kept moving. She cursed him, cursed her lack of strength.

"Ha!" he barked. "You are woman!"

A Blackfoot! Because her father had had a Blackfoot captive several years ago and she'd spent a great deal of time in the girl's presence, she'd learned their language. As comprehension sank through her, anger turned into hatred. A Blackfoot had destroyed her father!

"Not woman!" she taunted. "Cree! I spit on you. I—"

"I do not murder women!"

With that, he shoved her away from him, the force of his thrust unbalancing her and knocking her to the ground. When her elbow struck a rock, the knife flew from her hand. She desperately patted the ground around her but couldn't find it. When she looked up, she saw that the Blackfoot had left her and for this moment at least, no one was nearby.

It was a good place to be with Mother Earth beneath her and the stars overhead. If she clamped her hands over her ears, she might no longer hear the shouts and cries. She could look up at the stars and wait for—

Where was her husband? Shoving herself off Mother Earth, Little Rain stared first here and then there. By now her eyes had adjusted to the dim light and she knew her camp had been attacked by no more than eight Blackfeet warriors, but they'd come at night and on horseback while her people had been defenseless in sleep.

A woman screamed. A horse squealed. One man cursed and then another did the same and her attention was drawn first toward that sound and then by what she saw.

A naked man on foot had grabbed hold of a horse's rope and was trying to keep the animal close to him. Another man, painted for war and armed with a spear, sat astride the horse and was trying to bury his spear in the stander.

In the few days and nights she'd been Takes-Knife-at-Night's wife, she'd memorized his body; she was looking at it now. He was beautiful, his muscles taut, skin glistening, his black hair capturing the fiery glow. His bow and arrows were gone, but he held his knife between his teeth as if weapon and man were one and the same. She tried to tell herself it was enough and that her love for him would give him grizzly-strength.

Before she could order her legs to move, her husband managed to grab hold of the spear and, grunting, yanked his attacker off his horse. The two men went down together, the Blackfoot landing on top of Takes-Knife-at-Night. She ran toward them, willing the distance to become nothing.

Pounding hooves so close that they seemed to be on top of her caused her to stop in midstride. She was certain the horse would run her down; instead, its rider jerked it to such a violent halt that the horse's rump nearly dug into the earth. Feeling helpless, she waited for the rider to dismount and attack her husband while he remained pinned under his enemy. Instead, the young Blackfoot— she could see his youth in what she could make out of his features—remained frozen near the two men wrestling on the ground.

Why was he standing there?

Night Thunder had been certain it was Raven's Cry who'd been pulled off his horse. That, he told himself, was why he'd forced Deep Scar through the mass of bodies, but now that he was all but on top of them, he saw that he'd been mistaken. Whether afoot or on horseback, Middle River was a proven fighter; Middle River needed no help in—

—he could leave.

Turn around and run. Hide.

Save himself even if that meant spending the rest of his life in self-hatred.

Something touched him, not alive but not dead either. He felt a cold snout, the sensation of silky fur on his chest, looked into hot eyes. *Fight,* the creature seemed to say. *Fight and live!*

Not giving himself time to think, Night Thunder flung himself off Deep Scar and tore into the tangle of arms and legs. His fingers locked around what he believed to be a forearm. Whoever he'd grabbed fought with a strength greater than his own and the pounding fear he'd denied while dismounting reasserted itself. Releasing the thrashing arm, he stumbled backward, but before he could reach for Deep Scar's reins, he heard a gurgling sound like that of a deer whose throat has been cut. Frozen air swept over him, and he couldn't move. Instead, he stared down at the two battlers and waited.

He wasn't the only one watching. Without taking his eyes off the battle, he sensed the other presence and knew in his heart of hearts that his frozen state was being studied, not by Wolf spirit this time but by a Cree woman.

Moments passed—how many he couldn't say; then the naked man stood and looked around, his legs widespread and his body hunched forward as if ready for attack while the other man remained an inert lump. Middle River couldn't die! He was a Sun priest!

Disbelief hadn't yet become reality when the enemy warrior turned toward him and he saw that he was armed.

"Die, son of a dog!" the Cree bellowed. "Die and I will hang your scalp in front of my tepee!"

His brother's scalp had met that fate. It couldn't happen to him, it couldn't!

He thought he yelled but somehow the sound came out a howl. Hating both the howl and his terror, hating the Cree who had just killed Middle River, he snatched his knife from where it hung at his waist. The Cree held a spear—maybe Middle River's spear. Would he die with a Blackfoot spear in him?

The sounds of battle, he thought irrationally, were strange. Horses, yes, and sometimes a shout, but little else. Either the others had stopped fighting or he'd lost the ability to hear all but the most insistent of sounds.

"Did your mother open herself to a dog?" the Cree taunted. "Do you crawl about on four legs?"

"No!" he screamed.

"Ha! You lie! You are not a man." The Cree jabbed his spear at Night Thunder, forcing him to jump back. "Forever a boy because you sobbed and ran away instead of submitting at the Sun Dance."

"No!" If he'd dared, he would have ripped open his shirt to expose his scarred chest.

"Yes!" Once again the Cree thrust the spear and once again Night Thunder retreated. "Your father hangs his head in shame at the sight of you. He turns his back and—"

"No!"

Not thinking, Night Thunder hurtled himself at the taunter. At the last moment, he remembered the deadly spear and twisted to the side. Still, the spear found him, parting flesh and tearing along his ribs.

Pain exploded through him, but it was too late to retreat because his forward movement had carried him into the Cree. The enemy warrior stumbled but managed to remain on his feet while shoving Night Thunder away. Helpless, Night Thunder waited for the ground to slam into him, but what he landed on was soft.

Middle River's body!

Blood instantly soaked through his shirt, some of it his, some belonging to Middle River. He felt his strength draining away and desperately clung to it, gathered his muscles and pushed away from what had been Middle River. Fire burned within him with every breath he took, but the flames seemed to bring reason. He had to get to his feet, had to kill before he was killed!

The feel of his knife still in his hand first gave him courage. He was on his hands and knees like the dog his enemy had called him and was trying to decide how to stand without losing his grip on his weapon when something slammed into his wounded side and he was knocked off balance. At least his knife wasn't trapped under him, but the pain was so intense that conscious thought was impossible. He was going to die tonight—die with—

Through red-hazed eyes he saw that the Cree had straddled him and was reaching for his hair.

Scalped! Scalped alive!

As his head was being yanked off the ground, his attention fastened on his attacker's widespread legs and his manhood hanging unprotected between them. He had seconds in which to live unless—

Not fighting the grip on his hair, he allowed himself to be pulled upward. He didn't wait to see what the Cree intended to scalp him with but gripped his knife with all the strength left in him and drove it deep into his enemy, the motion long and slashing at the same time.

The Cree screamed and screamed and screamed, the cry more rage than anything else, but instead of jumping away, he continued to stand over Night Thunder while his life's blood spurted out of him. From where he lay, Night Thunder saw that he hadn't severed his enemy's manhood after all, but his knife had found an inner thigh and torn through the vein there.

After a moment, the Cree began to tremble and rock back and forth. The man tried to lift his leg but must have lacked the strength because he wound up dropping the spear and clamping his hands over his knees, his body sagging farther and farther forward while he panted like a buffalo calf run to the ground by wolves.

Just before the Cree fell, Night Thunder rolled to one side so that the dying warrior landed alongside Middle River. Blood still pulsed from the wound, but the Cree no longer seemed aware of what was happening to him. His bowels released their contents and that stench mixed with the smell of blood—his and Middle River's and his vanquished foe's—and Night Thunder felt his stomach begin to heave.

Despite the pain movement caused, he managed to scoot a little farther away before vomiting onto the ground. He was still heaving when a small but clawing and scratching body slammed into him.

9

Whoever was attacking him managed to bury strong fingernails in the side of his neck, but pain and battle gave Night Thunder unknown strength. He broke free by spinning beneath the weight and then shoved his fist into the Cree's throat. A strangled gasp told him that he'd at least momentarily robbed his attacker of the ability to breathe. His stomach continued to demand to be emptied, but he didn't dare be distracted.

Instead, he struggled to get his knees under him and looked around, desperately attempting to determine whether more danger waited. From what he could tell, he and Middle River had been the only Blackfeet to dismount. The others were bunched together in the middle of the Cree hunting camp, looking like buffalo protecting themselves from wolf attack. It was possible that no one had seen what had happened to Middle River and him, and with the sound of a roaring waterfall, he knew the folly of trying to call out.

Whoever he'd struck was still trying to breathe. His knife lay under his hand, and he wrapped his fingers around it, but in his mind, the knife became the spear that had wounded him, and he nearly threw it away.

The motionless bodies were too close to him, the smell of spilled blood hot and heavy in his nostrils. When he turned his head to one side and tried to breathe in untainted air, he was assaulted by the stench of the Cree's feces and his own rejected meal. His side pulsed; his head pounded, and if he wasn't afraid that shrieking would split his skull apart, he would have done so.

He'd seen death, had killed, had almost died himself and might be bleeding to death at this moment, and he couldn't fling what he felt into the night air so he did the only thing left to him, which was to hunch over the small, helpless Cree. Without any thought as to what he was going to do, he ripped the Cree's fingers off the vulnerable throat and shoved his knife close. His enemy's eyes blinked and focused and he realized in a dim and instinctive way that a woman had attacked him and he'd attacked her in turn.

"You killed him!" she sobbed, her voice made raw by his blow. "Murdered—"

"Silence!"

He thought she was going to obey, which would save him from having to acknowledge her further, but to his shock, she began digging at her own forearm with the nails that had recently punished him. He should leave her to her grief, but he'd already seen and smelled too much blood tonight and didn't want this reminder of what he'd been forced to do a few minutes ago to keep his life from ending.

When he slapped her hand away, it seemed to him that the woman snarled at him. The sound infuriated him and he dropped his knife, grabbed her shoulders, and began to shake her.

"Enough!" he insisted. "Enough or I will kill you."

The word *kill* became a burning branch in his belly and without thinking of what he was doing, he released one slender shoulder and reached for his weapon, but before he could pick it up, she lunged at him and clamped her teeth around his hand.

Shocked, he wrenched free but not before she'd pierced his flesh in several places. Hatred rose like a thunderstorm in him, and he shoved her with such force that the back of her head made a sickening thud as it struck the ground, but she didn't go limp, only stared up at him with a stunned expression. His knife remained in his hand, sharp and deadly.

"Kill her!" someone cried.

"Gut her!"

Where the words were coming from, he couldn't tell and even with her stretched out on her back, he knew better than to take his eyes off her. His wounded side screamed with every breath he took, and his hands had begun to shake.

"Kill her. Take two Cree lives tonight."

Yes, he could do that. Yes, he could slice her throat or open a vein the way he'd opened the warrior's, and if he was quick enough, her blood might not stain him, and if he refused to breathe, maybe he wouldn't smell anything. She'd die quick and silent—he'd demand that of her—and no strangled cry would follow him into tomorrow.

But before he could do as one of his fellow Blackfeet had just ordered, he realized he could no longer feel his fingers. Staring at them, he saw that the knife was slipping from his fingers. It thudded to the earth, and when the woman tried to reach for it, he again knocked her down. They glared at each other, wounded Blackfoot and desperate Cree, and in her eyes he saw that she'd forgotten her dead warrior and cared about nothing except staying alive. If he still had the strength, he could make a lie of her desire, but all he wanted to do was plant his feet under him and run into the night.

"Two Cree for two Blackfeet! Do it, Night Thunder! End her."

End? Make her nothing as his mother was nothing except memory?

"No," he heard himself say. "She will—live."

The Blackfoot had pitched forward onto his face almost before he'd finished speaking. Little Rain had been certain that those who'd called for her death would have immediately done so, but another warrior, a tall and powerfully built man, had joined the others, and they'd stepped back while he knelt beside the one who had killed her husband. The wounded Blackfoot was now trying to sit up but she didn't care.

Takes-Knife-at-Night was dead.

"We leave, now," the tall Blackfoot ordered as he supported

Takes-Knife-at-Night's killer. "Coup has been counted." He pointed at her husband's body. "And Red Mountain's death has been avenged."

"But Middle River—"

Before the tall Blackfoot could answer, an unseen Cree shouted. A mounted Blackfoot loudly explained that they were risking their lives by remaining here because at least two Cree women had run off and would bring back the rest of the tribe. Muscles straining, the tall Blackfoot handed the body of the dead Blackfoot to one of the riders and started to lead the wounded one to a horse.

"No," the one she'd nearly killed gasped.

He stood on uncertain legs, his side bleeding, looking around through eyes that didn't seem to focus. Finally spotting her, he lurched forward and grabbed her loose hair. Acting instinctively, she slammed her elbow into his wound, and he doubled over, hissing through clenched teeth. She made ready to run, but before she could escape, the tall Blackfoot clamped his arms around her.

"Night Thunder! Have you changed your mind? Do you want her blood spilled?" her captor asked.

"No," the one called Night Thunder gasped. "No."

"You cannot leave her," someone else said. "She tried to kill you, counted coup on you."

Night Thunder swayed, then lurched at her and tried to clamp a hand around her neck, but his hand trembled so violently that she could have broken free if the other warrior hadn't been holding her. He let out a sound that was more sob than curse. "I—take her with me."

"So be it," her captor answered and although she continued to fight, he quickly tied her hands behind her and lifted her onto his horse as if she weighed no more than a child. Then he helped Night Thunder mount and she and the band of murdering Blackfeet galloped away from the tepee she'd erected while it was still light, away from the bed she'd shared with Takes-Knife-at-Night. With her captor behind her, she couldn't see her husband's body, but she stared over her shoulder just the same, her heart breaking.

*   *   *

Was her father snoring?

Disoriented, White Calf sat up and tried to concentrate on her breathing. Pain lapped at her, the shards retreating and advancing but never going away. Once she might have told herself that she'd only been dreaming, but now she knew better than to waste time by trying to deceive herself.

Someone had been hurt; who that someone was she couldn't tell, but there was no doubt that at least one member of her people had been injured.

As wakefulness grew, she was able to eliminate those in camp because no one had cried out, and the shaman hadn't been summoned. How many warriors had accompanied Raven's Cry and Night Thunder on their revenge-hunt? It had to be one or more of them and if—

A sob built in her throat, forcing her to clamp her hand over her mouth. Pain ate at her with hungry teeth, and along with it came fear because pain this intense was capable of bringing death.

Perhaps had already brought death.

Resigned to what she had to do, she went deep inside herself to where the truth—at least some of it—lay. Her nostrils recorded sweat and the hot smell of blood. Her ears picked up a grief-wail, but that was all.

No, not all, because in the midst of all that darkness stood a shaggy form on four legs, its muzzle lifted to the sky.

Because they'd scattered the Cree horses before riding into the small camp, Night Thunder knew they wouldn't be immediately pursued. The thought should have given him a measure of comfort, but it was so hard to think with pain clamped onto his side like a coyote refusing to release a carcass. He understood that Middle River was dead, that he'd avenged the death and his own wounding by killing a Cree brave and taking a Cree woman captive but staying on Deep Scar was so hard and his heart still pounded like a wild thing.

Twice his mind emptied and he nearly lost his balance, would have if his legs hadn't known to remain clamped around Deep Scar. Whenever he touched his side, his hand came away wet and sticky and he had to fight to breathe. Most of all, he remembered that the woman had attacked him and he'd lacked the strength to subdue her.

It had been she who'd been watching while he fought for the courage to go to Middle River's aid; he had no doubt of that. If she ever threw that knowledge at him . . .

But he hadn't run. Instead . . .

If only he could remember what had happened.

"We have come far enough," Raven's Cry finally said. "It is time to rest."

Deep Scar must have understood his words because the stallion immediately slowed and then stopped, his head dropping as he searched for something to eat. By now dawn had touched the sky, making it possible for Night Thunder to see the Cree woman clearly for the first time. He was surprised by her youth and guessed her to be no older than him. One of her arms looked inflamed where she'd started to scratch herself, but he had no interest in her grief. When Raven's Cry slipped off his horse, he brought her down with him. Instead of trying to escape, she sank to her knees, her hands bound behind her and her loose hair streaming over her bent head.

"Night Thunder," Raven's Cry said. "I will help you dismount."

Yes, that was good. He would sit or lay and wait for his wound to stop bleeding and maybe someone would give him water and something to eat and—

He was jerked back to consciousness when Raven's Cry grasped his hands and began to gently pull. He felt himself start to slide but lacked the strength to keep his balance and would have fallen if his brother hadn't eased his way and helped him stretch out on the ground.

"I do not like what I see," Raven's Cry announced after examining his side. "Our father must tend to him."

No one acknowledged that he was conscious, and after a moment, he took in his surroundings. Middle River's body lay nearby and two braves were preparing to wrap him in his blanket. The captive who'd been quietly crying fell silent.

"Mother Earth, see this child. Hear his soul's crying and bring him comfort," Raven's Cry began in the sing-song that was a mourning lament. "Take him to your breast. Heal his wounds and let him join those who have gone before him."

Night Thunder swallowed, then forced his own words, his tone weaker than his brother's had been. "Mother Earth, look down upon Middle River. See that he died bravely." *Bravely.* "And—and smile upon him. His time with us is over. He awaits you."

The others took up the chant until at last they'd done what they could to ease Middle River's journey into the next world. Still, the thought of having to deliver the Sun priest's body to his family chilled him.

Chilled? It was so strange. One moment he couldn't keep his teeth from knocking together while the next he felt as if he might catch on fire. Although not all children survived to become adults, he'd never known a moment of sickness and had taken his health for granted, but he no longer could. Surely, he told himself, his father would see his need for medicine and lay his healing hands and herbs on him and maybe they would look into each other's eyes and see, really see each other. Time would pass and strength would flow back into his veins and he and Deep Scar would once more gallop across the prairie. Strong and healthy again, he would know what to do with his prisoner.

"I do not understand this," Blue Snake said loudly enough that it sent his head to pounding. "Raven's Cry, why did you not tell us that Middle River would be killed and your brother wounded?"

Blue Snake, who hadn't so much as moaned during his Sun Dance Ceremony, often walked at Chief Sleeps Too Long's side and his words echoed what came from the chief's lips. Night Thunder wasn't surprised to hear him criticize Raven's Cry's dreams— dreams that jeopardized Sleeps Too Long's leadership position in the tribe.

To Night Thunder's surprise, Raven's Cry didn't immediately answer. He tried to focus on his brother so he could see what existed inside him, but he couldn't keep daylight in his world and his side stopped throbbing only when he remained absolutely still.

"Answer me!" Blue Snake insisted. "Why should we trust your dreams?"

"Enough!" Raven's Cry shot back. "I answer to Middle River's parents, not you."

"Ha! You say that because you cannot face my truth!"

"Stop it!" Night Thunder ordered. He tried to sit up but lacked the strength. Falling back sent pain stabbing through him, and it was a while before he could continue. "Did you question when my brother led us to the Cree camp? No. You were the first to draw a weapon, but did you count coup? Did you step forward to avenge Middle River's death? No."

Blue Snake glared at him, but after a moment the hawk-nosed warrior turned his attention to his horse. Although he said nothing, Raven's Cry nodded at him and Night Thunder wondered if he saw gratitude in his brother's eyes. The Cree woman had begun to mutter to herself but although he wanted her to be silent, he understood she needed to mourn the dead Cree just as the Blackfeet had mourned Middle River.

After several minutes, Raven's Cry went about gathering a handful of grass and pressed against his side, keeping it in place by wrapping a strip of leather around him. Then he helped him drink from his water flask and offered him some pemmican. Although the effort of chewing exhausted him, he forced down the food.

"We cannot stay here," Raven's Cry said, his voice too low to carry beyond them.

"I know."

"You can ride?"

"I must."

Raven's Cry nodded, then indicated the Cree woman. "You lacked the strength to kill her?" he asked.

"I do not know."

"Hm. I ask you again, what do you want to do with her?"

"I—do not know."

"Remember, if you end her, two Cree will have died for two Blackfeet."

Forcing his vision to clear, Night Thunder concentrated on his captive. Her hair tangled around her face, but that didn't hide what was in her eyes. Although he'd readied himself for more of her hatred for him, it wasn't there. Instead, she reminded him of a child without a mother's comforting arms, an emotion that took him back to his own childhood. She fought her fear one wind-surge at a time, stood up to it and battled back, but the effort was exhausting her. He wished he'd left her where he'd found her.

"Brother," Raven's Cry whispered. "What do you say?"

"I will not kill a helpless woman. Tell me." He addressed the Cree woman. "Who was he, the one I killed?"

He didn't think she was going to answer him. If she hadn't, he would have left her with her warring emotions, but he saw her breasts rise and fall as she pulled in a great drink of air. "My husband," she whispered.

"He has no vision! Look at what happened and know that the truth of him stands before us! You say there is truth and wisdom in your son's dreams? I say his dreams are nothing!" At that, Chief Sleeps Too Long spat. Some of his spittle sank into the ground but a little clung to his chin.

"You lie!" Bunch of Lodges shot back. "Foolish words flow from you because you wish my son's gift for yourself."

Raven's Cry wanted nothing to do with the two powerful men's arguments. It had taken longer to return than he'd hoped because, despite his attempts to treat Night Thunder's wound, his brother had weakened from loss of blood and now fever burned in him. Fearful that he might start bleeding again, he'd kept Deep Scar at a slow walk.

His father should cease this wrangling and make medicine over his youngest son, but if he stepped between the two, the chief might lash out at him. Instead, he stood with his arm on Night Thunder's waist as the members of the tribe gathered around the just returned warriors. Loud wailing from Middle River's parents and brothers and sisters sliced into him, but expressing his sorrow and regrets to them would have to wait.

A number of children were staring at the captive—Little Rain she called herself—but she didn't seem to notice. She hadn't eaten in the three days and nights it had taken them to return home and had barely drunk enough water to keep herself alive. She was so small-framed that if she was trying to starve herself to death, it wouldn't take long. Still, no one would be foolish enough to allow her the opportunity to escape, which was why Long Axe stood near her.

"You think I want Raven's Cry's dreams?" The chief laughed and spat again. "Your son has nothing I would wish for myself."

Raven's Cry knew that wasn't the truth because he'd noticed the way Sleeps Too Long often studied his muscles when they sat naked in the sweat lodge and even when he'd been too young to join the warrior ritual, the chief had taken careful note of the youthful wrestling matches and races he'd almost always won because of his greater size and longer legs.

Rage turned Bunch of Lodges' features dark. "Red Mountain's spirit now sleeps in peace. Raven's Cry cannot be held responsible for the foolish actions of others that placed them in danger. My son"—he pointed at Raven's Cry "—led warriors into the heart of the enemy and Cree blood was shed. What must be has been done and I am content."

Night Thunder leaned against him and whispered, "It will never change, will it? The man has only one son. I am nothing to him."

Raven's Cry didn't bother to answer because they both knew it was the truth. Instead, he nodded at his friend Quail Legs, indicating he wanted him to help Night Thunder into the tepee they shared with their parents. Night Thunder's steps were slow and his clenched fists were proof of his discomfort, but he held his head high.

Many of the villagers were watching him, yet Raven's Cry cared only about the reaction of one. White Calf stood in the middle of a group of women, making no move to call attention to herself; still it had been so easy for him to single her out. She'd placed an arm around Middle River's mother's shoulder and was saying something to the older woman, but her eyes were on him. He saw no condemnation in her gaze, but maybe he was seeing only what he wanted to. Somehow he would have to be alone with her again, to find the courage to ask her to speak truthfully to him.

He would have sworn that the exchange with his brother and then his quick acknowledgment of White Calf had only taken a few moments, but in that time, Chief Sleeps Too Long had walked away from Bunch of Lodges and was stalking toward him.

"I will tell you this because it has been on many tongues and you will soon hear it anyway," the chief said. Then he paused and looked around, obviously making sure everyone was listening to him. "While you were gone, there has been much talk about what a fine chief you would make. Men and women, children even, point at the new horses and say the animals would not be here if not for you. They sang your praises and made much talk about the many coups you would count, the Cree blood you would shed. But you allowed Middle River to be killed and your brother wounded."

Had he? No matter how many times he'd asked himself why his dreams hadn't revealed death and danger, he still had no answer.

"I will not throw words at you, my chief." With an effort, he kept his voice calm.

"Because you know the folly of such a thing. Atch! I go to sweat and pray. Then I will know what must be done."

"Pray long and hard, Chief," Bunch of Lodges snapped, startling Raven's Cry because he hadn't seen his father coming. "Maybe this time the spirits will hear you when they never have before."

Sleeps Too Long whirled on the shaman. "Be careful, old man," he warned. "It is not for a medicine-maker to question the way a chief walks. Do not forget—" He tapped his chest. "I am chief because I am brave and have proven myself in battle, because no harm comes to those who follow me. That is how the spirits speak to me. They do not shine on your sons; they never will because you have displeased the spirits. *You!*"

A collective gasp followed by urgent whispering followed Sleeps Too Long's outburst. Although the Blackfeet rode willingly into war, among themselves they sought peace because the tribe's survival depended on unity. To have that change was dangerous.

"Father," Raven's Cry said with a calmness he didn't feel. "Night Thunder has need of your medicine."

Bunch of Lodges lifted his arms and raised his face toward the sky. "Hear me, *Na'pi*. This one whose name I will not speak today calls me an old man, but you are Old Man. This one spits on you. Punish him!"

"*Na'pi*, it is I, your servant. See me now as who I am in my heart, *I-so-kin'-uh-kini.*"

I-so-kin'-uh-kini, "heavy singer for the sick." With his hair done up in a huge topknot, a thick, black bearskin over his shoulders, and several fox pelts hanging from that, Bunch of Lodges looked every ounce the powerful shaman, but Night Thunder's attention was drawn not to his father and his long and extremely valuable medicine pipe but on Little Rain. Raven's Cry had brought her inside and ordered her to sit as far from the others as possible because his brother was concerned that her presence might blunt the power of his father's medicine, but Bunch of Lodges hadn't said anything.

Night Thunder lay on his sleeping blanket, naked from the waist up. From what he could tell, his wound had finally stopped seeping, but it hurt all the time, and he was bothered by its red and swollen appearance. He couldn't remember ever feeling this weak.

Bunch of Lodges knelt beside him and dropped a small pinch of sweet grass on the two hot coals his wife had placed on the nearby alter. As smoke rose from the smoldering grass, the shaman held his drum in the smoke, turning it from side to side and round and round to purify it. Then he put the drum down and did the same with his hands before rubbing his arms and body. Finally he picked up the drum again and began rapidly tapping it while chanting.

"Hear me, my spirit," the shaman began. "This is what you have always told me to do, and I have heeded you well. Help me now. Help me cure this sick one."

"He is your son," Raven's Cry whispered. "Call him that."

The drum fell silent, and, glowering, Bunch of Lodges shoved it at Raven's Cry. "I do medicine; do not disturb me," he insisted. "Even you must remain silent."

Reaching into the depths of the bearskin, Bunch of Lodges pulled out an eagle's wing and passed it through the smoke. Then, as he'd done over Red Mountain's body, he placed the wing's tip in his mouth, bit it off, and after chewing it awhile, he leaned close to Night Thunder's side and spit out the small lump.

Using the feather, he brushed off the mangled tip and then slowly, thoroughly slid the feather over Night Thunder's entire body, then repeated the ritual two more times. He said nothing.

When he was finished with that, he took the sacred pipe that had been in his possession since he'd become a shaman and was as valuable as many horses from his wife, lit it and inhaled. When he exhaled, he was careful to direct the smoke over the wound.

"I am done," he said. "My medicine is complete."

"You have not chanted." This came from Raven's Cry, and Night Thunder, who'd been mesmerized by everything his father had been doing, turned toward him. "Why not?"

"Because you disturbed my words."

"I only spoke the truth," Raven's Cry insisted. "Why will you not call him your son?"

"He is a patient. I am a shaman. It is enough."

"No, it is not!" Raven's Cry insisted. "It was Night Thunder who ended the Cree's life. If he had not done so, Red Mountain's spirit would still be crying."

"His carelessness allowed him to be wounded."

"You are perfect? You are such a mighty shaman that Red

Mountain did not die?"

Dirty Knee Sits gasped, and even the Cree woman who couldn't possibly care what was happening recoiled. Night Thunder wanted to warn his brother not to anger their father, but Raven's Cry had never spoken in his behalf before, and the knowledge awed him.

"When Night Thunder is well," Raven's Cry said, seemingly oblivious to the others' reaction, "we will hold a great feast and you will honor both of your sons."

"Do not tell me what I must do, child," Bunch of Lodges insisted.

"No, you are wrong." Raven's Cry's features softened and he now looked profoundly sad. "I say we will do this thing because then our chief will know that this family is of one mind. Thus, he will not challenge us."

Bunch of Lodges frowned, then after a moment, nodded. "I hear your wisdom, my son. It is good."

Raven's Cry too nodded. "And what your other son did," he asked, "is it also good?"

10

Because of Middle River's status as a Sun chief, his family decided his tepee should never be used again. As a result, it was moved a little distance from camp and carefully pegged down all around with stones piled on the edges. Although it wasn't part of the normal ritual, his family took care to repaint the buffalo tail decorations on the lodge's east side. Once that was done, Middle River's body was placed in the middle of the tepee and his weapons, war clothing, medicine, and pipe were stacked next to him. His father was the last to leave the final resting place, closing the door flap behind him with fingers that hadn't stopped shaking since he'd learned of his son's death. Then Middle River's war horse was killed and left nearby so he could ride it to Sand Hills.

In the future, only his family would mourn, but on the first night within his final resting tepee, everyone gathered around to wail and lament his loss. Because the clan would be leaving soon, it was important to leave Middle River with memories of his people. Bunch of Lodges and Dirty Knee Sits joined Raven's Cry, which meant Little Rain was alone with Night Thunder. Her hands had been untied on the way home, but with shock and grief enveloping her, she'd given scant thought to escape; besides, there'd been no opportunity. The Blackfeet were known to adopt captive women and children into the tribe, but she hated them so much that she was certain that would never happen. Either they'd release or kill her; tonight it didn't matter.

Night Thunder lay near the fire with his head turned so he could hear what was going on outside. He alternately shook with chills and sweated and he hadn't been able to keep down what little he'd eaten. She wished he would die.

She'd expected a Blackfoot tepee to be different from those of the Cree but although the designs on the outside were, inside they smelled the same and the same dried herbs and vegetables were stored on pieces of hide that had been treated just as the Cree did their own. The Blackfeet too had seats made of buffalo robes and lined the base of their tepees with cowskin to keep out the chill. There was no difference in the way Blackfeet and Cree fires burned or the path smoke took as it sought escape. Although her people had always joked that the Blackfeet were incapable of fashioning sturdy, handsome tepees, that wasn't the truth. The only difference was that at home, she'd felt at peace within the walls while now she was trapped.

"You do not want me here," she said, not bothering to keep her loathing of Night Thunder out of her voice. "Let me go."

"No."

"Then kill me."

"No."

"Why?" she demanded, exasperation creeping into her voice. "Your energy must go toward healing yourself. You have no need of someone who would finish what her husband began if she could."

He propped himself up on his elbow and regarded her through heavy-lidded eyes. "Why are you warning me? A wolf does not tell a deer what he is going to do."

Despite herself she laughed, the sound harsh. "You are no deer and I am not a wolf."

"Tonight I am a newborn fawn but you are right; you do not have fangs. Sharp nails, yes, but no teeth."

He glanced at his and Raven's Cry's bow and arrows near the

opening flap and she wondered if he could stop her if she sprang for them. Her fingers burned with the need to wrap themselves around a knife, but he'd certainly cry out and the others would kill her and despite what she'd told him, she didn't want to die.

Outside, a woman wailed, her cry sharp and so pain-filled that it was all Little Rain could do not to answer with a lament of her own.

"I was not given time to mourn my husband," she whispered. "I need—"

"You will not scar yourself!" he insisted. "I will not allow it."

"What? Why not?" she demanded. She no longer hugged the tepee wall as far away from him as possible but had scooted closer, telling herself she'd done so because she refused to be seen as a coward.

"I have seen enough tearing of flesh," he replied. "Often my father covers his legs but whenever I see them, I remember the blood that ran down them."

"I do not care what your father did. He is nothing to me."

To her surprise, he didn't become angry but only nodded before laying back down. He continued to look at her.

"What?" she demanded. "What do you want?"

"Nothing that will ever come from you; nothing I would ever tell you about. I must decide what I will do with you, but until then, I want you to remain silent."

How arrogant he was! Arrogant despite his ugly wound. "How will you silence me? You tell me you do not want to kill me but as long as I am alive, I will say what I must."

"No!"

"Yes!" Why was she arguing with him? Maybe, she thought, it was because otherwise she'd have to stare into a future without Takes-Knife-at-Night.

"No," he repeated, his tone calmer this time, either that or his outburst had weakened him. "Cree, I wished I never had to look at one of you again. I warn you; do not feed my anger or you will regret it."

She'd be a fool not to heed his warning; she had only to look into his feverish eyes to know that. The muffled cries continued, became her own grief. In her mind, she saw herself stepping outside and joining them, sobbing of what she'd lost, her love for Takes-Knife-at-Night and his for her—exposing herself to the Blackfeet.

"You speak of anger," she said because tears and sorrow were building up inside her and she couldn't think of any way to keep them at bay except by talking. "But you are not the only one who carries that inside."

"Because I killed your husband."

A burning brand shoved into her heart couldn't have hurt more; she fought the pain by throwing out more words. "Even before that I hated all Blackfeet."

"Why?"

She was on her feet before she knew it was going to happen, but although his gaze intensified, reminding her of an animal caught in a trap, she had no thought to injure him. Instead, she walked over to the fire and held out her hands, warming herself. Night Thunder's shaman father had purified his hands and drum in smoke before making medicine over Night Thunder, but maybe there was no way she could ever cleanse herself.

"The old ones say that Blackfeet and Cree have fought from the beginning of time, but I do not know about that." Her voice sounded hollow.

Drumming had begun. Although it was little more than a deep whisper now, it might become louder and he wouldn't be able to hear her. Whatever she said would have to be done now while she had the courage and desperate need.

"What I do know is that five moons ago my father killed a Blackfoot, but before the Blackfoot died, he made a cripple of my father. Since then his heart has been like a winter storm and I no longer recognize him. That is what matters to me, what has taken me down the path I now walk. To have you destroy my husband and be forced to—"

"Your father recently killed a Blackfoot?" he interrupted, his voice low and hard.

"Yes."

"Where did this take place?"

"Where? Near a creek, I believe. Yes, a creek which flows down from the Blue Mountains."

"Tell me, how did your father mark his arrows?"

A sudden chill took hold of her. She tried to tell herself she was simply reacting to the memories of what had happened to her father but knew different. Something was happening to Night Thunder. Whatever it was had taken away his fever and weakness and made his voice like a building storm.

"With woodpecker feathers at the end, not red or black feathers, but the fine gray ones near their legs," she told him.

"My brother Red Mountain died with such an arrow in him. He was killed because a Cree wanted his elk carcass, his!"

"No!"

"Yes. After he'd been shot, he ran at his attacker and stabbed him many times, cut into muscle and hit bone. Red Mountain was still alive when other Blackfeet found him, and as he died, he told them what had happened."

"Stabbed . . ."

"My brother was scalped—scalped alive."

No. No. No.

Despite her attempt to go on meeting her enemy's eyes, Little Rain's head sagged forward and she began to cry. Feeling overwhelmed, she struggled to remove her spirit from this place and return to the land of her heart. She remembered her father's laughter when she was a child, his love of games and the whimsical designs he'd painted on his horses, but those things were gone now, buried under the hatreds and fears of a man whose strength and laughter had been stolen from him in a single moment.

"Stop it!" Night Thunder demanded. "I will not have your tears!"

Something that might have been a small shaft of lightning that had found a home in her heart caused her tears to dry and she stared at her captor.

"My father ended your brother," she said. The revelation fed her courage and anger and she went on. "He was a fine hunter who once killed a bear who had tried to steal the fish he had just caught. He had no need to steal meat from a mere Blackfoot."

"There is no doubt that your father and my brother battled. That is the only truth which matters." Night Thunder sounded both numb and confused when she longed to throw the truth at him over and over again.

"Yes, it is."

Once again Night Thunder tried to sit and once again his strength failed him. She waited for him to throw his hatred at her, to be told that he wanted her dead as much as she wanted his death at this moment. Instead, he stared up at the top of the tepee, silent for a long time.

"Everything changed at Red Mountain's death," he whispered. "I thought it would be a glorious thing to die in battle, that my praises would be sung throughout the village and my body treated as if it was a sacred thing, but then I saw what remained of the boy I grew up beside."

Just as she'd seen her father's terrible wounds. "I . . ." She'd been about to tell him she understood but stopped herself in time.

"We could not keep the flies off him," he countered. "He looked so wasted, like an old man, no longer a fine young warrior. His mother, Dirty Knee Sits, cried until her voice became raw and my father—my father changed."

"So," she heard herself say, "did my father."

"Then he did not die of his wounds?"

"No." What had happened to her anger? She wanted it back because that way she wouldn't have to listen to Night Thunder's words or hear the pain in them or see darkness around his eyes. "But he became an old man. Wasted."

He wasn't looking at her. She told herself she should be grateful for that small amount of privacy. "I do not understand the way of the spirits," he whispered. "We have one, White Calf, who speaks the words of the spirits and now, maybe, the same is happening to my brother, but such things are beyond me."

His thoughts were taking him someplace she didn't want to go, and yet they'd become part of each other, and she had no choice except to listen.

"War and hatred between Cree and Blackfeet brought your father and my brother together," he said. "War is of man's making, but perhaps the spirits brought us together. I do not know what to make of that."

"Neither do I."

When Raven's Cry returned to the tepee, he immediately went to his brother's side. Night Thunder was hot to the touch and he sometimes muttered words that made no sense. Raven's Cry hoped their father would make more medicine over him, but Bunch of Lodges only said he'd done what he could and now things were in the hands of the spirits. It seemed to Raven's Cry that Bunch of Lodges avoided being near Night Thunder and so did his mother.

They said little, only went about their night preparations with heavy hands and tightly drawn lips. Neither of them offered the captive anything to eat so he did. She took the meat and water with a small nod of gratitude, her eyes looking older than they had when he'd first studied her. Something unspoken hung in the air, something that seemed to exist between his brother and the captive even though Night Thunder appeared unconscious, making him wonder what had passed between the two of them when they were alone together.

Before laying down for the night, he helped Night Thunder outside so his brother could relieve himself. When he asked if he should tie the captive so she wouldn't try to escape or kill them while they slept, he said no.

"Do not let your sickness steal your mind, brother," he warned. "Her husband fought bravely; she may do the same."

"No, she will not."

"How can you be sure?"

"She has seen enough killing. She will not lift a knife against us."

"Hm. Perhaps. But what if she tries to escape?"

"Then she does," Night Thunder said.

Certain that fever had been speaking for his brother, Raven's Cry warned the captive that the dogs would attack her if she tried to leave the tepee, and she couldn't make her way back to her people on foot. He said nothing about the possibility that she might try to steal a horse. If she'd taken his warning into her heart, she gave no sign, only studied the way Night Thunder stiffly settled himself back on his bed.

Despite his attempts to remain wakeful and watchful, sleep held Raven's Cry tight in its arms. When he woke, his first thought was that he hadn't dreamed. Sitting up, he saw that the captive was curled on her side, her lids drawn down in the way of someone who was trying to keep consciousness at bay. His parents hadn't yet stirred, and he got out of bed thinking to build a new fire so Night Thunder wouldn't be cold. That was when he heard his brother's labored breathing.

Hurrying over to him, he touched his forehead and was shocked by how hot, how sweat-covered it was. Straightening, he stalked over to his father and shook him. Bunch of Lodges started to slap his hand away but when he saw who it was, he stopped.

"Your son is worse," he said. "You must sing over him again."

Before the sun was high in the sky, Bunch of Lodges had performed the healing ceremony twice more, but it had done no good. Night Thunder no longer knew where he was and although he could be made to drink, he lacked the strength to chew. Raven's Cry had seen fever strip the life from a man or woman, even children, and his prayers echoed his father's. It seemed strange that he'd never thought of his brother in terms of love before, but he loved him today—loved him and hated what was happening to him.

Because having a Cree in the tepee might make it impossible

for the shaman's medicine to work, he took the captive to his uncle's place and, despite her protests, ordered her to remain there. He should have gone back home and encouraged Night Thunder to drink some more water, but the tepee's interior seemed grayer and darker than a somber day, and he needed to surround himself with space.

The Blackfeet were prairie people. He'd always accepted that and wondered how tribes like those who lived near the sea could stand to be surrounded by massive trees and close-growing ferns and brush. Being able to see into the horizon made it much harder for their enemies to approach undetected, but it was more than that. The great stretches of grassland were home and peace.

As he walked, he asked himself whether Night Thunder would ever again trod along ageless buffalo trails, then wondered whether his brother felt the same way he did about the prairie and why he hadn't asked himself that before. Maybe that's what he should do, go back to the tepee and help Night Thunder outside where the wind and earth and sky could speak to him. Still, he continued to walk.

A small, sharp-sided canyon like an open wound in the earth lay to his left, but just before that the ground rose up, and if he stood there, he could see almost to the ends of the earth. As he headed that way, he caught sight of a number of small birds scurrying through the grasses as they chased unseen insects. Despite his heavy and questioning heart, he laughed at their antics.

When, finally, he looked up again he saw that someone was standing on the hill. His hand instinctively went to his side where his knife rested, but surely no enemy would reveal himself while so close to the Blackfeet camp.

Walking closer, he recognized White Calf. Certainly she'd seen him approach, and yet she seemed lost either in her thoughts or what had caught her attention in the distance, and he was loath to disturb her meditation. To his surprise, she raised her hand, acknowledging him.

"I was listening to the morning," she said when he joined her.

"It speaks of the coming season when many animals sleep and others must spend all their time seeking food if they are to survive."

Her voice was like the wind, low and soothing and yet always different. She'd put a blanket on over her dress, giving her the appearance of being lost in it. Still, he half expected her to float above the ground like a weightless butterfly.

"How is your brother?" she asked, her question reminding him that he hadn't said anything.

"No better. Worse."

"Your father has sung his song over him and made medicine?"

"Several times, but the fire in him continues."

Closing her eyes, she nodded. She looked so peaceful standing there with her thoughts caught deep inside her that for a brief while he felt at peace himself.

"Perhaps he was wounded with a poisoned weapon," she suggested.

"Perhaps. I do not know what to do! I feel so helpless."

"I am sorry," she whispered. Her reaching out for him was such a fluid movement that he was barely aware of it until her small hand rested on his shoulder. "I wish you did not have to feel this pain."

"I do not care about myself." Her touch was like a warm bird's wing, and he was careful not to move. "I do not want my brother to die."

"Do you love him?"

"Love?" He whispered the word. "I do not know."

"I think maybe you do," she said as her hand slid off him; he felt the cold chill of that loss.

"What are you saying?" he asked. "You are not one who speaks simply because you enjoy the sound of your voice. Your words have meaning."

"I hope they do," she said, gifting him with a small smile. "I have watched you and your brother as I watch the others. Sometimes when I look into myself, I see darkness and danger and cannot bring myself to speak about that, but I do not always know who those things are for so I must study those around me because maybe the answer is in them. I have long known that you and Night Thunder are not close, that the air between you is heavy."

"What are you saying?" he repeated, alarm driving his words. "There is darkness around me and my brother? Death maybe?"

"I do not know." She pressed her hand to her forehead and was silent a long time. "My people wish for my thoughts to be simple and for me to know what tomorrow and all the tomorrows will bring and for those things to be good, but it is not so."

Maybe that explained his dreams. "You—you speak of heavy air between my brother and me. What does that have to do with his sickness?"

"Maybe nothing. Maybe I simply sense that it should not be so."

Her words were too vague when he needed something he could hold in his hand. Still, their time together felt like spring to him, and he didn't want that to turn into winter.

"What exists between Night Thunder and me does not matter today. All I want is for him to live."

"Bunch of Lodges is a powerful shaman. Perhaps he will be able to heal him."

Although he would never tell his father this, he now questioned the power of Bunch of Lodges's magic. "Perhaps," was all he said. Then: "I sent the Cree captive away because maybe she sickens my brother with her presence."

"No. She has nothing to do with it. When I looked at her, I saw only a woman mourning the loss of her husband. Listen to me. Dealing with her grief will make her strong, and if she is near Night Thunder, her strength might touch him."

"I will do as you say then. The sacred white calf speaks to you," he told her. "I beg you, ask Him what must be done to save my brother's life."

Instead of answering, she dropped to her knees and pulled a dried blade of grass out of the ground. She pinched it between her fingers, rubbing them back and forth until the blade had crumbled.

Then she blew on it and watched the wind carry it off.

"If I come into your tepee and make a different kind of medicine, Bunch Lodges will hate me."

"I do not care! Night Thunder must live!"

Raven's Cry hadn't asked what she planned to do, but if he had, White Calf wouldn't have been able to tell him much except that the wind had whispered to her to collect the leaves of the *na-wuh'-to-ski* plant and boil it in a small amount of water until she had a mush and cover Night Thunder's wound with it. Bunch of Lodges wasn't in the tepee when she, a downcast Little Rain, and Raven's Cry entered, but she'd just knelt beside Night Thunder when the shaman arrived. He glared at her but said nothing, only walked to the far side and sat. She wondered if he'd been at Red Mountain's burial place.

The Cree captive hadn't acknowledged anyone, and yet White Calf was intensely aware of her presence. Raven's Cry had been right to consider that Little Rain might have brought a malevolent spirit with her and that was why Bunch of Lodges's medicine hadn't worked, but White Calf felt nothing evil around the woman. Little Rain remained encased in grief, her thoughts going again and again to her dead husband, making White Calf pray the time would come when she could tell her that her husband's spirit had found peace because of Middle River's death. However, if she did, the captive might either not believe her or be frightened.

Shaking off the sense of solitude that so often surrounded her when she communicated with her spirit, White Calf concentrated on Night Thunder. His half-closed eyes briefly focused on her, but the effort was too great and he soon returned to the nothing place where he'd been.

Praying to the sacred white calf, she placed the mush over the hot and swollen wound. Then she sprinkled a little cool water over that. Night Thunder's muscles had jumped when she first touched him, but she now sensed him relaxing. Surely the cool poultice soothed his fevered side, and she had no doubt that the wind had spoken wisely to her, but her dreams of the death of the Blackfeet way of life—a death she didn't doubt—were proof of how little control she had over her world.

Outside children played, women gossiped, and men bragged, and she all too often found herself being distracted by Raven's Cry's silent presence. In the late afternoon she caught the sound of wailing and knew Middle River's family had returned to his tepee and were once again mourning his death, something they would do daily as long as the tribe remained here. One and then two of the dogs picked up the sound and then a man yelled, silencing them.

She remained beside Night Thunder, repeatedly dribbling water over the poultice. The second time she prayed aloud to Wind, Bunch of Lodges stalked out. A little later, Chief Sleeps Too Late poked his head in and informed Raven's Cry that he was expected to join Bunch of Lodges and others so they could discuss the risk of retaliation from the Cree. Raven's Cry asked if it would disturb her or cause Night Thunder harm if the captive remained with her. She told him no, then watched as he stood and walked outside, his movements graceful and sure.

"I have heard of you," Little Rain whispered unexpectedly when they were alone. "It is true that the animals speak to you?"

"Sometimes," she replied, reluctantly turning her thoughts from Raven's Cry.

"But—you are not a shaman, are you?"

"No."

"I do not understand."

"I do not either," she admitted, surprised she'd told the Cree that. "I believe I was given a gift when I saved the sacred white calf. I do not understand that gift, cannot guide it in any direction. It simply is. I have learned to accept."

Little Rain was breathing heavily now but, unwilling to be distracted from Night Thunder's condition, White Calf didn't study the other woman too closely.

"My husband is dead," Little Rain whispered. "Dead at the

hands of the one you are trying to save. How can I accept that?"

"Can you change what is?"

"N-no. I—I may have to stay here until he grows tired of my presence and sends me home or I anger him so that he kills me. This is not where my heart wants to be." She indicated her surroundings. "I do not understand Blackfeet ways. I do not want to!"

"But you must embrace the truth."

Sobbing softly, Little Rain pulled her knees up tight against her body and began rocking back and forth. Although she remained where she was, in her mind, White Calf walked over to the other woman and clutched her tightly.

11

The evening had been full of sweat baths and prayers, much feasting, and Bunch of Lodges' insistence that his oldest living son had proven himself to be a mighty warrior, but at long last Raven's Cry was able to take his leave and return to the tepee. He wanted to believe his parents cared how Night Thunder was doing, but instead of joining him, Bunch of Lodges and Dirty Knee Sits remained with those who were now talking about how many buffalo the tribe's arrows would find in the coming days.

Either White Calf or Little Rain had recently tended the fire. Red lights like infant lightning ran over the tepee's walls, reminding him of the time he'd taken a burning brand into a mountain cave. A foolish boy, he'd hoped to find a slumbering bear he could kill so he could wear its teeth as a necklace. Instead, he'd come across a pile of old bear scat and several bats who'd blindly flown around him, their tiny mouths open to reveal knife-edged teeth. When one passed so close that he felt the wind from its wing on his eyelids, he'd dropped the brand and run back into the sunlight.

Maybe if his brother was dead, he would run again.

After determining that Little Rain was either asleep or pretending to be, he approached White Calf who maybe hadn't moved in all the time he'd been gone. She reminded him of a wolf watching distant prey, silent and unmoving, yet missing nothing. He wondered if her thoughts had turned to him at all today.

"He is dead?" he made himself ask.

Although she looked up at him with her bright eyes, she didn't speak, and he knew he would have to learn the answer for himself. His legs felt heavy, and yet it was important to him that his moccasins make no sliding sound as he slid closer. Mothers sometimes sat over their sleeping infants looking for all the world as if they were content to spend their lives studying the tiny one that had come from their bodies. Night Thunder shouldn't matter that much to White Calf and yet it seemed as if they were no longer two separate humans but one. Standing over them now, he saw that they breathed at the same time.

"He lives," he whispered, shocked by his jealousy.

"Yes, he does."

"And is he—"

"I am here, my brother," Night Thunder said. His eyes opened, then a few seconds later, they closed. "Do not speak as if I am not."

Here but for how much longer? Afraid in a way that made his heart pound, he touched the back of his hand to Night Thunder's forehead. It seemed cooler than it had been earlier, but maybe he only felt what he wanted to. Because White Calf hadn't moved away from his brother, he had to lean closer to her in order to see the wound. The medicine she'd made was no longer on it, and the swelling had gone down; it wasn't as angry-looking as it had been.

"Your side?" he asked. "Is there much pain?"

"No, not much." This time when Night Thunder opened his eyes, they remained that way. "And my thoughts stay with me; I no longer feel as if I have lost them."

Telling himself he'd remained in the sweat lodge too long and that was what had weakened him, Raven's Cry sank to his knees near White Calf. He wasn't sure what he'd planned to say, not that it mattered because at that moment his shoulder brushed hers and he forgot everything.

"What did our father want?" Night Thunder asked, his voice low but strong. "I heard him ask you to come with him."

"He brags, that is all. And he insists that I hear every boastful word."

"His talk is still about you, is it not?"

Night Thunder sounded resigned, and he saw no reason not to tell him the truth. "I do not understand what lies beneath his words, but it is more than simple boasting. Do not bother yourself with an old man's talk. When you are able to leave here, you will tell everyone what happened and they will know the truth of it."

"Not the whole truth," Night Thunder whispered. "Some things a man must keep within himself. Things that—White Calf, I owe you my life."

My life. Night Thunder was right. How could he have forgotten that? Hoping to make amends, he turned toward the young woman. He was surprised and pleased to see that a small smile had transformed her usually somber features.

"I had my doubts," he admitted. "When I saw what you were doing, I asked myself what could be accomplished without our father's medicine pipe and feared—but I no longer do."

"I do not understand it either," she said as she reached out and brushed Night Thunder's hair out of his eyes. "But maybe it is enough to know that the fever is gone."

Night Thunder still lacked the strength to stand, and even the effort of talking tired him, but she was right; he would take each small gift the spirits gave them, and in the end, his brother would be whole again.

White Calf shifted her weight, signaling that she wanted to stand. However, she'd been kneeling for so long that her legs must have gone to sleep because she abruptly leaned forward and began kneading her thighs. Although he'd often dreamed of taking a maiden in his arms, Raven's Cry had never done it; still, he didn't hesitate from gripping her arms and helping her to her feet. She swayed, making him wonder if her knees might buckle, and he continued to support her. He'd always thought of her as a strong, straight woman, and yet she felt so small in his arms, almost as if she wanted to remain there.

"Thank you," he whispered, "for my brother's life." *And for these few moments together.*

Watching Raven's Cry and White Calf together had reminded Little Rain of the way she and Takes-Knife-at-Night had stood with their bodies touching, their souls speaking to each other, love crackling like a newborn fire. Raven's Cry had thanked the Blackfoot woman for saving his brother's life, but Night Thunder had murdered Takes-Knife-at-Night! If only her husband's weapon had found the young Blackfoot's heart!

When White Calf opened the door covering to leave, Little Rain noted that it was night again, not that it mattered because she couldn't empty her mind and order her muscles to relax so she could fall asleep. Instead, she listened to the low droning sound the brothers made as they talked and struggled against memories that both threatened to destroy her and kept her alive.

A little while later, the shaman and his wife came in, and she concentrated on what they were saying. From what she understood, there'd been much talk of buffalo hunting, but it would never be anything except talk until scouts reported that they'd found a worthy herd. Bunch of Lodges wanted Raven's Cry's to have dreams that would reveal where the buffalo were, but Raven's Cry told his father he had no control over what happened while he was asleep and couldn't say whether his dreams had meaning. Bunch of Lodges insisted Raven's Cry stop saying that. *His* son had been given a gift. He *had* to carry that gift into the future. Through all the talking, Night Thunder simply watched, making her wonder first what he was thinking and then why it should matter to her.

"Enough," Raven's Cry said at last. "You say I am one thing; I say that I may not be what you want of me. Tonight I turn my mind from that thing and give thanks to the spirits that Night Thunder did not follow Red Mountain into death."

When both Bunch of Lodges and Dirty Knee Sits nodded agreement, Raven's Cry told Night Thunder he'd help him outside so he could relieve himself, and then he wanted to be left alone so he could sleep.

"My thoughts are the same," Night Thunder said. "But I want Little Rain to come with us."

"No!" she gasped.

"Yes. You are my captive and you will do as I order."

"But—"

"You have spent too much time in here. Doing nothing except mourning." His tone softened. "The air tastes clean outside. That is where children play and laugh, where the stars show themselves. We both need that."

Clean, fresh air, a night sky alive with stars! How had he'd known how much she craved those things when she hadn't until he himself mentioned them?

After Raven's Cry helped Night Thunder to his feet, the three of them stepped outside. The Blackfeet village looked so different at night, all shadows and low fires instead of antlike activity and too many eyes on her, forcing her to remind herself that nothing had changed and she was still a Cree trapped in a Blackfeet camp. There were no great mountains of clouds tonight and although the faintest hint of day remained in the sky, it was already getting cold. Shivering, she took in all she could of her surroundings while the two men headed away from her.

A fat-headed dog slunk up to her and sniffed her legs but didn't challenge her, leaving her free to make her way to the rear of one of the tepees where she squatted and relieved herself. As she stood, her thought was that she'd return to where Night Thunder lived because there was nowhere else for her to go, but that was before the stars made their impact.

As a child, she'd tried to count them and, failing that, had entertained herself by creating endless shapes out of their placement. As she grew older, she saw the stars as part of her world and yet more so, objects of mystery and awe so far away that maybe not even eagles and hawks could reach them.

She and Takes-Knife-at-Night had stood under the stars before they were married and talked about how his hunting skills would keep their cooking pots full and how her belly would swell with sons and daughters. Although the pain of knowing she and the man she still loved would never again share his dreams with her nearly caused her to double over, she reminded herself that his soul had found its way into the sky by now. He was looking down at her, loving her and sending her his courage.

"What do you want me to do, my husband?" she asked. If the stars heard, so much the better. "If you wish me to join you, send me a message and I will provoke the Blackfeet into killing me. Or maybe I will seek out a rattlesnake or poison berries."

Clouds had been forming in the direction of winter storms and might soon cast a blanket over the stars, but for now the ancient night lights winked at her, challenged her to look deep into herself for the answer to her question.

"I do not want to die," she whispered, "especially from poison berries because that death takes so long. I should be eager to join you in the next world, my husband, but I look at this world, and I am not ready to leave it. The air—my captor said that the air would smell sweet out here, and he is right. Takes-Knife-at-Night, my lungs have not yet had their fill of air, and my eyes have not seen everything they want to. There are sounds of this world that I do not yet know about that I wish to hear for both of us. The time will come when I join you, but I want to bring you tales of a lifetime. I need . . ."

Restlessness drove her legs, and she began walking aimlessly. As the camp's sounds and smells became less, she felt as if her heart was awakening and being set free. Earlier, first to her disbelief and then horror, she'd found herself praying for Night Thunder to live when she should have wanted him dead. Surrounded by space and dark quiet, she told herself that the wounded Blackfoot must have cast a spell over her and turned her against her heritage, her husband. But she was beyond his reach now; he could no longer twist her thoughts.

"Stars, see me. Moon, hear my words. My lungs are no longer

full of Blackfeet air. My ears no longer hear their words. I am again Cree."

Cree! Her people had once made the vast woodlands closer to the rising sun their home. They'd roamed their land on foot and in canoes and depended on deer and wild rice to fill their bellies, but that had been before pale-skinned newcomers known as trappers had shown them that wealth lay in beaver pelts. As nearby beaver grew scarcer, her grandparents had moved into new country where they'd found Dakota and Assiniboine and now Blackfeet. The oldest Cree said that life had been better when they lived in the woods and not on the arid plains, but she'd never known anything else and didn't concern herself with what had been.

Instead, she'd learned that to be a Cree woman meant kneeling during childbirth and being surrounded by midwives, one of whom cut the navel cord. Later the cord was put in a decorated skin bag the child wore around his neck while the afterbirth was wrapped in a piece of hide and hung on a tree in the woods. A Cree newborn wasn't bathed but dried with soft wood or moss and when a few days old, was placed in a hide bag stuffed with moss. She didn't care how Blackfeet women gave birth or how they treated their infants, nor did it matter what they did to their dead—at least it hadn't until she'd been forced into a Blackfeet village.

Freedom was a wonderful thing, cool breezes for her alone, no one watching her, walking without wondering when she would be told that what she was doing wrong. Becoming Cree again.

How far had the Blackfeet taken her? As the warmth of freedom spread through her, she realized she'd gone beyond grief and shock and was now thinking about how she might return to her people. Night Thunder and his brother cared little what happened to her, either that or they were so wrapped up in what they were saying to each other that they'd foolishly allowed her out of sight. Either way, the experience of being alone had reawakened her mind, her will to live. Surely that was it.

She'd been grabbed at night, but despite that, she and her captors had traveled as fast as their horses could go until dawn when they'd stopped long enough to allow the animals to rest and eat, but then the horses had been forced to walk at a brisk pace until nightfall. They'd slept in a canyon with a nearly dry creek trickling through it. More traveling had begun at dawn and, despite another short rest the next night, the hard pace hadn't ended until they'd reached the Blackfeet camp late the following day. On foot, her return journey would take her more than twice as long but although she had nothing to eat or drink with her and the nights might be bitterly cold, she was now determined to return to where Takes-Knife-at-Night's bones waited for her.

White Calf had given her a pair of moccasins, and although she regretted taking advantage of the Blackfoot woman's generosity, she had no choice. The moccasins might not last, and she started toward where the horses were corralled. She was wondering how she might get her hands on a rope so she could control a horse, when she heard a youth laugh. A moment later another young man said something that caused the first to laugh even harder. Obviously the Blackfeet kept guards around their horses. She didn't dare risk being seen by getting closer.

The moon hadn't yet joined the stars and might not until the night was well advanced, and if the clouds continued to grow she wouldn't be able to see more than a few feet in front of her. Praying for her husband's spirit to show her the way and cover her in courage, she struck out as rapidly as she could without risking injury. If Night Thunder hadn't yet realized she was missing, he soon would, but he lacked the strength to come after her and maybe, she tried to tell herself, the others didn't care enough to leave their warm tepees to look for her.

The Blackfeet had set their camp near a small lake that summer had sucked nearly dry. The land around it was uneven with a number of rises and long, narrow valleys that were home to many small animals, but although surely buffalo had used the creek for as long as either the buffalo or the water existed, none were around it now. The constant climbing and then scrambling down increased her need to concentrate on her footing and allowed little time for wondering what she would do if she was pursued. Still, she was glad walking took so much effort because otherwise her determination might turn into uncertainty. She'd never been alone so far from home, and at night.

A whir of movement that turned out to be a low-flying owl was followed by the shriek of a dying rodent. Occasionally she kicked up insects hiding in the grass and once she heard a deer running away, but those things were part of her world and comforted her. No matter how many times she strained to hear approaching horses, she remained alone.

At least she believed she was until something that felt like cold fingers brushing the back of her neck caused her to stop midstride and spin in a circle that left her dizzy and without answers. She could, she tried to tell herself, be near an unseen deer or maybe a rabbit or mouse watched her from behind whatever shelter they'd chosen, but her body didn't fear those things.

Although she took a few more steps, the sense of unease didn't go away. Her heart picked up its cadence and the prickling along her spine intensified. Balanced on her toes, fingers clenched, she once again took in her surroundings, much slower this time. The clouds continued to build, but they hadn't yet swallowed the stars, which remained bright enough to paint her world as indistinct, silvery shadow. A jumble of boulders lay some distance to her right. On her left was a small group of trees which—

—no, not the trees.

Breathing through flared nostrils, she turned her attention back to the boulders. She still couldn't see anything beyond what she expected, yet her body now quivered, reminding her of a frightened deer a moment before it takes flight. What she didn't dare forget was that although deer had the gift of speed, she wasn't so blessed. Unarmed, she might—

—a wolf.

With air trapped in her frozen lungs, she strained to make sense of what stood on the boulders. She saw not so much a broad chest, large head, and strong legs but a powerful form that stared back at her as if content to do so for all the nights of its life.

A wolf was nothing to fear. Yes, she'd seen them attack buffalo calves and fawns and tear them apart almost before their hearts stopped beating, but wolves were wise and cunning creatures who wanted nothing to do with humans. They might regard people from a distance or even allow their curiosity to draw them just beyond range of an arrow, but they were unlike dogs who might bristle and growl. Instead, with a flicker of sleek movement, they disappeared whenever a human attempted to approach.

She would do that now, take those necessary steps and—

Although she didn't remember ordering her feet to move, she must have done so because she was closer to the wolf now, but it still hadn't turned and run.

"Go!" she yelled. "Leave me!"

In answer, the wolf lifted its head skyward, opened its mouth, and sent its howl out into the night. When it was done, it stared at her.

White Calf was standing alone near the entrance to the men's sweat lodge when she heard approaching footsteps. If her thoughts hadn't taken her beyond this place and time, she might have believed that one of her people was approaching her, but she knew it would be the Cree captive before the young woman hurried to the still-burning village campfire.

"They are not looking for you," she said. She kept her voice low, her movements slow and deliberate so as not to frighten Little Rain. "Raven's Cry wanted to, but Bunch of Lodges said he did not care what happened to you and ordered him to remain here. Night Thunder is too weak."

Little Rain stared at her but didn't say anything. From the way she turned her body this way and that while standing close to the fire, White Calf guessed she was cold. Still, it seemed more than that.

"You should go inside," she said.

"In—not yet."

Nervous energy radiated out from the young Cree, but although

White Calf sensed she needed and wanted to talk, the words would have to come in their own time. Because she'd only intended to be outside long enough to see if the night had any messages for her, she hadn't worn a blanket. Joining Little Rain, she too stared into the embers.

"Sometimes I think this is my favorite time," she said because revealing something about herself might help Little Rain relax. "When the day is done and all becomes quiet, I often stand out here by myself and think about the generations of Blackfeet who did the same and pray there will be more generations to come."

"I-I love morning." Little Rain kept her voice at a near whisper. "There is energy in dawn, that and promise."

"Yes, there is."

Little Rain sighed, then turned her back to the fire. Her attention immediately went to the darkness surrounding the village and she shivered. "If I tell you a thing, will you give me its meaning?"

"I do not know if I can."

"If not you, then who?" A note of desperation had crept into Little Rain's voice. "I wanted to run away. I cared not what would happen if I was recaptured, nor did it matter that I would have to travel for days and nights before I found my people; all that mattered was that I heard Cree sounds and thought Cree thoughts."

"But you returned."

"Yes." Another sigh followed by silence.

"What is it?" she asked. "Little Rain, a journey begun should be finished."

"I-I know, but this . . ."

"What?"

"It is my people's belief that wolves exist because Old Man Coyote so willed it. Warriors sometimes call on Wolf to give them speed and courage, but wolves must be summoned. They do not seek out humans. Perhaps—perhaps it is different in the land of the Blackfeet."

"No. It is not."

A squeak of alarm escaped Little Rain's lips, and she covered her throat with her hand. "No?" she whispered.

"Why do you ask?"

"If I say more, you will think me crazy."

"Listen to me. Many things happen within me for which there is no explanation. If I told you everything, you would say I have eaten of the crazy-making weed, but I know I have not."

"No. I would never—All know of your power."

White Calf didn't want to talk about herself. The truth was, she wished she could walk away from Little Rain and what she sensed the young woman was trying to tell her, but she couldn't. Instead, she waited.

"I ran," Little Rain whispered. "And when I was afraid I might fall, I walked. I listened to the night and felt peace but then—then I knew I was no longer alone."

She bent down and picked up a couple of branches, which she threw on the fire. The new flames seemed to mesmerize her. White Calf glanced at them, then stared up into the smoke. Smoke and clouds were so much alike; taken for granted, they revealed nothing, but if one studied them—if she studied them—sometimes they opened themselves up to her. The smoke was doing that now.

"You saw a wolf," she said.

"How—"

"It does not matter. Tell me, what did the wolf do?"

Turning away from her, Little Rain spoke with her face covered by night while the newly fed fire spat and cracked and clouds stole across the sky and began to swallow the stars.

"It—came toward me. I wanted to run, but my legs had forgotten how. I stood there believing I would die. Finally the wolf was so close that I should have felt its breath, but there was none."

She wrapped her fingers around her upper arms and hugged herself. "I saw teeth—great teeth, and in my mind, I felt those teeth sinking into me, but there was no pain. Instead—instead I felt great cold."

*   *   *

White Calf had no doubt that Little Rain had been visited by a sign from the spirits, which was what she'd told the young woman while they stood warming themselves by the fire. She'd even told her that Night Thunder and Raven's Cry had recently seen one of the beasts and it had acted in much the same way, but she had no idea whether it had been the same wolf, or what the message had been. She said nothing about her own disturbing Wolf-visions.

Little Rain had started to admit that she'd never had such an experience and feared the vision's meaning, but before she could finish, Raven's Cry stepped outside and said that Night Thunder had heard her and wanted her inside.

White Calf should have done the same because even with the fire, she felt chilled, but Little Rain and the smoke-figure had given her a great deal to think about and until certain things had a chance to become clearer in her mind, she didn't want to be distracted by her family.

A dog crept close and turned in a full circle before curling into a ball and lying down near her. It regarded her through slowly closing eyes, an occasional yawn telling her that she merited little attention. When the dog was asleep, she crouched and stared into the flames, at first seeing only coals and burning wood. Then, slowly but inescapably, the fire became the path Little Rain had taken, and at last she stood where the Cree woman had when the wolf approached her.

The wolf was a fully grown male, yet his coat showed no sign of the battles he must have fought and no warm breath issued from his black muzzle. In her mind, she crooned to it, and its ears twitched and its eyes held unblinking on hers. The eyes became larger, first darkening and then turning lighter and lighter, finally losing all color. Before long she was no longer looking into wolf eyes but into the heart of a snowstorm where fat flakes danced with ice pellets and winds fought with each other.

There were people in the middle of the storm, their shapes so indistinct that she couldn't tell how many were trapped in it. They trudged on heavy legs, backs bowed, fur capes pulled tight around haggard faces. They smelled of fear and desperate determination; and although she tried to free herself from the image, the howling gale assaulted her, and now it was her legs inside the thick but inadequate leggings, her eyes stinging from tiny ice shards, her heart and lungs fighting for life.

12

Night Thunder waited until morning to speak to Little Rain. In between snatches of restless sleep, he went over and over what had happened since he'd taken her outside last night, but as much as he wanted the truth from her, he didn't want it while his brother, father, and Dirty Knee Sits were around.

Now they were alone, the others having left shortly after dawn. Neither Dirty Knee Sits nor his father had spoken to him, Bunch of Lodges undoubtedly because he was angry over White Calf's interference. Raven's Cry had started to approach him, but their father had insisted they leave immediately for the sweat lodge.

Although he still felt newborn weak, he'd gone outside, ordering Little Rain to accompany him. She'd said nothing to him last night and had yet to break her silence this morning. He might have demanded she not keep her thoughts from him except that her eyes had the hollow look he'd seen in his father's when Red Mountain's body was brought to him.

As they headed away from camp, he noticed that Middle River's younger brother was staring at Little Rain, an unnecessary reminder of the hostility between Blackfeet and Cree.

"The Blackfeet do not seek revenge against women and children," he told her. "Warriors battle warriors; it is the way of men. But your husband killed a man much admired, and his family will not turn their backs on that."

"I feel their hatred," she said softly, her eyes fixed on the ground.

"Is that why you fled last night, because someone approached you?" he asked. As he expected, she shook her head.

"Why then?" he demanded.

"You do not know?" Stopping, she whirled on him. Anger had replaced grief. "I cannot believe that. Surely you know I want to be with my people."

Walking just beyond the village's confines had exhausted him, and he sought out a large rock to sit on. The boulder felt cold beneath his leggings, and the nearby grass was coated in a thin film of frost, but after his fever, the coolness was welcome. Although he indicated he wanted her to join him, she remained standing. If she started to run, he could never catch her. Still, despite the way she studied the distance, she remained near him.

"Why did you return?" he asked.

"I—I do not want to say."

"You talked to White Calf. My brother said he found the two of you together. If you opened yourself up to her, you can do so now."

"It is not the same," she said, shaking her head. "White Calf is a woman, one with a gift. I-I sought her wisdom."

"Why?" he demanded. Then he softened. "Listen to me. We are bound together, you and I. Our families have shed each other's blood, but that is not all. Last night when sleep would not come to me, I thought of that and now believe the spirits are responsible for our being together. Because this is so, we must speak the truth to each other."

He expected her to insist he was wrong. Instead, she sank to her knees and picked a frozen blade of grass, which she warmed by breathing on it. She didn't look at him as she told of fleeing into the dark last night of her determination to find her way home. Then she said that a wolf without the breath of life had blocked her way.

"I returned," she whispered. "I did not want to, but it was

what the wolf demanded of me and if I did not obey, it would have killed me."

"A wolf? You told White Calf this?"

"Yes. No. I think—I think she knew before I spoke the words."

"Ah. What did she say?"

"Only a little. She had just begun when your brother ordered me inside. She was not shocked; she did not call me foolish or say that I must be lying."

In other words, White Calf believed what Little Rain had told her.

"This is not the first time Wolf has shown himself," he admitted.

Her head came up and she stared so intently that he felt as if his soul was being invaded. "I know. White Calf told me," she said.

"White Calf—how can that be?"

"What do you mean? Did you not seek her wisdom about it?"

"No." A memory tapped at him, a sound he'd heard just before counting coup and attacking Takes-Knife-at-Night. "Your husband had wounded me," he forced himself to say. "Until this morning, I have not thought beyond that. But maybe my brother . . . and maybe Wolf spoke to her."

"Perhaps."

He went after the memory in his mind and tried to recall everything that had happened during those frantic moments, but the image failed; maybe he'd only imagined it.

"I must speak to White Calf," he said. "If, when he stood looking at me, Wolf had been trying to warn me that I would be wounded, I must have the wisdom to heed Wolf's message the next time he shows himself."

He waited for her to remind him that he'd killed her husband, but she didn't, maybe because she hurt too much for that, maybe because she was unable to take her thoughts off last night's wolf. His own head ached from everything it had tried to absorb.

"Will you try to escape again?" he asked because that was easier to talk about.

"What?"

"I ask, will you try to escape again?"

"If I say yes, you will throw ropes on me."

"You are in Blackfeet country; a Blackfoot wolf warned you to return to me. Only a foolish child would risk Wolf's anger."

"That or a woman who does not care whether she lives or dies," she whispered.

Was that possible? Looking at her, he tried to imagine what it was like not to embrace life. He'd never tell her that he'd fought her husband, not because he'd been driven by the desire to kill, but because terror had given him strength—at least he thought that was what had driven him.

"I do not believe you," he said. Although he'd only been sitting a short while, the frozen earth had penetrated him, and he'd begun to shiver. He tried to plant his legs under him, but they felt weak, forcing him to pause while he gathered what little strength he had. "If you wanted to die, you would have invited Wolf's teeth."

Her head snapped back, and her fists clenched. "I may be your prisoner, Night Thunder, but you do not own my thoughts, my actions. When I die, it will not be at the hands of a Blackfoot wolf."

"Perhaps that is not for you to say."

"Or for you either," she challenged. "You believe Wolf was warning you of danger? I say you are a fool if you think Wolf will keep you alive."

"You do not—"

"Listen to me! I did not want to think of the night my husband died, but it happened. And I remember something else."

"What?"

"Before you killed him—" She swallowed. "You stood like a small, frightened child, and I could taste your fear."

White Calf was puzzled to see Night Thunder and Little Rain together. From what she'd observed while she was caring for the warrior, she'd believed the Cree woman wanted nothing to do with her captor, yet as they returned to his tepee, she sensed that something with great meaning had passed between them. They were wary around each other, holding themselves separate from the other and maybe hating each other, yet connected in ways even she didn't understand.

Instead of asking Night Thunder whether he had further need of her services, she paced restlessly from where the horses were kept to the middle of the village and then back to the horses again. When one of the animals reached out to sniff her, she forced herself to concentrate on her last vision. Had there been horses in it?

Eyes open but unfocusing, she ran her hands over a strong, living shoulder and took a little warmth from the curious animal. No matter how many blankets she'd thrown over her, she hadn't been able to get warm last night. It was her vision's doing, icy fingers touching her despite her best efforts. Where had the Blackfeet been going and why were they out in the middle of a blizzard instead of safely inside their tepees?

The sound of her name being called both startled her and pulled her away from unwanted and maybe unanswerable questions. Chief Sleeps Too Long, his face painted with red and black stripes, was approaching her. Despite herself, she drew back as far as the horse's unmoving bulk would allow. Face painting occupied much of a warrior's time and competition to see who could make the most elaborate design was keen. Sleeps Too Long, however, was content with dark and bold slashes of color, but that wasn't why she didn't want him to get too close.

Not long after he'd counted his first coup by touching three armed Snakes while not receiving so much as a scratch, he'd married Big Dancer, the old chief's daughter. Everyone had said the two would produce sons worthy of becoming warchiefs, but although Big Dancer's belly had swollen numerous times, none of the babies had remained inside her long. Most had died without drawing breath, but two had struggled to live for several days, so small that Big Dancer had held them in the palm of one hand. Sleeps Too Long's father had insisted that Big Dancer didn't give proper thanks for the food his son provided, and as a result, the spirits caused the babies to be born before their time, but White Calf and the midwives knew different.

Each time she'd lost a child, Big Dancer's face and belly had been swollen and bruised and her women's place had looked wounded. After the last failed birth, Big Dancer had returned to her parents' tepee, and her voice was no longer silent. Her former husband, a man of great courage and leadership in war, brought violence to his marriage bed.

"I am humble before your power," Sleeps Too Long said, his mouth barely visible through the heavy painting. "Yesterday Night Thunder was close to death, but today he is able to walk."

"He is young and strong. With the right medicine—"

"The right medicine!" he interrupted. "Your wisdom is responsible, White Calf, only yours. Bunch of Lodges may be keeper of the medicine pipe, but his prayers and chants did not touch his son."

She didn't want to talk about this with Sleeps Too Long, but he was chief, which meant she couldn't turn her back on him. "I was not there when Bunch Of Lodges was making his medicine. I cannot say what he did."

"Ha! That is what he is proclaiming today. He boasts that his medicine and not yours saved Night Thunder's life. His words ring loud and none tell him that he is wrong."

If Raven's Cry's plea hadn't touched her heart, she'd never have entered the tepee and done what she had for Night Thunder because she knew she'd earn the shaman's wrath, but Raven's Cry was the shaman's son, and she'd told herself he would stand between her and Bunch of Lodges.

"I think of what you do and applaud your courage, White Calf," Sleeps Too Long said. "I stand in awe of your powers."

She couldn't remember ever having a private conversation with the chief and sensed that something unsaid was on his mind. While she waited him out, she continued to rub the horse's shoulder and scanned the distance.

"I was wrong to marry Big Dancer," he said. Another horse

approached them, but instead of welcoming its curiosity, Sleeps Too Long shoved it away. "She may be a chief's daughter, but there is no power in her."

"She is fertile. Many times she—"

"But she could not keep my seed within her until the birth-time came. That is why I divorced her."

"She says different," she retorted. "She says you were ungentle with her and that is why she left you."

Sleeps Too Long shrugged, and his features took on a pained expression. "I will not speak out against Big Dancer. Let her have her hate-filled words, words which run over her because she still grieves for our unborn children. I am chief and do not spend my time discussing what should have remained private between us."

He looked down at his hand, then started to lift it. Just when she thought he was going to touch her, he let it drop.

"Do not judge me harshly, White Calf. I, too, mourned my dead children; I grieved. When one after another they died, I died a little with them." His eyes briefly clouded. "Perhaps Big Dancer felt the pain of my grief and thought I meant it to become her burden, but it is done. Done. I am ready to begin again."

Both touched by his unexpected revelation and on edge, White Calf waited him out.

"You are different from the other women," he said.

"Yes."

"Just as I am more than simply a warrior." He pointed to in-dicate the front of his tepee with its many paintings indicating the number of times he'd counted coup. "I have spoken to your father."

"Have you?" Despite her effort to sound confident, her voice lacked its usual strength.

"You cannot be surprised, White Calf."

But she was because she'd often asked the spirits who she'd marry, only they'd remained silent.

"Your father waits for you," he said.

*   *   *

"But I do not wish to marry Chief Sleeps Too Long."

Grass Eater continued to smoke his pipe, but despite his immobile features, White Calf sensed that a great deal was going on inside him. Her mother had left as soon as she stepped inside, taking her younger brothers with her. Alone with her father, she wished they'd done this more often over the years so there'd be an easy closeness between them, but he'd always regarded her with a look of confusion on his face.

"He no longer has a sits-beside-him wife," Grass Eater said. "You would become that one."

"Father, I am White Calf, a woman who has been blessed by the spirits. I do not need a husband to have a place within the tribe."

"No Blackfoot woman remains unmarried even if she must share a husband because too many men have died in battle. That is our way."

"But I am like no other."

With a groan, he rocked forward. Once a fine horseman, he now spent much of his time sitting beside a fire. When she looked at him these days, she saw not the straight warrior he'd once been but a man aging too quickly.

"Why do you fight me on this, daughter?" he asked. "Having you has caused me to walk in a way no Blackfoot father has ever done before. You gave me much pride and when others spoke of your powers, my heart beat faster."

"I am glad," she said, meaning it.

"But your mother and I lay awake many nights talking about what your life would be like. We wanted your gift to remain so all could benefit from it, and yet you should not remain separate from all others."

It hadn't been easy being her parents, had it, she thought as she became aware of the sound of numerous horses approaching. Was Sleeps Too Long already bringing his bride-price horses to her father's tepee?

Grass Eater cocked his head and then nodded but didn't mention the disturbance. "Being true to our beliefs was not so hard when you were a child, but your body is now that of a woman. It is time for the next step to be taken."

Our chief is not a gentle man," she insisted. She had to speak louder in order to make herself heard because there was no end to the snorting and hoof stomping. "It matters not so much to the warriors who care only that he is able to lead in war and battle," she continued. "When I think of that, I know he is right to boast of his accomplishments, but Big Dancer left him."

"Yes, she did. And he has spoken to me of that."

"Has he?"

"Yes. He says that Big Dancer became so grief-stricken at each loss that she pummeled herself and would have scarred herself even further if he hadn't stopped her."

"She was torn in her woman's place," she insisted, trying to reconcile that awful image with what Sleeps Too Long had told her about the sorrow he felt for his dead babies. If whoever had brought the horses wasn't careful, they might knock over the tepee. "A tiny baby cannot do that kind of damage."

"I do not know. Women, not men, attend a birth. But a woman made crazy by too many deaths may harm herself in many ways."

Could that be what had happened? She didn't want to believe Big Dancer capable of that, but ever since she'd left Sleeps Too Long, the woman had spent most of her time by herself, doing little and saying even less except to proclaim her hatred of her former husband.

"I will not talk of women's things today," her father said. After staring in the direction of the greatest noise, he shook his head. "We must speak more of what way you will now walk, but first you must go outside. Then you will understand."

Understand what, she wondered. All she knew was that the tepee must be surrounded by horses but that couldn't be because not even the chief had this many animals. She waited for her father to stand; then they walked to the opening together, and he lifted the blanket.

Stallions, mares, and foals milled around, making it impossible for her to see anything else and yet she heard excited talk and laughter, proof that the entire village knew what was happening.

"I do not believe—" she began. "I am not worth—no woman is—"

"Look," her father said.

She did so, the realization slowly dawning that the horses carried not just Chief Sleeps Too Long's markings but the symbols Raven's Cry had recently put on the animals he'd brought back with him.

"Both?" she whispered.

"You have two suitors, my daughter."

Fog lay blanketlike over the ground when White Calf finally managed to slip way from the village. Despite her shock, she understood why everyone had laughed at the sight of so many horses bunched around a single tepee while the chief and a young, still learning warrior glared at each other. Sleeps Too Long had enlisted the help of several members of the esteemed All Crazy Dogs society in keeping his herd under control while Raven's Cry and his father were aided by a number of Mosquitos. Boys and girls ran back and forth in a futile effort to keep the horses separated, and although some of their parents chided them for adding to the confusion, most were too busy pointing and laughing.

She'd felt as overwhelmed as her father looked, but because being courted was a solemn occasion, she'd struggled to keep from letting her emotions show. If first one and then three stallions hadn't suddenly decided to try to mount a single mare, she might have had to suffer all those stares until she ducked back inside. Instead, she'd taken advantage of the diversion by darting away. Fortunately, no one had tried to stop her, and she'd kept on running until the din was little more than a murmur.

Two men wanted to marry her! She'd spent so much time wondering how she'd react when her first suitor approached her, and now two had demonstrated that they desired to mix their herds with her father's.

Shaking off the overwhelming thought, she put her mind to where she was walking. Little Rain might have come this way last night, her emotions still lingering in the air and on the grass; maybe that was why her thoughts felt like shattered ice. Had Little Rain loved her husband the way her parents loved each other? If she had, his death must have nearly destroyed her and explained why she'd curled in a silent ball while her captor fought for his life. And yet she'd summoned the strength to run away.

Run and then returned because of a wolf.

Maybe, White Calf thought ruefully, if she found the spot where the wolf had been last night, it would still be there and she could ask it which man she should marry. But wolves concerned themselves with killing and eating, not the joys and sorrows of a woman's heart.

"Mother Earth, please, hear me. I have been shown two paths today, two ways for my life to be lived. My father wants me to marry Sleeps Too Long; I know he does because that is who he talked about. But when I look at the chief, I think of what Big Dancer endured and I am afraid."

Hearing herself say that, she stopped walking. "What am I afraid of?" she demanded. "Sleeps Too Long has brought glory to the Blackfeet, and our enemies tremble when they speak his name. If I become his wife, I will tell him my dreams, and he will use them to make the Blackfeet even more powerful. That is good."

If Mother Earth was listening, she gave no indication. Instead, an angry gust of air swirled around White Calf, causing her to pull her blanket protectively around her.

"I do not know what kind of warrior Raven's Cry will be. My eyes have been drawn to him, as have the other maidens' eyes, because he is tall and handsome. But . . ."

Even before her voice had fallen away, she knew she wasn't alone. She hadn't come that far from the village and shouldn't be in danger from raiders from other tribes, unless Cree warriors had come looking for Little Rain.

The thought of becoming a captive of the Cree chilled her, and she made a careful survey of her surroundings. Her world was gray, dark and light, and every shade in between, but nothing that didn't belong.

Belong.

Perhaps Creator Sun had placed the great wolf there, she thought as her eyes brought her the truth. The creature couldn't have looked more a part of the prairie if it had been born of earth and dry grasses, its body made for traveling great distances, its keen nose capable of catching the most delicate scent, its eyes accurately recording all movement.

Little Rain had spoken of its aggressive nature and if it attacked, she couldn't possibly outrun it, but in the world of the People, there was little difference between a wolf and a newborn buffalo calf. All were sacred; all might add to her understanding of her world.

"Are you a spirit wolf?" she asked, trusting the wind to carry her words to it. "Who sent you? Was it Mother Earth? Perhaps Creator Sun sent you here for me to see. But it is not enough that we look at each other; we both know that. There must be more."

The wolf began walking toward her. Despite its heavy coat, she imagined the muscle and bone beneath the thick fur, blood pulsing through its veins. But if this was the same wolf Little Rain had seen last night, it might not breathe like a mortal wolf and thus would have no need for blood or muscle, or even bone.

"I want to understand." Her voice was less sure now, more awe-filled and a little afraid. "I must understand! But I do not."

The distance between them became less and less and then was nothing. The wolf's ears were tipped in black as dark as night and its pale eyes held secrets deep within them. She was acutely aware of its aloneness. Wolves lived in packs, but this one was by itself. If she was anyone else, she would tell herself it couldn't possibly need anything from her, but she was White Calf and maybe the wolf believed she was more animal than human, and around her, he wouldn't be lonely.

"I will not run as Little Rain did," she told it. "Is that what you want of me?"

No.

Feeling as if she'd been struck by lightning, White Calf struggled to swallow. After taking several less than steadying breaths, she clutched her courage to her, then reached out to touch the wolf. Its coat was almost too thick for her fingers to penetrate, but she pushed her way in until she found the breastbone. There was no beating heart. It smelled, not of the bodies of the creatures wolves killed and ate, but of winter snow.

"A spirit," she whispered. "Not mortal but truly a spirit."

Yes.

"What do you want of me?" she demanded with a little cry. Her own heart was beating so rapidly that she was afraid it would burst through her chest. "What is your message?"

When she returned to the village, White Calf did nothing to indicate she was aware that everyone was looking at her. Instead, she walked into the middle of the horses still around her father's tepee. Most ignored her. A few stretched out their noses to sniff her. Once, a pinto colt born in the spring, tried to take her blanket in its mouth. She gently pushed it away, then allowed the two herds that today had become one to surround her.

This decision was hers to make. Her time of being a woman alone was over, and what she did today would change her life. After gathering in a great, horse-scented breath that almost but didn't quite replace the taste of winter she'd carried back from her encounter with the wolf, she selected a horse that belonged to Raven's Cry. Taking it by the rope around its neck, she led it to where her father kept his horses and left it there. Only then did she acknowledge her two suitors.

"I have made my decision," she said. "I will become Raven's Cry's wife."

"No!" Sleeps Too Long bellowed. "He is unproven!"

"In your way but not in mine. Listen to me." She still felt

wrapped in wolf fur, still touched by the look in the spirit's eyes. "Listen and understand. Before Raven's Cry returned with the Snake horses, Bunch of Lodges asked me to find his son in my mind so he would know whether he was well. I did. A wolf was with him."

Raven's Cry didn't say anything, but when he nodded, she had her answer. He'd just come from the sweat lodge, and his naked chest still glistened with sweat, but cool mist surrounded him as the coming winter stole his heat. He hadn't begun to shiver.

"Wolf Spirit follows Raven's Cry," she said. "Today Wolf Spirit came to me. I heed Wolf's wisdom."

13

The feast to celebrate White Calf's marriage to Raven's Cry took place two days after she'd added his herd to her father's. Both sets of parents had wanted more time to prepare for such an important wedding, but that couldn't be because it was nearly time to move the clan to their winter home and, as a number of women pointed out, past time to hunt buffalo.

The braves, most of who were in camp now, took advantage of the celebration to dress themselves in their finest clothes, carefully comb and braid their hair, paint their faces, and then strut around anticipating admiring glances from the women. For the most part, the women were too busy to pay them much attention and the men turned to boasting about their hunting and fighting prowess or entertaining each other with ancient Blackfeet tales. Dirty Knee Sits ordered Little Rain to collect wood and help with the cooking, but even with the older Blackfoot woman watching her every move, Little Rain was aware of White Calf's comings and goings. Because there was no fresh meat in the tepee, Little Rain had mixed dried sarvis berries, chokecherries, bull berries, and red willow berries together with the sweet syrup from camas root and was adding that to a large stone bowl full of smoked meat when White Calf came into view wearing her wedding dress. Although White Calf hadn't had time to make a new dress, she'd added bright bird feathers and a long fringe to a ground-length one used only for ceremonies. Her hair was undone, allowing it to cascade down her back, and she held her head high, showing her long, slender neck; but Little Rain saw not a Blackfoot maiden but the way she herself had looked on the day of her own wedding.

Tears burned her eyes, but she didn't try to wipe them away because they'd only return. She remained crouched over her cooking as several women surrounded White Calf, the sound of feminine laughter soon filling the air. She too had been surrounded by giggling girls as she prepared to enter Takes-Knife-at-Night's tepee for the first time. They'd spoken of how handsome and brave he was, how no harm could possibly come to someone who'd proven himself to be a fearless fighter, how he would fill her belly with babies and leave her breathless from lovemaking.

Remembering the lovemaking—too little of it—she felt the strength go out of her legs and sank to the ground. She might never see where his family had placed his body, never wail over his bones, never touch the clothes he'd died in. Worst of all, maybe his spirit was searching for her in Cree land, not here among his enemy.

"Stand up!" Dirty Knee Sits ordered. "Be careful or you will burn the food."

Startled, she saw that the flames around the stone cooking kettle had grown dangerously high, but before she could put her mind to doing something about it, Dirty Knee Sits snatched up the kettle and placed it on the ground. She started to berate Little Rain, then stopped.

"You cry at my son's wedding? Perhaps you love him yourself?"

Little Rain shook her head at the impossible thought but didn't trust herself to speak. Dirty Knee Sits frowned. "You are Cree. Why should I waste my time trying to understand what happens inside you? You do not know our ways, do not belong here."

She was going to set her free? Before the thought had half taken root, Dirty Knee Sits shoved her, causing her to sprawl on the ground.

"Do not show yourself until the feast is over," Dirty Knee Sits ordered, her overly large lips flapping. "I do not care what you do, but I will not have your tears stain today." She clasped her hands to her breasts and smiled the smile of an animal who has hunted well. "All my life I dreamed that one of my sons would become a great man within the tribe. When I realized it would not be Red Mountain, I thought my heart would break, but my prayers have been answered. Raven's Cry has blessed the tribe with many horses and led the way to avenge his brother's death and now he marries White Calf. White Calf! Soon he will become chief and I—Go! I will not speak to a Cree about my heart's desires."

Only too glad to distance herself from the boastful woman, Little Rain handed her the stirring stick and started to back away.

"Wait!" Dirty Knee Sits called. "Do not try to run away again. Do not!"

"I—"

"If you do, my son will hunt you down and kill you."

Despite Dirty Knee Sits' order that she have nothing to do with the wedding, Little Rain didn't go off by herself. Instead, her wandering took her closer to the horses Raven's Cry had given to White Calf's father, and she stood there taking a small measure of comfort from their presence. The spirits had blessed today. Although it was cold, the sun was bright and the sky a clean blue that reminded her of the hot afternoons of her childhood when she and other girls had gone off to pick fruit but in truth had spent most of their time chasing butterflies and talking about boys.

As the realization that even back then she'd had her eye on Takes-Knife-at-Night sank in, the tears she'd hoped she'd left behind returned to fill her head and heart with pain. Surely White Calf wasn't in love with Raven's Cry the way she had been in love with the brave who'd become her husband. Not only couldn't she imagine anyone else being blessed the way she'd been, but neither White Calf nor Raven's Cry looked at each other with their hearts exposed.

Many marriages were like that, people brought together because the tribe would benefit from their union, and a marriage between those two surely strengthened everyone. Still, if they cared nothing for each other . . .

Blinking back the tears that wouldn't end, she struggled to concentrate on something, anything, else. All the horses here now belonged to White Calf's father but because Raven's Cry was becoming part of their family, the horses had remained his as well. Dirty Knee Sits had been right when she'd said that her son had been blessed. In truth, she'd never seen that many horses under a single ownership, never imagined—

A pinto stallion with a white mane and black tail caught her attention out of the corner of her eye. Suddenly numb, she turned and studied it. The horse wasn't particularly tall but so well muscled that it must be able to travel endlessly without wearying, she told herself, not yet ready to admit the truth of what she was seeing. Still, she made her way through the other animals until she could have touched the pinto. It studied her with white-rimmed eyes in that excitable way of stallions, and when she saw the whirlpool of hair at its shoulder, she knew.

A sob broke free, startling the horses around her. She reached out, but the stallion shied away and she lacked the strength to follow it. Instead she stood in the middle of the milling herd and cried the tears of someone who has lost everything. She was still there when Night Thunder found her.

Her first awareness of him came when she sensed that the horses were no longer solely interested in her. Her vision was too blurred for her to make out his features, but his slow way of walking told her enough. If she could have put her mind to it, she would have jumped on the pinto—Takes-Knife-at-Night's favorite horse—and galloped away, but grief had weakened her, forcing her to stay where she was while Night Thunder approached.

"Dirty Knee Sits told me she sent you away," he said, speaking just loud enough to be heard over the sounds the horses made. "I came looking for you."

Of course he had. She was his after all.

When he took her arm, she'd already prepared herself for the touch. What she hadn't expected was for his grip to be gentle, or for her to be willing to follow him. He didn't say anything until they stood on the far side of the herd with the animals between them and the village.

"I will not tell you not to cry," he said, "because if your tears dry now, they will only return. It is better to let them have their way and then be done with them."

She would never stop grieving for her husband, never!

"Little Rain, listen to me. I do not know what will happen to you. Perhaps the time will come when you will be returned to your people, but you are here now. This is your today. You must accept that just as I must accept certain things about myself."

Her tears had ceased while he was leading her away from the horses, but now they began again, and he regretted telling her what he had. Still, his words were the truth, and she needed to hear them, needed to make them part of her just as he'd been forced to listen as she told him that she'd been aware of his nearly numbing fear the night he defended himself against her husband.

"When Red Mountain was killed"—*By your father* "—I thought Bunch of Lodges' grief would never end," he said. "But today another of his sons is taking a wife and that has made him smile. You, too, will come to smile."

"How do you know?" she demanded. "Is your heart Cree?"

If anyone had been around, he might have slapped her to let her know that a prisoner doesn't throw angry words at her captor, but it was just the two of them.

"You know I am not Cree," he told her. "But I know what makes a Cree heart bleed."

She jerked away but took only that one step. Her ravaged face reminded him of a heartbroken child, and his first instinct was to hold her against him and try to comfort her. Instead, he kept his arms at his side and tried to remind himself that her husband had nearly killed him.

"Tell me," he said when he should have wanted nothing to do

with her. "What new grief touched your heart today?"

Her mouth opened and closed and he thought she wouldn't answer, knew it was better if they remained apart from each other like this, but then her eyes took on a lost and frightened look, and he felt himself being pulled into her emotions.

"You and your brother took my husband's horse." Her fingers trembled when she pointed. "It is now with your herd."

She was crying because of that? "Did we? I do not remember."

"Not remember," she whimpered. She began rocking back and forth and didn't seem to know what to do with her hands, which first clutched her elbows and then went to her waist. "Was killing my husband and capturing me such a little thing to you?"

No! But he wasn't going to bring up the terror that had gripped him and made everything else unimportant; it was almost more than he could handle knowing she'd seen his fear.

"That was not what I meant," he amended. "I do not remember much of what happened after your husband and I battled. The horses that were taken were my brother's doing. He is who placed them with White Calf's father's herd."

She nodded but her eyes remained dull. Going in search of her had weakened him when he needed to hold on to his strength so he could participate in tonight's feast. The female members of White Calf's family were busy erecting a small tepee for the newlyweds to use tonight. Perhaps he should have ordered his hostage to assist them, but grief had her in its grip and he wouldn't force her to help prepare another woman's marriage bed.

"The plains are so vast," he told her. "Blackfeet and Cree can ride for days without seeing each other, and there are more than enough buffalo for everyone. Yet you and I have been brought together, and men from both our families have spilled their blood so that blood runs together."

"I-I have thought about that."

"Have you? Tell me, do you believe this was the spirits' doing?"

"The spirits?"

"Nothing happens without reason," he pointed out. "Everything we do and that is done to us is because the spirits so will it."

Her gaze settled on him at that, and he felt her mind reaching for his. The sensation left him vulnerable, but even if he hadn't said what he had, the truth would have been there.

"I do not want to think about that," she whispered. "I must walk through today, only one day at a time. I will not look behind me or try to see into tomorrow."

"I do not believe you."

"What?"

An excited shout spun him around, but when he realized it was only Quail Legs calling to Raven's Cry who'd just emerged from his tepee wearing a new fringed shirt and leggings decorated with porcupine quills, he dismissed what was happening in the village.

"You say that you care nothing about the breaths you must take tomorrow or the ones you took yesterday, but I do not believe you," he said. "The ancient ones made us who we are, all of us, Blackfeet and Cree, and we can never forget that. Neither can we turn our backs on what must be done to ensure our children's lives."

"Your words are too heavy," she insisted. "I do not wish to hear them."

"What you wish and what is are not the same." He grabbed her arms and pulled her close. Although she could have broken free if she'd wanted, she didn't try. "My brother will become a husband before this day is over. Tonight he may place new life inside White Calf. I ask myself what that child's life will be like. Will he know nothing except war with the Cree? If so, he must have the wisdom and courage to face his enemy just as Raven's Cry and White Calf must have the strength to go on if he is killed as Red Mountain and your husband were."

Silent, she stared up at him. His words swirled around him, and he wasn't sure he fully understood them, or why he'd said anything to her.

"This horse," he indicated the pinto, "does not care whether it belongs to Blackfeet or Cree, but you and I are not horses. We bleed Blackfeet or Cree blood. And sometimes that blood runs together. When that happens, those who live, grieve, and that grief is the same."

"No! It is not!" she insisted. Jerking free, she backed away from him and stood there looking like a wild horse preparing to bolt despite restraining ropes around its neck and legs. "You lost your brother, but I saw my husband killed, saw life draining from the man I loved and could not help him. Before that I watched my father become twisted and bitter. You carry one sorrow, but I live with two. And I hate you for it!"

He could have killed her. In fact, with her outburst echoing inside her, Little Rain was surprised that Night Thunder hadn't put an end to her. Several years ago her tribe had attacked a band of Shoshone and captured several women. Although the women were eventually adopted into the tribe, for awhile they'd lived in fear of their lives, slinking around like dogs fearful of being kicked, eagerly doing whatever was demanded of them. A child at the time, she'd had little to do with the Shoshone women, but she had noticed how hard they'd worked and how grateful they'd been for every bit of food they were given. She should have learned from them and kept her mouth closed and her thoughts to herself.

But how could she when Takes-Knife-at-Night still walked beside her and she'd become his killer's hostage?

As she sat a short distance from where dozens of laughing Blackfeet sat gorging themselves, she struggled to keep from thinking about Night Thunder's words by watching Raven's Cry and White Calf. Both were dressed in their finest clothes and seemed to enjoy having so much attention heaped on them, but they seldom looked at each other and sat surrounded by their respective families. Even as preparations for her wedding had been taking place, she'd spent every possible moment with Takes-Knife-at-Night and when his arm brushed hers or he leaned down to hear what she was saying, the blood pounded in her temple.

That was what Night Thunder didn't understand.

Although he sat next to his brother, taking his turn smoking and praising Raven's Cry's accomplishments, she carried on her silent and unwanted argument with him. He had lost a brother, but had he ever felt capable of flying simply because Red Mountain looked at him? No! Had he clung to Red Mountain at night and told him things he'd never told another human being? No! Had he dreamed of walking through all the tomorrows of his life with Red Mountain? No!

She must have been staring at Night Thunder for too long because he suddenly straightened and stared at her, but instead of glaring at her or ordering her to leave, his features seemed to soften. Then he pointed upward, and she followed the line of his finger to where a hawk floated in an effortless circle.

"When your sister married, I knew what I would tell her, but I cannot give you the same words because you are different."

White Calf nodded but couldn't think of anything to say to her mother. Although hardly anyone had left the feasting area, they were all too full to go on eating. It was night and the central fire glowed and crackled from the many branches that had been thrown on it. Soon she would be expected to walk away from the merrymakers and join this man called Raven's Cry in their first night as husband and wife.

"I wish this had not happened so fast," her mother went on. "When I married your father, we had spent many days talking and getting to know each other so that when the time came for us to make love for the first time, I was not afraid of him."

"I do not fear Raven's Cry. I would never marry a man I did."

Laughing softly, her mother gave her a fierce hug. "I told myself I would not say anything, that whichever man you married had to be your decision, but when I knew it would not be our chief, my heart was happy and I gave thanks to the spirits."

"Did you? What would you have done if I had chosen Sleeps Too Long?"

Still laughing, her mother shrugged. "Then I would have told you what was on my mind."

White Calf couldn't help chuckling. "I thought so."

"Yes, I am like that, a woman who says what she thinks. Only, my daughter, it is not so easy today."

From where he sat across the campfire, Raven's Cry glanced at her and then went back to talking with his brother. "What do you mean?" she asked, wondering which of them would be the first to start toward the tepee they'd share as man and wife.

"White Calf, you were such an easy child, laughing and happy even though your curiosity often got you into trouble, and I thought I would never be able to trust you around fire."

"I remember," she admitted. "I kept wondering if I would turn the color of flames if I stepped into them."

"And no matter how many times I ordered you to stay away, you were determined to learn the truth for yourself."

"Just be glad I finally put that thought behind me."

"Yes." Her mother sighed. "You did because you saved a white calf and everything changed for you, changed about you."

This must be what her mother had wanted to talk to her about. Giving her her undivided attention she said, "After that things were different between us. We were no longer simply mother and daughter."

"No, we were not because the spirits had taken you for their own. I was happy for you and felt blessed, but I also wanted back my little girl. For you to be like all others."

Because this wasn't the first time her mother had admitted that, White Calf wasn't shocked. "I am still your daughter. That will never change."

"But it will because tonight you become Raven's Cry's wife."

He was looking at her again, this time with a questioning look in his eyes. "Yes. I will."

"I want to tell you what it is like to be a wife, but because you are like no other, I cannot use the words I did with your sister."

"I know what happens between a man and a woman when they share the same blanket," she whispered. "I have heard—"

"You have heard your father and me making love; I know that," she said with no sign of embarrassment. "But the spirits guide your steps and sometimes show you the way into tomorrow. It is said that the same gift has come to Raven's Cry. Maybe the two of you are like no others. Maybe—maybe what happens to you in bed has never happened before."

"Mother."

"I have to say those words," she went on hurriedly, "because maybe it is so. I—I just want you, my daughter, to understand that."

Acutely aware of the attention he was drawing to himself, Raven's Cry nevertheless walked over to White Calf and held out his hand. After the smallest of hesitations, she took it, but as she got to her feet, she looked down at her mother, not him. Neither of them spoke as they made their way through the sprawling mounds of people who'd all but eaten themselves into a stupor. Quail Legs called out that he hoped Raven's Cry would have the strength to stand in the morning; that was followed by raucous laughter from everyone, but if White Calf was embarrassed, she gave no indication. Instead, she unexpectedly drew closer to him. Looking around, he saw that they'd just passed Sleeps Too Long and that the chief wasn't smiling.

"He is not our concern," he whispered. "Not tonight."

"But later he will be."

Because she was right, he simply lifted the blanket that covered the opening to their new home and watched her step inside. Ever since she'd placed his horses with her father's herd, he'd been the object of uncounted jokes about how to put his manhood to best use. Someone had suggested he tie a bone to it so it would remain pointed and at the ready at all times. Another warrior had insisted that exposing it to cold air was what it took to keep it healthy, while someone else argued that heat and not cold served the same purpose. His father had given him a handful of duck down which he'd blessed and told him to surround his organ with that. Although the down still cradled him, he'd felt no stirring to life tonight.

White Calf turned toward him in the darkened space; they'd

need a fire for heat before morning, but he had no desire to chase away the night.

"My father is most pleased that you chose me," he said. His voice caught and he had to struggle to get it going again. "He made much medicine to assure that would happen."

"Did he?" She too sounded unsure of herself. "If-if he had not wanted this marriage, would you have offered up your horses?"

He didn't answer because the truth was he'd stepped from being a youth into manhood so suddenly that he hadn't had time to fully comprehend the change. "What I know is that I had a dream, two dreams, and they became the truth. I do not know why I now walk the same path you do or if . . ." He'd been about to admit that he still doubted his dreams, but he couldn't tell anyone that.

"I do not remember when my head was not filled with what others cannot see. Perhaps it is easier for me."

"Perhaps," he said, surprised by her understanding of what he was going through. "Tell me, when you wish to see what does not exist here and now, how do you tell that to happen?"

She stared to sit down on the blankets they would share, then straightened. "It is not like that. Sometimes, but not often, I can make myself take that walk. People ask me this and that and I try to give them the answers they seek, but sometimes the truth brings pain. It is easier for me not to search, but even if I do not, sometimes things come to me."

"Like visions of when pale-skinned ones take our land."

"Yes," she whispered. "When I feel that coming over me, I want to run, and with all my heart, I want to be like everyone else."

His two telling dreams had led to a great number of horses and a successful raid on the Cree. True, his brother had been wounded and Middle River killed, but coup had been counted and Red Mountain's spirit was at rest. Still, if he knew that his dreams would show the end to the Blackfeet way of life, he would fight and curse those dreams.

"Your dreams are like fire," he said. "Fire brings warmth but it can also burn."

"You understand," she whispered.

He was now sorry that they were standing in darkness because he wanted to see the look in her eyes, to know without reservation that they were no longer strangers.

"I believe it is right for us to be married," she said. Her voice remained soft and hollow. "Together we will have wisdom that a person alone cannot."

Reaching out, he first found only air, but then his fingers brushed her, and he drew her close to him. When he'd first seen her in her wedding dress, he'd been afraid she wouldn't want to remove it for him or that he wouldn't be able to spill himself inside her, but he no longer was.

"I do not care about that tonight," he told her. "Tonight a man and a woman will become one. That is enough."

"Yes." Her voice quavered. "It is."

White Calf and Raven's Cry came together in a jumble of half-discarded garments, fumbling hands, and soon, deep and rapid breathing. They trembled and drew back, reached out, then retreated again. Then he ran his tongue over her ear and she laughed; his laugh followed hers and they were no longer awkward. As she spread her legs and his manhood searched for and found its home, they clutched each other, kissing, exploring, learning.

When the lovemaking was over, he held her in his arms, his heart beating next to the ear she'd placed on his chest. They remained like that, breathing as one, until they heard the wolf howl.

In a nearby tepee, Night Thunder and Little Rain too heard the cry.

14

Big Wind Plains had been named by Teton Indians who'd been the first to resign themselves to the fact that the wind here never ceased blowing. In summer, its heat instantly dried a horse's sweat as soon as the animal stopped running, but its winter breath came from the land of the Eskimo, so fierce that snow swirled in endless circles instead of coating the ground. Still, grass grew sweet and thick and buffalo had been coming since the beginning of time to fatten on it.

In his dream, Raven's Cry had been riding the Cree pinto and had had so much trouble controlling the headstrong animal that he'd paid little attention to where he was going. When the prairie stretched in front of him without end, his first thought was to let the horse run until it could no longer catch its breath. Maybe then it would understand that it had a new owner, but before he could give the beast its head, he spotted a distant darkness. Curious, he dug his heels into the pinto's sides, and suddenly the stallion was no longer fighting him but prancing lightly as a well-trained horse awaiting its rider's command does.

"You see the darkness too, don't you," he said. "Are your eyes keener than mine? What waits within the ground-cloud?"

Instead of answering, the pinto started forward, not trotting but gliding as if its legs had become wings. Raven's Cry felt himself rising and looked down to see that he and the pinto were no longer on the ground but drifting above it. The wind seemed to be pushing him from behind, yet the pinto's mane and tail hadn't become wind-tossed. In the vaguest of ways, he knew this wasn't happening, that the warrior known as Raven's Cry wasn't astride a ghost horse with the power to fly, but he'd seek the truth later. For now he'd sit straight and strong and see where he was being taken.

The dark mass became larger and larger like black water shooting up from the earth, yet he knew it wasn't water. The pinto soared higher into the sky and then he was no longer on horseback but settled between the outstretched wings of a white-headed eagle. Giddy with excitement, he buried his fingers in the eagle's feathers and peered down through eyes that had grown as sharp as those of a bird of prey.

He was flying over a vast herd of buffalo, bulls and large cows leading the way while calves brought up the rear. Like ants marching over leaves, they trod over Big Wind Plains, not stopping to eat and yet not stampeding either. There was a cliff at the far end of the plains and if they kept on, they might fall off the cliff and buzzards would pick their bones clean, but the prairie was so vast that he wondered if they might grow old and die before they reached its end.

"Where are you going, Buffalo?" he asked.

Home, came the reply.

"But buffalo are like the Blackfeet, always moving, always seeking new land. Tell me, where are you going?"

This time there was no answer, and as the eagle kept pace with the herd he saw that some of the calves had stopped and were looking behind them. A bull bellowed but instead of obeying his command to catch up, the calves started stampeding in all directions.

It was then that he saw Blackfeet hunters galloping after the calves.

* * *

White Calf lay on her back staring up at the smoke hole. Night had just begun to give way to day, but there was no reason for her to get up; besides, Raven's Cry had flung his arm over her during one of his restless movements and she might wake him if she tried to move.

Because her father snored so loud that he sometimes kept everyone from sleeping, she'd wondered if Raven's Cry might too, but although she'd roused several times during the night, his breathing had lulled her, not alarmed her. Even when he'd thrashed about, and she'd waited for his dreams to be done with him, she'd been a part of him. It felt strange to share her bed with another human being and even stranger to allow him access to every part of her. She'd told her mother she was ready for marriage, and even when Raven's Cry reached for her that first time she'd believed she'd known what would happen next, but she'd been wrong.

Barely aware of what she was doing, she lay her hand on her husband's forearm, concentrating on the soft hairs, smooth skin, and firm muscle. His arm was heavy on her ribs and she'd lost a little sensation there but had to admit she didn't mind. Still, she'd been motionless for so long that her own muscles felt jumpy and she slowly straightened her legs. Only then did she become aware of the soreness at the apex of her thighs.

She was no longer a virgin. The soreness and the bit of blood she'd shed were proof of her new status. Last night she'd been too aware of Raven's Cry to think beyond him, and after they'd made love, she'd been so tired that sleep had come easily. Now, waiting for him to join her in the morning, she tried to concentrate on what remained the same about her. She was still White Calf, still visited by visions and dreams, still set apart from all others. That shouldn't be hard for her to remember.

But she hadn't slept alone last night and knew the feel of a man's hands on her breasts, a man's organ joining them together.

"Big Wind Plains is a five-day hard ride from here," Chief Sleeps Too Long insisted. "I say it is foolish to send all our hunters and the women necessary to butcher buffalo so far simply because Raven's Cry says he had a dream."

"Are you saying my son lies?" Bunch of Lodges demanded.

Instead of answering, the chief, who'd been sitting at the place of honor in the middle of his tepee, looked around at the assembled warriors. His attention only briefly touched Night Thunder, but that was all it took for Night Thunder to sense Sleeps Too Long's anger. Every male old enough to have participated in the Sun Dance had crowded into the tepee and although their collective body heat was more than enough to keep the morning chill at bay, Sleeps Too Long had put fresh wood on his fire as proof that the women of his family provided for him even through his wife had left him. The smell of sweat made Night Thunder half sick.

"On his wedding night, Raven's Cry dreamed of a great herd," Bunch of Lodges continued. "I am shaman and I say only a fool does not believe that his dream was sent to him by the spirits."

Sleeps Too Long grunted and leaned over to whisper something to his friend Blue Snake. Then he looked over at Raven's Cry who sat to his father's left. From what Night Thunder understood, Raven's Cry had told their father about the dream as soon as he left White Calf's side this morning. Bunch of Lodges had immediately prayed to Sun and Old Man, his prayers loud enough that they'd attracted the attention he surely wanted. As word of Raven's Cry's dream grew, the tribe members had clamored around him. Chief Sleeps Too Long must have realized that prestige and power was shifting to Raven's Cry because he'd ordered every man to his tepee for what he'd called the most important of discussions.

"I do not turn my back on this dream," Sleeps Too Long insisted. "I have not said this. But if there truly is a great herd there, we must take full advantage of it. It is not enough that just the hunters and butchering women go to Big Wind Plains. I now say that this is a journey for the whole village. The Snakes claim Big Wind as their own. However, if they see so many Blackfeet, they will hide from us."

"But that will slow us down," Raven's Cry insisted. "The buffalo were on the move. They may be gone by the time we arrive, and in my dream, I saw no Snakes."

"Maybe," Blue Snake spoke up. "But I add my voice to our chief's. There are no buffalo here."

A number of the older men agreed with Blue Snake, then Sleeps Too Long thrust his hands over his head, silencing everyone.

"Listen to me," he said. "I accord Raven's Cry much respect. He has proven himself and without his vision, we might never find the buffalo we need, but he is not chief; I am. I say that today the women will take down the tepees and tomorrow everyone will start toward Big Wind."

Blue Snake tapped him on his shoulder. Once again the two whispered among themselves. "The hunters will go on ahead," Sleeps Too Long continued, "and when we have found the buffalo, we will send a runner for those who will do the skinning. If someone believes different, now is the time for them to say so."

Raven's Cry slowly got to his feet. As was custom, he'd smoked from the communal pipe and passed it to his left, thus freeing himself to speak.

"My chief is right," he said. "The hunters must go to Big Wind, but the women have been speaking for a long time and we must listen to them. I say hunters and a number of women will start for Big Wind. The rest, however, must begin the journey south. When we have finished hunting, we will join the rest of the clan where the sun shines on us and there is not so much snow. What say you, Chief? Do we heed the women's words? My wife's words?"

Sleeps Too Long grunted but didn't argue. Instead, he waited until the pipe had passed to him and then smoked.

"I hear your words, Raven's Cry," he said. "They are wise."

As talk turned to successful hunts in the past, the assembled braves' excitement grew. Someone threw back the blanket door, but there still wasn't enough air, and if he'd been able to move, Night Thunder would have hurried outside.

"Do you have enough arrows?" Quail Legs asked him. "The herd your brother spoke of is so large that it will take all our weapons to bring them down. What horse will you ride? Surely not the ugly one your father gave you. Maybe your brother has a few left after gifting White Calf's father and will let you have one of them."

The joking was good-natured, but Night Thunder was barely able to summon a brief smile. He'd felt close to his brother when Raven's Cry helped him back to the village and would always be grateful to Raven's Cry for insisting their father acknowledge that he'd killed a Cree, but since then, Raven's Cry had grown distant. Of course, he told himself, if he had just taken a wife, he wouldn't have time for a younger brother. Still, he felt cut off from the boastful talk and loud planning and gave little thought to the respect Sleeps Too Long had accorded Raven's Cry. It wasn't until the warriors began leaving the tepee that he admitted his brother had very little to do with his mood.

He'd heard a wolf last night. It seemed that a wolf, maybe a spirit wolf, was around all the time now, but no one had mentioned the sound this morning. Maybe his father and Dirty Knee Sits hadn't heard it, and his brother and White Calf might have been too occupied with each other to notice anything else, but Little Rain had sat up and listened for a long time. Spirit wolves did nothing without reason, but what had been behind the haunting cry?

Instead of joining his father and brother, he walked behind the tepee and stared in the direction of Big Wind Plains. When the traveling was over and if Raven's Cry's dream had foretold the truth, he would join the other warriors in hunting buffalo.

Hundreds of buffalo with sharp hooves, deadly horns, and swift danger in their every movement.

Was he the only one to fear the hunt?

Angry at himself for allowing the coward's thought, he turned back toward the village. Quail Legs had been right. If he was going to participate fully in the hunt, he needed to check his weapons and, if there was time, fashion a few more arrows. Those things were men's work, but he could order Little Rain to supply him with the materials he'd need. Besides, keeping her busy might not allow her time to think about what she'd be doing if she was back with her people.

To his surprise, he spotted her, not standing off by herself as usual, but in earnest conversation with Feather Tickles, an attractive, shy young woman well-known for her hide-tanning skill. Although she'd been courted by several men, Feather Tickles' father, Jumper, hadn't accepted any of their gifts. Instead, he'd made no secret of his desire to have her marry a wealthy and highly regarded warrior even if he already had a number of wives and children.

It was said that Feather Tickles had tried to convince Jumper that she would be much happier married to a warrior her own age and position, but so far he'd refused to listen to her. More than one person had speculated as to whether Feather Tickles might become old while waiting for someone Jumper approved of. At one time Night Thunder had fantasized about what it might be like to have Feather Tickles as his wife since he was drawn to her quiet, gentle nature, but as a young and untested brave, he would have been rejected.

He couldn't imagine what Little Rain and Feather Tickles might have to talk about, but then the ways of women weren't often known to him. They spoke of things that men kept to themselves, shared secrets, and talked about the most intimate details of their lives, whereas a man didn't expose himself like that.

With a mental shake of his head, he started toward his tepee, then stopped. There hadn't been the opportunity for him to ask Little Rain what she thought of last night's wolf call. As soon as she and Feather Tickles were done talking, he'd call her to him and ask . . .

Had Little Rain just washed and braided her hair? Maybe she had on a dress different from the one she'd been wearing when she'd been captured and that was what was different about her. Whichever it was, it struck him that although he'd always been aware of how attractive Feather Tickles was, today she was a small gray wren next to Little Rain.

*   *   *

The Blackfeet tepee was much more than just a home; it also served as a sacred place. Made of six to twenty-eight buffalo skins, the floor symbolized the earth, the sides reaching to the sky. The roundness served as a reminder of the sacred life circle that has no beginning and no end. Each tepee had an earth alter where incense was burned and prayers spoken. The floor represented the earth and the walls the sky, while the poles portrayed the pathway between the two realms, linking the Blackfeet to WakanTanka, the great mystery.

However, as the women went about rapidly dismantling their tepees and preparing them for travel, no one spoke of solemn occasions. Instead, a sense of excitement permeated the village. Caught up in the prospect of a successful hunt, Night Thunder was painting a buffalo head symbol on Deep Scar's rump when he heard several men call out and scrambled to his feet.

A half-dozen horses all tied together were being led toward Feather Tickles's father's tepee, which already lay on the ground. Surprised that anyone would take time for courting with the village on the move, Night Thunder left Deep Scar and hurried closer. Chief Sleeps Too Long, bedecked in full headdress, bone and teeth necklace, and a ceremonial shirt, rode at the head of the small herd. He paid no attention to those around him but stared straight ahead until his horse was only a few feet away from Jumper. Then, with utmost solemnity, he handed the lead rope to the older man. At first Jumper seemed unaware of what was happening, but Night Thunder suspected that was only because he didn't want to appear too eager.

"I am a man alone," Sleeps Too Long said in a loud voice. "My bed is cold at night and I have no children to help me when I become an old man. I look at your daughter and see a strong woman. She has learned the skills of womanhood well and would be worthy of me."

It seemed like a boastful speech but Sleeps Too Long was the chief, after all. Night Thunder wondered how Jumper would reply, but instead of saying anything, Feather Tickles's father only folded his arms across his chest.

"My old wife left me," Sleeps Too Long went on. "I did not want her to, but she was unable to give me children and it is not right for the chief not to have children. Even before that one returned to her parents' tepee, I had decided I would take another wife. White Calf was wrong not to choose me and may one day admit her error, but I will not sit alone and wait for that time. Feather Tickles's hips are wide. Her breasts are large enough to hold much milk. Yes, she is worthy of me."

"But you say she is worth only six horses." Jumper looked angry. "You offered more for White Calf."

"Because White Calf is different. Feather Tickles is a woman like every other woman and would be honored to have me choose her. Besides, a chief does not remain chief if he gives away all his horses."

From the way Jumper nodded, it was clear that he agreed. "You wish to marry her today?" he asked.

"Yes. Our journey begins tomorrow and it may be many days before all our people are reunited. I want my wife to skin the buffalo I bring down, want a child to begin to grow within her before winter."

Several women giggled at that, prompting Night Thunder to look around for Feather Tickles. She was still standing with Little Rain, but the two were so far away that he couldn't see the expression on her face, not that what Feather Tickles thought or did was his concern.

"What do you say?" Sleeps Too Long demanded. "A chief has much to plan before a hunt. I do not have time for endless talk."

"Have I asked such a thing?" Jumper glanced around, but if he was looking for his daughter, he hadn't found her. "You are a man of quick ways, decisive ways. I understand that."

"Then do you understand that I must have my answer now?"

Jumper shrugged. Night Thunder thought he looked like a male grouse who has run a female into the ground.

"I have long waited for this day," Jumper said as he took the lead rope from the chief. "I have seen you staring at my daughter, but I did not want her to marry you if she could not be your sits-beside-you wife. Now she can."

Out of the corner of his eyes, Night Thunder saw Feather Tickles cover her mouth with her hand. At the same time, Little Rain put her arm around the other woman's shoulder.

"Why were you with her?" Night Thunder demanded of Little Rain. "What did Feather Tickles have to say to you?"

It was late afternoon now, and although a few were still hurrying around getting ready for tomorrow's march, most of the women were preparing dinner while the men sat in groups boasting about how many buffalo they'd kill. Even the elderly men who wouldn't accompany them were engaged in the conversation. Feather Tickles had joined her father shortly after he'd taken possession of Sleeps Too Long's horses and Little Rain had gone to help Dirty Knee Sits. However, although he couldn't fault Little Rain for the way she'd conducted herself, she was his hostage and responsibility and should have asked his permission. Besides, he needed to understand what was different about her today.

"We spoke of women things," Little Rain said, her eyes downcast. "Not things that would concern a man."

"I will be the one to decide that. If you think you can get Feather Tickles and other women to speak against me—"

"No. No. It is not that."

"Then what?"

"You will not tell Sleeps Too Long?"

That made him laugh. "The chief and I are not like brothers, not like cousins even. These days he has no love for Raven's Cry and surely feels the same toward me."

"Is he a good man?" she asked.

"Sleeps Too Long? He is a fearless leader."

"That is not what I asked." For the first time since they'd started talking, she met his gaze. "Is he a good man?"

"Why?"

"Because Feather Tickles does not want to marry him. She is afraid of him."

Little Rain's eyes reminded him of deep pools of water. He tried to tell himself it wouldn't be like that if the sun was high in the sky but maybe daylight and shadows had nothing to do with his reaction.

"Afraid?" he mouthed, distracted.

"She says that his first wife was not cast out because she could not give him children but that he beat her and she fled."

"Feather Tickles spoke of this to you? You are not a Blackfoot."

"No. But I am a woman. Feather Tickles cannot speak to her mother or the other women of her family because all they want is for her marriage to bring prestige to them, but she could not keep her fears to herself."

"And she chose you?"

"Is that so hard for you to accept? Maybe." She seemed to be answering her own question. "I must remember that I am the spoils of war to you. When Feather Tickles and I looked at each other, we saw only a woman's heart, nothing else, but you will not understand that."

He wasn't sure what, if anything, he understood this afternoon. He wanted to talk to her about the wolf, demand that she tell him if her people were going to come after her, insist that she never mention his moments of terror to anyone, important things, but her voice and eyes and body distracted him. If she'd cast a spell over him—

"Feather Tickles knew I would not take her words to her father," Little Rain went on. "That is why she told me what she did. She—she loves her father but she does not feel close to him. When she was a child, they played and laughed together, but now that she is a woman, she had become his possession."

"Has she?" was all he could think to say.

She nodded. "It is her belief that her father now looks at his life and knows he will never be a wealthy or powerful man and that eats at him. He has only one way of gaining prestige and that is by having her marry well. Who better than the chief?"

Suddenly bored by the conversation, he shrugged. "Who Chief Sleeps Too Long marries is not my concern.

"That is what Jumper told Feather Tickles."

At first her simple words made no impact, but as she continued to stand before him, they seemed to take on a life of their own. "Feather Tickles believes her father does not care about . . ."

"Her heart is not his concern. Whether she laughs or cries is not his concern.

"That is not right," he heard himself say. "A father should—Enough! I do not know what a father should do or say or think!"

"Night Thunder," she murmured, "I understand."

Something with featherlike strength touched his forearm. He didn't have to look down to know she'd brushed him with her fingertips. They both stared at what she'd done.

"Do not walk away from what you feel," she whispered. "Remember, I have seen you and your father together. A man who cannot hold his father's love in his hand is a man alone."

He couldn't speak.

"I know." Her whisper trailed off until he could barely hear her. "Because that is the way of a woman who has seen the man she loves killed."

She shouldn't have told him anything, Little Rain berated herself that night as she lay under the stars, the dismantled tent ready to be tied to a horse in the morning. She'd said what she had, not just because she'd wanted to place distance between herself and Night Thunder—which she did because she felt exposed around him—but because his words had been so heartfelt and she'd cared and—

No, she didn't care what happened to him!

She would never care.

15

Many generations ago, the Blackfeet had lived near the North Saskatchewan River, but they'd gradually worked their way westward until they reached the Rocky Mountains. Because game was abundant, they remained there until they obtained horses. Horses gave them a freedom they'd never known before and they ventured out onto the plains.

Now the country that was home to the Blackfeet extended from the Saskatchewan on the north to the Yellowstone on the south, and mountains acted as guardians around broad prairies. Some of those mountains were so tall that their snow-capped peaks reached into the clouds while smaller ranges were made up of pine forests. Still, it was possible to travel for days seeing nothing except brown plains marked with yellow bunchgrass, bluestem, cordgrass, and prairie snake. Occasional winding river valleys broke up the monotony as did the red, gray, and brown ravines with their wind and rain-carved walls. The Blackfeet and other Indians used the sharp ridges and square-topped buttes rising out of the flat earth to guide themselves, often stopping to leave gifts for the spirits at the base of short, sturdy trees with gnarled trunks and thick, knotted branches created by the endless wind.

Although White Calf was his wife and she was now his family, Raven's Cry rode beside his father and brother, the rest of the tribe moving like a river around them, dust puffing up from hundreds of hooves, dogs yipping, children laughing, the traveling so much a part of their lives that no one spoke of wanting to return to where they'd spent the summer. Before long the hunters would break off from the rest but for now the entire clan was together.

The shaman had indicated he wanted Raven's Cry with him, and it was somehow easier to listen to Bunch of Lodges' boasting than try to think of something to say to the woman he'd made love to last night.

"Our chief is a fool," Bunch of Lodges said. "He took his horses to Feather Tickles's father because he did not want people to laugh about how White Calf chose you over him. And the things he said to Jumper! To hear Sleeps Too Long talk, he rejected White Calf, not she him. Does he truly think anyone would believe that?"

"It does not matter," Raven's Cry said. He had no doubt that if others had been around, his father would have kept his thoughts to himself, but the tribe had spread out since morning with the slower horses and walkers falling farther and farther behind. "He married Feather Tickles. Perhaps she will give him children and he will be content."

Bunch of Lodges spat. Fortunately, the chilly wind didn't blow his spittle back at him. "He thinks Feather Tickles is as good as White Calf? Ha! A chief should choose his wife more carefully."

Both his parents loved to gossip, but although talking about someone else was a favorite Blackfeet occupation, he'd known that those he talked about would do the same about him, and that had kept him silent.

"I say it because it is the truth," Bunch of Lodges continued. "Our chief is a fool."

"He is a proven warrior. He—"

"His time is coming to an end."

"What do you mean?" Night Thunder asked as he pulled his horse closer to Bunch of Lodges. Wind-tossed dust billowed around all of them, forcing Raven's Cry to squint so that his brother was more blur than reality. He wasn't surprised to see Night Thunder on Deep Scar. "You did not make medicine to make him sick, did you?"

Bunch of Lodges snorted and slapped his thigh. "There is no need although it would be an easy thing for me to do. Night Thunder, look at your brother. See the wisdom in him. You must know that he is no longer simply another warrior. His dreams have given him great power and that power will only grow. And he has taken White Calf as his wife. Soon everyone will want him and not Sleeps Too Long as chief."

Raven's Cry tried to catch his brother's eye, but Night Thunder had turned his attention to the horizon and his lips were drawn tight.

Our father's words are not mine, he thought, wondering if they might possibly reach his brother. *I walk softly in this new way the spirits are taking me. I do not boast and brag. I do not—I do not yet believe.*

It seemed strange to have her pick of the horses, but although her father had tried to talk her into taking five or six with her, White Calf had been content with one, a roan with white legs and an equally white blaze down her long, narrow face. She'd called the mare Snow Feet although given the way the mare loved to prance, perhaps she should have called her Dancing Legs. Maybe her husband—husband?—was displeased by her choice and that's why he was riding with his father instead of by her side. Just the same, she had to admit it was easier not to have him close by. She wasn't sure how it had come about, but she found herself riding a few strides ahead of Little Rain. She'd slowed Snow Feet so the Cree could catch up, and although they'd said little for a long time, she felt comfortable in the other woman's presence.

Little Rain rode a strong-headed pinto stallion, and when she'd asked her about it, Little Rain had explained that the horse had been her husband's and Night Thunder had given it to her.

"He is a gentle man," White Calf said. "Gentle and quiet."

"Gentle! He killed my husband!"

"He is Blackfeet just as your husband was Cree."

Instead of saying anything, Little Rain stared off into the distance. After a quick glance at her husband, White Calf did the same. She'd been so busy getting ready to leave this morning, that she'd paid scant attention to the sky. As she now did, her earlier vision came back to her in freezing clarity. It had been a small group, no more than three or four. Like storm-trapped trees, they'd bent low over their horses in a futile attempt to protect themselves from the worst of the wind.

A wise man finds shelter during a storm, so what were those dream people doing out where the blizzard could attack them? Drawing on the unwanted memory, she forced out more and more details until she was certain that all of the riders hadn't been warriors and that fear had ridden with them. The sky had been an eery mix of black and purple with clouds so dark that they seemed born of the underworld.

With a shock, she realized that today's clouds held that same hue.

"I do not like this," she said, barely aware of who she was talking to. "We are out in the open. If it storms, we cannot hide from it."

"You speak as if you have never been in snow before," Little Rain said. "A storm is nothing to fear."

"Not an ordinary storm, but one created by an angry Wind Maker is far different."

Holding up a hand to shield her eyes from the swirling dust, Little Rain focused on the cloud-mountain building in the distance. "Why would Wind Maker be angry at the Blackfeet?" she asked, challenge clear in her voice. "You are Blackfeet and the spirits sent their dreams to your husband."

"You make fun of us," White Calf said. "Do the Cree think so little of the Blackfeet?"

"I say only that the Blackfeet are no more than the Cree."

Despite herself, White Calf was glad Little Rain wasn't so weighed down by grief that she couldn't think beyond it. The pinto was becoming harder and harder to handle, obviously made excitable by the gusting wind. White Calf pulled her blanket up around her neck, but that did little to keep her warm.

"I do not want to fight with you," she told Little Rain. "It is for men to fight and kill and be killed. Women raise the tribe's children."

"Except that those children grow up to kill and be killed and our tears never end."

Little Rain opened her mouth to say something else, but at that moment, the pinto reared and she was hard-put to remain seated. A moment ago, White Calf had wanted to turn her back on the Cree but, knowing how easily Little Rain could be injured or killed if she was thrown off, she no longer did. By forcing her quieter mare closer to the pinto, she managed to limit its movements. Little Rain wrapped the jaw rope around her hand and pulled, forcing the pinto to arch its neck. Then she leaned forward and spoke quietly into a twitching ear.

"You do not want to fight me, horse of my husband," she crooned. "He loved you and you loved him. Do not forget that. Do not forget him or that I lay with him. Listen to me. Listen. He was your master and now I am. Serve me well and I will not let anything happen to you."

Although the pinto's hooves continued to stab the earth, its eyes no longer showed white.

"That is is right. That is good," Little Rain went on. "Listen to me. Listen and believe. You know the taste and feel of the wind. You have lived through winters and smelled spring's sweetness. Accept what is. Do not fight. Accept. Just accept."

"He has heard you," White Calf said once Little Rain had the young horse under control. "He may have a stallion's wildness, but he understands a woman's voice."

"I wish it was not so. I wish my husband was . . ." Leaning forward, Little Rain fastened her arms around the pinto's neck in a fierce hug. "But what I want and what is are not the same," she whispered. "This horse may want to run with the wind, but he cannot. I must learn the same thing."

"You already have," White Calf told her. "You may shed tears, but you do not hide from the truth."

"No," Little Rain said, "I do not."

Following that, the two women rode in silence for awhile as they alternatively studied the darkening sky and each other. Finally White Calf acknowledged the Cree's glance with a smile.

"I think we have thrown enough words at each other," she said. "Because we are Blackfeet and Cree we think we must be enemies, but that is not a blanket I wish to wear."

"Me either." Little Rain's smile, while not as open, couldn't be mistaken for anything else. "Yesterday I spoke to Feather Tickles and she spoke to me and I saw in her, not a Blackfoot, but a woman. The same is true of you."

Pleased, White Calf started to nod. That was when the wind changed its song and for a moment became an angry roar. The cry was low and full-throated, ancient, trailing over the prairie as if it had been waiting to be heard since the beginning of time. As alarm snaked through her, she stared into the clouds and distant nothingness until she spotted a loping figure. Gusts threw up dust-billows and caused the grasses to twist and turn wildly, but the creature moved effortlessly, untouched. It held its head high and proud, legs churning in an ancient rhythm. Then it howled.

"Wolf," she whispered to Little Rain.

"Wolf," Little Rain whispered back. "Again."

Well before darkness settled over the prairie, Chief Sleeps Too Long ordered everyone to stop for the night. Because he'd chosen a sloping canyon for them to sleep in, they were protected from the worst of the wind, and the fire horn holding a live coal quickly became several large blazes. Despite the biting cold, Raven's Cry didn't smell snow and hopefully they wouldn't have to erect their tepees. Dinner consisted of pemmican. Following that, the men filled their pipes with *kinnikinnick* and relaxed over the mix of tobacco, herbs, and dried barks.

Raven's Cry, however, was too restless.

Although caring for the horses had been left up to youths, he wandered over to where they were tied. He'd seen Little Rain's pinto act up several times, but the stallion seemed to have forgotten its earlier fright and, despite its short rope, was trying to mount a mare.

He hadn't been at all like the aggressive stallion when his body had joined with White Calf's. Certainly he hadn't squealed or tried to bite her and she hadn't kicked at him. Still, once they'd taken off their clothes and reached for each other, he'd known he wouldn't be able to stop.

His father never had sex with his mother any more; it seemed impossible that a man and woman could lie under the same blanket and not be driven by need and yet—

"Did you hear it?" White Calf asked, startling him because he'd thought he was alone.

What, he almost asked before he realized what she was talking about. "The wolf. Yes, and so did my brother although our father gave no sign."

"Hm. Some may think it was the wind, but I knew better."

"Tell me, what does it mean?"

Instead of answering, she briefly leaned against the nearest horse and smoothed her hair out of her eyes. The wind had chapped her cheeks and she would have to rebraid her hair, but even in the growing dark, he thought her beautiful.

"I do not know," she said, reminding him that he'd asked her a question. "I have asked the spirits to tell me what is behind this wolf spirit, but they are silent in that."

"In that? What about other things?"

"Other things?"

He'd hoped she'd know what he was talking about without his having to lay everything in front of her, but either she didn't know his thoughts or was forcing him to be honest—and vulnerable. If anyone had told him how exposed he would feel around a wife, maybe he wouldn't have given into his father's pressuring. Just the

same, having someone to sleep with was good and the maleness in
him was content.

"I dreamed of a great herd and a successful hunt," he said. "But
is it possible that you have seen something different?"

"Different?"

"White Calf, we are husband and wife. It is our people's wish
that our separate magic touches and becomes one. I need to know
if that is going to be."

Straightening, she gave the horse a pat before starting to wander
off. He kept pace, wondering if they might walk together in silence
until they came to the end of the sheltering canyon.

"I had a vision," she whispered.

"What! Tell me!"

"It was not what you think; not what you want."

Did all women say things that made little sense or was it only
her? "Tell me," he repeated.

Sighing, she stopped and faced him. A little light remained in
the sky, but none of that touched them down here. The wind, cold
and strong despite the stone walls, pushed and pulled but he'd
stand here as long as she did.

"My last vision came before your dream," she said. "It—it returned the night we became husband and wife."

The same night he'd "seen" the buffalo herd. "Why did you not
tell me?"

"Because your thoughts were full of what had come to you."
He heard her draw in a deep breath. Then: "And because I did not
want to admit what I had seen."

"Will you tell it to me now?" he asked.

"Yes." She drew out her reply. "But not because I want to."

There were her confusing woman's words again. "Why? Do you
believe it is something I have no right to know?"

"No. No, it is not that at all. It is because I do not want to hear
them. Raven's Cry—" She rested her hand on his shoulder. "I am
afraid."

"Of what?"

"Of the truth," she whispered. "I was looking into the future; I know that. I saw snow and a storm like a grizzly's teeth. A few people on horseback were in the middle of that storm. There was no escape for them, and they were cold, so cold that even if they had been able to build a fire, it might not have warmed them. Fear had been painted on their faces and had found its way into their hearts. Their horses had their heads down and then . . ."

"What?"

"And then one of the horses fell and could not get up."

"Did it die?"

"I do not know. One horse became two and soon none could move and the people were left alone."

"Tell me about those people."

Her grip on his shoulder tightened. "They were Blackfeet."

Although he'd already sensed that, he felt as if he'd been struck. "Their names," he whispered. "Who are they?"

"I—I do not know."

"Is that it or were you afraid to look into their faces?"

She hadn't answered him, but as he pulled the sleeping blanket over both of them, Raven's Cry admitted he was glad White Calf hadn't. He stretched out on his back and stared upward, trying to ignore the warmth beside him. Before, he'd wondered if he'd resent having to share his sleeping place with a woman, but already his body acted as if she'd been there forever. Still, although she wouldn't turn her back on him, he fought to keep her impact from taking over everything.

"I love being part of a hunt," she said unexpectedly. "Everyone with the same thoughts and determination. I remember the first time I saw my father ride after a buffalo. He looked so magnificent and brave that it never occurred to me that he might be injured."

"Because you were a child then."

"Yes," she admitted, then hurried on. "From where my mother and I stood, we could see him and his brothers as they brought down a lone cow. Afterward the men cheered and then gave thanks to Buffalo for providing for us and from where I was, I did the same. My mother hugged me and laughed, but when I looked into her eyes, I saw tears. When I asked her about them, she said that a woman who loves a hunter does not let him know that she fears for his safety because her fear may weaken him."

"Your mother loves your father?"

"Just as he loves her. Does that surprise you?"

"Their marriage was arranged. They did not choose each other."

"I know." She sighed. "My mother told me that she barely knew the name of the man who had become her husband, but on the first night they spent in their own tepee, he brought a motherless puppy into it, and by the time it had been fed and had fallen asleep in his arms, she knew she could laugh and smile with him. Love grew from that."

Her words struck him as incredibly wise, but he didn't say so because that would take the conversation too close to the journey the two of them had to take as husband and wife.

"A puppy? Why did he not simply give it to a bitch to suckle?"

"My father is a gentle man. Children delight him and when my youngest brother was born, it was he who got him to smile for the first time. I think, even on his wedding night, he could not turn his back on an orphan."

Was that what White Calf wanted in a husband, someone who put a puppy before himself? "I am not your father," he told her. "My ways are not his."

"I know," she whispered.

"Do you?"

"What do you mean?"

She'd been curled beside him, one arm tucked under her head, her slow and even breathing whispering across his neck. Although he longed to touch her, finishing what they'd begun had to come first.

"I am Raven's Cry," he told her. "No other. My ways are my ways. I do not want you to say that I am like my father or uncles or grandfather. The steps I choose are my own."

"So are mine," she told him, her words barely audible.

"Of course they are," he replied without thinking. "You are White Calf."

He sensed her shaking her head. "The woman known as White Calf is only part of who I am. Inside . . ."

"Inside, your heart beats in a way that is yours alone. Sometimes its cadence makes you brave. Sometimes it makes you fearful."

She gasped. "How do you know that about me?"

How indeed he asked himself even though he already knew the answer. Unwilling to give up that much of himself yet, he turned toward her. His breathing's rhythm was the same as hers, in and out together. "I cannot look inside you," he told her. "Are you afraid that I can?"

"No. No," she repeated, her tone even less sure than it had been a moment ago. "I do not fear you, Raven's Cry."

He would never want that, never. "I do not know what it is to be a husband," he heard himself admitting. "I do not know what you want from me or I from you. It . . ."

"We have begun a new journey," she said after they'd been silent for several moments. "Always before we have walked alone or with our parents, but it is different now. And my dreams have not told me how this journey will be walked."

"Neither have mine," he told her, laughing a little at himself because his dreams were like newborn infants next to hers.

"Maybe that is better." Lifting her head, she brushed her lips against his shoulder.

A shiver that had nothing to do with the wind and waiting winter caught him in its grip, he could barely speak. "You do not want to know whether we will have children or how many? Whether they will play or fight together?"

"No. Not tonight."

"Then what do you want?"

She showed him.

16

White Calf and his brother were making love. When they'd crawled under their blankets near the communal campfire, Night Thunder hadn't paid any attention to what they were saying to each other, hadn't cared that the speaking had stopped, but now—

Teeth clenched, he turned his back on them and pulled his own blanket over his ears, but he could still hear their quickened breathing and frenzied movements. So, he decided, could anyone else sleeping nearby. There'd been no need to pitch tepees that would only have to be dismantled in the morning, but the lack of privacy—

What was it like to bury oneself inside a woman's softness? The older braves bragged about their baby-making abilities, and like the rest of the young men, he'd listened to their every word and tried to imagine doing the same thing to his wife, but he had no wife, only his body's growing need for release.

Not caring what his brother and White Calf might think, he scrambled to his feet, shoved into his moccasins, and because the night was cold, wrapped his blanket around his shoulders. At first he had no thought beyond putting distance between himself and sounds of something he had yet to experience but filled his thoughts more times than he could remember; then as he made his way, his feet brushed something. Looking down, he realized it was Little Rain.

"Get up," he ordered in a harsh whisper. "Come with me."

She muttered something he didn't understand, not that it mattered. When she didn't move quickly enough for him, he yanked her blanket off her and grabbed her shoulder. She jerked away from him, then hurried to her feet. Without acknowledging him, she too put on her moccasins and picked up her blanket, which she draped around her. After a glance at the mound that was White Calf and Raven's Cry, she stalked away.

Overtaking her, he indicated with grunts and gestures that he intended to head away from the encampment and expected her to accompany him.

Night was a time for calming, for the forgetfulness of sleep, rest, and renewal. Instead, he felt as if he might fly apart. Raven's Cry was no more than six moons older than him. They'd been children together, had left that childhood behind during the same Sun Dance ceremony, but since then things had happened so quickly that he felt dizzy and sometimes lost.

"Where are we going?" Little Rain asked.

"Away."

"A-way?"

"I do not wish to be part of my brother's wedding nights."

"But—where will we go?"

"I do not know! Do not question me!"

Instead of following meekly the way a hostage should—at least the way he'd hoped this hostage would, she stopped and faced him. "I do not want to spend the night walking in the dark. It may be what you wish but—"

"What I wish is what you will do," he insisted, the ridiculous words echoing around him. He couldn't say why he'd ordered her to accompany him, just that maybe he didn't want to be alone with his thoughts, and she was the only one he could be around who would keep her knowledge of what he said and did to herself. And maybe, he admitted as she stood looking up at him, her slight but soft woman's body calling to him, he wanted what his brother had.

"Is that what you think?" she asked, her voice trembling a little. "That you can treat me as if I am not human?"

"What I think is that you are my hostage to do with as I wish."

"No!"

She started to back away, but he grabbed her wrist and hauled her with him as he stalked farther and farther from the others. Although her feet dragged, she didn't fight him. He shouldn't care what she was thinking, but putting his mind to what might be going on inside her was easier than dealing with his own tangled emotions. No one had ever feared him, but then he'd never been in a position of power before. Acknowledging his control over her made him strong, allowed him to step beyond boyhood and the fears he'd been forced to weather when his life was in danger. Let her be afraid tonight. Let him be the warrior.

"I will bring down many buffalo," he said, speaking more to his budding courage than to her. "I will ride close to a stampeding bull and bury my arrow in its heart and all will acknowledge my courage. I will do those things. I!"

"Why—why are you telling me this?"

Why? "Because it is time for you to know who has taken you hostage," he insisted. "You think I am a boy but—"

"No." Digging in her heels, she tried to stop. "I never said—"

Hadn't she? Confused, he jerked her close but didn't try to get them moving again. The sky was alive with stars, some looking so close that he half believed he could touch them, most so far away that they were part of a world beyond his comprehension. When he took in a measured breath, the air was so cold that it made his nose and eyes ache.

"I am a man. A warrior," he said.

He waited for her to reply but she remained silent. She hadn't seemed that much smaller than him before, but tonight with the stars and moon barely touching her outline, he half believed he could pick her up and carry her for as long as his restless legs needed to walk. As a child, he'd paid little attention to the girls his age. While he was learning the skills of hunting and fighting by playing at such things with his companions or watching the village's men, the girls had been helping their mothers with women's duties of food preparation, sewing, and tepee building, and he hadn't been interested in their activities, but it was different these days.

Too different.

"Soon I will take a wife," he told Little Rain. "And when I do, my wife and I will have our own tepee. It will not matter what my father says or thinks, and I will not care whether my brother makes love to White Calf."

"Why are you telling me these things?" She repeated her earlier question.

Maybe for no reason beyond her being the only person with him. Maybe because she was the first woman he'd touched. "Do not question me. You belong to me."

"I do not!" With her free hand, she tried to pry his fingers off her wrist.

"Yes! You do."

As if giving weight to his words, he captured her other hand and pulled her against him. Layers of buffalo hide were between them, but that didn't stop him from feeling her heat, her softness and strength. It was becoming harder for him to breathe and his manhood instantly became huge and hard.

She shrank away from him. "No," she whimpered.

"Do not tell me what I can or cannot do! You are mine."

"No! No, I am not. My husband is—"

"I killed your husband!"

Like a blast of winter air, his words slammed back at him and for the first time in his life, he hated himself. But before he could tell her that, she stopped fighting him and came at him with punishing feet and then clawing fingers. Breathless and pain-filled from the blow she'd delivered between his legs, he released her.

"I will not hear that again!" she screamed as he continued to give way, protecting his throbbing manhood at the same time. "My husband lives still in my heart. I will not have you touch him there! I will not!"

Although he shook his head from side to side, she managed to bury her nails in his neck. Galvanized by this sudden new pain, he surged forward. Because he was bent over, his head caught the underside of her chin and she went down as if he'd struck her with a rock.

Panting in a desperate attempt to keep the agony she'd inflicted from overwhelming him, he stared down at her through blurred eyes. She'd already begun to move, but he could tell she was stunned. Her dress was bunched high on her thighs. As the pain between his legs lessened, he became aware of how much his neck stung.

"You—you are a fighter," he gasped. "I will not forget that."

"I hate you!"

"There is no need to tell me what I already know," he informed her, every word an effort.

Touching his neck told him two things: she'd drawn blood and the sweat on his hands made the scratches sting even more. When she'd first kicked him, he'd thought he'd die, but although he wasn't sure his now deflated member would ever harden again, he had no wish to inflict the same damage on her.

"Kill me," she hissed. "Kill me now so I may join Takes-Knife-at-Night."

"No."

"I dare you!" She started to sit up, but the movement must have made her dizzy because she fell back again. "A warrior—a real warrior would not have allowed me to live after what I did to you."

True, someone like Chief Sleeps Too Long would have already buried his knife in her throat, but no matter how angry she made him, he couldn't imagine doing that. Did knowing his weakness make her the strong one, he wondered. He understood almost nothing about her while he was unable to keep anything from her? Confused, he dropped down beside her, careful to remain out of reach.

"Only the oldest Blackfeet embrace death because it is preferable to becoming helpless," he told her. "You are young, healthy. You should want to live."

"What do you know of what I want? And why should it matter? You took me because the others said you should. I am a burden to you, a burden!"

She was that all right, but when he looked, really looked at her, he was forced to admit how much a part of his life she'd become in the few days they'd been together. After hearing his brother with White Calf, he should have wanted to be alone, but he'd brought Little Rain with him, and not just because she was his responsibility.

"Why do you want me to hate you?" he asked.

Although he repeated his question a few minutes later, she gave no indication she'd heard. Instead, she struggled to cover her legs and then sat up. Despite the poor lighting, it seemed to him that the flesh under her chin was swelling. She touched herself there as gingerly as he'd examined his scratched neck. Finally, ignoring him, she stood up. At first she swayed and he readied himself to catch her should she fall, but her will was strong.

"I want to go back," she whispered.

"To my people? What do you want with them?"

"Nothing, but I do not want to stay here with you."

She'd already made that painfully clear, but if they returned, he would only have to listen to Raven's Cry and White Calf.

"You will do what I tell you, when I tell you," he said.

"And if I do not?"

Why was he arguing with someone with no more say over her life than one of the horses they'd taken from the Snakes? "Do you want to fight again? This time I will know not to let you kick me."

It couldn't be, but he thought he heard her chuckle. "I want to be left alone," she said.

"A moment ago you said you wanted to return to my people. Which is it?"

She'd been moving her head from side to side, but now she stopped and stared at him as if she'd never seen him before—either that or because she hated him for having asked the question.

"I want there to be nothing between us. For us to have never been."

So did he, but instead of telling her that, he stepped toward her, his eyes never leaving her legs. His member still throbbed and the thought of her striking him again made him shudder. Still, a part of him he didn't understand wanted to touch her, wanted more than that. She didn't shy away when he brushed her hair off her shoulder but stared at him the way a wild horse stares at the brave who has roped it.

"If I keep you with me," he said, "you will be adopted into the tribe. By next winter you will no longer be Cree but Blackfoot."

"No!" She started to back away but stopped herself with what he guessed was a great effort of will. "I was born Cree. My heart will remain Cree forever."

"And if you never see your people again? How will your heart beat then?"

"Why are you doing this to me?" she sobbed, her sudden tears shocking him. "Do you want my heart to break?"

"I want you to accept what is."

Her head shaking slowly from side to side again, she squeezed her eyes shut as if trying to will her tears to remain inside her, but they continued to fall.

"Take me," she hissed. "If you want to spill yourself inside me, I cannot stop you, but you will know that I hate you for it and that I will hate you for as long as I live."

"I do not push myself on unwilling women," he told her when the truth was, he'd never had the opportunity to slip inside any woman.

"You tried a few minutes ago."

He wasn't sure what had taken place just before she kicked him, not that he was going to admit that to her. "Think what you will," he said.

"I know what happened. You—you will not rape me?" she asked, her voice unexpectedly small and weak.

She was his to do with as he wished. A hostage was simply that, the spoils of war or battle or the result of a raid, not as valuable as a horse but sometimes worth bartering about. At least that was what he'd always believed, but he'd watched her mourn her husband and knew that her heart beat the same as his.

"No, I will not rape you."

Little Rain had still been shaking when she and Night Thunder returned to the others, but after a while, he'd fallen asleep and his slow, easy breathing had calmed her. She'd been aware that she'd dozed off, but her sleep had been fitful, interrupted every time someone shifted position or snored. Although the cold air of dawn had made her gasp when she got up to help with morning food preparations, she'd been grateful for something to do.

Smoke rose from several small cooking fires and mixed with the fog that had crept over them during the night. The camp dogs were prowling as close to the fires as they dared, and the five nursing Blackfeet babies somberly regarded the activity from their cradle boards. As the rising sun showed the horizon in greater and greater detail, she listened to quiet female voices, occasional yips from the dogs, the men's deeper conversations. The way the Blackfeet went about beginning their days while on the move was little different from that of the Cree, a fact that both surprised and comforted her.

When Night Thunder had first brought her to his people, she'd been in shock and had paid little attention to what went on around her, but time was separating her from the worst of her pain. Last night her captor had told her that she might spend the rest of her life with the Blackfeet. This morning she looked about her and tried to imagine never seeing anything except Blackfeet faces and hearing Blackfeet voices for the rest of her life.

"Little Rain, where are you going?"

Startled, she focused on the woman who'd just spoken. White Calf, her hair tousled and her cheeks looking chapped, was looking at her, and she realized that she'd started to wander toward a rocky outcropping.

"Nowhere," she assured White Calf. "I have no thought to run. I simply—"

"Whether you remain here or leave is not for me to say," White Calf told her. "But your eyes say that you are troubled. If your thoughts wound you, perhaps you want to talk about them."

The idea of telling White Calf what was on her mind had never occurred to her, but the Blackfoot woman was what she'd been not so long ago, a bride. Maybe White Calf would understand. Maybe.

"I—I do not know. I—so many things . . ."

"Many things. Yes, I know what that is like," White Calf said with a small smile. "Do what you must." She indicated where Little Rain had been walking toward. "Sometimes being alone is the best thing, but if you do not find peace out there, what you tell me will not pass beyond my lips."

Could she tell White Calf that she hated her husband's brother, Little Rain thought as she struck out for the rocks. Only she didn't hate Night Thunder, nothing that simple. She'd challenged him to ravage her last night because if he had, her emotions where he was concerned would have been simple and clean. She'd want him dead. But he hadn't touched her again, and that confused her.

"My husband, hear me." Although White Calf hadn't accompanied her, she kept her voice low. "Please hear me! My heart is yours. It will be yours for as long as I live. I do not want to stand near another man, not the man who killed you! Please, show me the way to walk."

The tears she'd finally mastered last night returned before she'd known they still lurked. Maybe she'd left the others because some part of her had sensed the coming tears.

"I want to go home," she whimpered. "I want to step into yesterday and have Takes-Knife-at-Night beside me. I want to be a Cree, only a Cree."

Her plea, useless as it was, served as the release she'd needed and she sank to the ground, sobbing. Her eyes burned, her lungs ached, and her heart felt as if it was being ripped apart, but she didn't try to hold back, made no attempt to protect herself from the too-long pent-up rage and grief and, ultimately, saying good-bye to the man she loved.

When at last she was able to concentrate on her surroundings again, she straightened, opened her eyes, and stared at her now red-tinted world. The land here was no different from what she'd seen her entire life, and her people went on buffalo hunts that accomplished the same things. They cooked in the same ways and although the Blackfeet decorated their arrows in ways the Cree didn't—

Someone was coming toward her. Because she still didn't trust herself to speak, she looked around to see if there was somewhere she could hide, but before she could put thought into action, she realized that the approaching stranger wasn't Night Thunder or one of the other warriors but a woman. It wasn't White Calf because this woman was shorter without White Calf's long arms and legs. Then she heard the woman's labored breathing and who she was no longer mattered.

The newcomer didn't walk so much as stumble, but whether it was because she was paying no attention to where her feet were going or something else bothered her, Little Rain couldn't say. Despite the bowed head and shuffling gait, she took her to be young. She wore a dress but not a blanket for warmth, and Little Rain could now see that she had on only one mocassin. Standing, she waited for the woman to notice her, but she only came closer and closer until she knew it was Feather Tickles who'd just become the Blackfoot chief's wife.

"Are you all right?" she asked, alarmed by the sight of Feather Tickles's blackened eye and swollen nose.

Feather Tickles let out a squeak of alarm and whirled away like a deer about to run.

"Please, do not be afraid. It is me, the Cree hostage. I will not harm you."

"I—I . . ." Feather Tickles clamped a hand around her throat. "I thought I would be alone."

So did I. "There is room here for both of us," she pointed out.

"But you are hurt. What happened?"

"What?" Feather Tickles blinked, then gasped and moved her hand from her throat to her injured eye.

"What happened to you?" Little Rain repeated.

"I—he . . ."

Feather Tickles was staring at her, yet Little Rain wasn't sure whether the other woman was really seeing her.

"Who?" she prompted.

When Feather Tickles didn't answer, she stepped closer. Dried blood clung to Feather Tickles's cheek and covered what she feared might be even more injury.

"Who did this to you?"

"My—Chief Sleeps Too Long."

Although she'd already suspected that, she couldn't suppress a gasp. *Why,* she longed to ask, but she wasn't sure Feather Tickles was capable of answering. Instead, she slowly extended her hand so the injured woman could see that she wanted to touch her. When she took her hand, Feather Tickles stiffened but remained where she was.

"Sit down," Little Rain ordered. "Otherwise you might fall."

Feather Tickles started to obey, but then she straightened. "If I stay here," she whispered, "he will find me."

Alarmed, Little Rain stared back at the camp, but she didn't see anyone heading their way.

"No, he won't," she said in what she hoped was a comforting tone. "You are all right. I promise; you are all right."

"He hurt me."

Feather Tickles started rocking back and forth, and Little Rain wrapped her arm around her and pulled her close. She smelled sweat and the scent of a man's spilled seed. "I know he hurt you," she whispered. "But he isn't here now. You are with me. Safe."

"No. No. No."

What had gone on between Feather Tickles and Sleeps Too Long was too horrible for Little Rain to think about, but because the young woman's condition terrified her, she forced herself to stay where she was. Feather Tickles was shivering. When Little Rain removed her blanket and wrapped it around Feather Tickles's shoulders, she gave her a look of gratitude she would never forget.

"He—he—I think he must hate me," she whimpered.

"You do not know that," Little Rain started, then stopped because now that Feather Tickles had started to talk, she would simply listen. "Why do you say that?"

"I—I wanted to be a good wife. Before I went to him the first time, I prepared myself for him and put on my finest dress."

Little Rain had done the same in preparation for becoming Takes-Knife-at-Night's bride.

"I was happy to have been chosen. Even though he had wanted to marry White Calf, I felt honored. To be the chief's sits-beside-him wife . . ."

"I know," she muttered. "I know." Her words, she believed, didn't matter. What Feather Tickles needed to hear was a sympathetic voice. "But it was not as you expected?"

Feather Tickles shook her head. When she shuddered, Little Rain hugged Feather Tickles to her again and wondered how long she could ignore her growing sense of discomfort at being ill-dressed against the cold.

"He wanted me to—I wanted to be his woman and to have his seed inside me so I might give him a child, but he wanted . . ."

Hadn't Feather Tickles's female relatives prepared her for the realities of marriage? But no woman expects to be beaten.

"Do not go back to him," she said firmly. "Return to your parents' tepee and tell everyone that you will not be Sleeps Too Long's wife."

"I cannot!"

"Yes you can. He had no right to—"

"My father will be shamed."

"Because you left a man who hurt you? I cannot believe—"

"You do not understand!" Feather Tickles interrupted.

Her outburst seemed to exhaust her, but Little Rain waited her out, rubbing her still trembling shoulder as she did. She could see the injured eye and nose, but if the way Feather Tickles had been walking was any indication, she'd been hurt in other ways. Little Rain had taken little note of the Blackfeet chief beyond coming to the conclusion that he was a man quick to anger and do battle. Those things, she now understood, carried over to his relationship with his new wife.

Feather Tickles spoke so softly that Little Rain had to strain to hear her, but it wasn't long before she understood that Feather Tickles's father wouldn't be alive if Sleeps Too Long hadn't killed a buffalo that had gored Jumper's horse.

"My father owes his life to the chief," Feather Tickles said. "He believed the debt would never be repaid, but when Sleeps Too Long brought his horses to him, he said that the time of giving gifts without end to Sleeps Too Long was over. Now—my father will not let me into his tepee again."

There was more than one way of being trapped. She might be a prisoner, but Feather Tickles too had nowhere to go.

"Talk to your husband," she said although she couldn't imagine ever speaking to the man who'd done this. "Tell him—"

"I tried!"

"What?"

"Last night was not the first time." Feather Tickles stared at something maybe only she could see. "After—the day I stepped into his tepee as his wife, he took me the way a stallion takes a mare. He made me bleed, grabbed my breasts and squeezed them. Bit me. I begged—I cried and I begged but he did not hear. He did not care."

"Why?" Little Rain demanded, not that she expected Feather Tickles to understand the man she'd found herself married to. "Why was he not gentle?"

"I do not know. I tried to ask but he . . ." She started to bury her face in her hand but gasped and Little Rain guessed she'd jarred her injuries. "At first his manhood was limp and useless. It came to life when he hit me, and he was happy. He will not change. I cannot stand—he will not change."

Feather Tickles had begun to moan to herself, but although she hated the sound, Little Rain didn't try to silence her.

"Your father must be made to understand what happened," she said, not sure Feather Tickles could hear her. "Welcome you back."

"I—I told my husband I would not stay with him. He laughed and said he would tell everyone that he had rejected me, and I was not worthy of being anyone's wife. And—and he would insist my father give him twenty horses as payment for my unworthiness."

Jumper wasn't a wealthy man. He had nowhere near twenty horses and a man with a debt he cannot pay is a man who can never again hold his head high.

"I do not want to live."

Although she tried to hold onto her, Feather Tickles broke free and staggered out of reach. The blanket had slipped off her shoulders and lay in a heap on the ground, but she made no effort to pick it up.

"I do not want to live," she repeated. "There is no place for me in this world."

17

Night Thunder was sitting with the other hunters when Little Rain found him. She'd hoped to avoid Chief Sleeps Too Long, but that wasn't possible and now she couldn't keep her eyes off the man. This morning he was smoking his pipe and laughing at something someone had said, looking as if he had nothing on his mind. But she knew what he was capable of, and that's what gave her the courage to approach Night Thunder. Ignoring the men's stares, she leaned close to Night Thunder.

"Please," she gasped, afraid her voice would carry. Out of breath, she had to suck in air before she could continue. "Please, I must speak to you. Alone."

"What are you—" he began, looking irritated. Then he frowned and studied her. "We are planning the day. Raven's Cry has consulted his dream and—"

"I need your help. Please. I would not approach you if there was any other way. Believe me, I do not want—"

Before she could finish, he stood and without saying a word to the others, grabbed her wrist and strode away, taking her with him. Half afraid of him, she hurried to keep up.

"What is it?" he demanded when they were by themselves. "If you seek to shame me—"

"No. It is not that at all." Despite the sense of urgency that had compelled her to run all the way back to camp, she wasn't sure how to begin. "It—it is Feather Tickles. I am afraid for her. I tried to stop her but she would not—if she tries to kill herself—"

"Feather Tickles? You should be speaking to her husband."

"Her husband! You have not seen what he did to her."

His features suddenly grim, Night Thunder looked around. "Where is she?"

Rushing her words, she told him what had taken place between her and the other woman. When she described Feather Tickles's injuries, Night Thunder clenched his teeth but didn't say anything until she'd finished.

"She said she did not want to go on living," she wound up, afraid they were wasting precious time. "Because of her father's debts to Sleeps Too Long, she believes she would be cast out of his tepee if she tried to return home. She is a woman who belongs nowhere, a woman in despair."

"I want to tell you you are wrong," Night Thunder said, "that our chief would not do such a thing to his wife." She readied herself to tell him she knew otherwise, but he went on. "But Sleeps Too Long is a man given to quick anger, a man who boasts of his prowess in bed."

"Prowess! He is brutal! I know because I have seen. Night Thunder, please. If she tries to take her life, we may already be too late."

"Where is she?" he repeated.

"There." She pointed, startled by how far she'd come from where she'd left Feather Tickles. "I tried to make her return with me, but her strength—"

"Desperate strength," Night Thunder finished for her. When Little Rain had first approached him, he'd been both shocked and embarrassed to have his hostage burst into the middle of a warriors' conversation, but the look in her eyes had made an impact he couldn't ignore. Now he understood what had driven her.

Not bothering to explain what he intended to do, he hurried toward Deep Scar and the other horses; Little Rain kept pace. Not taking time to look for the pinto stallion, he indicated one of the horses belonging to his father and she mounted it at the same time he sprang onto Deep Scar's back.

It wasn't until the horses began galloping that he fully realized what he'd done. What went on between his chief and his new bride was none of his concern, and if Blackfeet wanted to end their lives, it wasn't for others to try to stop them. Still, he dug his knees into Deep Scar's sides. When he looked over at Little Rain, he knew she was responsible.

After last night, he'd been glad to discover her gone this morning. He'd wanted to concentrate on his brother's dream, wanted to feel like a hunter, to prepare himself for the danger and excitement of the hunt, but those emotions had evaporated like mist under a hot summer sun because of the look in Little Rain's eyes.

Again he glanced at her. As before, her attention was on what lay ahead of them, and he told himself he meant nothing to her and she nothing to him. He'd just begun to repeat the silent message when alarm spread over her features, and she jabbed a finger at something in the distance.

At first he didn't see what had caught her attention, but when he followed the line of her finger, he unconsciously slowed. The dark, distant shape could, he told himself, be a coyote or deer or antelope, but when he felt his gut tighten, he knew different.

"Wolf," he said.

"Wolf," she repeated but didn't slow.

The sure-footed horses easily, cautiously ate up the distance, but the wolf merely waited for them, its form becoming more and more distinct as they neared. He cursed himself for leaving camp without his bow and arrows but reassured himself that he at least carried his knife at his waist. When the first deep howl reached him, he slowed even more, not surprised to see that Little Rain was doing the same.

"There was no wolf before?" he asked.

"No. At least I did not see him."

Him. Not just *a* wolf but *him.* Stopping, he concentrated on the watching beast. Yellow eyes returned his gaze. He'd been close to wolves in the past and knew their eyes spoke of courage and a little curiosity along with a simmering distrust of man, but it was different this morning. Even when he lifted his fist and shook it, the wolf gave no indication that he feared anything. Neither did he hate.

"You are sure this is where you left Feather Tickles?" he asked as he forced himself to take in the rest of his surroundings. An arrow might reach the wolf, but only if he was armed and put every bit of strength he possessed behind the act. Did the wolf know he didn't need to fear that?

And maybe this was the same wolf he'd tried and failed to kill before.

"Over there." She pointed toward a stretch of ground level except for a tiny hill created by some burrowing creature. Just beyond that was a particularly dense and tall clump of grass. "That is where Feather Tickles was."

Splitting her attention between the still motionless wolf and the grass, Little Rain urged her horse into a slow walk. He wanted to join her but didn't dare allow himself to be distracted from the predator who'd started howling again, the sound going on and on until he felt as if his ears would shatter.

"What—" Little Rain hissed. "What is this? I do not understand."

Do not ask me to explain the unexplainable. A moment later he heard her gasp, then she slid off her horse, but instead of continuing on, she stood motionless. The howl stopped, then began again, low and breathy like the wind.

Something lay in the middle of the tall grass.

He dismounted, settling his fingers over his knife handle as he did. He felt both powerful and weak this morning, his shoulder muscles burning at the thought of hurtling his knife at the wolf. If it came any closer, he would let it fly. At the same time, the hated and all too familiar fear gnawed at him and threatened to suck all strength from him. His mouth dried and he could no longer feel his legs.

"Feather Tickles."

The despair in Little Rain's voice made enough of an impact that he was able to regain a little control over his emotions. She paid no attention to the watching, waiting, wailing wolf as she made her slow way through grass that brushed her hips. When she reached the mound in the middle of the cluster, she stopped and stood with her head bowed, her arms wrapped tight around her waist. A barely audible whimper became a moan.

Feather Tickles was dead. Even without touching the young woman, he knew she couldn't have survived what had been done to her throat. The flesh had been torn apart and her life's blood soaked the ground under her, red becoming brown as the earth absorbed what she no longer needed.

"It killed . . ." Little Rain took a shuddering breath. "It killed her."

Another wave of fear slammed into Night Thunder and spun him around. As he turned, he tried to remind himself that he'd taken his attention off the wolf for only a few seconds and it had been showing no signs of attacking, but the image of what had been done to Feather Tickles made that impossible.

No longer howling, the wolf might have been a rock painting. Not even its eyes blinked and although the breeze was brisk, its fur remained unruffled. Its mouth hung open, but not so much that he could see its tongue and only a glimpse of teeth served as proof of what it was capable of—what it had done.

"Feather Tickles," Little Rain sobbed. "No. Please, no!"

Although he didn't dare take his eyes off the wolf, he realized Little Rain had dropped to her knees and, unmindful of the gore, was pushing the hair out of the dead woman's eyes. Her useless but gentle gesture struck him with the force of a blow.

A bellow of rage that must have come from him shattered the air. Panting in the wake of that effort, he leaped toward the wolf, hurtling his knife at the same time. The weapon sliced through the air as clean and deadly as the straightest arrow. Striking the wolf full in the chest, the blade buried itself in the dark coat. Night

Thunder waited, waited for the beast to begin writhing. He had no doubt that his weapon had found vital organs. Blood might continue to pump through the heart, but that would only extend the wolf's agony.

Nothing.

No! Not again!

Reaching down, he scooped up a rock and prepared to heave it at the head, not because he cared how long it took the wolf to die but because a predator who has already killed today might spend the end of its life taking out its revenge on the man who has killed it.

And on Little Rain.

A sideways glance told him she'd seen what he'd done. If she knew she was responsible for his having thrown his knife, so be it, and if she believed fear had driven him, he couldn't change that.

The rock felt solid and potent, and with Little Rain looking up at him, he began to advance on the wolf. The wind stung his face, but the wolf continued to exist in a pocket of calm.

Either that or it didn't exist.

His legs tingled, and the dread that had captured him not so long ago lapped at him with a hot tongue. His head pounded, forcing him to wince, but he struggled to ignore the pain because allowing himself to be distracted might be the last mistake he'd ever make.

The wolf was granite, powerful and compelling, and he wondered if it might have cast a spell over him and that was why he continued to approach it. He saw the knife hilt sticking out of it, foreign and deadly, yet somehow a part of the creature. The creature's coat was black tipped but lighter underneath, so thick not even the fiercest winter could penetrate.

The knife had.

Or had it?

"Night Thunder!" Little Rain gasped. "Do not get any closer."

What she said made a great deal of sense and echoed what his brain was screaming at him, but his body had a will of its own.

Either that or he'd fallen under the wolf's spell and—

Closer and then closer still he came, but although the wolf continued to look at him through unblinking eyes, it didn't seem to care that the man who'd wounded it—if he had—was so close he could nearly reach out and touch it. In a way that defied comprehension, Night Thunder now knew without a doubt that the wolf wasn't breathing. He couldn't see anything except the knife handle. The blade was long enough that it might have pierced, not just one lung but both of them, yet no blood marred the flawless coat.

"What are you?" Night Thunder demanded, shocked that he could speak. "Who are you?"

The nose might have moved just the slightest bit but maybe he'd imagined it. His fingers around the rock ached, and he laughed at himself for thinking that this small stone could bring down a creature that weighed nearly as much as he did and could outrun a horse.

"What do you want with me? With the Blackfeet?"

Nothing.

"Leave us!" His head screamed and he lowered his voice, but now that he'd begun to speak, he didn't know how he was going to stop.

"You killed Feather Tickles. She meant you no harm and you have no need of her flesh so why—"

"Night Thunder, please."

Whatever Little Rain wanted of him would have to wait; didn't she know that?

"My knife wounded you. How dare you defy it! How dare you!"

Maybe the wolf found that funny because its mouth curled upward, revealing perfect teeth.

"Night Thunder?"

Little Rain wasn't that far behind him, but she belonged to the world he'd always known and understood while this creature—

"What are you?" he asked it. "Why are you here? Why do you not feel . . ."

His free hand was reaching out. Both fascinated and appalled by what he was doing, he watched his fingers extend toward the great mat of fur over the powerful shoulder. Feeling himself begin to tremble, he tried to order himself to increase his grip on the rock, but all his body wanted to do was touch the wolf, try to make sense of it.

Little Rain took a ragged breath. His own oxygen-starved body cried out for the same thing, but he couldn't remember how to make his lungs work.

You are not of my understanding, he told it. *Beyond anything I have ever known. Why do* . . .

His thoughts splintered and despite eyes that refused to focus, he realized that the wolf was becoming less and less distinct. In the middle of winter, the air sometimes became so cold that what little moisture was in it froze into tiny ice crystals. Maybe the wolf was turning into ice crystals, breaking apart, losing touch with the earth and yet not flying.

Once again Little Rain sucked in a breath and once again he ignored her. He could no longer tell where the frozen air ended and the wolf began. It was as if they'd become the same, each taking from the other.

"Wolf," he whispered. "Wolf."

Little Rain knelt and tucked grass around Feather Tickles's body as if trying to warm the other woman. The Cree hadn't spoken since they'd left where they'd last seen the wolf, but neither had he for the simple reason that he hadn't been able to think beyond the weight and reality of the knife he once again carried. What he knew wasn't nearly enough, just that when the wolf no longer existed, his weapon had fallen to the ground, and when he picked it up, there'd been no blood on it, and it had been winter-cold.

His first clear thought had been to jump on Deep Scar's back and gallop away. Whether Little Rain accompanied him or remained behind didn't matter because the important thing, the only thing, was putting distance between himself and what defied all understanding. But the horses had been nervous and when he'd given up trying to approach them, he realized Little Rain had remained beside Feather Tickles's body.

"Was she afraid?" Little Rain asked in a whisper. "When she saw the wolf, did she cry out and try to run away?"

"I do not know."

"She must have," Little Rain went on, her gaze still on Feather Tickles. "If it had been me—if I had been there, would the wolf have killed me as well?"

"I do not know." He had to stop saying that; a man doesn't admit his lack of understanding.

"I know you do not," she said, her tone gentle. "I did not expect . . . There is no explanation for what happened here today, what we saw, is there?"

"No. There is not."

Little Rain was small of stature, but from the first he'd been impressed by her strength and courage. Now, however, she reminded him of a lost child.

"Will we tell your father?" she asked.

We? She was right; this was *their* experience. "I have not decided."

She nodded as if he'd said something full of wisdom, and he suddenly realized how much she understood about his relationship with his father. All the time he'd been recovering from his wound, he'd given her little thought beyond believing she was too much in shock to be aware of her surroundings, but he'd been wrong.

"What about White Calf?" she asked as she pulled Feather Tickles's dress up around her throat. Now that he could no longer see what had killed the chief's wife, the injuries to her face made a chilling impact.

"White Calf?" he repeated.

"I would like to talk to her about what happened, but if you do not want me to—"

"No. It is all right. If anyone can understand this"—he touched his knife—"my brother's wife can."

"I hope so." She pressed her palm to Feather Tickles's forehead.

"I pray this one was not afraid when the wolf attacked."

"Not afraid? Of course she was."

"Maybe."

"What do you mean, maybe?" The crawling sensation across his shoulders and at the base of his spine kept much of his attention on their surroundings, but if the wolf wasn't done with them, surely he wouldn't have disappeared.

"If I say, you will ridicule me."

How honest they were around each other. "No," he told her. "I will not."

"I think—" After giving Feather Tickles's shoulder a pat, she stood. "I was little more than a baby when my grandmother died," she said. "She had been ill for a long time, and nothing the shaman did took the pain from her belly. I remember—my grandfather had taken her outside because he did not want her to die in his tepee and have to get the women to build him another—I remember not wanting to touch her because I was afraid her pain would become mine. That was my childish belief."

Mouth soft and vulnerable, she looked down at her hands. "I do not fear a body that has been claimed by death," she whispered. "I may not understand why death comes, why we cannot live forever and have to grow old, but once life has left a person, the body is no more than an animal carcass."

He'd never seen it that way. In fact, for a whole day after his mother's death, he'd prayed that his father's medicine-making would return her to life. By the time Red Mountain had been killed, he'd known better than to pray for the impossible.

"I want—" Little Rain started. "I want to believe that Feather Tickles breathed her last in peace."

He could have reminded her of the young woman's mutilated throat but didn't.

"I think—this is what I will believe. This woman who I call a friend knew there was no place within the Blackfeet for her. She prayed to be taken to another place and the spirits sent a wolf to answer her prayer."

"You cannot—" he began but then stopped. What was the point of telling her that she was speaking nonsense when there was indeed a wolf who existed but did not, who hadn't felt the knife in him.

"I do not want to stay here," he announced. "Our horses want to leave and we would be wise to heed them."

Little Rain nodded. When her eyes flickered to where the wolf had been, he realized her disbelief matched his. And despite his earlier thoughts, what had happened this morning couldn't be kept between the two of them; his father would have to be told, but not yet. Not until . . .

Not until he was capable of speaking the words.

"Night Thunder?"

"What?" he asked, his tone sharp because she'd cut into his thoughts.

"I cannot lift her by myself."

She'd already knelt again and had begun sliding her hands under Feather Tickles's body. Steadying himself for what had to be done, he joined her and maneuvered the dead weight onto his shoulder. Standing took all the strength in his legs, and he was glad when Little Rain steadied him by clamping her hands against his side to help balance him.

The look they shared lasted only a heartbeat and then he heaved what remained of Feather Tickles onto Deep Scar's back.

18

"I divorced her. She is not mine to bury."

"She walked out of your tepee. Do not say she is not your responsibility."

Chief Sleeps Too Late's face flushed and he clutched his smoking pipe so tightly that Night Thunder thought it might break, but he didn't regret what he'd said. He'd ridden Deep Scar on the way back to the camp to make sure Feather Tickles's body didn't slide off, but now he'd dismounted and had confronted the man who'd barely glanced at what remained of his wife. Little Rain stood by his side

"I saw what you did to her." He made sure his voice carried so everyone would hear. "Beating one's wife is the way of a coward."

"Me, a coward? Ha! What do you know of courage?"

"I counted coup and revenged my brother's—"

"Have you gone to war, Night Thunder? No! When you have led warriors into battle, then I will listen to your words."

"You will listen now," he insisted, puzzled by where his courage was coming from. "Feather Tickles loved to laugh and was a willing worker, but you ended that. Look at her face."

Although Feather Tickles was past caring, he gently lifted her head from Deep Scar's side. The still-gathering Blackfeet crowded close to see, then stepped back to allow Jumper to gaze into his daughter's sightless eyes. The brave cried out, then bowed his head.

"Are those the marks of a woman who has spent the night with the man she loves?" Night Thunder demanded. "No. Those things were done to her in anger and because our chief cared nothing for his new wife."

"Silence!"

Although he whirled around, he already knew who had spoken. His father, his hair matted and tangled around his temple, was stalking toward him.

"You will not speak those words to your chief," Bunch of Lodges ordered. He tried to run his fingers through his hair, then after slapping the greasy mess, gave up. "You brought her body back. There is nothing left for you to do."

Nothing? His body felt as if it might fly apart if he didn't get Sleeps Too Long to admit what he'd done; still, he was already losing some of the strength his outrage had given him.

"I will not turn my back on this," he managed, his gaze leveled at his chief. "It is not the way of a Blackfoot man to beat his wife."

"She displeased me."

Displeased? Before he could throw the word back at Sleeps Too Long, he caught a warning look from his brother. Raven's Cry had been standing with White Calf, but now he joined their father, his body angled so that it served as a shield between his two relatives. Raven's Cry's silent stare said it all; it was bad enough that he'd attacked the chief in public, but if he now ignored his father, the unity the tribe depended on for survival was in jeopardy.

What he felt, what Little Rain thought, what had happened to Feather Tickles, didn't matter. Still . . .

"When Little Rain saw her this morning," he said once he trusted himself to speak. "Feather Tickles was crying. She said she could not return to her husband's side. The Cree told me that thing and I believe her; Feather Tickles's face does not lie." He indicated the body. "Now she will not have to. This is all I will say on the matter."

"You have said more than enough," Sleeps Too Long shot back.

"You say your hostage spoke to the woman who was my wife, that she was alive a short while ago. What killed her?"

By way of answer, Night Thunder lifted the blanket from around Feather Tickles's throat. Several women gasped and then everyone pressed forward for a closer look.

"Wolf," Raven's Cry said.

"Yes, Wolf," he replied.

Stepping close, his brother touched him on the shoulder, but he only shook his head.

"Whether you speak or not on this does not silence the questions," Raven's Cry said. "Or my belief that a spirit wolf was responsible."

A spirit wolf seemed such a simple explanation when there was nothing simple about what had happened. The thing he found both hardest and easiest to accept was that Feather Tickles had prayed for death and her prayer had been answered—by the creature that had been following them.

When Raven's Cry looked over at White Calf, she walked over to where Deep Scar stood and touched Feather Tickles's temple. "She does not cry," she said solemnly. "She is at peace."

True to his word, the chief made no plans to bury his dead wife. According to him, she hadn't fulfilled her marriage responsibilities and thus he'd rejected her. Although many muttered that Sleeps Too Long had been too quick to turn his back on his marriage and a number of the warriors cast disapproving glances his way, no one confronted him. Night Thunder wasn't surprised. Sleeps Too Long might shock and anger the others, but no one, not even White Calf or Raven's Cry, was willing to step forward and challenge his right to be called chief, because without his leadership the clan might not have survived recent attacks from the Crow and Tetons.

After lifting the body off Deep Scar, he laid it on the ground. Wailing, Jumper knelt beside his daughter, then began tearing out chunks of his hair. Blood ran into his eyes, and he seemed nearly unconscious with grief. By contrast, Feather Tickles's mother stared without blinking at her daughter, her face sickly pale.

Little Rain and White Calf stepped forward and wrapped the dead woman's body in several blankets, their movements in perfect unison. Burying her with the ground this hard or building a suitable raised platform would take time they didn't have, but no one argued when the women collected rocks and covered Feather Tickles so animals couldn't disturb her.

"Find peace in this place," White Calf said as she stood over the mound, one arm draped around Jumper's shoulder, the other resting on the back of Feather Tickles's mother's neck. "Here you are safe from winter's wind and will again feel summer's heat. You will not be lonely because our prayers are with you. Journey into the world that waits for all of us and when we have died, we will join you and we will all laugh together."

"Speak of the wolf, please," Jumper whispered. "White Calf, please tell us why a wolf would do this to our child."

White Calf nodded, but it was a while before she spoke. "When I touched Feather Tickles, I found what Wolf had left behind of himself. He is not yet ready to reveal the truth about himself; perhaps he never will, but I know one thing. He may not be a spirit."

"How can that be?" Night Thunder demanded before he could stop himself.

"Listen to me," White Calf continued, her tone both gentle and somber. "Wolf spoke to me in his way, as a *Sta-au'* might."

"The ghost of an evil one who has died?" Bunch of Lodges challenged. He'd been standing off to one side, but now he stalked into the middle of the group. "That cannot be! My magic, which is powerful, keeps the *Sta-au'* away. If one is here, it is because someone does not walk the way he or she should." He kept his hard gaze on White Calf.

"I do not have the answers." White Calf returned the shaman's stare. "I do not know what is happening. I simply say what I feel and I feel a *Sta-au'* walking among us."

"No!" Jumper gasped.

"What Wolf did to your daughter is not evil," White Calf said.

"She asked for death and it was given to her. Perhaps not all ghosts are evil."

Was that possible?

As soon as prayers for Feather Tickles were over, it was time for the clan to split up, hunters and helpers continuing after buffalo while the others headed south. Usually separations like this were taken as a matter of course, but a death caused by a ghost or spirit wolf had made an impact on everyone. As a consequence, good-byes took longer and there were more promises to pray for one another. Bunch of Lodges led a prayer to Sun, loudly reminding Sun that he, as shaman, was filled with wisdom and kindness and had always been good to those who did right; the People were good. He didn't look at the chief while he was saying that. Neither did he acknowledge White Calf.

Once the children, elderly, and infirmed had left with all the clan's possessions except for a few traveling tepees, Raven's Cry offered to go on ahead toward Big Wind Plains.

"My dream is not clear," he admitted. "It still tells me that we travel in the right direction, but I do not know how far we will have to ride before we find the buffalo—or whether they have moved on."

"Alone?" Sleeps Too Long questioned. Since Night Thunder had confronted him, the chief's eyes had darkened and somber lines pulled down the corners of his mouth.

"Yes. I will return when the buffalo have revealed themselves to me."

"Take White Calf with you," Sleeps Too Long ordered. "Together your magic will be even greater."

Around his wife he felt, not strong, but weak and vulnerable. Maybe it wouldn't be like that once he was used to sleeping with her, but these nights he felt as if there was nothing she didn't know about him, nothing he wouldn't give her. He told his chief that this was his dream and his to follow, alone.

"Why marry White Calf if you treat her as if she was like all other women?" Sleeps Too Long looked around at the others, smiling a little when a couple of them nodded.

"What comes of my marriage with her is like a tree just beginning to grow," he replied. "I pray it will strengthen and that the Blackfeet will be blessed because of that strength, but one cannot order a tree to become full-grown before its time."

To his relief, Sleeps Too Long hadn't argued with that, and Raven's Cry had taken advantage of the momentary silence to turn his back on the group.

Now, hours later, he was tired of riding and despite his heavy blanket, he felt chilled. New Snow continued to walk where he guided her, but she showed no interest in her surroundings other than laying her ears back whenever the wind threw debris at her. The sky was heavy and dark, weighing him down and making him ask himself whether he was on a fool's mission.

"They come so easily," White Calf had said of her visions last night as he held her in his arms. "Even when I do not want them, they come."

Was that the way it was supposed to be for him? He'd told the others that he continued to dream of a great herd but no one, not even White Calf, knew that nothing had come to him last night.

"Are you there, Raven?" he asked aloud. "Do you see me and know what I am doing? Do you know my fears?"

His brother feared going into battle; although Night Thunder hadn't said anything, his eyes had given him away. Hiding from death made no sense because it touched everyone and what greater glory could come to a warrior than dying in battle?

But the others were depending on him to lead them to the meat they needed to stay alive. What if he failed? What if his dream hadn't been sent to him by the spirits and meant nothing?

"Raven, listen to me. Mother Earth, hear this child. I was shown the way to the Snake horses. Thoughts became images in my mind and I believed and that belief became the truth. I want it to happen again. I *need* it to happen again!"

New Snow's ears flicked back toward him. "I do not speak to

you," he told the mare. "Your spirit is strong, but it cares nothing about buffalo meat. Those are concerns of the Blackfeet, not horses."

White Calf's prayers were always to the sacred calf responsible for her name but should he be praying to Raven?

Raven had the power to give people far sight. Often a man going to war wore a stuffed raven's skin so if he got close to the enemy, the skin would warn him of danger. A number of ravens flying over lodges, crying as they went, was proof that someone would soon bring news from far away. Ravens sometimes told of nearby game by calling to a hunter and then flying away, coming back again and again until the hunter knew where to go. But there weren't any ravens around today.

"*Na'pi,* Old Man, do you hear me? Surely you are not playing a joke on me. I trusted in my earlier dream and it came true, but now—"

Were the spirits making a fool of him, he wondered, the thought chilling him even more than the cutting wind. Whoever found *I-nis'-kim,* the buffalo stone, had great power with buffalo; but although he'd always searched for one of the small sacred rocks when he was on the prairie and listened carefully for the faint chirping sound like that of a little bird, which meant a *I-nis'-kim* was nearby, he'd never found one.

He shivered, suddenly so cold that he looked around to make sure a blizzard hadn't struck. As his thoughts about *I-nis'-kim* returned to him, he recalled an ancient story about a winter when the buffalo had disappeared and the snow was so deep that the People couldn't move.

The hunters had killed elk, deer, and small game but finally none of those were left and the people began to starve. A woman cooking a small jackrabbit had heard a beautiful song and had followed the sound to a cottonwood tree where she'd found a strange-looking rock. When she picked it up, the rock had told her to take it to the village and teach everyone the song she'd just learned. Finally she was told to pray, not to starve, and for the buffalo to return and by morning everyone's heart would be glad.

The old story had fascinated him and he'd asked to have it told over and over again, not certain whether it had been the truth or simply a way of entertaining people, but that had been when the buffalo were near and the responsibility for finding them hadn't been his. Now that, like his knowledge of Old Man and the power of ravens, swirled around him like random dust devils.

He'd been traveling through a narrow slit cut into the earth because grass grew thicker there and cushioned his horse's way, but as he came to the top of a rise, he urged New Snow to the highest point. In the distance, the clouds were so dark that it seemed as if night had reached up and was trying to devour the prairie, but it was lighter overhead. He could go in one direction or another, follow the slit or veer off and pick up one of the seemingly endless paths left by generations of buffalo, but those options were the meanderings of a mind looking for something to do when his people's very lives might depend on what he found today.

Straightening, he lifted his head toward the heavens and sucked in frigid air, concentrating on the route it took on the way to his lungs. "Hear me, Raven. Listen to my words and know that I have need of your wisdom and guidance. I am not an insect driven by the wind. I must have purpose and my people's bellies must be filled. Show me! Please, show me!"

The snow-heavy clouds sagged, putting him in mind of a woman's belly swollen by the child inside. Although he wanted to sit tall and proud while praying to his spirit, he felt weighed down by the clouds. They pushed at him, challenged him to fight them, and because he was merely a man, he slumped forward. As he did, New Snow shied to one side, snorting unexpectedly.

After resettling himself on her back, he looked down at what had startled her. A buffalo skull, bleached white with empty sockets and wide, curving horns lay in stark contrast to the dark growth surrounding it. The head was pointed in the same direction the wind was blowing.

After studying it a moment longer, he turned New Snow that

way and urged her to pick up her pace. As he left the skull behind, he first muttered a prayer of thankfulness to Raven and Old Man and Sun and the other spirits and then prayed that this was indeed a sign.

When Raven's Cry hadn't returned by nightfall, Chief Sleeps Too Long told the others that there'd be no more traveling toward Big Wind Plain today. Although he wondered whether the chief believed his son was out there wandering about aimlessly, Bunch of Lodges, who'd spent much of the day looking for signs in the heavy clouds, didn't argue with him. Whether he revered the chief or not—which he didn't—Sleeps Too Long was right. It made no sense to keep on the move when they didn't know where they were heading.

"I have faith in him," Bunch of Lodges proclaimed loud enough for everyone to hear. "My son will not fail his people."

"I never said—" Sleeps Too Long started, but Bunch of Lodges waved him off.

"A man's relationship with his spirits is a sacred one, and it is even more so for my son," he continued. "Raven's Cry has been blessed. The spirits have told me so! But"—he glared at the chief—"perhaps the spirits will not bless those who question his power. I trust. Those who do the same will be rewarded. Those who do not . . ."

He deliberately left the rest unsaid and was rewarded when the two braves who'd been flanking their chief stepped away from him.

Looking as alone as a lame buffalo who can't keep up when the rest of the herd travels on, Sleeps Too Long nevertheless lifted his spear high overhead.

"I am chief," he proclaimed. "I have made a decision. That is all I am going to say."

If it was, Bunch of Lodges thought, that would be one of the few times Sleeps Too Long didn't fill the air with his nonsense. Turning his back on the chief as if he was of no consequence to him, he stalked toward where his wife was setting up their tepee.

He should have ordered her to continue toward their winter home. In fact, he'd given it serious thought, thinking how peaceful it would be without her complaining, but in the end, he'd told her to accompany him because although her hands no longer had the strength necessary to cut meat from a buffalo's carcass, she could cook for him and make sure he had a warm place to sleep, thus freeing him to pray and make magic.

When he saw White Calf working with Dirty Knee Sits, he paused, remembering that White Calf had glared at Sleeps Too Long when the chief denied any responsibility in his wife's death. The realization that White Calf was disgusted with the man who'd tried to marry her filled him with a sense of power. He'd been concerned that she might regret her decision regarding which suitor to accept, but he no longer did.

Without waiting for the women to acknowledge him, he announced himself with a loud belch. Dirty Knee Sits barely glanced up, but White Calf watched him with a wary alertness that belied her casual stance.

"What have your visions told you?" he demanded of her. "Will we see my son before morning?"

Although she'd expected the question, White Calf felt herself tense anew. Since marrying Raven's Cry, she'd been even more aware of Bunch of Lodges' hostility toward her, only maybe hostility didn't say it all.

"I have been given no vision of him," she explained as concisely as possible.

"Perhaps you did not seek one."

"Why would I not do so?" she countered and immediately regretted it. She had so much to learn about the shaman and didn't dare ever forget that he'd had many more years in which to perfect his skills. "When I try to find him in my mind, I see only swirling darkness."

"Atch! This cannot be!"

"It is not what I want," she admitted. "But perhaps the spirits do not want me to know too much about my husband."

Bunch of Lodges considered that. "Ah, yes. You speak with wisdom since that is why they did not tell me my oldest son would be killed."

"It is wise of the spirits," she said, nodding because he was. "It would cause too much pain if we knew when those who are important to us face danger or death."

"Hm. Do not forget, the spirits are not always kind. If you displease them, they will seek revenge."

Surprised by how he'd turned the conversation on her that way, she shrugged and went back to helping Dirty Knee Sits secure the lodge pins on the small tepee they'd be using tonight.

"I only mean to pass my wisdom onto you, White Calf," he went on. "It has taken me many years to earn the spirits' ears. They listen to me. You cannot yet expect the same."

"Perhaps." Then because wondering where Raven's Cry was and whether he would be warm and dry tonight made her edgy, she pointed out that her pathway to the spirits had been forged when she was much younger than Bunch of Lodges had been.

"Be careful what you say, White Calf," the shaman warned, his voice sharp-edged. "We are Mother Earth's children, and She does not want us to argue among ourselves. Wisdom belongs to those who have lived many years, thus you can never hope to stand side by side with me. The Blackfeet may speak reverently of your gift of sight, but it is I they come to when they need healing or magic done. I."

She couldn't argue that. Besides, with worry gnawing at her belly, she couldn't concentrate on what she might have said in response. She needed to pray to the sacred white calf that Raven's Cry be guided safely back to her. "Look" for him the way she had several times already today, and maybe this time she would find him.

The first snow had fallen during the night. A layer no thicker than the width of a single finger covered the tepee and ground when White Calf got up at dawn the next morning. Although she'd been aware of the wind during the night, it had settled down, reminding her of a sleeping animal. Maybe winter stood between her and visions of her husband.

And maybe what she felt for the man she'd just begun to share herself with left her so confused that even the sacred calf couldn't see through that confusion.

Raven's Cry's horse was short-legged, but the mare's feet were broad and solid, which meant she shouldn't have trouble keeping her balance. And if Raven's Cry had decided to travel on foot to spare New Snow, his powerful muscles wouldn't fail him.

Why then did fear grip her?

Too restless to go back inside where Bunch of Lodges might be waiting for her, she struck out toward the horses. They seemed unconcerned about the cold, but then their coats had become thick and heavy over the past few weeks. Even this spring's foals were so shaggy that they put her in mind of bears. Creator Sun had chosen well when he designed horses; the same was true of the rest of the earth's creatures. Only humans, hairless and unable to subsist on grass and without sharp teeth or claws for hunting, were ill-equipped for survival. The why of that had long troubled her, but because the spirits had never answered her questions on that matter, she'd had to be content with the thought that perhaps humans had more wisdom and thus knew how to take from their surroundings and prosper.

But did she want wisdom when fear was part of it?

"White Calf?"

Her heart thudded painfully, then slowed when she realized that Little Rain was coming toward her. Because Little Rain was heavily bundled, for a moment she tried to convince herself that the approaching figure was Raven's Cry's, but she already knew different.

"You are out early," she said to the other woman.

"So are you. The horses are fine?"

"Yes."

Little Rain nodded. "I saw you leave and . . . The horses seem so content. It does not matter to them that winter has arrived."

Something about Little Rain's tone held her attention. "I was thinking the same thing," she admitted. "Thinking that it is good to be a horse who does not look ahead to blizzards or times of no food. Only this moment matters to them."

Little Rain flashed a smile. "Perhaps I envy them. Are you all right?"

"All right?"

"You had to sleep alone last night."

"I slept alone for a long time before I became Raven's Cry's wife."

"True. But your heart is uneasy."

"Uneasy? No. I—"

"It is all right," Little Rain interrupted. "On the last night of his life, my husband left my side and stepped out to face those who had attacked us. When I saw him reach for his weapons, I tried to keep him with me, because I was afraid he would be killed." She drew in an unsteady breath. "It is for a woman to fear for the life of the warrior she loves."

Loves?

"A woman in love is like a bird who can no longer fly," Little Rain continued. "We are trapped by that love."

"Trapped?"

"I speak from wisdom. What you feel for Raven's Cry is still growing, but if you do not kill it, it will continue to bloom. Although the flower that is love is beautiful, there is no escaping it."

Little Rain was speaking nonsense; at least that's what she tried to tell herself. But the Cree had loved her husband; her grief had made that all too clear.

"Do you ever wish it was otherwise?" she asked.

"Yes. But I would not trade the time I had with my husband. We were one and I will never forget that."

"One? I cannot imagine—"

A sudden shout stopped White Calf midsentence. Her heart struggled to free itself from her chest, and although she didn't know what was happening, she started running toward the sound. At last only a few feet separated her from the excited voices and the snow seemed to part and she saw Raven's Cry.

A sob caught in her throat and it was all she could do not to throw herself at him.

19

Snow had been spitting during the day, the flakes small and hard. White Calf imagined that the smallest children were running around chattering about how much fun they'd have if a true storm overtook them while they were still in the country's colder regions, but although their parents might be tolerant of their loud voices and excitement, they wouldn't share the youthful enthusiasm.

"I hoped there would be no storm until after the hunt is over," she told Raven's Cry as they lay together that night. He'd ridden with the other hunters all afternoon, and this was the first opportunity she'd had to speak with him. "It is right that the rest of the tribe is heading toward warmer land."

Raven's Cry muttered something she took to be agreement.

"What is it?" she asked. "You have been preoccupied."

To her exasperation, he nodded but didn't say anything. However, in the short time they'd been husband and wife, she'd discovered ways of capturing his attention. She now used one by running her hand over his belly until he drew her against him, more than a little surprised at how easily her body had accepted his right to it. If it had been her bleeding time, they would have slept apart because she was unclean then, but she didn't need to concern herself with that tonight.

"I have been watching our chief," she told him, her voice low even though they had a small tepee to themselves. "Watching and trying to understand him."

"What? Why?"

Men! Why was it so difficult for them to know what went on inside a woman's mind and heart? "Because of what happened to Feather Tickles. She was his bride; he had just paid a price to make her his, and yet he had no hand in her burying and has not mourned her death."

"The horses he gave Jumper are his again; he is happy."

"Happy? He has said nothing to you or the other warriors about what he feels?"

"He says she brought about her own death by going where a wolf was. You know that."

"And he accepts no responsibility for what happened to her?" Instead of waiting for her husband's reply, she went on. "Big Dancing was right to leave him. I only wish Feather Tickles had done the same. If she had, she would still be alive."

"Hm. Perhaps."

What was wrong with Raven's Cry? Although he was now fingering her breast, he still seemed distracted.

"Your father struts about like a bull elk these days," she said because maybe a change of subject would catch his attention. "Some say he is too old to be part of a hunting party, but he is so proud of your dreams that no one could prevent him from coming along. My husband, your visions of the buffalo herd, do they remain with you always?"

"What? Why do you ask?"

"Because I want to understand your gift. Did you think I would not?"

"White Calf, I . . . You are full of talk. It has been a long day and I thought you would be tired."

"Sleep waits for me, yes, but I—I missed you today."

"Missed? I did not go anywhere."

But you have.

*　　*　　*

They'd made love on the hides that protected them from the cold and ungiving ground and had fallen asleep with their bodies wrapped together. Several times Raven's Cry must have dreamed because he'd moaned and moved about, waking her. Her hand resting on his ribs, she'd waited out his restlessness, relaxing and falling back asleep only when he once again snored lightly.

In the morning she asked him about his dreams, but, his features tight and unmoving, he said she must have been mistaken because he remembered nothing. Snow hadn't been falling when they first woke up, but the small, sparse flakes began again as dawn gave way to day. There was little wind, and despite the cold, no one spoke of winter.

Instead, as everyone gathered to eat, Raven's Cry announced that he intended to go out alone again today.

"But the scouts—" his father began.

"I do not fault their ability to track, but whenever I try to take my thoughts to the herd, all I see is them," Raven's Cry explained. "I do not want any more distractions."

He hadn't looked at her during his short speech, but as he took off, White Calf asked herself if he considered her the greatest distraction. She first occupied herself with getting ready to travel and then, once they were underway, she asked Little Rain if it was any different when the Cree went after buffalo. Little Rain admitted she'd only been on two small hunts before her marriage, neither of them with the great potential of this one.

After that White Calf couldn't think of anything to say and Little Rain didn't seem interested in conversation either. The snow was like dripping water, part irritant and part fascination. Her mount plodded on, uninterested in anything except doing what was expected of it, and she allowed herself to be lulled by the easy rocking motion. Morning finished itself and gave way to midday and still the group rode toward Big Wind Plains where Raven's Cry had told them they'd find the buffalo. By the time the sun began its downward slide, there'd still been no sign of her husband.

The first time her mind floated out seeking Raven's Cry, she pulled it back because she refused to question his decision, not ask herself if he was safe. But he'd left without speaking to her and his silence made a bitter taste in her mouth. He wasn't displeased with her; she didn't believe that. Yet he hadn't wanted anything to do with her.

An unusually fat flake landed on the tip of her nose and she wiped it away. She tried to recall what Raven's Cry had been wearing, but she'd been so concerned with the look in his eyes that she hadn't noticed. She could do that, she told herself. "Look" for him and when she had, satisfy her mind on that one thing but nothing else.

She "found" him easily, a solitary figure astride the mare he loved. They traveled as one, the horse with her head high and alert, the man well-protected against the weather but a little concerned with the heavy clouds. Like New Snow, Raven's Cry kept his attention on his surroundings, watching, listening, mentally pushing against the dribbling snow, as if by doing so he could make his world as clean and clear as it was on a summer-dry afternoon.

Although she sometimes sensed what went on inside another person's mind, she hadn't wanted to do that with her husband and refused to probe. Just the same, the way he carried himself told her a great deal. He was like a hungry coyote searching for something to fill its belly, not yet desperate but too driven to notice whether its legs were tiring.

New Snow dropped her head, intending to grab a chunk of grass as she passed, but Raven's Cry didn't let her, yanking on the single rope with unaccustomed force. Startled, New Snow pranced. Raven's Cry cursed, his voice bouncing against the flakes and then dying. White Calf clung to the echo of his outburst, learning a great deal.

"What drives you, my husband?" she muttered. "You are like a man too long without a woman and yet you released yourself inside me last night. Your body should be at peace."

Raven's Cry's searching became more intense, more disjointed. He pulled New Snow this way and that, eyes straining and now red-tinged. He smelled of determination and, although she struggled to deny it, fear. Sometimes a Blackfoot or dog or horse became blind; her husband was like that, lost and angry because he couldn't find what he was determined to.

She could, would help. Leaving him, she "floated" and waited for the senses she didn't understand and yet accepted to tell her what she needed to know. It didn't take long, an easy push through the few flakes to where the buffalo herd walked and fed and waited for the wind to drive them on. They weren't ahead of Raven's Cry but to one side and slightly behind him and if he continued in the direction he was going, he would miss them.

The vision of hunger and despair, of desperate men and women pushing themselves through a relentless blizzard slammed into her. It had done no good to try to deny it! None at all.

But this was a baby-storm and no one was starving—yet.

Returning to Raven's Cry in her mind, she touched him with her thoughts but hopefully not with her fear. *Go this way,* she begged him. *You will find what you need. What we must have.*

When he dismounted, Raven's Cry wasn't sure his legs would hold him. He was struggling to control their weary trembling when White Calf hurried toward him. He thought she might hug him in front of everyone and knew he'd embrace her in turn, but in the end, she simply grasped his forearms. When he looked down at her, he saw moisture shining in her eyes—that and something else.

Even if he'd been able to tell her how close he'd come to missing the herd and that the knowledge continued to eat away at his confidence, there was no time for them to speak in private. Night Thunder took New Snow's reins but didn't lead her away. Instead his brother stood waiting along with the rapidly assembling members of the hunting party.

"I found the buffalo," he said simply when it hadn't been simple at all.

"Where?"

"How many?"

"Are they fat?" The last came from his father.

"You were gone a long time," the chief said before he could answer his father. "Were they that well-hidden?"

There'd been times he'd lost the distinction between snow and the whiteness he knew existed only in his head, but whether the herd had been trying to hide from him, he didn't know.

"They move," he said, not answering his chief's question. "Not fast, but this storm continues to grow and may be replaced by one with more teeth. If that happens, it will be hard to overtake them. Besides, it will be dark soon and if the buffalo do not sleep but continue to travel and the snow covers their tracks—"

"He is right," Bunch of Lodges proclaimed. "And he was right to hurry back to us. We cannot lose them, we will not!"

Creator Sun had fashioned the first buffalo from mud and blew life into the creature's nostrils. Then he'd caused it to fall asleep and removed a rib and used that to create a mate for it. This flesh food also provided the People with clothing and the means for carrying foodstuffs. Rawhide became pole hitches, horseshoes, shields, and blankets. Hair became the stuffing for pillows, to pad saddles and make ropes, fashion headdresses, and ornaments. Even the tendons were transformed into needles and the hooves were used for rattles and glue. No warrior killed a buffalo without thanking Buffalo Spirit for the gift.

As Raven's Cry expected, the chief immediately began making plans to take off. The hunters would set forth on their fastest horses so they could cover as much distance as possible before dark, the women following with the pack horses and what they needed for butchering. Someone would be dispatched to take word of what they were doing back to the rest of the tribe.

"My son needs to sleep," Bunch of Lodges argued.

"Let him catch up once he has rested," the chief countered.

"And if you cannot follow his tracks? Only my son can show the way."

My son, Night Thunder thought, his stomach clenching in a way that was all too familiar. He'd taken charge of his brother's horse because it was expected that of him. He'd listened while the chief and other warriors made plans because no one cared about the opinion of someone untested in hunting. As long as he wasn't given the task of carrying word to the elders, infirm, children, and new mothers, he didn't care.

"I will be ready," Raven's Cry said, ignoring his father.

"So be it." Sleeps Too Long shrugged. "How my arms ache to release arrows and watch them find a living heart! I want to look into the eyes of a buffalo I have just killed and know my people will grow fat on his flesh."

Sleeps Too Long's love of killing was legendary. He was happy shedding the blood of an animal but even more pleased if he killed an enemy. No wonder he'd been made chief. No wonder everyone listened to his wisdom and often put that wisdom before anyone else's.

"It will take the women a long time to catch up," Dirty Knee Sits whined. "If we had a little help with—"

"You have your job, Wife!" Bunch of Lodges snapped. "Do we ask you to join us in the danger of hunting?"

"I simply said—"

"I know what you are thinking! Nothing would please you more than to make the men do your work. Even with the Cree to help, no one is slower. You are too old to be part of this; I should have ordered you to remain behind."

"*I* am too old? How long has it been since *you* hunted? Your knees will creak and frighten the buffalo."

The shaman's nostrils flared, reminding Night Thunder of how often his father and Dirty Knee Sits fought. She should know better than to make fun of her husband, the shaman, but she seemed to delight in doing so; and for reasons he might never understand, his father never truly challenged his wife.

"If my husband says the men must not waste time in taking off after the buffalo, we will do as he says," White Calf pointed out before Bunch of Lodges could say anything. "It is always the way of women to follow a hunting party."

Dirty Knee Sits grumbled that it would take even longer to get underway because it was snowing, but no one paid any attention to her. Instead, Chief Sleeps Too Long asked Raven's Cry if he'd come across fresh tracks and that was how he'd known where to locate the herd.

"That has always been my way," Sleeps Too Long said with a speculative look in Raven's Cry's direction. "It is such a simple thing that even a child can do it. But—" He paused, looking around to make sure he had everyone's attention. "Maybe you do not need to use your eyes because your dreams supply all answers."

"Maybe."

"Maybe? You are not going to say?"

Raven's Cry rubbed the back of his neck, but when he yawned, Night Thunder didn't believe he was that relaxed. "I keep my own counsel, my chief," Raven's Cry said. "Now I wish something to eat."

"You did well with our chief," Bunch of Lodges said as Raven's Cry ate. "Silenced his boasting and foolish questions."

White Calf had given him a bowl of pemmican and then handed a like amount to his father and brother while his mother continued her grumbling. Excited by the increased activity, the horses whinnied. Men called back and forth to each other as they collected their weapons. As for himself, he could only hope he would feel revived once he'd filled his belly.

"I do not wish to speak to Sleeps Too Long," he admitted. "The man pushes his way into things that are not his concern."

"He believes being chief has given him the right to do and say anything he wants."

He nodded agreement with his father's observation. White Calf, however, did more than that.

"He does not understand that he is not all powerful," she said, seeming not to care that the chief might overhear. "Yes, he has had much success in war, but he brings his battles into his tepee; that should not be."

"And into his bed," Little Rain whispered as she and White Calf exchanged a look.

"Little Rain, we cannot change what happened to Feather Tickles," Night Thunder warned. "Do not try to walk into the past."

"I do not," she said with more spirit than she'd shown just a few days ago. "But if the Blackfeet walk into the future with Sleeps Too Long as their chief—"

"What the Blackfeet do is not your concern, Cree!" Bunch of Lodges interrupted. "Do the chores that are assigned you and remain silent. That is all I want from you."

"Father," Night Thunder warned. "She is my responsibility, not yours."

Bunch of Lodges angrily pointed out that he wouldn't have had to say anything to Little Rain if Night Thunder had done his job, but Raven's Cry couldn't concentrate on the argument. He'd walked away from Sleeps Too Long, not just because he wanted to eat, but because he'd been afraid someone would ask too many questions about the dreams that must have led him to the herd.

There hadn't been any more telling dreams and he'd come so close to missing what was vital to the tribe's survival.

Because he no longer had to concentrate on finding his way in the dark, Raven's Cry managed to doze a little as they traveled. The snow, what little there was of it, was simply an irritant. New Snow had been tired and tender-footed so he'd left her behind with White Calf. The stallion he rode had a broader back with a thick neck and a mane he could bury his fingers in. His father rode ahead of him on a young mare and all his stallion wanted to do was keep pace with her. Once they were closer to where he'd seen the herd, he would take the lead, but that wasn't necessary yet. Night Thunder was beside him, silent in contrast to the boastful conversations all around. Finally he roused enough to acknowledge his brother.

"Are you praying to your spirit?" he asked. "Is that why you have so little so say?"

"I am thinking."

"About what? Perhaps you wonder, as I do, if our father should be doing this."

"No. I am thinking about the hunt."

"Hm. Do not let it consume you. Just because this is your first one does not mean you do not know what to expect. How many times have we heard hunters boast? Thanks to their never-ending words, even a small child knows what is done, where to aim an arrow."

"No," Night Thunder said slowly. "That is not it. I am also remembering . . ."

"What?"

"When I counted coup."

Momentarily confused, he started to ask his brother to explain himself. Then he caught Night Thunder's expression. "Your memories weigh you down," he said. "Are you not proud of what you accomplished?"

"Of course I am."

"Then what?"

Night Thunder sighed and Raven's Cry thought he wouldn't answer but after glancing at their father who was now talking to Quail Legs, he said, "I tell myself that hunting and counting coup are not so different. They are both dangerous and a warrior may die doing either thing."

"Yes."

"Is that all you can say, yes?" Night Thunder snapped.

"What more do you want?"

"I do not know! How easy it is for you, brother. You have your dream messages and White Calf. You are tall and strong and our father smiles at you. I envy you."

Would he if he knew the truth? "Why? I walk the same ground you do. What wounds you wounds me."

"But you do not take fear of that wounding deep inside you," Night Thunder said softly. Then he dug his heels into Deep Scar's sides and galloped away, his form disappearing in the white.

* * *

The storm had grown needle-sharp teeth by the time the warriors were within striking distance of the buffalo. They set up a crude camp in the dark, planning to sleep until dawn. Buffalo were quick to stampede and before they'd been gifted with horses, the Blackfeet had had to sneak up on their prey with wolf hides draped over them as disguises or depend on ice, deep snow, or a steep cliff they could drive the animals over, but now they could run them down. They'd do so in the morning when their horses were fresh.

Because there was no covering beyond the slight rise they'd put between themselves and the wind, the hunting party kept warm by sleeping packed back to back. They took turns staying up with the horses because even the most well-trained mount was known to break its restraining ropes if frightened or in an effort to find shelter.

When his time came to watch, Night Thunder discovered that no matter how close he stood to the horses, he was unable to see them clearly. It was as if the storm and dark had swallowed the animals, leaving behind little except their sounds and smells to tease him. True, he held onto the rope that tied them together so he knew they hadn't somehow worked their way loose, but his hands had become numb and he half believed the rope too was an illusion. He couldn't feel his nose or cheeks, and when he pulled his blanket close to his face, he was so clumsy that the blanket kept sliding down and he had to secure it over and over again.

His mind had become as numb as his nose and fingers. He vaguely recalled saying things to his brother that he now regretted but for a long time couldn't remember what they'd been. He could only hope Raven's Cry had been so tired that he hadn't paid attention. Something about fear . . .

In an attempt to keep his mind from closing down completely around the hated word, he struggled to recall what his father and the chief had said to each other, but the closer he tried to look back, the clearer Little Rain's image became.

What was it White Calf had said, that a ghost might have been responsible for Feather Tickles's death, only the wolf that had killed her, the wolf that had become part of his and Raven's Cry's lives, wasn't evil. It had . . .

. . . been there when he'd found the courage to count coup and attack Takes-Knife-at-Night.

"We will ride at both sides of the herd," Sleeps Too Long announced as the warriors looked out at the dark, constantly moving mass. "Thus if they stampede, they should run in a straight line. If they do not, we will gallop to the front and turn them upon themselves."

Even the shaman nodded agreement. The snow was up to the horses' hocks by now and the buffalo looked more like endless white boulders than living animals, but the storm had ceased and the buffalo were taking advantage of the lull in the weather to feed. Even from here, Night Thunder could hear countless teeth pulling at grass.

There were many kinds of buffalo, old bulls no one bothered to bring down because their hides and meat were too tough, three and four year olds with silky, thick fur perfect for blankets and robes, mature cows known as Big Females and the dangerous Horns Not Cracked, which were adult males. At first they all blurred together in his mind and vision, but as he concentrated, he saw that most of the calves grazed near the center of the herd while many of the bulls were to the left. It was past breeding season, which meant the bulls cared for little except regaining the weight they'd lost while chasing the females. Still, he had no desire to go near the Horns Not Cracked when there were so many fat cows.

"My mouth waters," someone announced. "I may not wait until the meat is cooked before filling my belly."

"Ha! I will be so busy bringing down buffalo that I will not have time to eat."

"I prayed over my arrows and kept them close to my heart during the night," Quail Legs admitted. "Today every one of them will find a buffalo's heart."

Blue Snake insisted he had the most arrows and intended to bring down more of the beasts than anyone else. Although he joined in the good-natured laughter which followed that boast, Night

Thunder's tongue felt as if it was stuck to the roof of his mouth. Maybe it would be different if he could recall the thought that had come to him while he was guarding the horses, but he couldn't.

"Buffalo Spirit!" Bunch of Lodges called out in a loud sing-song that silenced everyone. "Look down on us and know our need. Feel our courage. Speak to your children and tell them to give themselves up to us so that our people will be fed. If you do this thing, we will sing your praises during the many feasts to come. Look down on us and see that the Blackfeet shaman is among the hunters. And his son who you have blessed with telling dreams."

Although the others had their eyes on Bunch of Lodges, Night Thunder snuck a glance at Sleeps Too Long. The chief glowered.

"We go now!" Bunch of Lodges finished. "Our strength is great, and I, *I* have prayed!"

Propelled forward by the force of his father's words and the now galloping horses, Night Thunder leaned low along Deep Scar's back, his attention fixed on the great herd. No one had yelled yet, but the buffalo abruptly stopped eating and looked around, their eyes already showing the white of alarm. Several bellowed at the same time. One and then maybe as many as twenty bulls wheeled and pounded toward the rest of the herd. A cow squealed.

A pounding, drumming sound began, the heavy thunder of countless hooves on frozen earth. Bellowing and snorting, the herd whirled first one way and then the other like a great mound of leaves caught in a twisting wind, bunching closer and closer together. Night Thunder gripped his bow in one icy hand, an arrow in the other, his full quiver lashed to his back.

Run away!

No!

He became part of Deep Scar and the stallion part of him. They galloped as one, death only a misstep away. As a small boy, he'd once fallen into a storm-swollen river and been borne far downstream before he managed to drag himself onto shore. Today felt like that, not enough within his control, too much happening too fast, needing to do one thing.

Out of the corner of his eye, he saw his father bearing down on a yearling, the older man's solid weight slowing his horse's movement. The shaman's back was straighter than it had been in years, his shoulders squared. Blood-lust contorted his features, the emotion touching his son. Because Bunch of Lodges had pulled his bow tight, Night Thunder did the same, seeing in his mind the upcoming kill and then—

—and then the past slammed into him.

He'd shot a wolf, not once, not twice, but three times. His arrows had sped true and fast—he knew they had—and yet they hadn't found what they'd sought. Instead, he'd been forced to stare into the pale and deadly eyes of something that couldn't be killed.

Today was different! Please, Mother Earth, make it different!

Screaming, he focused on the nearest animal. The huge, snot-flinging cow ran with mad determination, massive head low and swaying, snow splaying around and then behind her. He noted the wildly twitching tail, steam bursting from widespread nostrils, open mouth. Closer, closer, so close now that he felt both the buffalo's heat and her panic. She was everything, his world, massive. His father, old with unused muscles, could hunt. So could he!

His arms burned with effort; his thigh muscles shrieked. Deep Scar, his wonderful, faithful horse hugged the cow's side and kept pace with her, blowing out his own clouds of spent air.

"Now!" Night Thunder screamed. "Now!"

His words sent strength and decision throughout him; he first stained and then released the arrow. It sailed straight and strong, burying itself deep in the great shoulder. For maybe three heart-beats, the cow continued her headlong run, then staggered. She regained her footing, but her next breath sprayed blood. Of its own accord, his hand reached back for another arrow, but by the time he'd readied it, the cow was slowing.

She died by degrees, first her shoulder muscles, then her tail, and finally her head. She was barely standing now, her eyes rolled back and unseeing. Bloody drool ran from her open mouth, her fat body shuddering. He felt himself fall with her, felt her pain and despair and then acceptance and was surprised to discover he was still on horseback looking down at the heaving side and jerking legs.

"Turn them!"

Pulling himself free of his death-caused spell, he quickly took in what was happening. The herd had split apart with the bulk of the animals racing for open ground. The rest, no more than twenty, remained trapped by the warriors on either side of them. Despite the confusion, he spotted his father and two other warriors who raced after the larger number, but why should he try to join them when there were enough buffalo nearby? Still, three braves couldn't possibly stop or even turn that many animals and the odds against the men increased the danger.

His mind was made up for him when another cow, this one smaller but with a rich, winter-thick coat tried to run past him. Her pounding gait was a storm that sucked him along, mindless, full of what he'd just accomplished. Without needing to be urged, Deep Scar turned toward her and Night Thunder sighted down the line of his arrow.

The cow might have lived if she'd whirled and hidden herself in the midst of her kind, but she galloped straight and unswerving, which made it a simple matter for him to fix on the vulnerable place just behind the shoulder. Once again he pulled his bow taut and then gave it freedom. Once again his arrow sped where he'd willed it. Once again white breath became blood speckled. Although this cow ran longer and took longer to fall, in the end, the result was the same.

Looking down at what he'd done, he wanted to remain where he was while Deep Scar sucked in air and he accepted the simple and wonderful fact that instead of running away, he'd stayed and killed two buffalo this morning; but suddenly someone screamed, the sound so loud and sharp that even the relentlessly pounding herd didn't bury the human sound.

"Father!"

Startled, he looked wildly around, spotting his brother. Raven's

Cry had already whipped his stallion into a frantic gallop and was pounding toward where Night Thunder had last seen their father.

Deep Scar responded instantly, running clean and strong and effortlessly while dodging around the calves that lagged behind. Someone called out Bunch of Lodges' name and a brave who'd been about to launch an arrow at one of the calves jerked his horse to the left and then charged after Raven's Cry.

The fleeing buffalo had become a dark, rushing current that hid the ground and either scattered or trampled snow. They were a flood, unstoppable and deadly, terrifying and terrible. A swift horse might overtake them, but no one was trying to follow them now. Instead, as one, the hunters galloped in same direction as Raven's Cry.

"Father! No!" Raven's Cry screamed.

Torn Ear, the shaman's horse was down and half buried in crimson snow and trampled ground. Even before he reached him, Night Thunder saw the great, tearing wound in the animal's side, and in his mind, he relived what must have happened. The horse wasn't particularly fast and no longer in its prime. Age and the shaman's growing weight had slowed Torn Ear, and he'd gotten too close to a buffalo. When the animal hooked its horn in its tormentor's direction, Torn Ear had been gored.

Where was Bunch of Lodges?

If he'd had any hand in making Deep Scar halt his headlong gallop, Night Thunder couldn't recall. He was on his feet and running now, bow and arrow dangling from his fingers. Panting, he dropped to his knees beside Raven's Cry, only then seeing the mud-splattered figure under Torn Ear.

Bunch of Lodges, his father, stared up at him. If it hadn't been for the way his mouth sagged open and the broken blood vessels in his eyes, Night Thunder might have believed that the shaman had fallen asleep under his horse.

Dead. My father is dead.

A sound like an infant trying to draw its first breath pulled him from the thought. Bunch of Lodges' lips flapped shut and then parted and the tortured breathing sound was repeated. Raven's Cry and he said nothing to each other, but when he slid his hands under Torn Ear's body, his brother did the same. Their eyes, shocked and understanding at the same time, met. They heaved and lifted together and someone else was suddenly there to grab Bunch of Lodges' shoulders and yank him out from under the dying animal.

His father screamed, the cry ending in a gurgle.

"Father!"

"No, this cannot happen to our holy man!"

"A sign. I say it, a sign!" The last was spoken by Chief Sleeps Too Long.

Whether this terrible injury to the Blackfeet shaman was a sign of displeasure on the part of the spirits or not didn't matter to Night Thunder. He needed to touch his father so he'd know how strongly the older man's heart beat, to hear his singsong chant and believe it would continue forever, but Raven's Cry was the one who had placed his ear against Bunch of Lodges' chest. His features were intent, his mouth pale.

"He lives," Raven's Cry whispered. "He will not die. He will not!"

Night Thunder scooted closer, and when his knee bumped his father's limp hand, he picked it up and gripped it. Baby-strength fluttered through Bunch of Lodges' fingers, and his aimless eyes focused, briefly.

20

White Calf couldn't breathe. Gasping, she opened her mouth and a few flakes found their way onto her tongue. They momentarily distracted her, and she concentrated on the cold taste, but when that was gone, she went back to fighting for air.

The other women sat on their horses either checking the progress of the pack animals or talking among themselves. None of them had had the air stolen from them; only she felt trapped.

Forcing herself to calm, she clamped her fingers around her throat and massaged until the taut muscles relaxed and blessed relief flowed through her. The feeling that she'd been about to die had taken over before. When those horrible sensations first came over her, she'd fought them the way a hamstrung deer continues to fight the wolves that are killing it, but she'd learned that was useless.

After assuring herself that she was safely astride her horse and able to breathe again, she gave into the unwanted but inescapable things taking place within her. She was no longer White Calf, no longer a woman accompanying other women through an early winter storm but a Blackfoot warrior. She didn't know who she'd become and didn't want to know because pain had become everything to that man.

Snow. Darkness. Snow and darkness. Cold and fear. Hot agony

that made the cold unimportant. Other voices, male voices all yelling at the same time. The smell of sweating buffalo and horses and men. Vastness beyond the darkness and eyes like burning embers but no body.

She was a hunter and there were buffalo all around, but she could no longer hunt because something horrible and deadly had been done to her and she was afraid and angry and alone despite the presence of those responsible for the sweat-smell.

Most of all she was dying.

Not Raven's Cry!

Please, not Raven's Cry!

"No!"

Someone had cried out, but it wasn't him and that was all Raven's Cry knew. Snowfall might have become a blizzard, and that was why he couldn't see the details of his father's outline but that, like whoever had yelled "no," didn't matter. What did was that Night Thunder's hand rested on Bunch of Lodges' chest, and his hand didn't move.

"Our father is dead," his brother whispered.

Dead? The word and the emotion behind it meaning nothing to him, he stood and gathered up his weapons without knowing he was going to do those things. Whatever buffalo had gored Torn Ear was safely hidden in the middle of the rapidly disappearing mass. If someone died in battle the way Red Mountain had, his relatives were expected to avenge the killing, but there was no way of singling out the beast responsible for his father's end. Still—

"What are you doing?"

His brother's unexpected question stopped him, but he didn't bother to turn around—either that or he was incapable. "We have not killed enough buffalo," he said into the wind. "Our people will starve if we do not bring down more."

"What?" Chief Sleeps Too Long gasped. "You will not at least say a prayer over your father's body?"

"There is no time." He indicated the living, snorting wave rapidly being swallowed by the endless white. Snow, which he hadn't been aware of before, now fell curtainlike around him, isolating him, yet he realized that every member of the hunting party had stopped their hunting and had already or were now gathering around their dead shaman.

"My brother is right," Night Thunder said; he still knelt in muck and blood. "Look. Already too many are beyond our reach. We must—"

Night Thunder didn't finish but instead pushed himself to his feet and vaulted onto Deep Scar's back. He held aloft his weapons. "I ride! I hunt!"

That should have been for him to say, Raven's Cry reminded himself as Night Thunder galloped away. He was older and stronger, unafraid, and yet Night Thunder was already racing toward the few buffalo he still might be able to overtake. He looked around for his horse, momentarily confused because he expected to see New Snow, then remembered that the mare was with his wife.

The stallion whistled in alarm and tried to jerk away when he yanked on its rope, but he refused to let go. It took two tries before he seated himself, and then the worthless creature fought his insistence that it race after Deep Scar. Finally, though, he forced it into a gallop.

His father's dying hadn't taken long, had it? It seemed that only a moment had passed since he'd seen Torn Ear go down under the buffalo's assault, only a moment to hurry to his father's side, no more than three or four heartbeats in which to force Torn Ear's body off Bunch of Lodges. But he must be wrong because the buffalo had gotten so far away.

Not all of them. Night Thunder had almost overtaken the small group that had been separated from the herd and in a few more seconds—

His brother was no longer a youth astride a disfigured castoff of a horse. He'd become part of Deep Scar, part of the tide of movement made up of fleeing buffalo, gusting wind, and snow. Still,

Night Thunder stood apart from the terrified creatures, a determined figure urging his mount closer and closer to the dangerous tide. Yelling, Raven's Cry took off after, not the buffalo, but his brother.

A calf with a swollen and gunk-matted eye trailed the others, but Night Thunder wasn't trying to bring down the easy prey. Instead, he pounded after a huge cow whose legs seemed bent on beating the ground into submission. Closer and closer Night Thunder came to the cow, his body as sleek and deadly as any arrow. Despite the countless shattered emotions bombarding him, Raven's Cry admired his brother as he never had before, wished they were riding side by side, sharing the same determination.

Night Thunder's arm that was holding his arrow shaft and bow string tensed. At the same time, he straightened his other arm, muscles long and strong. Deep Scar now matched the big cow stride for stride, the horse's hoofs beating their own wounds into the earth.

"Kill! Kill and make this your revenge for our father's death!" Raven's Cry bellowed.

Maybe the arrow itself heard, because it shot forward as if it had become as a diving hawk, parted first hair and then hide and finally sought its deadly home in the buffalo's core. For three strides, the cow seemed invincible, all muscle and might. Then her tail shot straight into the air, the ponderous head swung in the direction the arrow had gone in, and the strength went out of her hind legs. She continued to drag herself on her too-small front legs, but because her head was tucked back against her, she turned in an awkward circle toward Night Thunder. Sensing what might be danger, Deep Scar veered away. At the same time, Night Thunder catapulted himself off his horse's back and ran at the cow.

"Feel my wrath!" Night Thunder bellowed. "Eat my arrow and feel it tear your heart apart!"

The cow's front legs continued to churn but her increasingly useless body had become too heavy to allow forward movement. Her head hung down so that her jaw dragged on the ground.

Raven's Cry thought he heard a gurgling moan coming from the creature, but with so much noise all around, he couldn't be sure.

Night Thunder drew his knife, and although it was obvious that the cow had been mortally wounded, he slashed at her throat. It seemed to Raven's Cry that killer and killed were looking into each other's eyes, the message between them unfathomable but lasting forever. Blood poured from the new wound and instantly stained the snow a wet red. Night Thunder scooped up a handful of the crimson snow and held it over his head.

"Hear me, Father! I have avenged your death. You are at peace."

Raven's Cry was about to repeat what Night Thunder had said when he sensed movement behind him. The few other buffalo who'd been running with the one his brother had just killed had scattered like a covey of birds that has sensed danger. Five of them raced to overtake their companions, but one had fallen back and seemed intent on running over the dying cow.

"Night Thunder, look out!"

At that, Night Thunder whirled. Despite the blanket of falling snow, Raven's Cry saw the startled and helpless look in his brother's eyes.

"Run!" he screamed, but of course it was too late.

The panicked buffalo pounded relentlessly forward, its too-short legs grinding, its head and shoulders reminding Raven's Cry of a boulder rolling downhill. It breathed in great whooshes of sound that exploded as white mist around it, and it cared not at all that a man on foot stood in its way.

Still, the charging buffalo must have sensed the presence of its fallen companion because at the last moment it tried to turn direction, but its heavy body continued forward.

Forward and over Night Thunder.

Even before the buffalo rushed on, Raven's Cry catapulted himself off his horse and ran to his brother. Night Thunder lay on his side, his legs half bent under him, his arms folded toward his head as if he was trying to protect himself.

"No!" Raven's Cry yelled. "No!"

Night Thunder's fingers twitched. Not thinking what he was doing, Raven's Cry grabbed his brother's hand and pressed it against his chest.

"You are not dead! Listen to me. You are not dead!"

His brother was trying to breathe but managing only painful gasps. Thinking he had to give Night Thunder's lungs more room in which to work, he eased him onto his back. Night Thunder's chest rose and fell, rose and fell and no blood gushed from him. However, because he wore a heavy shirt, Raven's Cry knew that it might be hiding fearful wounds.

"I—I . . ."

"Do not speak!"

Night Thunder blinked but gave no other indication that he'd heard. Now he breathed in short, painful gasps and clenched his teeth so tight that the muscles around his mouth stood out.

"You will not die," Raven's Cry ordered. "I will not lose you too."

"I—"

"No! Save your strength."

When it first started falling, the snow had come down in small, tight chunks like fine ice. Now perhaps Cold Maker had tired of that creation and had decided to make his children fatter and more of them. The falling white cloud felt heavy on the back of Raven's Cry's neck and he leaned forward to shield his brother's face from it.

"You will not die," he ordered. "I will not let you die."

"He lives?"

When had the others reached them? He tried to concentrate, but taking his eyes off his brother was too much of an effort and maybe Night Thunder would live only as long as they remained connected in this way. He couldn't remember when Night Thunder hadn't been part of his life. They'd grown up together, sometimes fighting, eating side by side, and boasting of all the things they'd do when they became warriors.

Neither of them had expressed fear about the Sun Dance and

when he was done with his sacrifice, he hadn't told Night Thunder about white-hot pain and sickness in his belly and helplessness, but when, later that same day, it was Night Thunder's turn to treat his torn chest, their eyes had met and they'd each known what the other had experienced.

They'd been united by survival, that unity lost as they each struggled to find their way in the world of warriors.

They'd just become men, both of them. He would *not* finish the journey alone!

"Bring blankets," he ordered because Night Thunder had begun to shake. "And find shelter from the wind."

"I am leader!" Chief Sleeps Too Long stood so close to Night Thunder's head that he could have stepped on him. "I will decide what we must do."

"Not this time!" Raven's Cry retorted. "Not this time!"

The women arrived before nightfall. By then nothing remained of the herd and even their hoofprints had been buried under the relentless snow. Although a number of buffalo had been wounded, only four had been killed, three by Night Thunder. The hunters had managed to find enough brush and tree limbs that they'd been able to construct a lean-to, which they'd placed between Night Thunder and the worst of the wind.

When Raven's Cry pulled up his brother's shirt, he'd discovered that three of the charging buffalo's hooves had landed on Night Thunder's chest. Night Thunder's flesh had been pierced twice and all three wounds had already become deep, dark bruises. Night Thunder admitted that it hurt to breathe, but he wasn't spitting up blood and hadn't fallen into unconsciousness.

Their father's body lay where it had fallen, a blanket over and around him and the snow falling on top of that.

"It cannot be!" Dirty Knee Sits sobbed when she learned what had happened to her husband. "He cannot die. Not him! Not the shaman!"

"Our shaman is dead!" another woman cried out. "May the

spirits take pity on us."

"Pity!" Chief Sleeps Too Long snapped back. "The spirits are angry. That is why Bunch of Lodges was killed and why we killed so few buffalo."

"Do not say that!" Raven's Cry ordered. "No one knows the thoughts of Mother Earth or Creator Sun."

"Not them," the chief hurried. "I say we have been tricked by Thunder, only Him. Thunder Spirit made us believe Raven's Cry had dream magic but it was a lie, and now we have been punished for our stupidity. It is so! The greatest harm came to Raven's Cry's brother, did it not?"

"And Night Thunder killed the most buffalo. What do you say to that?"

The argument raged around her, but Little Rain paid little attention to it. Because her people shared the same belief in this, she had no doubt of Thunder's ability to make the lives of anyone who had angered him miserable, but whether Bunch of Lodges was alive or dead meant little to her. In truth, maybe her life would be easier without him. But without Night Thunder—

Although they should have already begun butchering the buffalo, none of the women had started toward the cooling carcasses. Instead, they wailed over their shaman's body and cast hesitant glances at Night Thunder. She told herself to walk away from this thing that had nothing to do with her, to take a knife and begin stripping the hide off the nearest buffalo. Instead, when she had the knife in her hand, she found herself walking to the lean-to and looking in.

Night Thunder's eyes were open although she wasn't sure how much he saw. White Calf was with him.

"I felt pain," White Calf whispered as if to herself. "I knew something horrible had happened. That is why I told the others to hurry."

Like the other women, Little Rain hadn't questioned White Calf's insistence on speed. This thing that White Calf knew and yet didn't know hadn't mattered to her; she would simply do as the others did—at least that's what she'd tried to tell herself.

"I am thirsty," Night Thunder whispered.

As White Calf lifted the water-filled bladder to his lips, Little Rain tried to turn away. Instead, she stood on legs that didn't know what to do with themselves and felt the weight of the skinning tool she carried and asked herself whether Night Thunder was dying.

"Two." White Calf's voice was even fainter than it had been a moment ago. "One wounding and one death but two men feeling pain."

"Not for long," Night Thunder managed, wincing. "The shaman's heart beat only a few times before he died."

White Calf nodded as if that piece of information was vital to her. "It does not matter. He no longer feels anything."

Bunch of Lodges was truly dead, as dead as Little Rain's husband. Wanting numbness, she stood over Night Thunder and fought her memories of Takes-Knife-at-Night's dying, but when she'd turned away, they were replaced by thoughts of whether Night Thunder's soul would soon begin its journey to the afterworld.

And who would wail over his body.

"A skinning knife," Night Thunder said unexpectedly. "Little Rain, is it for the buffalo I killed, or for me?"

Was that what she'd been thinking? Uncertain, she held out the knife so they could both see it better; it felt so heavy that she was afraid she would drop it.

"I do not kill an enemy who cannot defend himself," she told him.

Night Thunder didn't know who'd built the fire the hunting party now sat around, but he was grateful for its warmth and to his brother for helping him over to it. His chest felt as if someone had thrown rocks at him, and he wished he didn't have to breathe. If his father was still alive, maybe Bunch of Lodges would have made medicine over him. He would have thanked him for the effort because those things were expected of both of them; maybe they'd talk, really talk, and father and son would become friends. But that would never happen.

Raven's Cry and White Calf had gently examined his wounds and bruises and they'd all agreed that the buffalo's hooves hadn't destroyed what he needed to remain alive, something he'd already discovered for himself. He wondered if Little Rain was disappointed.

"We must speak of this," Chief Sleeps Too Long said from where he sat with his back to the wind. It was no longer snowing, but the wind might blow forever.

"Some may believe I have no right to say what I am," the chief continued. "That my words come because Raven's Cry and I sought the same wife, but that is not so."

His father's body hadn't been moved from where he'd died, and no plans had yet been made for his burial. As befitted a man of his stature, the tongues of the slain buffalo would be cut up and held up to the heavens in his name. Dirty Knee Sits had raked her forearms with her fingernails, and the long scratches now caught and held firelight. Still, they'd bled only a little, nothing like the scars she and his father had inflicted on themselves when Red Mountain was killed.

The chief stretched his pipe toward the fire, then inhaled. "It is bad that the Blackfeet have lost their shaman. Bunch of Lodges should not have come on this hunt. Hunts are for the young and strong, but he insisted, saying he would share in his son's glory. I say he took the risk because he knew Raven's Cry could not follow his foolish buffalo dreams into the truth and sought to give him guidance."

Night Thunder was used to the twists and turns in Sleeps Too Long's logic, but he couldn't keep up with them tonight. Part of his inability to concentrate was a result of his injuries, but he also remembered how Little Rain had looked as she stood over him with a knife clutched in her fingers.

"Thunder is displeased with us," Sleeps Too Long continued.

"So is Storm Maker and maybe Old Man as well."

"No!" someone gasped. "That cannot be."

"Yes it can," Sleeps Too Long retorted. The fire danced with the changing wind, now bathing the chief's face in red. "Listen to my wisdom. Listen and believe."

Raven's Cry should say something. How could his brother sit silently beside White Calf?

Sleeps Too Long spat and the flames instantly absorbed the moisture. "Perhaps Raven's Cry's dreams about the Snake horses was a gift from the spirits, it is not for me to say," he continued. "Perhaps his dreams were a test."

"A test?"

The chief glared at whoever had spoken. "Thunder and Storm Maker and Old Man wanted to see if we were so foolish that we would believe Raven's Cry had gone from being a youth to a wisdom-speaker simply because Bunch of Lodges's blood runs in his veins. Think of that thing! Raven's Cry was not quick to find his spirit, was he? No. He had to remain on his quest long after most boys had completed their journey. Perhaps the joke did not come from the spirits after all."

Sleeps Too Long surged to his feet and stalked toward Raven's Cry. As he did, the blanket he'd draped over his shoulders fell to the ground dangerously close to the fire.

"Tell me, Raven's Cry!" he ordered. "Did you stumble about like some blind mouse, walking aimlessly until you happened upon the hidden horses and then returned with lies about dreams?"

"No!"

"No?" Sleeps Too Long taunted. "What about your visions of buffalo? Why did you not know your father would be killed and your brother injured? You said we would have enough meat to last the winter, but four buffalo is not enough."

Had someone done something to the fire, Night Thunder wondered as everything darkened, but no one else seemed to notice that blackness had taken over. Instead, everyone remained motionless except for their eyes, which flickered from Sleeps Too Long to

Raven's Cry and back again.

"Raven's Cry must leave!" Sleeps Too Long insisted. "He is like Thunder Spirit, a bringer of death and danger."

"No!" White Calf gasped.

"Yes! Look!" Sleeps Too Long jabbed a finger at Bunch of Lodges' body. "Our shaman is dead. Look!" Eyes flashing, he indicated Night Thunder who felt himself sagging, sagging.

"Cast out the evil one! Before it is too late!"

21

Despite Chief Sleeps Too Long's harangue, no decision was reached about whether Raven's Cry was still a worthy member of the Blackfeet tribe. Most of the warriors and women were still in a state of shock over their shaman's death while a few like Blue Snake agreed with his chief that a shaman on a hunt with his sons wouldn't be killed unless those sons had done something to displease the spirits, either that or Bunch of Lodges' medicine had deserted him, thus causing his death. The matter might have been discussed far into the night if Dirty Knee Sits hadn't started crying for her husband again.

At first Raven's Cry resented his mother's intrusion because not allowing Sleeps Too Long the opportunity to speak at length wouldn't change the chief's mind. Besides, he doubted that his mother's grief was as intense as she made it appear. However, he felt weary both in body and spirit and needed to rest before asking the same questions of himself that his chief had.

Although the buffalo were gutted so the meat would remain fit to eat, preparing the carcasses for travel would have to wait until daylight. In the meantime, aided by the light of the campfire, the women managed to erect three tepees. Raven's Cry thought some of those without shelter might elect to spend the night in the one White Calf and Little Rain had put up, but no one did. Even his mother had decided to sleep with other relatives.

"There is nothing you want?" he asked Night Thunder once his brother was settled on the bed Little Rain had laid out for him. "You are warm enough?"

Night Thunder indicated the mound of fur tucked around him. "Perhaps the spirits smile at us a little after all," he said morosely. "At least this time my injuries are not so serious that I have need of a shaman."

"You do not know that. Not all wounds show themselves early."

"True." Night Thunder glanced over at Little Rain who knelt nearby but was staring into space, seemingly oblivious to her surroundings. "But I asked my body to speak to me, and I am content with the answer."

He wasn't sure about that. It was possible his brother was keeping his concerns to himself because he, like their chief and undoubtedly others, feared that malevolent forces surrounded him.

"I want honesty between us, Night Thunder," he said. "I do not want to wake to find your body cold."

"Neither do I." Night Thunder laughed but the sound didn't reach his eyes. "Go to sleep. Perhaps you will not dream."

"What?"

"Of what happened today. That is all I mean."

Once again Raven's Cry wasn't sure he could fully believe his brother, but whatever they had to say to each other should be voiced when they were alone.

White Calf was already under the blankets they'd begun sharing the day of their wedding. The small fire she and Little Rain had built in here would have to be stoked during the night, but he felt warmer than he had all day, stiff and worn out. Old. Because there was nowhere else for him to go, he slipped in beside her, his hip grazing hers. She started but didn't draw away. If she no longer wanted to call him her husband . . .

"You and the other women came so fast," he said because the most important words wouldn't come. "And you were running. Did you know . . ."

"I knew someone had died," she whispered, her voice unsteady. "I did not know who."

"You thought it might be me?"

She didn't answer, and her silence left him feeling adrift. Not sure he had a right to do this, or if he ever could again, he placed his hand over her waist. She remained motionless, not tense, and he slid his hand upward until he found the warm, moist heat under her breast.

"I do not wish to share my body with you tonight," she said.

"Because I have become less to you?"

"A great deal happened today, and that is more important than our making love."

"Can I believe you?"

She sighed and covered his hand with her own. Her grip was strong, hard. Maybe desperate. "I do not lie to you, Raven's Cry. I would never do that. The way you carry yourself and the words you speak tell me that you wonder if our chief speaks the truth, that you doubt yourself."

He didn't want this. If it was possible, he'd forget himself in her, bury his body against her and think of nothing except her and the humming energy her presence always awakened in him.

"What the spirits think and do is beyond our comprehension," she continued after a short silence. "I—while we were hurrying to you, I looked for Wolf in my mind, thinking He might speak to me because . . ."

"But he did not show himself?"

"No. I do not understand that. Maybe it is a test. Maybe—We must live our lives as best we can and remain true to the ways of the Blackfeet; that is all anyone can do."

"Sleeps Too Long—"

"I spit on him!" she hissed. "He should not have said—Husband, why did you not scar yourself? Your father is dead."

He'd seen his mother rake at her arms, but it hadn't occurred to him to do the same. Shocked, he remained silent.

"Your brother was hurt and you were concerned for him," she

said, her words flowing over him. "I understand that. I also understand that what our chief said wounded and angered you but demonstrating grief is the way of the People. It is not a path we must be shown."

Suddenly he no longer wanted to touch her. Alone now, he stared upward to where smoke escaped and the wind challenged the topmost flaps and poles.

"I do not condemn," she said with her mouth close to his ear and her warm breath teasing him. "And I do not say what your feelings should or should not be. I ask the thing I did because perhaps my questions will allow you to see what lies within you."

She was so wise, much wiser than he would ever be.

"When your father fell, what did you feel?" she asked.

"I could not believe—I did not want to believe."

"Ah. Yes, of course. But what else?"

If he slid his hand between her legs and begin the exploration that had turned her into something wild the last time they were together, would she cease her unwanted words?

"Nothing," he lied, then hated himself for having done so. "You ask too much of me, White Calf. A buffalo gored my father's horse and it fell on him. Everything happened so fast and when Bunch of Lodges was dead, Night Thunder rode after yet another buffalo like a crazy man and I tried to follow him. My father's blood was on my hands. I needed to revenge his death by killing buffalo until none were left alive." He felt exhausted.

"What Sleeps Too Long said about your dreams did not occur to you then?"

He'd lied a moment ago; he had to lie again. "No. White Calf, I had dreamed. I shared my dreams with my people. That is all."

"Is it?"

He came within a heartbeat of ordering her to be silent, but she spoke before he could.

"I dreamed too," she said softly. "No, not a dream but something else. I became a man, a hunter of buffalo. That man was wounded and dying and I feared it was you. My heart . . ."

Reaching out, she wrapped her suddenly cold fingers around his forearm, her grip numbing his flesh. "But I did not tell the other women that. I simply said that something I could not see but was had come to me and that we must hurry."

"No one doubted your words"— he wasn't sure why he was saying this, maybe for himself—"because you are White Calf."

"But many now doubt your dreams and that is not an easy thing."

No, it is not, he almost told her.

I doubt them too, he thought. *And if you do, that is even worse.*

By morning Night Thunder was so stiff and sore that he gasped when Raven's Cry helped him stand. Nearby, White Calf studied him with sober eyes.

"You do not have to do this," she said. "The others will understand if you do not attend your father's death ceremony."

"Will they?" Although Little Rain was standing apart from them, she too was staring at him. "Perhaps. But I will not. What about you, Little Rain? Do you intend to accompany us?"

"I will do as you order."

"Not this time. Today you must decide whether you will take this walk with us."

I hate you, her eyes said, but when she blinked, that changed and now her eyes were telling him she wished it was as simple as hating him. Her attention dropped from him to her hands, which were pressed over her belly as if she was trying to protect herself.

"I envy you," he said. The effort of talking exhausted him but was keeping things inside any better? "Today you can walk along whatever path you wish. My brother and I do not have that choice."

"Bunch of Lodges is nothing to me," Little Rain said. "He barely acknowledged my existence."

"Then stay here. What you do does not matter to me."

He didn't want to lean on Raven's Cry's arm as they stepped outside, but he'd become an old man during the night. The air was so cold that at first his lungs screamed from the pain of having to take it in. His moccasins crunched through the layer of ice that had formed on the ankle-deep snow, making travel even more difficult. The patient horses tethered to one side of the collection of tepees were half hidden behind the mist of their breaths, and he was thankful they'd known to grow their winter coats. Further on, the inert mounds identified where the buffalo had been left. He could hardly believe that he'd brought down three of them, and his brother none.

"I do not want this," Raven's Cry said to him. "During the night I told myself that the morning would find our father alive, that surely a simple buffalo could not have killed him. But those things were a falsehood."

Unaccustomed to such openness from his brother, he could only concentrate on the effort of walking.

"Tell me," Raven's Cry continued. "Will you truly mourn his death?"

"Do not ask me such a thing!"

"I have a right."

Yes, he did. "Perhaps I do not have the answer," he admitted. "At this moment, I feel nothing—nothing except my bruises."

His brother nodded at that. Chief Sleeps Too Long, Blue Snake, Quail Legs, and the other warriors were already standing around Bunch of Lodges' body. Dirty Knee Sits knelt at her husband's head, her graying hair hacked off. Her eyes were red and swollen, but she wasn't crying now. Instead, she seemed somehow removed from what was happening, as if frozen.

He didn't have to turn to know that Little Rain had followed him after all because he felt her presence in his nerve endings and the back of his neck told him that she was staring at him. Raven's Cry was walking so slowly that the tribe's oldest woman could have kept up, and for that he was grateful. Now that they were where the others could see them, he no longer held onto his brother but concentrated on putting one foot in front of the other.

So that frozen lump under a new horse blanket was his father, all that remained of him. Maybe he should have drawn blood on his arms and legs but if he had, it would have only been because it was expected of him, and today he wouldn't do that.

All eyes were on him and Raven's Cry as they made their way to Dirty Knee Sits. Raven's Cry helped her to her feet and then White Calf was there to put her arm around the older woman and lead her away so the men could do what had to be done. He didn't know who had taken responsibility for cutting down four straight saplings and driving them far enough into the ground so that a bed made of rope and strips of leather and branches could be fashioned at the top. Stones had been piled around the base of the saplings, but he wasn't sure they would support his father's weight. Bunch of Lodges' horse, its gored side an open and frozen wound, lay nearby so his father could ride it during his journey to the spirit world. Once they were back with the rest of the tribe, there would be an elaborate ceremony to mark his passing, but this was all they had time for today.

His father . . .

. . . being lifted in Raven's Cry's arms, and with Quail Legs' help being settled into the newly made bed.

. . . sagging into his new home and testing the saplings but not collapsing them.

Motionless.

Dead.

"See what we have done, Old Man," Sleeps Too Long began. "Sun, look down on us and know that we are doing everything we can to walk the way we always have."

"It is not enough," Blue Snake said in response to a glance from his chief. "We have lost our shaman, a fearful thing, but even before that a ghost walked among us. That ghost's poison was greater than Bunch of Lodges."

"No!" Dirty Knee Sits insisted. "My husband's medicine was the most powerful. He—"

"Once, yes," Sleeps Too Long interrupted. The breach of etiquette that dictated that everyone be allowed to speak in his or her own time didn't go unnoticed. "But no longer. Do you think I wish to say this?" He shook his head. "But I must. We found buffalo beyond counting at Big Wind Plains; perhaps Raven's Cry's dreams were indeed responsible. But many, many of the beasts should have fallen. They did not—because evil walks among us."

Everyone's attention turned to White Calf as if she could explain the unexplainable, but instead of answering, she stared off into something only she could see.

"Someone has displeased the spirits," Sleeps Too Long continued. "I fear the Blackfeet have lost their way."

The break in the weather was a brief one with snow returning not long after the burying ceremony had been completed. Raven's Cry had gone off somewhere by himself and Little Rain and White Calf were with the other women as they prepared the meat for carrying to the rest of the tribe. Little Rain had built a hot fire, which warmed the air around Night Thunder, and although he hadn't felt particularly tired, he dozed off. He woke a little while later thinking that he should go look for his brother. However, when he stepped outside, his attention was drawn to the white-coated pier where his father lay.

Although they were far from the Sand Hills, his thoughts went to that bleak, sandy country northeast of the Sweet Grass Hills. The soul of a Blackfoot was its shadow. After death, the shadows of good people congregated at Sand Hills even though it wasn't a place for the living to go because no animals or water were there. Children were told that if they were good, their souls would spend eternity there, and despite the monotony, at least they wouldn't be alone.

It wasn't the same for those who'd been wicked. Instead of being welcomed at Sand Hills, bad people took the shape of ghosts and were compelled ever after to remain near the place where they'd died. Because they are unhappy, they envy those who are happy and continually lurk about the tepees of the living, seeking to do them harm. At times they simply play such tricks as tapping on lodge skins and whistling down smoke holes. However, if a fire is burning within, they won't enter.

Outside, in the dark, they could be dangerous. Although that was more true of the ghosts of enemies who have been killed in battle, all bad souls are to be feared because they can shoot invisible arrows into people thus bringing sickness and death, hit people on the head and cause them to become crazy, even paralyze limbs and pull faces out of shape.

Those ghosts walked, not on the ground, but above it. Sometimes they even talked to people, particularly those they'd hated while alive. It was also said that the soul of a dead person might take over the body of an animal; no one doubted that some owls are the ghosts of medicine men.

Night Thunder quickly looked around, but he'd never seen an owl during a storm and there wasn't one about this morning. Still, he was left with the question of whether his father's soul was on its way to Sand Hills or even now was thinking of a way to punish the son who hadn't followed in his footsteps.

"Listen to me, Father," he said into the swirling flakes. "Do not forget that it was I who went into the Cree village and killed a warrior, thus bringing peace to Red Mountain's soul. I pray you and Red Mountain are together and happy. I cannot do more than I have. I do not deserve your hatred and anger."

Could his father hear him from here? If Bunch of Lodges' soul was just beginning its journey from his unneeded body, maybe he was still nearby. Despite his fear that his father's ghost might grab him, he began the slow and laborious walk to his resting place. It occurred to him that he might have been wounded, not because of the ghost Sleeps Too Long had mentioned, but because Bunch of Lodges' ghost emerged even as the body was dying and had found its way to the buffalo and had been riding it when it trampled him. If that was so, maybe the ghost was already satisfied.

It shouldn't matter to a body whether it was left in a lonely place or buried close to a village, but Night Thunder couldn't help wondering whether the solitude bothered his father, whether he would find a way to remain near his sons.

"Can you see me?" he asked once he was looking up at his

290 // Vella Munn

father's motionless figure. "Can you hear me?"

Because he'd spoken to Red Mountain and his mother's bodies and gotten no response, he wasn't surprised when nothing except the wind filled his ears. The difference between day and night was little this morning, the gray clouds making the world nearly as dark as it was after the sun went down. He felt closed in and trapped, yet he lacked the energy to try to break free.

"Did you fight death?" he asked. "When it came, did your heart struggle to go on beating or were you content to let everything end? I think—if I had lived a life full of accomplishments but my body was no longer able to continue that way and the time was coming when I could no longer perform the duties expected of me that I would welcome death."

A gust shook his father's resting place, causing him to jump back, and it took several deliberately deep breaths for him to calm himself. He'd already said things to his father that he never could have while the man was alive, but the most important things still remained within him.

His eyes burned. He could have told himself that the fierce weather was responsible, but he didn't. Before, he hadn't been able to make himself touch his father's body, but he did so now. Working his fingers under in the blanket, he probed until he touched a cold leg.

"Were we really that different? When you first looked at me, did you think that I was part of you, or because you already had two sons, did it not matter?"

A groan escaped him. He barely felt the cold, but that wouldn't continue for long. Still, he was no longer sure why he'd come here.

"I hope your soul is on its way to the Sand Hills. Others will say you were a great shaman, and it is not for me to think different. You did good during your life, healed injuries and took away sickness. You knew a great deal about herbs and other medicines, and if Red Mountain had lived, your knowledge would have been passed onto him. Because of you, our people knew which way the spirits wanted us to walk. No matter what the chief says, I believe in the power of your magic." He paused, then finished. "This is all you will hear from me, that I wish you peace."

He wasn't alone. For an instant, he thought his father's ghost had appeared, but when he whirled and spotted the gray shape sliding out from the white curtain that defined his world, he knew different.

The wolf looked as powerful as it had when he'd seen it before and might have been listening to him for a long time before making its presence known, its feet silent on the cushioning snow. Almost accustomed to the ghostly creature now, he stood with one hand still on his father's leg and studied the wolf's smooth, slow approach. The small ears were pricked forward, head outstretched as if impervious to the storm.

"Are you after my father's body?" he asked, half believing the wolf would answer. "Is that how you maintain yourself, from eating the flesh of a Blackfoot shaman?"

The wolf didn't answer.

"Do not try because I will stop you," he warned. "I will not allow my father to be torn apart and his bones scattered. I am his son and I vow, he will not be treated like your kill."

When they were closer than they'd ever been, the wolf stopped but continued to regard him with eyes that didn't judge.

"Did you hear my words? Is that why you revealed yourself, because what I said has meaning to you?"

Nothing.

"What do you want from me?"

Still nothing.

"You stalk me; I feel stalked by you. I want to understand but you have told me nothing. What is it you want of me!"

Snow, bent and buffeted by the wind, slapped at the wolf but the creature seemed not to care. By contrast, Night Thunder felt a shiver run up his spine.

"I will not stay out here while I wait for you to reveal your meaning to me. You must have heard what I said. Find the truth of me in those words. Know—know that I make a vow today."

The great gray head tilted to one side.

"That is what you want?" He could barely form the words. "To hear my vow?"

The steady and challenging stare continued.

"All right! All right, I say it! Listen to me, Bunch of Lodges. Listen to me, Wolf. Some day, I pray, I will become a father. And when that time comes, I will embrace all of my children. They will be equal in my heart and none will walk alone the way I have."

Little Rain was waiting for Night Thunder when he returned. She'd spotted him as he came out of the tepee and although he'd soon walked out of sight, she'd guessed he was going to his father's grave. She told herself she didn't care why he was doing what he was, that his relationship with Bunch of Lodges was none of her concern. Still, she'd left her work and been standing near the door flap when he returned. That he failed to acknowledge her until they were only a few feet apart told her a great deal and yet not enough about what he was going through.

"You should be with the other women," was the first thing he said to her. He'd placed his blanket over his head so she could barely make out his features and his voice was muffled.

"I will return to them, but first . . ."

"First what?"

"I . . ."

"You want nothing to do with me," he told her. "I would think you would stay as far from me as possible."

He'd killed her husband; she would never forget that! "I have no choice," she threw at him. "I am your prisoner."

"Today I do not have the strength to hold a puppy."

He was right; she couldn't pretend otherwise. Under his covering he trembled but whether from the cold or his injuries she couldn't tell. His stance was wide, his arms outstretched as if to balance himself.

Without taking time to study the wisdom or know the why of what she was doing, she reached out and took his hand. He looked down at what she'd done but didn't try to draw away.

"You must rest," she told him. "Come inside with me."

"Inside?" He glanced over his shoulder, then concentrated on her again.

"Yes," she said as she wondered if she'd have to speak to him the way one does to a small child. "Your people need you. You must take care of yourself."

That must have made sense to him because he obediently followed her into the tepee and when she indicated she wanted him to sit down, he did that too. His body sagged, and she drew off his blanket, relieved to see that his cheeks were red and chapped looking, not pale.

"I saw you walk toward your father's resting place," she admitted.

"Did you?"

His eyes reminded her of red-hot coals. They burned with something that wasn't fever but consumed him just the same. That, she now knew, was why she'd waited for him. Despite everything that stood between them and everything she hated about him, he was in torment and she didn't want that for him.

"You were not able to say what you wanted to him earlier?" she asked. "You had to be alone with his memory because too much is unsettled between you?"

"What do you care?"

I don't. Except if she told him that, it would be a lie and she didn't want lies today.

"I do not know," she admitted. "But it does matter to me. I think—I think . . . My father once loved life but after he was wounded, he became bitter. I hated seeing him change. I hated even more knowing I could not reach him, could not help. I think—it was the same for you and your father."

"Bunch of Lodges was not a bitter man. He was not crippled."

"No," she admitted. "But you could not reach him."

He wanted to touch her. She knew that as she'd never known anything in life, but taking his hand earlier had been dangerous, and she wasn't about to take another chance. Still, there were things she could and had to say.

"I know the pain that brought you to his resting place because I have felt the same pain. You will never be able to make your peace with your father, and perhaps neither will I." *Because maybe I'll never see my people again.* "Because of that, both our hearts bleed."

"Bleed?" he whispered, but he didn't seem to be asking a question of her.

Despite the effort it took, he got to his feet and paced to the far end of the tepee.

"Wolf came to me," he said.

Although shock coursed through her, she simply nodded.

"I spoke to my father, but it was Wolf who heard."

"What were your words?"

A shuttered look came over him, and she knew he didn't want to tell her, but she continued to stare at him while she again asked herself why this should matter to her.

"That I wanted things to have been different between my brother and me. And I vowed it would not be like that for my children and myself."

My children.

There wasn't enough air in here and what there was tasted hot. Desperate for what her lungs craved, she bolted for the door and stepped outside. Opening her mouth wide, she breathed deeply, barely seeing the small Blackfeet tepees or the storm that kept her with them.

"What is it?" Night Thunder demanded. He grabbed her arm and forced her around.

"No-nothing."

"I do not believe you. You wanted the truth from me, but when I gave it to you, you fled."

His hand burned where he gripped her, causing her to try to pull free. "I did not flee. I—I simply needed air."

"Ha!" He stepped even closer until it felt as if she was becoming part of him. "You are lying, and I will not allow that. I will not!"

A moment ago he'd been wrapped within his own agony and her heart had gone out to him, but now he was a Blackfoot warrior, and she was afraid of him. Once again she tried to jerk free.

"No!" he insisted as he tried to force her back inside. "Do not fight me."

"Let me go. Please, let me go!"

"No."

"I hate you! You think you can control me. Do whatever you want with me!"

They'd been engaged in an unequal struggle, but although he could have easily forced her to do his bidding, he abruptly released her. She scrambled away but didn't try to run.

"Do not be afraid of me, Little Rain," he said softly. "The other day I nearly took you against your will, but it did not happen then, and it will not happen now."

That's what he thought? That she'd rushed out here and then fought him because she was afraid of being raped?

The low hum of male voices reached her, and without looking at the chief's tepee, she knew the braves were coming outside. She could hide behind that distraction, but if she did, she'd only be putting off what she had to tell him.

"You spoke of your children," she whispered. "Children not yet conceived."

"Yes?"

Her hand stole to her belly.

22

Raven's Cry had kept his head high during the brief gathering, but the effort cost him. The rest of the warriors, along with half the women, would be taking off after the buffalo herd as soon as possible, but not him. His brother was in no shape for a long ride or dangerous hunt; it wasn't the same for him.

"I am sorry," Night Thunder said. They were sitting alone in the tepee, the wind buffeting it forcing them to speak louder than usual. "I should have been there for you."

Both numb and as tense as a deer who has just caught the scent of a cougar, he shook his head. "I do not wish you speaking for me. If the others no longer want me in their midst, I will not force myself upon them."

"Our father's death was not your doing; in their hearts, the others must know that. Perhaps Bunch of Lodges was careless or maybe age had slowed him and taken the sharpness from his eyes."

"Perhaps," he muttered, not sure what he believed. "But that is not what the warriors choose to believe."

Although he'd prefer to be by himself, he'd come in here to inform his brother that they'd be traveling with the women who were going to overtake the rest of the tribe and to ask if Night Thunder was able to travel today or would he prefer to wait until tomorrow. Night Thunder had pointed out that the unrelenting storm made getting the meat supply to the others urgent, and he felt strong enough. Now there was nothing to do except step back outside so the remaining women could begin dismantling the tepee.

Night Thunder could have made him go by himself, but to his surprise, his brother joined him. They stood with their shoulders nearly touching as the hunting and butchering party mounted. The women who weren't traveling with them called out encouragement, which was followed by loud but somber boasts. No one spoke a warning. No one mentioned the dead shaman or looked closely at the brothers.

Raven's Cry was distracted by the sight of White Calf standing apart from the others, her head bare despite the weather. The day he'd taken his horses to her father seemed so long ago; it belonged to a time of innocence and discovery and honest talk about her great power and what he'd once believed had been his own but no longer did.

Instead of taking off, the mounted Blackfeet remained in a tight bunch while gust-driven snow attacked them, all of them staring at White Calf.

"They want her to go with them," Night Thunder whispered.

"I know," he said. Then, although he wasn't sure why, he started toward his wife.

When he was a few feet away, she smiled at him, but the gesture lasted only a moment. "I do not wish this for you," she said. Her gaze strayed to the storm-shrouded horizon, then back to him. "You should be with them."

"Not today." *And maybe never again.* "You know why they wait, do you not?"

Her features remained immobile, making it impossible for him to tell what she was thinking.

"I have failed them," he went on, not sure their conversation was private. "They turned to me for guidance, but the herd I told them about was not to be."

"Yes it was! Do not blame yourself for what happened afterward."

How he wanted to embrace her words, but if he did, would he be burying himself in her, hiding behind her, less than a warrior?

"I know what happened," he said.

"We all do, but not all of us think about it in the same way." Her fingers were so close to his that he half believed they were intertwined. Still, she'd made no effort to touch him. "You are my husband, and I want to hold my head high when I speak of you."

"But you cannot," he snapped. Then, although it tore him apart to do so, he stepped away and looked down at her. When he spoke, his words held no warmth. "I do not want you with me, have no need of you."

Her shoulders hunched, then straightened. "I do not believe you."

"Then you are a fool!" The wind pitched his words with more force than he'd intended. "You are White Calf. Now that Bunch of Lodges is dead, there is none above you. You know where your place is."

She continued to stare at him without blinking, her gaze tearing into him and forcing him to battle her impact.

"Snow covers the buffalos' tracks," he went on. "Without you, they will never be found."

Insanely, he wanted her to tell him that her place was beside him, but she'd already tried to do that and he'd rebuffed her. Surely that was why she held herself stiff and straight, her features immobile and unreadable.

"Go!" he ordered.

Little Rain was carrying the child of the man he'd killed.

Night Thunder had briefly forced the knowledge away because he believed his brother needed him, but when he saw Raven's Cry and White Calf momentarily together and then the way she'd turned her back on him, he was once again reminded of how much distance could exist between two people. For reasons he didn't fully understand and weren't his responsibility, Raven's Cry and White Calf had separated, and she was riding off with the warriors. By contrast, Little Rain remained with him, but the chasm between them couldn't have been any less.

"How long have you known?" he asked her once the buffalo meat had been loaded onto the pack horses and they were underway.

"Does it matter?"

"Yes!" he snapped although maybe she was right. "You are not to keep anything from me."

She clenched her teeth but instead of glaring at him, looked back at the three horses she was leading. Two were weighed down with meat while the third pulled the tepee-laden travois. The animals' heads were lowered against the weather, and they required constant urging to keep going. A silent Raven's Cry led the way. Dirty Knee Sits, the only woman not responsible for a pack animal, rode behind her son. Although the group of two men and five women remained within sight of each other, they struck him as lonely and isolated human beings with nothing except winter to keep him or her company. Was it the same for the others or had White Calf's presence given them strength?

"What will you do when my child is born?" Little Rain asked, her question nearly lost under the howling wind.

"Do?"

"I must know," she insisted. "Will you try to kill it?"

A Blackfoot would never end a child's life. If it was different for the Cree, he didn't want to know that, and he told her so.

"Even your enemy's child?"

"Do not ask me such a thing!"

"I must." Even with the wind making hearing difficult, he caught the desperation in her voice. "Night Thunder, I tell you this. If we are still together when my child is born and you speak or act out against it, I will kill you."

"You kill me? Tell me, Cree, were you raised to become a warrior? What do you know of fighting and war-making?"

"It does not matter," she shot back. "This child is everything to me, and that will give me strength. I will become a mother grizzly who attacks all who come close to her cubs."

He believed her.

A grateful Chief Sleeps Too Long asked White Calf to ride beside him and then thanked her over and over again for bringing her magic to the hunting party. She said little except to explain that she'd do what she could, and when he finally fell silent, she turned her thoughts to where the herd might be now and what the creatures were doing.

At least she tried to.

Raven's Cry didn't want or need her around. She'd told him she didn't believe him, but that had been because she hadn't wanted to hear his words, hadn't wanted the pain they brought her. How could she pretend to know anything about the near stranger she found herself married to? Besides, maybe his dreams *had* failed him. If that was so, would he change from the courageous man she'd started to fall in love with?

Frightened by thoughts of what those changes might be, she settled herself on her horse and stared through slitted eyes at the swirling snow that was her world. Every time the storm slackened, she told herself that its energy had spent itself, and the sun would return to melt the drifts, but then new strength surged through it and she despaired of it ever ending.

She wouldn't look into the storm. Instead, she'd search for buffalo. Pray to her namesake and give thanks for past meat-gifts and then think of nothing except the massive beasts whose presence meant life and whose absence signaled starvation and death.

Yes, yes. They were out there, far away because they'd stampeded for a long time, bunched together in a great mass as they waited out the wind and snow—snow which covered the ground and hid all proof of their journey. Occasionally one or more would break away to feed, but they must feel lonely or be cold because before long, they rejoined the group.

She told Sleeps Too Long that and then when he pressed her for details, asked him to be quiet while she tried to determine exactly where the buffalo were. The unrelenting whiteness made that difficult, and the prairies for as far as her mind's eye could see were all the same. Despite the urgency clawing at her, she felt herself becoming lost in the sameness, relishing it, even drawing strength from vast, flat stretches and smells as old as the earth itself. This land was more than where her people lived; it was her people, their mother and father, children and ancestors and she would never want anything else.

Someday that would change. Someday the pale-skinned strangers of her nightmares would sweep over the world of the Blackfeet and destroy it, but, she fiercely reminded herself, she lived only in today. The buffalo and eagles, antelope and wolves, grasses and plains and precious water existed in this moment, and she took from their wisdom.

"I see a place where the ground sinks down into itself," she said more to herself than Sleeps Too Long. "Here the rocks push through the earth and leave nothing for the grasses to hold onto."

"The buffalo are there?"

"No. They have moved beyond it and stand near a small lake fed by a thin creek." She paused, concentrating. "The water in the lake dances with the wind, but it has begun to freeze around the edges; the buffalo will wait out the storm there because they have feed."

"There are several creeks ahead of us, White Calf," the chief pointed out, his tone hesitant and respectful. "Some trail down from the mountains in the direction of the great sea while others come from the land of forever winter. We cannot find the buffalo if we do not know more."

He didn't have to tell her that, but she didn't bother reminding him, just as she didn't tell him that he sounded less like a chief and more like an unsure, questioning child around her. It pleased her to think that Sleeps Too Long, a man given to such violent ways that his wife sought death to escape him was in awe of her. For a moment, she entertained the thought that she could send him out into the snow to his own death because she'd "seen" where the land dropped abruptly away at the edge of a gully, but if she did, his horse would die as well. Besides, her body had been created to give life, not take it.

"The water whispers of what it has seen along its journey," she told him. "It speaks softly, shyly, its words made sluggish by cold but . . . Yes, it came down from a mountain, the mountain known as Old Raven."

She needed to listen and observe a little more to be sure, but before long, Old Raven Creek told her that the hunters should turn away from where the sun was so that the wind came at them from the side and then continue in a straight line. The ground would buckle and dip a number of times, but before nightfall, they should overtake the herd.

"You have no doubt?" Sleeps Too Long asked. "I—I do not question you, but you have never been here before, have you?"

"No," she admitted. "But my eyes see it as if I was standing there now." What she didn't tell him was that the effort had exhausted her. "The buffalo are patient and willing to remain where they are until the storm ends, but when it does, they will grow restless. You must hurry."

He grunted agreement, then gathered the others around him. She let him take over the telling, not because she cared whether he presented himself as a leader, but because her thoughts were being drawn away from the buffalo.

In her tired mind she'd turned around and was riding back the way she'd come. The wind slammed into her exposed face, but she struggled to keep her eyes open, and finally the snowflakes parted and she "saw" the group making its way to the rest of the Blackfeet.

Raven's Cry, her husband, led the way. He was followed by his grieving mother, only when she believed no one was looking, Dirty Knee Sits' tears dried and her eyes grew bright. Night Thunder and Little Rain had been riding together, but they'd separated, each of them trapped inside dark thoughts.

They weren't alone. Wolf followed them.

Only, something else was out there. A force, a power, relentless, dangerous . . .

Whatever it was appeared to her as dark shadows without form but although that alarmed her so much that she felt she would scream, she didn't dare take the time to study shadows for the truth behind them. Not with the wolf stalking her husband and that dark force terrifying her.

"You are to sleep with Dirty Knee Sits."

Little Rain eased her tired, cold body off the horse that had once been her husband's but couldn't summon the energy to face Night Thunder. The snow had finally, thankfully, stopped, but although the sun had struggled to appear, there'd been no warmth in its muted light, and all she could think about was helping build a fire before dark.

"Did you hear me?" he demanded. "I do not want you near me. Wherever my brother's mother sleeps, that is where you will be."

"I understand."

"Do you?" he challenged, forcing her to lift her head. Tightness around his mouth and new depth in his black eyes told her that the journey had been difficult for him, but he'd been able to dismount without help and stood as straight as ever. He reminded her of a bear, and although she told herself it was because his coat was so thick, she knew that wasn't all of it. He'd become fierce today, fierce and distant. Perhaps she wasn't the only one capable of turning into a grizzly.

"Yes," she answered. "I do. You do not want me."

"Or your child."

Of course he wouldn't. Still, hearing him say that hurt. "Then let me return to my people. My father will pay you a number of horses for my return, and we will be done with each other."

"Do not tempt me, Little Rain."

"Tempt? If you wish me out of your life, it is an easy thing to do."

"But not tonight and not here."

She opened her mouth, but before she could speak, Dirty Knee Sits called for her. Night Thunder shrugged and then dismissed her with a sharp wave. As she started toward Raven's Cry's mother, she noticed that Raven's Cry was standing off by himself, looking as lonely as she felt. Perhaps he regretted sending White Calf with the hunters, not that she should concern herself with that.

"A woman in mourning does not work," Dirty Knee Sits informed her. "Especially if her husband was shaman. I wrap grief around me and until it is gone, I must be waited on."

Because she was in no position of knowing whether that was how Blackfeet women handled widowhood, Little Rain simply nodded, then went about setting up the tepee with fingers so numb that the task took twice as long as it should have.

The shelter was really no different from the ones she'd helped build and maintain and frequently move as a Cree, but the work was usually shared by two or more women. Having to erect it on her own took what remained of her strength, and by the time she'd stumbled inside with an armload of damp branches, she was too tired to care about finding something to eat.

"Finally." Dirty Knee Sits held up the fire horn that held the carefully tended coals used to start new fires. "The other women are already warming themselves. I thought this coal might burn itself out before you had fuel ready for it."

Dirty Knee Sits could have tended to that chore herself, but instead of pointing that out to her, Little Rain knelt close to the glowing ember and breathed on it until the handful of dried grass she'd carried all day caught fire. The grass flamed the branches, which hissed and snapped but soon began giving out heat.

"Ah." Her features an image of contentment, Dirty Knee Sits stretched out her legs and then reached forward trying to touch her feet. "They are so cold. I should have worn warmer moccasins."

From where she sat, Little Rain saw that the older women's toes were colorless and she was shivering. She scooted closer and pulled Dirty Knees Sits' feet onto her lap, shocked to find them nearly as cold as the ground they'd been passing over.

"That is not good," she muttered. "You could have given yourself frostbite."

"I know." Dirty Knee Sits sighed. "I wanted to tell my son so he would stop and help me warm them, but our people need the meat, and I did not want to slow him. Besides, I am Raven's Cry's mother. I want him to be proud of me."

Wasn't it Raven's Cry who should be worrying about his ability to hold up his head? Keeping the question to herself, she said that Raven's Cry had done an admirable job of leading the group today. At that, Dirty Knee Sits smiled broadly. Her smile faded when Little Rain mentioned that Night Thunder had shown courage in keeping up with them despite his bruises.

"What Night Thunder does or does not do is of no concern to me," Dirty Knee Sits said. "His mother died when he had seen seven winters. He no longer had need of a mother, and I did not call him my son. Why should I?" she asked fiercely. "I already had two fine sons."

Two. Red Mountain and Raven's Cry. "Seven is not so old. Did—did Night Thunder mourn his mother's death?"

"Mourn?" Dirty Knee Sits frowned. "I do not know."

"But you must remember."

"It was a long time ago. Why does it matter to you?"

The question slammed into her, forcing her to ask it of herself. "I—I am Night Thunder's. He can do with me what he wills, grant me my freedom or keep me with him. I seek to understand what kind of a man he is."

That must have made sense to Dirty Knee Sits because she leaned back on her braced arms, sighed, and stared upward.

"I have never known him, not really. I did not want his mother living inside my tepee, sharing Bunch of Lodges' bed."

"That—sometimes that is hard to do."

"For me it was," Dirty Knee Sits admitted with no sign of embarrassment. "Morning Willow came from a poor family. Her father had only one horse that was too old for hunting, and Walks-All-the-Time was barely able to kill enough rabbits and prairie dogs to feed his family. Sometimes other warriors took pity, not on him because he carried his hatred of his life like a great stone, but on his wife and children."

Lips pursed, she shook her head. "His wife was a sickly creature who nevertheless kept giving him babies. She finally died when Morning Willow was nearly marrying age."

"Why did Bunch of Lodges marry Morning Willow?" Little Rain asked. "He is—was a wealthy man, a shaman with great position who was respected by everyone. If her family was poor—"

"Beyond poor, but when you look at Night Thunder, what do you see?"

"See? I—I do not understand."

"Think!" Dirty Knee Sits insisted. "Look at him with a woman's eyes and tell me what you see."

"He—he is handsome. Not as big and strong as Raven's Cry, but his eyes are—are beautiful. He carries himself proudly. At least he does when he is not wounded."

"Beautiful eyes, yes. What else?"

Not sure where this was going, Little Rain nevertheless reached inside herself for an image of the man who'd turned her life in a direction she didn't want.

"His voice is low and soft, calm like a lake. His hands and feet are large and sure. There—there may be times when he doubts his abilities, but his body is always ready. He—he easily killed my husband." Her throat tightened and she couldn't speak.

Dirty Knee Sits looked as if she wanted to disagree with what Little Rain had said but couldn't. "And he heals easily from his injuries," she admitted reluctantly. "In that way, he is unlike his mother, but in many ways they were as one."

"Morning Willow was beautiful?"

"Beautiful?" Dirty Knee Sits spat the word. "If my husband was still alive, he would tell you she was, but I will not say that."

Because you envied her. "I—maybe I understand," she tried. "I look at White Calf and know I will never have her gift. It leaves me in awe of her."

"Do you hate White Calf?"

"No. Of course not. Why should I?"

"If you and White Calf wanted the same man, you would."

An image of what things must have been like when Morning Willow was alive formed in her mind. Dirty Knee Sits might have been Bunch of Lodges' sits-beside-him wife, but that didn't mean she wasn't jealous of the beautiful woman she had to share her husband with. The situation had been even harder for Dirty Knee Sits to stomach because, although Morning Willow's family had been beneath her, her husband had chosen her because of what she was physically.

"I hated Morning Willow," Dirty Knee Sits hissed. Pulling her now warm feet free, she reached for the evening's food supply. "My husband stepped on my pride when he brought that child into our house, said I did not satisfy him in bed and that he wanted another who made him feel like a stud. A stud! Maybe once but no longer!"

Because Bunch of Lodges was dead or because his manhood had failed him before that? "Night Thunder knew how you felt about his mother?" she asked because that question was safer.

Dirty Knee Sits shrugged and shoved a fistful of pemmican in her mouth. "It does not matter."

"And his mother, how did he feel about her?"

Again Dirty Knee Sits shrugged. "He loved her, he had no choice."

"No choice?"

Dirty Knee Sits looked as if she wanted to be done with the conversation. "Morning Willow was so young when Night Thunder was born. What did she know about raising a child? All she ever wanted to do was hold Night Thunder and sing to him and give him her breast. She had her work but did she do it? No! Instead she devoted all her time to her only child. She would not share him with Bunch of Lodges, but my husband did not care because he had my sons. Because I did everything I could to make them first in his eyes."

"I will tell you this," Dirty Knee Sits went on, "and then I am done. I did not shed a tear when Morning Willow died. She had cried and begged Bunch of Lodges to give her another child but none grew inside her. Or in me. I did what I should and conducted myself as a shaman's wife but not Morning Willow. Instead, she and Night Thunder became like one. Separate from all others. My husband's face darkened when he saw that, but I did not care. I had given him two sons, not just one like her."

"How—how did she die?"

Dirty Knee Sits turned her attention from her meal to the small but hot fire. She stared into it for so long that her features seemed to absorb the deep, dancing reds and oranges and she looked, not like a new widow, but like a ghost herself.

"Morning Willow tripped and fell into a fire. She was so badly burned that not even her husband could save her."

"I—I thought she was sick."

"Not sick enough."

23

If he'd prayed for the storm to end, he might have been able to take the current lack of snowfall as a sign, but Raven's Cry's thoughts had been on the hunters, not the weather. He'd willed those who didn't want him with them to be able to see far into the distance because that way, they'd know where to go to find the buffalo, but then his mind had turned to White Calf—turned and stayed there.

Success lay in her hands. Only she had the gift, only she could guide the hunters to success. His dreams had become less than mist.

Feeling as if he'd grown too large for his body, he paced first one way and then the other, oblivious to the sounds of activity inside the hastily erected traveling tepees, even the warmth they provided. He'd seen wild horses attack their restraining ropes and understood what made them risk a broken leg or neck. If it had been possible for him to fly—

Night had already descended, and he should have made his peace with the darkness, but it gnawed at him, turning restlessness into caution. Surely there were no Snakes or Cree around, and he had nothing to fear from one of his own. Yet, he'd grown up knowing that only a fool turned his back on wind-whispered warnings.

The snow had frosted over and crunched with each step he took. If someone or something was out here with him, he should be able to hear that person or animal's approach.

Belatedly stopping his energy-expending movement, he turned an ear into the now gentle but bitterly cold breeze. Awakened from their storm-imposed hiding, a couple of owls called out. If they were hunting prairie dogs, they would be unsuccessful because those small creatures were now under at least two feet of snow, perhaps already hibernating.

A frown wrinkled his forehead as he pondered whether what he'd heard had been a burrowing owl. The tiny, sharp-eyed creatures made their homes deep in abandoned prairie dog holes and should have been just as trapped as the rodents, but maybe they'd known to flee their nests in time.

The distraction caused by the mysterious ways and wisdoms of owls didn't last long. Something in the distance made a muted crunching sound, and he immediately turned his mind to determining what was responsible for that. By concentrating on the hesitant yet measured beat, he realized he was listening to a gently stepping deer and silently laughed at himself. A man who grows alarmed because he shares the night with a deer is a fool.

Either that or he blinds himself to what might be danger after all.

A moment ago he'd told himself that he and the others had nothing to fear from wild animals or members of other tribes, but how could he have forgotten about the wolf?

His hand slipped to his side, and he relaxed slightly when he felt the weight of his knife. Holding it in front of himself, he turned in a slow half-circle, thinking to return to his brother so they could discuss his unease and determine what, if anything, they should do. He kept his movements sure and purposeful, his shoulders squared and his head high. Still, he felt vulnerable.

"Raven's Cry?"

The unexpected voice hit his senses like a lightning bolt, and it was all he could do not to cry out in alarm. Staring ineffectively into the night, he struggled to determine where the woman—that was all he knew about the newcomer—was.

"Raven's Cry, I have returned."

His wife. Although White Calf expected a response, he had to wait until he could trust himself to speak.

"What are you doing here?" he asked harshly, unable to shake off the sensation that she wasn't the only one nearby. "I ordered you—"

"I did what was expected of me, Raven's Cry," she interrupted. "Not because you ordered me but because I am Blackfoot. There was no need for me to remain with them."

He'd determined that she was standing between him and the closely grouped tepees, which shouldn't have been possible because he'd just come from that direction; but although his eyesight was keen, she existed as nothing more than a soft voice. Perhaps she'd learned new ways of moving from ghosts and shadows.

"You found the buffalo?" he asked.

"I told the others where to travel in order to find them."

Of course she had. It had been a simple matter for her to spread her gifts over the plains and call up the creatures that had killed his father and nearly done the same to Night Thunder. Although it was irrational of him, he cursed her, half believed she was responsible for the death and injury.

"You should have stayed with them," he told her when the question should have been how she'd fared during her solitary journey. "What if the buffalo move on?"

"They will not. Raven's Cry, you did not want me to return?"

He didn't know anything tonight, anything except that her voice called to him just as one owl calls to another and when they find each other, they are no longer lonely. Guided by what his nerves and muscles and maybe even his bones were telling him, he unerringly made his way to her. She wore several layers of clothing that should have made her appear as bulky as a bear, but the small form that was all he could see of her sang of the woman in her. If she touched him, would he catch fire like a tree struck by lightning?

Cautious, he held back from any contact with his wife. She was power and strength while he'd proven himself to be as weak as a newborn. Until the time came when he was once again her equal, he'd keep distance between them, and if that time never came—

"Wolf has been following you," she said.

"What?"

"When I was done with the buffalo, I brought my thoughts to you. I saw you and Night Thunder and the women and, keeping pace, Wolf. There was—I wanted to tell myself that Wolf was simply watching, but I knew different. My husband, this sudden winter frightens me. It came to me earlier, warning of danger and death. Wolf's eyes speak of those things. He—his presence this time foretells death."

That couldn't be! How could she possibly know what a spirit creature might be warning of?

The answer came easily, unwanted but easily. She was White Calf.

Without bothering to tell her what he was going to do, he brushed past her and strode toward his tepee. He sensed her presence behind him, and although he didn't want the feeling, he was grateful that she was coming with him.

He also sensed they weren't alone out here.

Dirty Knee Sits was snoring. Little Rain turned onto her side and pulled her blanket over her exposed ear, but that didn't do enough to muffle the sharp snorts. Next, she tried calling out to Dirty Knee Sits although that might waken the two other women they were sharing the tepee with, but that made no difference either. Finally she decided to shake Dirty Knee Sits because that had sometimes silenced her father.

Sliding out of bed, she padded over to the new widow with gray-streaked hair. Dirty Knee Sits' snores made her think a hibernating bear couldn't possibly make any less noise, not that she could imagine herself ever telling Dirty Knee Sits that.

Her first shake resulted in a quick series of snorts followed by undiminished sound, but when she once again rocked Dirty Knee Sits, the older woman turned onto her stomach and her breathing became much quieter. With a sigh of gratitude, Little Rain started back toward her bed, but before she could reach it, she heard a long, low howl.

Ignore it, she ordered herself.

The cry was repeated, distant and cold and challenging. Was it possible that the creature was approaching the horses? She didn't think a guard had been posted.

After slipping into her moccasins, she hurried outside. The moon was a child tonight, not quite half full and somewhat obscured by lingering clouds. She chided herself for not taking into consideration how cold it would be, but it would only take a moment to take a look at the horses. If she saw anything that alarmed her, she'd tell Night Thunder and Raven's Cry.

At the thought, she found herself looking over her shoulder at the tent where the brothers were sleeping. White Calf had returned earlier in the evening, but she hadn't spoken to her and so she had no idea what had happened while White Calf was with the hunters. She should have been grateful that Night Thunder hadn't wanted her near him tonight, and yet . . .

What did it matter what Night Thunder did or thought? She'd check on the horses and then—

Alarm surged through her when she saw that all of the horses were awake. Although none had yet snorted or stamped their hooves in alarm, the moon revealed their widespread nostrils and constantly moving ears. The next wolf call spread over her, not a threat, but as if the creature had found a cloud or fog to send his cry out on.

She felt it seep into her and imagined it doing the same to the horses, maybe lulling them, when to let down their guard might risk their lives. It was all but impossible for her to do anything except listen and feel part of the lonely, ageless sound.

Not sure what if anything she had in mind, or why she should concern herself with Blackfeet horses, she took a tentative step toward the closest animals. One started to extend his muzzle in her direction, then suddenly flung his head high and shied to one side. As he did, she saw the shape huddled just beyond the horse.

Impressions came too quickly and made too little sense. The shape was straightening and revealing itself as a warrior, but it was neither Night Thunder or Raven's Cry and there were no other men here.

No other Blackfeet men.

"Attack!" she screamed. The cry lent strength to her legs and she bolted for the tepees. "Help! Attack!"

Another shape materialized out of the darkness to her left. She reacted by whirling away from this new danger, but as she did, her feet sank into the snow and she lost her balance. Still calling out in alarm, she struggled to right herself. The man who'd just surprised her reached for her, but he too was slowed by the uncertain footing.

"Die Blackfoot squaw!" the man bellowed. "Die!"

"I am not Blackfoot!"

"Not—" he started but she couldn't hear the rest of what he was saying because someone burst out of the closest tepee. She recognized Raven's Cry's tall, sturdy shape followed close behind by Night Thunder.

A harsh series of cries that made her wonder if they'd been attacked by the mystical and terrifying Below Ground people slashed the night air. Several horses bellowed in alarm, while still others screamed as if they'd been attacked by cougars, and the man who'd come after her was momentarily distracted from trying to silence her. Compelled on by fear, she fought the snow. By the time she'd regained her feet, people were running about with burning branches that illuminated the chaotic scene.

The small camp was under attack. By how many of the enemy she couldn't tell, but because the one man was so close to her, she identified his face markings as belonging to the Snakes.

Snakes? Braving the weather to avenge the taking of horses they'd once claimed as their own?

Before she could reach the nearest tepee and whatever she might find inside it with which to defend herself, the Snake warrior lunged and grabbed her hair.

"I am not Blackfoot!" she repeated, but either he didn't believe her or it made no difference to him.

Despite her attempts to resist, he hauled her to him. The pain in her scalp brought tears to her eyes. A bow and quiver full of arrows were slung over his back, but what frightened her was the sight of the knife clutched in his free hand, and she forced herself not to fight.

Instead, she waited until he was so close that she could smell his sweat and the fat he'd coated his face and arms with. When his knife-wielding hand snaked toward her, she wrenched herself to one side, her muscles and nerves screaming.

To her horror, he retained his grip on her hair and she wondered if he'd ripped out a great handful. She couldn't think to breathe, couldn't remember why she'd thought she'd stand a better chance of survival if she didn't fight until he was ready to bury his knife in her.

Once again his weapon began its deadly descent. Once again, she fought his control over her. Still, something sharp penetrated her dress and then the flesh on her shoulder, but she felt no pain.

"No!" she screamed, her cry giving her strength. His face filled her vision, but although she quailed at the look of triumph in his eyes, she refused to be overwhelmed. Her hands had been in the snow long enough for cold to seep through them, but she ignored the loss of sensation and came at his eyes with clawed fingers.

At the last moment, he snapped his head back so that her nails dug into his cheeks instead, but his angry grunt told her she'd inflicted pain. He shouted, the words garbled.

Beyond her, people ran here and there, some fighting, all yelling. The horses continued their frightened whinnies, adding to the din. She wanted to be gone from this tornado of battle, to run and run and then run some more. Instead, she struggled to keep her fingers buried in the Snake's flesh.

He cursed and struck the side of her head. Red exploded inside her. She screamed.

Suddenly she was free. Her scalp felt on fire. That, combined with the blow the Snake had just inflicted confused her, left her unable to decide whether her life was still in danger. Struggling to concentrate, she pushed herself to her knees, then hung there half buried in snow while she waited for her vision and mind to clear.

Her attacker was now locked in battle with another man. The newcomer was barefoot but armed with a knife that looked a twin of the one that had been used on her. It wasn't until someone ran past with a burning branch that she had enough light to see who'd come to her aid.

Night Thunder had thrown himself on the Snake and knocked him off balance, but the Snake was larger and perhaps more experienced in battle because he'd already managed to wriggle out from under Night Thunder. They looked like battling elk who have reared onto their hind legs so they can attack with deadly antlers, only the men's weapons were their knives—the very weapon that had crippled her father.

She nearly screamed a warning to Night Thunder but held back because she was afraid she'd distract him. He was ill-dressed for the cold but seemed as oblivious to that as he was to anything except the man he was trying to subdue.

No, not subdue. Kill.

The Snake quickly transferred his weapon from one hand to the other, dodging back at the same time. He might have been taunting Night Thunder to come after him, but he'd miscalculated his footing. As had happened to her, the Snake sank into the snow. He remained on his feet but was distracted just long enough for Night Thunder to lunge.

Night Thunder too was hampered, not just by the quicksand of snow but his bare feet as well. It didn't matter when he'd stopped feeling them, just that they'd become like dead stumps at the end of his rapidly numbing legs. Before long he'd be unable to run or hold his own in a hand-to-hand battle. That was why he'd thrown himself at the Snake who'd been trying to kill Little Rain.

Despite his awkward assault, he hit the Snake with enough force to buckle the other man's knees. Once again they went down together, but this time Little Rain wasn't in his way. He drove himself into the Snake, his frozen feet churning. Flat on his back now, the Snake stared up at him. Blood ran from several deep scratches under his eyes. Night Thunder caught a blur of movement that his nerve endings sensed was his enemy's knife, but he hadn't lost hold of his own weapon, and in that brief moment before the Snake's stone blade found him, he slashed at the exposed throat.

The Snake bucked and thrashed. A sound like drowning bubbled up from deep inside him and exploded in a froth of blood. Both fascinated and horrified, Night Thunder stared at the gaping wound and the red current flowing from it. He thought to move off the dying Snake only when the man's limbs began a palsied trembling.

He tried to stand, but he was now numb and useless from the hips down. Something small and warm settled beside and around him and he realized that Little Rain was helping him to his feet.

"You are all right?" he gasped.

"Yes." Her voice carried a hint of tears and terror. "You killed—"

"Yes!" Wonder filled him, wonder and pride and an awful sickening in his stomach.

She was silent for a moment and then: "You cannot stay outside the way you are. You will freeze."

He was half frozen already and thought to tell her that, but he could hear his brother's deep, urgent voice out there in the dark and knew he was needed. Still, he squeezed Little Rain in relief and gratitude and other emotions he didn't understand before pulling free and stumbling back into the shelter he'd so recently left. Breathing heavily, he yanked on his footwear and shoved his arms into a second shirt but a robe would only get in the way. After grabbing one of the butchering knives, he ran back outside.

He couldn't tell whether any of the women was Dirty Knee Sits but wouldn't be surprised if she was hiding. Although the moon and firebrands helped, he wasn't sure how many Snakes were out there. One of the figures had to belong to his brother, but there was so much confusion that he was certain a number of Blackfeet women were trying to repulse the attackers.

If anything happened to White Calf—

Unable to accept the possibility that she was as mortal as his father had been, he looked to where he'd left the Snake's body. Little Rain was no longer there.

"The horses! Stop them!"

He was running toward the makeshift corral before his brain registered that a woman had called out the warning.

The Snakes' intent had been to sneak up on the sleeping Blackfeet and grab both the precious meat supply and horses before anyone knew they were there. They might have been successful if Little Rain hadn't heard them and sounded the alarm. Now the raiders were trying to accomplish their goal while fending off attack by two warriors and a number of angry, determined Blackfeet women.

A couple of Snakes were trying to cut the horses loose and lead them away while the rest gathered up the buffalo meat bundles and secured them to their own mounts. Although they might privately curse the bone-numbing cold and the war chief who'd convinced them that sneaking up on sleeping Blackfeet would be easy, several had seen one of their companions killed and were now even more determined to make their enemies pay for taking so many Snake horses, thus humiliating them.

Raven's Cry's first thought had been to protect the horses, and he'd been running toward them when he'd spotted his mother standing in front of her tepee, arms flailing, long hair swirled around her neck. He'd ordered her to go back inside, but before she had, she'd pointed at the mounds of buffalo meat and a trio of shadowy figures around them.

He'd cast around trying to locate his brother; when he hadn't seen him, he'd started toward the raiders. However, instead of running away, they'd stood their ground, grinning and taunting him to take on all three.

As he stood staring back at them, White Calf joined him.

"They are armed," she hissed. "Bows and arrows as well as knives."

"I know." How could he have been so stupid as to have left his weapons behind?

"No!" she warned when he took a forward step.

"Did you hear your woman?" one of the Snakes taunted. "Listen to her, child, and you may live to see the morning."

"Ah, the mighty Blackfeet. Mighty but so stupid that they sent only two warriors to accompany the women on their journey to the rest of the clan."

Despite the storm, the Snakes had been watching them? If that was so, maybe they knew that Bunch of Lodges had been killed.

"Why did you not know?" he demanded of White Calf. "Your visions—"

"White Calf!" a Snake interrupted. "She is here?"

Before he could say anything, he sensed increased commotion from where their horses were being kept. To his horror, he realized that several were already being led away and that the Snakes were lashing the rest together.

"Raven's Cry! Come!"

Catapulted by his brother's command, he grabbed White Calf's wrist and hauled her with him away from the Snakes. Those he'd accepted responsibility for would be hungry if they lost the meat, but without horses they would be defenseless, at the mercy of winter.

White Calf shook free, then matched his pace as they slogged through the knee-deep white that lay between them and the horses. Looking back over his shoulders, he was surprised to see that the warriors who'd been taunting him were now hurrying to their own mounts. If they were afraid of incurring White Calf's wrath—

One of the Blackfeet stallions had broken free. Terrified, it first bolted after those already under Snake control and then whirled and thundered back to those it had left behind. As it did, it bumped into a mare who went down in a swirl of legs. Squealing, she righted herself and joined the stallion in a mad dash.

Their route was taking them straight for Dirty Knee Sits' tepee. Without giving himself time to think, Raven's Cry charged the two runaways. He managed to grab the rope around the mare's neck, but the stallion veered toward him, forcing him to jump back. Regaining his balance, he sprang toward the mare and scrambled onto her back. She thundered after the stallion, snow flying out behind her in dirty clouds.

He hauled on the rope, then, when it came loose, cursed the inept Snake who'd tried to control her; there was no way he could ride after the captured horses on a mount he couldn't control. The mare slowed when the stallion ran in front of her, and he took that opportunity to dismount. He began running back the way he'd come, but although he remained in the trail made by the two horses, he was much slower than he needed to be.

More shouts briefly drew his attention to where he'd first been confronted by the Snakes. In the short time he'd been gone, they'd finished lashing the meat supply to their horses and were trying to leave. Several Blackfeet women had stepped forward to block them but backed away when the Snakes forced the horses at them.

His brother was in the midst of the Blackfeet horses, fighting with someone. He cast around trying to locate White Calf but everything was in turmoil. Frustration weighed him down yet he plunged on, his legs burning from the exertion. He thought he heard his mother scream but couldn't recognize her in all the turmoil.

Someone—the form was short and round enough to be his mother—had fallen and another woman was trying to help her stand. They were in the way of several rapidly advancing horses, and might be crushed if they didn't get out of the way.

Calling out a warning, he changed direction.

Dirty Knee Sits had wrapped her arms around Little Rain's arms, trapping her. As Little Rain tried to pull free, she heard someone yell, "Look out!," and twisted in the older woman's grip. Horses, wide-eyed and snorting, were heading for them.

Spinning back toward Dirty Knee Sits, she used all her strength and then some to drag the older, heavier woman with her. They stumbled and fell, righted themselves and began running. The snow clawed at her, but she fought it as fiercely as she'd once fought Night Thunder.

Dirty Knee Sits began to pitch forward, but Little Rain yanked her upright and now propelled her ahead of her. She must have buried her mocassin in mud because she felt it being sucked off. Momentarily trapped, she yelled at Dirty Knee Sits to keep running.

Before she could free herself, the Snake riders were upon her. An arrow was being aimed at her.

"Die Blackfoot! Die!"

"I am not Blackfoot!" she screamed although maybe he couldn't hear her and what did it matter?

To her surprise, the Snake warrior lowered his weapon. Moonlight glinted off his teeth.

"What then?"

"Cree."

"Cree!"

As his laugh echoed around her, she wrenched upward, freeing her foot but leaving her mocassin behind. When he saw what had happened, he laughed again.

Then he rode down on her, leaned low over his horse, and wrapped his arms around her waist. She felt herself being lifted and thrown face-down in front of him on the horse's neck. The animal grunted, and she felt the sound throughout the length of her.

24

White Calf stared at where she'd last seen the Snakes. She could still hear them, but the night had claimed them—them and the meat and horses.

"We were fools," Night Thunder said, his tone sharp with a hint of desperation clinging to it. "We are in land the Snakes want to claim as theirs, but we did not set out guards to watch for them."

"The storm—" Raven's Cry started and then stopped. He'd already looked at her several times and was doing so again, but she refused to meet his gaze.

"We thought our enemy would not venture out in the storm," Night Thunder finished.

It had been more than that, and White Calf knew it. Her people depended on her to warn them of danger, but instead of looking inside herself, or taking her thoughts to her surroundings, she'd allowed herself to be distracted by Raven's Cry, to worry about him and think endlessly of him. Yes, she'd shown Chief Sleeps Too Long where to look for the rest of the buffalo, but when she'd "seen" a wolf following her husband and sensed the mantle of death around it, she'd hurried back to him.

She'd been content to ride and sleep by Raven's Cry's side, and told herself that he and the others were safe as long as she was with them and then listened to her husband breathe and watched him walk and prayed he'd want to bury himself inside her.

She'd forgotten to be White Calf.

One of the women who'd been gathering up what little remained of the food supply announced that there was barely enough left to feed the group today and nothing to take to the rest of the clan.

"What are we going to do?" the woman asked. "I fear facing my sister and her children knowing they will go hungry."

"Perhaps our warriors will be successful," Dirty Knee Sits suggested. "They will return—"

"When?" Night Thunder snapped. He'd barely taken his eye off where Little Rain had been standing when the Snake warrior grabbed her. Still, White Calf had no idea what he was thinking. "There are only a few women to prepare the meat, and if they are successful, many carcasses. They will feast and wait out the storms before thinking to come back because they believe we have supplied the others. It might be many days."

Jaw muscles clenched, Raven's Cry nodded. "I take responsibility for what happened," he said, each word slow and measured. "And I will go after what is ours. I vow—"

"No!" White Calf gasped, startled out of her silence. "It is too dangerous. Wolf's warning of death—"

"What would you have me do, White Calf?" His tone was so harsh that she couldn't remember what it sounded like when it was gentle. "Return to my people empty handed?"

"They are my people too."

"Are they?" He blinked, and she wanted to tell herself that he regretted having attacked her, wanted to but couldn't.

"Yes." Although she was so weary she didn't trust her legs to hold her, she stepped closer to him. He had a scratch on his cheek and his knuckles were scraped. Still, he stood above the others, everything about him commanding, and she loved him.

She also had failed him.

"I am sorry," she whispered. Just the same, she knew everyone could hear her. "I sensed danger—death—in a stalking wolf that existed inside my mind, but I did not seek the truth behind that sign. Instead, I told myself no harm would come to—to anyone if I was with them. I was wrong."

"We are all alive."

She gave Night Thunder a grateful look for having said that. "And you killed one of the enemy," she told him. "That is good."

"What about Little Rain?" Raven's Cry asked. "They took her."

"Took?" Night Thunder echoed. "Perhaps she went willingly."

In the turmoil, four horses had been left behind. Night Thunder stood with a calming hand over a young stallion's nose. He hated the thought that Deep Scar was with the Snakes, then vowed he wouldn't rest until his favorite mount was back with him— and the pinto that had belonged to Takes-Knife-at-Night. For now he refused to think beyond that.

"At least we are not on foot," Raven's Cry pointed out. "These may be packhorses, but they will carry us after our enemy."

Night Thunder grunted his agreement, but too much was going through him to say anything. He still shook with excitement and dread and concern and other emotions he couldn't identify in the middle of the night. The Snake he'd killed lay where he'd fallen, ignored by the women. With a minimum of discussion, he and his brother had made the decision to take off after the Snakes. They'd have to leave the women behind, but if the women started at day-break, they might be able to overtake the rest of the clan before night. Neither he or Raven's Cry had said anything about how the empty-handed group would be received.

"It is possible that the Snakes who ran off with our horses will remain apart from the rest of their tribe," Raven's Cry said. "They may believe they will have a greater chance of escaping us that way."

"They are right."

Sensing his anger, the horse he'd been holding shied. He forced himself to calm, aware that if he allowed his thoughts to fasten onto Little Rain, he might not win the battle.

"You have another thought?" his brother asked. "Perhaps now

that you have twice killed, you believe you are ready to lead."

"This is not the time to talk of that," he retorted, then glanced around, acknowledging the others. "We did not think with the heads of seasoned warriors," he admitted. "The way Sleeps Too Long would have. The Snakes took advantage of that, but we will do what we must."

Raven's Cry too had been taking in his surroundings. Now he studied the sky. "The clouds are lonely children, but they may again grow strong. We must move and act swiftly. You are ready to ride?"

He indicated his bow and full quiver. "I am ready."

Giving weight to his words, he swung onto the stallion's back. His brother would ride the mare he'd had to jump off earlier, which left just two horses for the others, and he didn't envy them having to drag the tepees over the snow. However, they didn't dare risk remaining here.

Raven's Cry mounted, the movement sleek and sure. He wore a cap made of badger skin with the ears intact, which gave him a fierce look. Nothing remained of the smiling man who'd risen from his marriage bed after that first night. He too was heavily armed.

"Wait!"

At the order, Night Thunder clenched his teeth and waited while Dirty Knee Sits hurried up to them.

"You cannot go at night," she chided. "How can you find your way?"

Raven's Cry pointed at the fresh wounds the Snakes and horses had left in the snow. "Even a small child can follow this, Mother."

"And if you overtake them? How will you—"

"Mother!" Raven's Cry warned. "Do not tell a warrior what he must do."

"You are my son! I have already lost one son and a husband. I will not be left alone. I will not!"

With cold clarity, Night Thunder understood that Dirty Knee Sits was more concerned about who would provide for her than the risks her son might be taking.

"You are not alone," he said, although a glare from Raven's

Cry told him that his interference wasn't wanted. "White Calf will be with you, as will the other women."

"White Calf? Was it she who saved me? No. It was Little Rain, only now she is gone."

"Little Rain?" he asked, bewildered. "What did she do?"

In Dirty Knee Sits' rambling way, she explained that she would have been trampled under a Snake horse if Little Rain hadn't pushed her aside and then confronted their attacker. As befitting a woman of her age and stature within the tribe, Dirty Knee Sits had sought to protect herself but not Little Rain.

"She was like a warrior. She did not run or call out for help."

"Not run?" he questioned. "You may say that, but she went willingly with the Snakes."

"You do not know that," Raven's Cry pointed out. "Did you see what happened?"

"What I know is that she is the only one who is no longer here. I heard her tell the man I killed that she was not a Blackfoot. I say she told the same thing to the man she rode away with. She chooses the Snakes over us; so be it."

So be it.

Although Raven's Cry had been certain that only he and his brother would be riding off in pursuit of their stolen horses and goods, they'd gone no more than a few steps before a mounted White Calf overtook them. Like him and Night Thunder, she was dressed for winter. She also carried two skinning knives lashed to her waist.

"I will not argue this with you," she said when he tried to wave her away. "Tonight I go with you."

"You belong—"

"I belong with my husband!" Although barely any moonlight touched her face, he thought her features had darkened. "I told the women I needed one of the horses, and they did not argue with me. They would not. Raven's Cry, this time I will not close my senses to whispers of danger."

"There are whispers?"

When she didn't immediately answer, her silence filled him with foreboding, and he strained to see into the distance where a Snake might be waiting in ambush.

"Wolf," she said. "Wolf is still here."

"What—"

Before he could finish, she held up her hand, stopping him. The frozen crust over the snowpack cracked and hissed, and a lone owl hooted.

"I have been standing off by myself," she said, "but even so, it is hard to be alone. I feel fear and anger, yet that is not all."

"The Snakes?"

She frowned. "No. Not Snakes but . . ."

He wanted to say or do something to stop the chill down his spine that had nothing to do with the weather, but what would trying to argue her down accomplish?

"There is no heartbeat."

"A wolf without a heart?"

"No, not Wolf."

Not a spirit and not the enemy? "I do not understand."

He thought he'd spoken clearly, but she didn't seem to have heard him. As he'd just done, she scanned her surroundings. She seemed to have shrunken inside her heavy clothing, and yet her huge eyes glittered. It was right that the moon had buried so much of its light in them.

"No heartbeat and no breath," she continued. "No warmth and yet there is sound."

Raven's Cry sucked in his breath. If his mother was still within earshot, for once she wasn't saying anything.

"Danger walks with it—whatever it is," White Calf whispered. "No, not walk. Floating. Charging sometimes. Turning and twisting. Powerful."

She was frightening him, and from the way she hunched in around herself, he knew she'd scared herself.

"I have never felt anything like this. Never known . . ."

"Stay here," he commanded her. "Do not risk—"

"No!" Her head snapped back. "It makes no difference. The danger is everywhere."

His jaw muscles worked, but he couldn't make himself speak.

"We will do this together," she finished.

By dawn, the wind had picked up. It grew in strength throughout the morning, forcing the three to ride close together and hunched over. At times, the wind tore at the snow with such force that it was thrown about in great swirls, all but obliterating the tracks they were following. The horses had to be prodded, and the humans stared out at their world through lids drawn down as far as possible, blankets pulled tight around them.

Although White Calf rode beside him, Raven's Cry made no attempt to speak to her. He occasionally glanced at her, but with so much of her face covered, he couldn't read her expression. Still, tension draped every line of her body, and for the first time in his life, he wished she'd never come across the sacred white calf.

For several hours, he'd comforted himself with the knowledge that the sky remained clear; then he'd cursed to himself when he spotted the first dark clouds. Although he tried to deny it, they now reminded him of a great buffalo herd sweeping over the plains, eating everything and leaving no room for anything else. The cloud-mountains seemed hard pressed to carry their own weight, sagging so low that he half believed he, his brother, and his wife would be swallowed by them.

He felt buffeted by icy gusts, half numb with nothing except determination to keep him going. Fighting the numbness, he tried to put his thoughts on his wife and how hard this journey must be for her, but she'd already told him she would stay with him and—no, not with him. She was here because she hoped her presence would be enough to keep death from attacking, because, maybe Wolf would—

"Raven's Cry, stop."

Pulled out of himself by his brother's order, he discovered that

Night Thunder had halted and was staring intently at the approaching storm.

"We cannot keep moving," Night Thunder said. "Wind Maker walks among us. When it begins snowing—"

"It has not yet," he tersely pointed out.

"But when it does, we must take shelter."

"What are you saying, that you want to turn back without what was taken from us, what will keep our people from starving? Are we less than the Snakes? Fools they will laugh at for—"

"No! Never. But—White Calf, what do you say? Will this journey kill us?"

It hadn't been that long ago that Night Thunder wouldn't have dared ask her something like that, but so much had changed in recent days.

"I do not know," White Calf said, her head cocked to one side.

"Hm. Tell me, if you were alone, what would you be doing?"

"I am not. It does no good to ask such a thing." She had to yell to make herself heard over the angry wind.

"True," Night Thunder said with what might have been a smile. "Still I would like to hear your words."

"No, you do not want to know this thing." She took a deep breath. "I am afraid."

"Afraid to speak?"

"No." She shifted her weight and stared off into the distance. "Of this storm. I think maybe this is the danger I sensed earlier."

Night Thunder stared fixedly at him, but Raven's Cry didn't take his eyes off White Calf.

"But although I may fear Wind Maker's strength, I am first and always a Blackfoot," she continued. "My people need horses and food. Nothing else matters."

"You speak wisely," Night Thunder said.

"Wisely? Maybe." She frowned. "What I know is that my heart and not my head drives my words and that may be the greatest danger."

He'd been a small, curious child when he'd stuck his hand into a prairie dog hole. The impulsive gesture had earned him a severe bite that had left two fingers red and swollen. The harsh, driving air was much more powerful than prairie dog teeth could ever be, yet there was a great deal that was the same about them. He'd been trapped until he'd pulled his hand out of the hole. Now Wind Maker held him in the same inescapable grip.

"Do what you must, my brother," he told Night Thunder. "You still feel the effects of the buffalo attack. No one would fault you if you turned back."

"And you?"

"I cannot return to my people empty handed. I will not."

"Neither will I."

Such brave words, Night Thunder chided himself as snow—stinging ice pellets really—began attacking him. He was proud of both his brother and himself for putting the tribe's needs beyond their own safety, but mixed in with pride was the reality of what surrounded them. He didn't need White Calf's magic to know they might not be alive by the time the storm spent itself. Hadn't he twice seen horses who'd frozen because they'd been unable to find shelter? Even the mighty buffalo turned their backs on Wind Maker's rage.

But Raven's Cry was right. If they didn't go after the Snakes, their people might starve and they would never be able to call themselves warriors.

His horse had already tried to stop more times than he could count. When the creature did so this time, he started to dig his knees into its side, then forced himself to study what lay ahead of him.

The trail left behind by the fleeing Snakes had been as clear as a mountain stream only a little while ago, but the path was rapidly disappearing under fresh snow. That, combined with the wind's sweeping action, would soon erase it. Still—

"It is no good!" Raven's Cry called out. "Soon we will no longer be able to see anything. Surely the Snakes have taken shelter. We must do the same."

"No!" Panic he refused to acknowledge bit at him. "No!"

"Night Thunder!" It was White Calf. "Your brother speaks wisely."

He didn't want wisdom. He wanted to plow on, to find the thieving Snakes and exact vengeance on them. Ignoring the other two, he urged his horse on, but the miserable beast responded by planting his feet and refusing to move. He'd just lifted his hand to slap the horse's rump when White Calf's mount stepped in front of his.

"You cannot find her this way," White Calf said.

"Her?"

"Little Rain."

Little Rain had nothing to do with this, nothing! No matter what others might have said, he believed she'd chosen the Snakes over the Blackfeet. Why shouldn't she? The Snakes had no reason to be at war with her family and would probably allow her to return to the Cree as soon as the weather allowed. He was shed of her—and of her child.

"Whenever I look at you, I feel her presence," White Rain was saying. Raven's Cry had joined them, and the three of them stood close together, solitary figures surrounded by nature's strength.

"She has become part of you, Night Thunder," White Rain continued. "You may tell us that she has not, but you cannot tell yourself the same thing."

"She left."

"Left or was taken away?"

"It does not matter!" he snapped although it did, a great deal. "Why should I care what happens to her?"

The snow felt like frozen grains of sand being hurtled at him by an angry giant. Not long ago he'd been able to make out his surroundings, but everything was becoming lost in white. As lost as he felt.

"We will die if we stay here!" Raven's Cry yelled over the wind.

"We must have shelter! There!" He pointed. "Boulders we can hide behind."

Boulders or buckled earth, it was all the same Night Thunder thought as he and the other two urged their horses toward what little shelter the land might provide. What Raven's Cry had spotted turned out to be a stony projectile as tall as a chief's tepee and almost as wide at the base. It was so situated that the wind slammed into it, leaving a pocket of calm if not warmth behind it.

The horses immediately bunched together, noses touching even before their riders had dismounted and pressed their backs against the rock, Raven's Cry and Night Thunder on either side of White Calf.

"Wind Maker is filled with rage," Raven's Cry said in an almost conversational tone. "What have we done to displease him?"

"Not rage," White Calf said. "Wind Maker rejoices in his strength. Winter is his time, and the cold feeds him when all others hide from it. He is laughing and shouting in joy. Listen to him."

Listen to Wind Maker's joy? Still, as absurd as it seemed, Night Thunder found himself doing just that. The screaming washed over him, causing him to pull his covering even tighter around him. He felt surrounded by the storm, by his clothing, by relentless white and howling wind. Despite the outcropping, snow continued to pummel him, and he wondered if it might go on forever. Might hold him in its belly until he no longer felt like a Blackfoot warrior and became part of the wind.

Little Rain didn't have a blanket.

"You are all right?" Raven's Cry asked him. "Protected?"

"It is better here," he acknowledged. He wanted to thank White Calf for not letting him plunge on into what would have been his horse's and his death, but she knew so much about him that surely she'd already felt his gratitude.

"The Snakes are not fools," she said, and he knew she was speaking to him. "They too have found shelter."

"Can you see them?"

When she didn't immediately answer, he told himself she was

seeking out the raiders and that her knowledge would make it possible for him to find the Snakes once they could move on.

"No," she said, the admission hollowing him out. "But although the Blackfeet may never understand the ways of the Snakes, our love of living is the same. Besides, they do not know we are following them so why should they hurry?"

That made sense, only the storm took so much energy from him that it was nearly impossible to concentrate. Thinking to renew himself, he concentrated on the feel of the rock against his back, his legs that were slowly disappearing under new snow, air's cold path into his lungs.

Little Rain didn't have a blanket.

"She should not have gone with them," he said. Only now that the words had escaped did he realize how much he needed to say that.

"No," White Calf agreed. "She should not have."

"They cannot care what happens to her. Winter attacks them, and they will do what they must to protect themselves, but her comfort and safety means nothing to them."

"True."

He didn't want White Calf to agree with him. Instead, irrationally, he wanted to be reassured that Little Rain was at least as safe as he was.

"She will freeze."

"Maybe."

"But not just her."

White Calf slid her hand into his and squeezed. "No," she said so softly that he wasn't sure whether Raven's Cry could hear. "Her baby too will be harmed."

"She—she told you about that?"

"No, but I knew."

"Because of your gift?" he asked, envying her.

"No, not that." There was a hint of a smile in her voice, and she continued to grip his fingers. "The truth was in her eyes, Night Thunder. She had the look of a woman whose thoughts now go both inside and beyond herself, who has been taken into the future and knows she no longer lives just for herself."

Little Rain's features had told White Calf all that? "I did not see those things," he admitted.

"Because your thoughts are on yourself. But I am a woman."

"What does that—"

"A woman knows her body will some day carry life. A man can never fully understand what that means, but it forces and allows women to be more than themselves."

He didn't have the energy to think about the differences between men and women or whether he was missing something because he was unable to nurture the way women did.

"I hoped she would come to me," White Calf was saying. "I would like to believe that time would come and she would not have to walk her journey alone, but maybe it will never be."

Because Little Rain was no longer with them. Because she might not survive the storm.

"At least she told you," White Calf said.

"Because she had to. Not because it was what she wanted."

"Hm. And what about you?"

"Me?"

"That child's father is dead because of you," White Calf pointed out unnecessarily. The screaming wind tore at but didn't kill her words. "You put an end to him because that was what you had to do as a Blackfoot, but he lives on through his child."

He didn't want to hear this but didn't know how to silence her.

"If Little Rain gave birth in a Blackfoot camp, what would you have done?"

25

The day passed before the new storm showed any sign of slackening. The prairies that were home to the Blackfeet had always been windswept places; White Calf had known that from earliest childhood, her grandparents having passed on the stories of their grandparents and their grandparents before them. She'd never told anyone this, but even when the future stretched into the time when the prairie no longer belonged to the Blackfeet, Wind Maker remained.

Her prayer was that the wind would always carry memories of her people.

Now it was nearly dark, and although she was weary of sitting, she didn't dare walk away from their makeshift shelter because if she did, she risked getting lost. Still, she could make a journey in her mind. Neither Night Thunder nor her husband had said anything for a long time, and by the cadence of their breathing, she knew they'd fallen asleep. She envied them their forgetfulness, but it was no use to think about that, not when she had work to do.

Although there must be life and living things beyond her, when she first "stepped" into the vastness of her surroundings, she felt utterly alone. It was said that Below Ground people often ventured out to observe what Wind Maker had created but even they must have been awed into silence by today's rage.

Still, she had no choice.

The new snow had packed down in places, but in others, the wind had scraped the ground nearly bare. By contrast, many grasses and rocks were now buried under drifts nearly as tall as her. Still, she was weightless in this journey and thus easily floated over the never-ending white that blanketed everything. She didn't have to breathe, didn't have to think about her empty belly. She was and yet she wasn't, spirit and soul and very little else. This land was hers, freeing her to run as effortlessly over it as an eagle soared.

She loved seeing summer's insects, all except for mosquitos. The multitude of moths and butterflies sometimes captured her attention, and she accepted that there must be a need for the flies that congregated around scat, but her favorite small creature had always been the long, skinny walkingsticks who could change their color to blend in with their surroundings. They looked so much like the prairie grass they clung to that they went unnoticed unless they moved.

Where were the walkingsticks now? What happened to the delicate wings of moths and butterflies when snowflakes pelted them? It seemed impossible that they could survive such a savage attack, and yet they had to leave something of themselves behind, or there wouldn't be any to welcome next spring's warmth. Frowning, she vowed to pay closer attention to the life cycles of the tiny creatures she'd always taken for granted.

Night Thunder was right to worry about Little Rain. He might not admit he cared what happened to his hostage, but the truth of his feelings rode on his every word and the concern in his black eyes. If she put her mind to it, she might be able to "find" Little Rain, but the effort would leave her exhausted when she had to know whether she and Raven's Cry and Night Thunder—mostly Raven's Cry—would survive. Besides, learning Little Rain's fate wouldn't change anything.

The snow of her mind wasn't cold; it simply existed, simply was. Although new flakes continued to join those that were already there, she no longer felt buffeted by the storm, and her eyes had taken on the ability to "see" through and around and past the un-relenting white.

She and the two braves weren't alone after all. The burrowing creatures had gone to sleep for the winter, but their presence still made an impact on her senses, as did the few antelope who'd been heading south when the early storms hit. She felt sorry for the antelope who lacked a buffalo's vast storehouse of fat and would grow weary from pawing through snow for something to eat, but she couldn't lead them to safety. A buck, worn out from rutting, had stayed behind when the rest of his kind left for a warmer place. He'd belatedly become aware of the danger he was in and had started to hurry after the others, but it might be too late for him.

After sending a message of concern and a prayer for courage to the buck, she began a slow, thorough study of her immediate sur-roundings. It didn't take long to conclude that they'd been wise to seek shelter where they had because the strange formation was the largest wind barrier around. They'd been heading toward forested foothills, but it would take the better part of a day to reach them. The trees—

When the first prickling of alarm came, she shook it off, but despite her effort, it returned. Danger waited for her in the form of murderous teeth and a nose so keen that it was aware of everything within shouting distance and maybe beyond. The wolf was the same one she'd "seen" before, the one who'd been following her husband and his brother and had caused her to leave Chief Sleeps Too Long.

Wolf and his death message.

Despite the fear she couldn't deny, she began "walking" toward the patiently waiting creature. Snow wasn't embracing him so much as he embraced it, and his fur absorbed flake after flake until she half expected him to turn into a frozen mound.

"I do not understand the truth of you," she said into the night. "You exist and yet you do not. You are a wolf and yet not one of your kind. Perhaps they do not know of you?"

Because she didn't need to concern herself with keeping herself warm, the part of her that walked the prairie cast off her blanket so the elements could more easily reach her and so, hopefully, her senses would absorb more.

"Wolf is a hunter. A killer. But he loves his children and cares for them. He brings down newborn fawns and takes them to his den so his children can live. Does that bother him? Does he seek the reason for what must be? When one wolf finds a mate, nothing except death will separate them. They are not loners but crave the company of their own kind. They have the capacity to care and yet they must kill."

The wolf waited.

"Which are you, Wolf? Gentle or deadly?"

No answer drifted to her.

"Are you here to pass your courage and strength onto me and those with me, or are we to fear you?"

Fear.

Hating the answer, she held out her hands to ward it off, but that didn't stop the silent echo.

"Fear *you*," she managed.

No.

"What then?"

Death.

"D-death? Mine?"

No answer.

"Night Thunder's? Raven's Cry's? Please, not his."

Still nothing.

"Whose? Please, whose?"

Death.

When Raven's Cry stirred, White Calf held her breath and hoped he'd go on sleeping, but he stretched and briefly leaned against her.

"You did not sleep?" he asked as he drew away.

"No," she told him because she couldn't lie to him.

"Hm. It is dark. Does night still have a lengthy journey?"

She told him yes but couldn't think of anything else to say. As she'd expected, her journey had left her spent. Her eyes ached from trying to penetrate the gloom and her cheeks and nose felt as if they'd been rubbed raw. Only the side that was pressed against her husband was warm.

"I hope the Snakes have found no shelter," he said. He spoke in a near whisper, and she guessed he didn't want his brother to hear. "I would have no regret if they all froze."

"Perhaps they will."

Her words caught his attention because it wasn't like White Calf to speak ill of anyone.

"You are thinking of Little Rain and wanting no harm to come to her?"

"No. Not . . ."

He'd been trying to accept his new wife's wisdom, her long silences, and the way her eyes sometimes fixed on things he believed he would never see, but the storm had worn him down, left him without enough in reserve.

"What is it?" he pressed. Night Thunder's deep breathing ceased, and he knew his brother had come instantly awake. "What is it?" he repeated.

She told them what had taken place when her spirit walked the prairie, her voice low and deep, gentle yet heavy. Because he'd seen the wolf himself, he easily imagined what it had looked like and even understood its disregard of the elements. What was beyond his comprehension was how the creature had communicated with White Calf.

At least he tried to make himself believe it was beyond his comprehension.

"How do you know he was warning of death?" he demanded. "Did you hear his words?"

"No."

"No!" He pounced on that. "Then how—"

"I know, Raven's Cry. I know."

How was it possible for her to silence him so easily? He struggled through his splintering thoughts for yet another argument to throw at her, but even as he did, he knew it didn't exist.

"Whose death did he speak of?" Night Thunder asked. "You have not said."

"Because he would not, or could not, tell me."

As her words faded away, she shivered, making him wonder whether her mind's journey was responsible or if she was keeping something from him. It would be so easy for her to do, so easy for her to travel beyond the world he knew.

"Perhaps if you had stayed longer, the truth would have come to you," he ventured.

"Perhaps, but I did not want to."

"Why? Do—" His throat closed and he fought to go on. "Are you in danger?"

Instead of clinging to him as a new wife sometimes did, she wrapped her arms around her knees, hugging herself, separate from him.

"Maybe," she said.

Rage flashed through him. In his mind's eye, he saw himself aiming an arrow at the wolf's heart. Even if it meant that all other wolves would stalk him and take out their revenge on him, it didn't matter as long as she was safe. But his brother's arrows had been useless against the spirit-creature.

"I think—" She sighed. "I wonder if death walks among us but has not yet chosen who it will take. Perhaps that is why Wolf was unable to give me the answer I asked for. And maybe . . . maybe the time has not yet come for me to know."

Either possibility made terrible sense; he wouldn't make the mistake of trying to tell her otherwise. When her body spasmed for the second time, he wrapped his arm around her shoulder. It seemed that she leaned into him a little and yet something remained between them.

She was White Calf. He couldn't take her burdens from her so she could rest and find peace any more than he could face Wolf for her. Still, he told her that he wanted to be informed before her mind went on another of its searching journeys.

"It would make no difference," she told him.

"Why not?"

"Because—" She lowered her head until it rested on her bent knees and when she spoke, her voice was muffled. "Because it is not a Blackfoot journey. Only I can walk that way."

Only her. Not her husband with his earthbound feet and useless dreams.

Death.

Death.

Night Thunder rolled the word over and over in his mind, but although he strained to make an image of it, the heavy, freezing, blowing night that surrounded him remained inside him as well.

He'd left his brother and White Calf long enough to relieve himself but was once again huddled against their rocky protection. His feet had become numb, and he pulled first one and then the other close so he could massage warmth back into them. They'd eaten a little after taking shelter and the snow had provided them with enough to drink although the act of holding snow in his mouth to thaw it had chilled him.

It was dangerous to allow sleep to take him too deep into its belly. If he gave into his body's need, he might not feel the night's icy grip until it was too late. Still, it was so hard to remain alert.

In an effort to keep his mind occupied, he told himself several of Old Man's tales. It disturbed him that they were all about the struggle to survive, but he took comfort in legends about how the chief of wolves had kept Old Man from freezing, how he'd used the fat from a bear he'd killed to cover all other animals with fat so they could withstand winter, the time he'd spared the life of a pregnant cow elk.

Old Man had not always been wise. There'd been times when coyotes or wolves or bears had stolen his food, and when he'd taken Sun's leggings and tried to hide from Sun, the leggings had caught fire while he was wearing them, but tonight Night Thunder refused to dwell on Old Man's foolish side.

Old Man was the creator. It was He who'd made all people,

animals, birds, and fish. Without him, there would have been no prairies, mountains, or streams. Old Man could never die but he'd long ago left the Blackfeet and gone to the West where it was said he lived in the mountains. Before he'd gone, he'd told the ancient ones that he would always take care of the Blackfeet and would eventually return.

He'd also said that when he did, he would find the Blackfeet changed.

Did Old Man exist for the Cree?

The unwanted question caught Night Thunder unaware, and he surged forward, cursing to himself. White Calf and Raven's Cry demanded to know what was wrong, but he felt too exposed and vulnerable to answer. He'd thought he could banish thoughts of Little Rain from his mind by recalling the stories of his childhood but he'd been wrong, as foolish as Old Man sometimes was.

If it wasn't for the storm, he would have walked out into the night and kept on walking until exhaustion overtook him. Instead, he had no choice but to remain where he was, to think and be swamped by those thoughts.

So much had changed about him recently. His belly and nerves remembered the feel of fear, and if it had been earlier, he might not have had the courage to track the Snakes, to face the fact that he and his brother would have to attack and perhaps battle the Snakes if they were to recover what was theirs. Fear, like the freezing wind, waited out there, but it couldn't reach him tonight. That might be because the storm had numbed him, but he didn't think so. Rather, he'd been forced to face danger and had survived. He'd risked his life but hadn't died. That might change tomorrow; tonight might be the last he would spend on this earth, but it was enough. He took comfort from that.

And tried to grab hold of what had stood beside him during those moments of danger and looming death.

The Snakes had been in the open when the storm hit, but they'd pushed the horses into a hard gallop that had taken them into a grove of trees growing along a creek. Someone had tried to start a fire with the coal they'd brought with them, but the wind had blown it out. With the loss of that hope came a resigned silence broken only infrequently as one or another of the Snakes said something in a short, sharp tone that was answered in the same way.

The man who'd forced Little Rain to go with them had at least given her a blanket and his spare moccasins, even if they were so big that she could hardly keep them on. Once they stopped moving and inactivity made her more vulnerable to the cold, her captor hadn't objected when she'd dug through his supplies for a beaver skin cap and pulled it down around her ears.

The horses had bunched tightly together, their backs to the worst of the relentless gusts. Although she couldn't see them, their constant movement and complaints made it impossible for her to dismiss their presence. It was the same with the Snake warriors who'd pulled themselves into a close circle. She'd joined them, adding her own warmth to the shared but scant heat.

Because her clan hadn't had much to do with the Snakes, she understood very little of what they said and darkness prevented her from communicating through sign language, even if she'd been so inclined.

Would the night and the howling fury ever end? She'd been in storms as fierce as this one, but always before she'd been surrounded by her people and the warming fires had never gone out. Even the unwanted time she'd spent with the Blackfeet hadn't prepared her for this—this silent, miserable waiting.

To her surprise, she found herself longing for the company of a woman almost as much as she longed for her body to stop shivering. Dirty Knee Sits had never done anything to make her feel welcome, but she hadn't rejected her either, and she'd been content to share in the chores that filled her days and sometimes her mind. In contrast, White Calf had reached out to her and made her feel that whether she was Cree or Blackfeet didn't matter. Warmed by the memory, she sent White Calf a silent message of thanks.

When her thoughts first turned to Night Thunder, she reined

them in with a will born of denial, but cold had seeped into her, leaving her weak. The young Blackfoot brave would never be Takes-Knife-at-Night, and she couldn't imagine herself wanting to share her body with him, yet he'd shown her the man beneath a warrior's mask, and bit by bit she'd stopped throwing up defenses designed to keep him at bay. He knew how much she hated the changes in her father, that she wanted to blame the Blackfeet for Weasel Tail's bitterness but that it hadn't been that simple. Beyond that, Night Thunder knew she'd try to kill him if he did anything to injure her unborn child.

A long, hard, convulsive shudder surged through her. Without wanting to, she nevertheless leaned against her captor. He'd layered himself with several blankets, which prevented her from tapping much of his body heat, but he stopped the wind on that side from reaching her and maybe if she—

Grunting, he clamped a hand over her bent knee. The grip might have been painful if she hadn't been numb. Then he turned toward her and said something she didn't understand but caused the man next to him to snort with laughter. Before she could think how to stop him, her captor yanked at the length of skirt over her legs and slid his hand under the soft hide. She sensed more than felt his fingers' relentlessness movement until, to her horror, he reached the warmest part of her. With a gasp, she jerked away, only to be rudely stopped by the man on her other side who wrapped his arms around her, his palms pressing painfully against her breasts.

Someone she couldn't see but whose presence she sensed all too clearly said something that caused the men to laugh. Half sick with fear, she tried to wrench free.

"No!" she sobbed. "No, please!"

"Silence!" one of the men snapped in Blackfeet. "You—are—dog!"

"No!" It didn't matter how the man had learned those few Blackfeet words. All that did was making herself understood. Begging if necessary. "I am not a—I am Cree."

"Cree, no. Blackfeet dog. Bitch."

The man who'd imprisoned her said something to whoever had called her a bitch. The response resulted in harsh laughter that struck her like knife stabs. When members of one tribe captured a woman or child from another tribe, the captive was usually treated with respect, but if too much hatred existed between the two tribes—or if the captive was the only woman in a band of warriors, she might be passed around them.

Little Rain had heard of that happening only once, years ago when the Snakes had attacked a small group of Tetons, leaving just one woman alive. It was said that after four days of unending rape, the young Teton had gotten her hands on a knife and plunged it into her own heart.

The hand between her legs started to move again, invading. Screaming, she fought to twist away, but the arms around her made that impossible.

Fear was like a raging river determined to suck her down into its depths. She thought of her innocent baby, her dead husband, Night Thunder who could have done anything he wanted to her but instead had looked deep into her eyes and perhaps had been touched by what he'd seen there.

These men knew nothing about her and didn't care.

"We have de-cided," the interpreter said. "You will—warm us."

No! A sickening image of what Feather Tickles looked like shortly before she'd killed herself filled Little Rain's mind's eye. Whether she lay passively or fought would make no difference because the Snakes chose to believe she was a Blackfoot and nothing would give them greater satisfaction than punishing a Blackfoot woman.

The thought of being beaten stole the air from her lungs, but not because she was afraid for herself. Her unborn child's life was at risk.

"Not Blackfeet!" she repeated. "Cree. I am Cree."

"You live with Blackfeet. You are Blackfeet."

They didn't care. They'd needed something other than the

storm and the risk of freezing to think about, and she was providing them with it. Fear continued to threaten to drown her but she fought it because her child's survival depended on it. She didn't know where the courage to stop struggling came from, but she willed her muscles to cease straining and lay passively in her captors' grip, waiting, praying. The one who had hold of her breasts said something she didn't understand.

"Why you no fight?" the interpreter asked.

"I am as dead. If you rape me, you will be raping a dead woman."

More grumbling and intense conversation followed that. The man who'd taken her from the Blackfeet still had his hand on her most private part, but he'd stopped trying to force a reaction from her. Despite her pounding heart and the fear eating at her sanity, she was grateful for that.

"You not dead. We will make . . ."

It didn't matter that he didn't have the means of expressing himself because she knew what he would have said, that they'd force her to fight and when she did, they'd laugh and abuse her and—

Before she knew it was going to happen, she was being yanked to her feet. One captor now had hold of her right arm while the other tugged on the left. Still, she willed herself to remain limp while she wondered if they were going to tear her apart.

A heated argument broke out between the two men and was punctuated by harsh comments from the other warriors. The man who'd grabbed her must have won because the other abruptly released her, and she felt herself being dragged around so that she now faced her captor.

His quick breath rained down on her, warming her face but chilling the rest of her. Because she continued to sag, he had to hold her up, her weight pulling him off balance. When he started to release her so he could get a better hold on her, he spread his legs slightly.

She didn't think, simply acted, her knee slamming upward with every bit of strength in her desperate body.

Grunting, he fell back, dragging her with him, but she wrenched free and ran. Ran with death behind and around her.

As the night and storm swallowed her, she drank in freezing air and snow pellets slammed into her exposed eyes and cheeks and nose and chin.

26

In the time of White Calf's grandmother's grandmother, there'd been no horses. The People hadn't known it could be different so they were content to spend their lives running after buffalo and other game. They never settled in any place and kept their belongings simple because there was only so much they and the dogs could carry. As a consequence, going north in the winter was something they did only when pursued by another tribe.

White Calf's grandmother's grandmother had been an old woman and her husband was already dead when she agreed to accompany a group of hunters who'd located a small elk herd at the base of Raging Snow Mountain. Her children and grandchildren hadn't wanted her to go, but Moon Singer had believed that many of her people wouldn't make it through the winter without food. Besides, she'd lived a great number of years and was willing to take the risk if it meant those she loved would be safe.

An unexpected storm had hit as they were butchering the three elk the warriors had brought down. The Blackfeet had taken shelter in a cave and lived off the elk meat for awhile, but almost before the first storm had ended, another took its place and then another until there were drifts higher than a man's head.

The Blackfeet hadn't brought along snowshoes because the shaman had said they wouldn't be needed, and the hungry hunters had had to make their way out of the mountains by plunging through the drifts. Two of the People hadn't made it, a youth who'd broken his ankle and Moon Singer who'd told the others to leave her behind when her strength gave out.

Because an ancestor's soul lived forever and might hear and see a great deal, White Calf sometimes spoke to Moon Singer. In the past she'd asked Moon Singer if she was content, surrounded by her children and grandchildren and able to ride ghost horses, but as dawn struggled to make itself known, White Calf sent out a prayer that if she, Raven's Cry, and Night Thunder froze here, their ancestors would show their shadows the way to acceptance.

Instead, Moon Singer sent her a dream—maybe a dream—that caused her heart to briefly stop beating and then pound raggedly. Frightened both by the dream and her heart's reaction, she clasped her hand over her chest. As she did, Raven's Cry, who'd been sleeping beside her, stirred and then sat up.

"What is it?" he asked.

"No-thing."

"Do not say that, White Calf. Your heart races. Do you see into the future?"

"No."

"Then what?"

She and Raven's Cry were strangers to each other, like solitary eagles who nevertheless shared the same sky and maybe the same view of the world. One eagle might fight another for food, but if they were male and female, the spirits would bring them together, and these former adversaries would mate and risk their own lives to care for their young.

"The future, yes," she amended. "But after our time. Our grand-children—"

"Ours? Yours and mine?"

"I do not know!" She was irritated by his question, either that or frightened by it. "It does not matter."

"Not—I am sorry. I did not mean to stop your thoughts."

They weren't simple thoughts; they were something much more

horrifying. Her first impulse was to jump to her feet and run, but she'd be forced to take her images with her when she'd do anything not to be alone with them. Besides, she needed her husband's warmth.

"I do not want to say this."

"If that is so, then I do not want to hear it, but the burden should not be yours alone."

Wondering if he now truly understood the weight of what others called a gift, she sagged against him. She'd meant for the contact to last only a moment while she gathered herself for what had to be said, but before she could separate herself from him, he wrapped his arm around her.

The wind she'd come to hate was unsatiable. Even a grizzly or cougar eventually tired, but there'd never been a time when she wasn't aware of the air that moved restlessly across the land. Sometimes, like today, it turned into a monster.

"I have been with my grandmother's grandmother," she began. "Moon Singer was alone when she died. Maybe that is why she came to me, because she was lonely. I wish—I wish she had not."

"Why?"

Night Thunder, huddled nearby, had asked the question, but she barely acknowledged him and spoke to her husband. "Moon Singer took me into the future," she explained. "She showed me the—a time of many tears and death for our people."

Momentarily unable to go on, she waited for the men to tell her they didn't want to hear this, prayed they would do so, but they didn't.

Feeling as if she'd never spoken before and had to fight to form each word, she brought them with her into that unwanted time. The whites who'd taken over Blackfeet land called it the winter of 1883–1884, but to the Blackfeet that the whites had named the South Peigans, it was known as Starvation Winter. The Peigans had been forced farther and farther north, hunted by the army and civilians alike. The diseases the newcomers had brought with them exacted their own toils, the great buffalo herds had been depleted,

and those that remained weren't in the inhospitable land the Peigans had been forced into. Treaties with something the soldiers
called the United States had been signed and orders given that made
the Peigans dependent on government rations, but those pitiful
supplies were uncertain.

There were no successful buffalo hunts during Starvation Winter and what little the government provided wasn't enough to keep
the People alive. By the time it ended, six hundred Blackfeet men,
women, and children were dead.

"I hear the crying," White Calf managed around her tightened
throat. "Mothers crying for their children. Men wailing for their
fathers, chiefs, and shamen. What warriors that are left hate what
has been done to them, but their empty bellies eat the hatred and
leave them weak. Defeated."

"This cannot be!" Night Thunder exclaimed. "Surely you do
not see—"

"She does," Raven's Cry interrupted. White Calf had been shaking all through her telling, but now she lay motionless and spent
against him. "I hate her words," he admitted, "but I cannot call
them false."

"No? Ha! I wish there was no one named White Calf," Night
Thunder said, his words an explosion. "I curse her and everything
she says."

"Do you think I want this?" White Calf moaned. "If I could, I
would cast this thing called a gift from me. If I thought I could turn
my people toward another future by driving a spear through my
mind and heart, I would. Sometimes—sometimes I wish I had
never been born."

But if she hadn't, Raven's Cry thought, he wouldn't be holding
her this morning.

Neither his brother nor White Calf had said anything after that,
leaving Night Thunder alone with his own thoughts. Although
she'd spoken little about the suffering during Starvation Winter,
he'd all too easily imagined the look of desperation in the eyes of

those who were dying. In his own mind, he'd felt despair and un-relenting hunger and cold and heard too many unanswered prayers.

The only way he could deal with those things was by insisting that they take off after the Snakes now that it was light. Their horses were hungry and not inclined to travel, but they were well-enough trained that before long, they no longer tried to stop. Raven's Cry and White Calf had slept next to each other last night, and he'd joined them because they needed to conserve and share each other's heat, but he couldn't detect any closeness between his brother and his wife this morning, perhaps because they were as trapped within themselves as he felt.

The Snakes were his enemy. They were, he told himself, lazy and useless. Instead of going after their horses when they'd first lost them, they'd waited for the Blackfeet to round them up and then stolen them away. Being lazy and too stupid to understand the danger in an unexpected storm, they'd feel no urgency about getting back to their village, and if he continued on his relentless pursuit of them, he'd eventually overtake them.

Them and Little Rain.

White Calf believed that someone would die, that that had been Wolf's message, but it wouldn't be her or his brother or himself. Or Little Rain. It wouldn't!

Maybe—yes!—White Calf's vision had meant that he would kill a Snake! That's what he told himself as the cloud-hidden sun struggled upward, what he made himself believe.

His legs were numb, and it hurt to breathe and the clouds once again spit snow, but Night Thunder forgot those things when the Snakes and their horses came into view through the mists of swirl-ing snow that was being ripped from the earth and tossed about by the wind. A quick glance at Raven's Cry and White Calf told him they'd seen the same thing. He'd been afraid they wouldn't be able to overtake their enemy before the Snakes reached the safety of their village after all, but the extra horses had forced them to move at a slower pace than their pursuers.

"Not yet," Raven's Cry warned as he started to urge his horse forward. "First—White Calf, look into tonight. Find your way to it. What do you see?"

White Calf closed her eyes, swayed slightly, then caught herself by wrapping her fingers in her horse's mane. She didn't say anything.

"Earlier you spoke of death," Raven's Cry prompted. "Does death still walk among us?"

The unrelenting wind tore at his eyes despite his attempts to keep his lids as closed as possible. Just the same, Night Thunder knew he hadn't mistaken the distress on her face.

"Yes." The word was more emotion than sound.

"Whose?" he asked.

"I do not know. I—It is here, heavy and dark, like a stalking wolf. But I still cannot tell who it waits for."

Raven's Cry grunted and then pointed at the Snakes who appeared like dark shadows moving through a white world. As the older brother, Raven's Cry should be leading the way, but Night Thunder didn't care about that. The Snakes might believe they had nothing to fear from the Blackfeet. If that was true, they wouldn't be looking behind them. And if they did, what did it matter because death was going to visit one of them today—brought by a Blackfoot warrior named Night Thunder.

A Snake death, none other!

Not Cree, no, not Cree!

He couldn't remember how long it had been since he'd last seen Little Rain. She'd been part of his world such a short period that having her gone shouldn't feel wrong, and yet he didn't try to tell himself otherwise. She'd left him, he reminded himself, ridden away with the Snakes, and he needed to know why. That was all he wanted from her.

And if she'd been an unwilling—

By taking advantage of the occasional brush and swirling snow, he, Raven's Cry, and White Calf managed to come up on the right side of the Snakes. By then their horses were breathing heavily from the exertion, but the Snakes couldn't hear them over the wind's roar and the sounds the other animals made. Only a lazy arrow's distance now separated him from his enemy, yet the poor visibility forced him to strain to see. He felt trapped in the storm, part of it and yet not, exhausted from fighting its strength.

The Snakes were all there, every one of them on horseback as they led the rest of the herd. They traveled with their heads down, hunched forward as if trying to make themselves one with the animals. Deep Scar had to be among them, but he couldn't make out his horse. None of the Snakes spoke or looked around, almost as if they'd gone into hibernation.

Little Rain wasn't among them.

Shocked into immobility, Night Thunder stopped urging his horse on, and the mare immediately halted. With every second, the distance between him and those he'd been pursuing increased, but it no longer mattered. Little Rain, gone. Gone where?

"What is it?" Raven's Cry hissed.

When he didn't answer, Raven's Cry brought his horse alongside, and a moment later, White Calf joined them. No one said anything until the storm had once again swallowed their enemy.

"What is it?" his brother repeated. "Do you fear—"

"Fear?" *What was that?* "I did not see her."

Little Rain couldn't have taken off on her own. He knew that as surely and deeply as he knew that if she was alive he would find her. And if she wasn't—

"What did they do to her?"

Neither Raven's Cry or White Calf answered.

"Dead? She trusted them and they betrayed that trust?" He wondered aloud. "If they have killed her, I will—I must revenge her—"

"No!"

Hearing that, he whirled on White Calf. Instead of cowering before his anger, her eyes blazed and looked capable of melting the snow that fell between them.

"I will kill—"

"No," she repeated. Although she'd spoken more softly this

time, the word lashed at him. "A wolf kills because he must," she continued, "but you are a man, not a wolf."

"Listen to her," Raven's Cry insisted. "Do not forget why we are here."

How could he care about meat or horses or even revenge when he felt as if someone had thrust a spear into him? The storm had been all-powerful, and he'd felt like a leaf being blown about by it, but that was nothing compared to the tornado of emotions now attacking him.

"Night Thunder. Night Thunder, hear my words." It was White Calf. "Our people have placed their lives in our hands. We cannot return empty handed. And if you give into your anger, it may kill you."

"I do not care."

"I do," Raven's Cry countered. Then, before he could move away, his brother reached out and yanked the horse rope out of his hand.

"You speak like a man who has eaten too many fermented berries," Raven's Cry said. "We are after what was stolen from us, nothing more. If you die, your death will have been for nothing. And if you kill a Snake, his friends will come after us. A Snake heart stops beating and then a Blackfoot and then another Snake. It may never end."

"It has always been that way. I—"

"Not any more," Raven's Cry insisted. "And certainly not now."

"You are not chief. I—"

"But someday I will be, and when that time comes, the Blackfeet will walk my way."

"He is right," White Calf said once Raven's Cry's words had fallen away. "One violent act follows another. It never ends unless someone turns in another direction. Night Thunder, you are not a man of violence. I have seen the fear of death in your eyes and cannot believe that no longer exists."

He remembered the fear all right. In truth, he'd once believed he'd have to battle it for the rest of his life, and yet it no longer existed for him. If he'd thought he could save Little Rain's life by rushing into the middle of the Snakes, he would do so with no care as to the consequences, but she wasn't there, and thus the Snakes didn't matter—unless they'd already killed her.

"I will force them to tell me what happened to her," he insisted.

"You think they would? Even if you, I, and my wife were able to overcome the Snakes, what makes you believe they would hand you the truth?"

He had no answer for that, only the horrid realization that Death walked the prairie.

Little Rain's?

White Calf's mind felt as if it had been invaded by icy blasts. Still, she struggled to think as the wind buffeted her and her legs lost the ability to sense her horse's movements. They'd gotten close enough to the Snakes that she'd been able to count their horses and come to the chilling realization that they were all there. Surely Night Thunder must have come to the same conclusion and knew that if Little Rain was still alive, she was on foot.

If?

Was it possible for one to cease to be human and become one with the wind? She'd seen leaves thrown about so violently that they tore apart and the tiny pieces scattered over the prairie. Today's gusts weren't the strongest she'd ever experienced or even the coldest, but always before, she'd been able to take shelter. Never before had continuing to battle winter been so important.

Was Little Rain alive?

She'd already asked her spirit that question more times than she could remember, and yet she did so again. As before, she felt herself pushing against the great, dark mass that was death, but it kept her on the outside and mocked her, challenged her.

Before she could prepare herself, something hard and heavy slammed into her heart with such force that she nearly cried out. She wasn't afraid to die, and if Wolf's message had been about the end to Little Rain, perhaps it had already come, but there were two other possibilities, Night Thunder and Raven's Cry.

Hear me, Spirit. Please, hear me. These men ride because they will not fail their people. They risk everything so others will live. I ask nothing for myself and will not fight if you have chosen me. If death has taken Little Rain, I pray her going was gentle, but a warrior seeks a violent death.

Please, not Raven's Cry! Not my husband!

Startled by the intensity of her emotion, she slid her hand over her heart, but that did nothing to quiet the pain. She didn't dare risk looking at him, couldn't bargain with death so it would choose her instead of him and yet—

A wolf has been with us. Not any wolf, but a spirit creature. Wolf, come! Walk with Raven's Cry and lend him your courage and strength. Do this thing for me. Please.

But the wolf didn't make its presence known.

His ears had been full of storm-sounds for so long that Raven's Cry had forgotten what silence could feel like. From earliest childhood, he'd been aware of Wind Maker's power and had accepted it, but today he wanted to beat his fists against Wind Maker and demand He put an end to what raged around them.

White Calf rode beside him, and yet she felt as far away as Little Rain did. He tried to put his mind on what they would do once they'd again overtaken the Snakes; instead, over and over, he heard himself saying that one day he would be chief.

Chief when he had no power beyond the strength in his body? Chief when his boasting of magical dreams lay crumbled around him?

To counter the unanswerable questions, he breathed deep and long, following the frigid air's path into his lungs. The simple act put him in touch with his body, and he took inventory of muscles honed by a lifetime spent surviving his world. As a child, he'd never lost a wrestling match and could manage the wildest horse. He'd turned his back on those simple realities while in pursuit of something beyond himself, beyond understanding, but he now knew that his dreams held no power and if they briefly had, that gift had been taken from him.

He had to accept what was.

Had to live with his limitations and inability to match what came so naturally to White Calf.

"We must act now," he told his wife and brother. "If we wait, we will be too close to the Snake camp, and the journey back to our people will take too long."

White Calf said nothing; Night Thunder merely grunted his agreement. Then, because they were both looking at him, he explained that he'd been here a couple of summers ago with some other youths and remembered that a wide depression lay a short distance beyond the slow-moving Snakes. As soon as the Snakes dipped into it, they would be able to overtake them with less risk of being seen. The Snakes didn't matter today, only the packhorses with their buffalo meat burdens did. The attack would be swift and sure, lead ropes grabbed followed by instant retreat.

That said, he searched inside himself for the slightest hint of hesitation, but there wasn't any. How could there be when so much was at stake and he had so much to prove, both to himself and White Calf? His only doubt was whether his brother was ready.

"I long for this," Night Thunder said as if in answer to his unspoken question. "Nothing means more to me than having my revenge."

"Do not let your need to prove yourself rob you of wisdom," he warned.

"I have already heard those words," Night Thunder shot back. "And I have not forgotten them. But what I do today is for Little Rain."

"Not for your people?"

"I am Blackfeet! Always Blackfeet! Do not try to step inside me and tell me what my thoughts must be!" Night Thunder snapped.

You are right. I am sorry. "Stay here," he ordered White Calf. "We will not—"

"No," she interrupted in that calm but immovable way of hers.

"I will not remain behind."

"But—"

"Listen to me, Raven's Cry. I came with on this journey because it is my duty and I . . ." Her voice trailed off and even with the poor visibility, he knew she was struggling with something.

"Blackfeet women are more than mothers," she continued. "More than the builders of tepees and preparers of food. When we must, we fight."

"Night Thunder and I are not going to do battle," he said, although of course he couldn't be sure of the confrontation's outcome.

"Maybe. Maybe not," she said. "It makes no difference. I am going with you."

Because she had no faith in him and believed his life depended on her being by his side. But much as he raged against her for thinking that way, he didn't try to argue her down because she was right. She soared with eagles while his feet were sinking into soft sand.

As Raven's Cry turned his back on her and plunged into the endless white, White Calf's heart went out to him, not just in regret for what he believed he'd lost, but also because her fear for him knew no bounds. She should have told him and Night Thunder about her futile attempt to reach out to Wolf so they'd know to be even more cautious, but the words had refused to come. She wanted to tell herself it was because the men needed to remain sure and confident, unafraid, but that was only part of why she remained silent.

Maybe Wolf hadn't answered her because she was already dead to the spirit. If that was so, whether she remained behind or rode beside her husband made no difference.

27

Once the Snakes disappeared into the depression in the earth, Night Thunder urged his tired horse into a canter. After a momentary hesitation, Raven's Cry joined him with White Calf riding close behind. Night Thunder kept his attention on the snow-covered ground ahead of them. Just the same, enough of him remained apart from the act that he was acutely aware of his brother's presence.

They rode horses that were the same size with the consequence that, as always, Raven's Cry was taller than him. In the past he would have both resented and been grateful for that difference, but today it didn't matter.

The hard and driving snow slammed into his exposed face, but he merely shielded his eyes as best he could with a cupped hand and closed his thoughts around what it was to be a warrior. The world was white and endless, ancient and new, and he loved it. Even with dread about Little Rain's fate clawing at him, he loved the storm's strength and his ability to survive it. If he died today, he would die part and parcel of this land; he asked for nothing more.

When they reached the lip marking the depression's beginning, Raven's Cry pointed first to the right and then the left, indicating they should separate and approach from two directions. Then his brother gestured to White Calf, silently letting her know he wanted her to continue riding ahead—into the middle of the Snakes.

Was his brother courting White Calf's death? Denial came almost instantly as Raven's Cry's plan became clear. If White Calf rode, shouting, into the middle of the raiders, her unexpected presence would hopefully startle them and perhaps panic their horses. Before they could figure out what was happening, he and Raven's Cry would attack from either side. Their goal was simple, grab the packhorses and run, if possible. If not, they would fight like the Blackfeet braves they were. If the spirits remained with White Calf as they always had, she could easily plow through the Snakes and disappear untouched. And if not—

Without saying anything, Raven's Cry swung his horse away and quickly disappeared into the storm. Night Thunder did the same, silently cursing because he wasn't mounted on Deep Scar. His last glimpse of White Calf was of her leaning low over her horse while she prodded it into a hard run.

Alone, he counted off the amount of time it would take her to reach the Snakes, then as his horse began the sliding descent into the narrow valley, he unsheathed his knife and held it ready because with the poor visibility, he didn't dare risk an arrow striking either his brother or White Calf.

For too long there was nothing except his white-coated world and then, suddenly, he heard White Calf's seemingly endless, high-pitched shriek and spotted the Snakes and horses. Heard them.

Although he couldn't make out White Calf's form, he guessed she'd already ridden into the middle of the Snakes because they were no longer plodding ahead but stopping and whirling and shouting while trying to retain control over their startled horses.

A Snake warrior leading three pack animals was closest to him. Fastening his attention on the lead rope, he galloped at the Snake and with a short, slashing motion, severed the rope. The packhorses stopped almost immediately, but instead of going after them, with a quick prayer for forgiveness, he bore down on the Snake.

When he was close enough to touch his enemy, he again lifted his knife, but although he was tempted, he didn't aim at a human chest. Instead, he drove the tip into the horse's flank, careful not to lose hold of his weapon.

Squealing, the frantic animal bucked and whirled as if trying to bite its wound. Unprepared, the Snake struggled to remain seated. As he did, Night Thunder opened his mouth and howled, the sound long and low and yet sharp, a wolf cry. Snorting now, the wounded horse dropped his head and plunged into the storm.

Although the three pack horses were milling about, he doubted they'd stampede for any distance because they were tired and being lashed together prevented them from moving about freely. Still, their presence created the distraction he needed.

Leaving them to their inexplicable fears, he strained to locate the rest of the Blackfeet horses. However, the wind and snow made that difficult, and he rode in a searching pattern until he found himself only a few feet from five riderless horses. These too were tied together but unburdened; one was Deep Scar, his head high and eyes alert.

Whoever had been in charge of the five had left them, a realization that sent dread burrowing deep inside him, because if the Snake had attacked Raven's Cry or White Calf they might need him.

"Raven's Cry!" he called. "Where are you?"

His brother didn't answer, but he caught the urgent sounds of struggle, and although he wished he had time to climb onto Deep Scar's back, he pushed his mount in that direction. Finally the storm gave up enough of its secrets that he spotted White Calf. She was still mounted but fighting someone who'd grabbed her hair and was trying to drag her toward him.

"Raven's Cry!" he bellowed when maybe he should have been calling to the sacred white calf "Raven's Cry!"

He was four horse lengths away from White Calf and then three but before it became two, something materialized at the corner of his eye. The shadow revealed itself as a well-blanketed Snake on a tall, black horse, and he immediately whirled to face the new danger.

Blood pounded in his temple, and his lungs could barely keep up with his body's need for air, but he felt alive! Alive and strong, determined. Staring into what might be his death and not flinching.

"Run, Snake!" he taunted. "Run now or begin your death cry!"

A short distance away, Night Thunder's warning and the challenge he'd just issued echoed inside Raven's Cry. He stared frantically in the direction the words had come from, but the storm was playing a deadly game with him, making it impossible for him to make sense of what he needed to. He wanted to demand that Night Thunder tell him more, but that might draw even more Snakes to his brother.

The snow was a blanket, sheltering fog and night. Feeling invisible, he slipped through it as his eyes and ears and nose groped for understanding. A prayer chanted inside him, not that he would live to see tomorrow, but that his brother and wife would.

Then he heard White Calf cry out, the sound much different from when she'd been trying to confuse the Snakes.

Rage and fear blinded him, stripped caution from him, killed the prayer. He dug his knees into his horse's heaving sides, not caring whether he was risking the animal's life during the blind rush. His wife needed him; nothing else mattered.

There, movement that didn't dance to the wind's tune. People on horseback, snow falling and coating them and the snow being thrown off by the frantic struggle. The smallest figure was bent low over its horse and then he could see the figure's long braids and a large hand wrapped around the locks.

White Calf screamed again. The sound ended in an explosion of air as she was hauled off her horse and struck the ground. Snow billowed up around her, half swallowing her and, she hoped, hopefully cushioning her fall. Her attacker had already catapulted off his horse and was following her down.

Raven's Cry felt his thigh and calf muscles gathering. At the same time, the fingers that gripped his knife tightened and, giving no thought to personal danger, he dove at the struggling figures.

He hit the Snake in the side, which sent both of them tumbling on top of White Calf. He could barely feel her under the thick layers she wore and prayed she hadn't been injured. Only after wrenching both himself and the Snake off White Calf did he realize he'd lost his knife. Cursing himself, the storm he hated with every fiber in him, and the Snake he hated even more, he plunged his hand into the snow and searched frantically, but his fingers were already becoming numb, and if he didn't find his weapon soon, he wouldn't be able to use it.

Something bit into his side, the sudden sharpness turning him into an animal under attack. He spun away from what might kill him, but instead of running like a terrified deer, he plowed his feet into the snow and faced his foe. Something that rivaled a growl escaped his throat.

The Snake was armed with a short knife that hungrily lapped up the flakes falling on it. The weapon was so close that if Raven's Cry could have lifted his legs, he could have kicked it out of his enemy's grasp, but the snow that was both friend and foe held him prisoner.

The same was true for the Snake, a reality that might save his life. White Calf had gotten to her knees and was staring up at him through eyes that were as dark as winter clouds. Her look turned him hungry with the need to protect her, and, still growling, he lowered his head and drove himself into the Snake's belly.

Even as he propelled his knife forward, the Snake was being bent backward; Raven's Cry wrenched himself to the side, the act freeing his feet. By contrast, the Snake remained rooted in place, his knees giving way as Raven's Cry ground into him, muscles straining to bridge the impossible gap, straining and then losing the battle.

A bellow of pain and anger buried itself in Raven's Cry, and if White Calf said anything, he couldn't hear her. He thought he heard something snap and wondered if he'd broken the Snake's knee, but he didn't dare think about that as long as his enemy remained armed.

His madly searching fingers found thick fur and beneath that hide which made it impossible to inflict any more damage than he already had. He was too close to the Snake to keep him in focus and prayed the Snake was at the same disadvantage.

Feel my strength, my weight! Buckle beneath it!

A sudden warning screamed inside him, spun him in a new direction. Another Snake had joined the first, but instead of coming to his companion's aid, the newcomer had grabbed White Calf around the throat. Her mouth hung open in a silent scream, and for a moment their eyes met, saying nothing and everything. Then she began sliding inside herself, her world narrowing down to nothing except a fight to breathe. To survive.

Night Thunder! Where are you?

Heedless to any danger to himself, Raven's Cry returned his attention to the Snake he'd been battling, not because White Calf didn't matter but because dead, he'd be no use to her. He'd been afraid to reach for the enemy's knife because its deadly blade might cripple him, but that was no longer important.

The crippled Snake responded to his first desperate grab for the weapon by swinging it in an arch that forced Raven's Cry to retreat, but before the Snake could bring the weapon back around, Raven's Cry lunged.

His numb fingers closed around a thick wrist and he squeezed with all the strength in him, nails grinding into and tearing vulnerable flesh. At the same time, he again bore down on the Snake, pressing against his knees, punishing.

"Aye!" the Snake bellowed.

Raven's Cry twisted his hand first one way and then the other as if it was possible to tear his enemy's wrist apart.

"Aye!"

Sweat poured off Raven's Cry but cooled the moment air reached it; still he continued to feel bathed in sweat, was strengthened by it.

Under his fingers, he felt the Snake's grip slacken and then release. Through dimmed vision, he saw the knife begin to sink into the snow. Releasing the Snake's wrist, he plunged his fingers after the weapon. He thought the blade had punctured the webbing between his thumb and forefinger, but he couldn't be sure, and it didn't matter.

The handle was a lump around which his fingers awkwardly clung. White Calf's mouth was still open, her fingers clamped around the dark paws that shut down her throat. She looked at nothing.

Brother, I need you! Brother, are you alive?

The wounded Snake beneath him cried out at the same moment Raven's Cry did and their voices rose together to split the frigid air. Lost to everything except his wife's need, he again wrenched his feet free, took a stumbling, thudding step, and drove the knife at her tormentor.

With a bellow like a dying buffalo, the Snake released White Calf. Although everything he was and had ever been screamed at him to see to her needs, Raven's Cry didn't dare allow himself to be distracted. Instead, he split his attention between both the man thrashing in the snow while trying to grab hold of his knees and the one staring at the steaming, crimson flow coming from his chest.

There'd been nothing except this battle, this place, this moment, but now Raven's Cry became aware of heaving breaths exploding from deep chests—his and the two Snakes and, please, White Calf's. There was another sound, a rapid plunging and sucking muffled by snow.

"Raven's Cry, now!" Night Thunder commanded. "We must leave!"

Alive! You are alive! He wanted to sing his gratitude and thanks and relief but White Calf hadn't moved and that terrified him. A moment ago, the warrior he was had known it was vital to keep his eye on the enemy, but the Snakes now became nothing. His burning leg muscles screamed in protest as he forced himself toward his wife, and then his arms felt full as he lifted her and held her against him.

She wasn't breathing.

"White Calf, no! Not you! No, not you!"

"Raven's Cry, we must—"

"I cannot leave. Not without her."

He would cover her body with his, wrap himself around her so no Snake weapons would ever find her. In his dream world, she would remain safe and warm, needing nothing except him.

It would be the same for him. Forever.

"Raven's Cry, we must—Hand her to me!"

Yes, that made sense. Yes, he could do that, ignoring his waning strength and tortured muscles and lifting her up so that Night Thunder could haul her on horseback with him. She looked like summer-dry grass untouched by a breeze and he thought he would die from looking at her ruined form . . .

. . . and then the grass stirred.

Despite the turmoil and urgency, Night Thunder had managed to round up a total of seven horses after wounding but not killing the Snake who'd confronted him. Deep Scar was the only horse who hadn't first fought him. Instead, rumbling low in his throat, the stallion had pressed his head against his chest. Then Night Thunder had breathed into his horse's nostrils and they'd remained together for precious seconds before he'd mounted him and gone looking for his brother and White Calf.

When he'd seen that White Calf was indeed alive, Raven's Cry had clamored onto the nearest horse's back, grabbed two of the lead ropes, and galloped after his brother and his wife. Their progress put him in mind of deer trying to plow through endless powdery snow, but the Snakes weren't following them—maybe because he'd crippled their leader.

Once he'd been certain of their safety, he'd asked Night Thunder to stop. His wife was still fighting to breathe, the sound hurting him as much as it must hurt her, but at least she had the strength to settle herself on a sturdy pinto. When she straightened and looked at him, really looked at him, he extended his hand to her and she took it. From then on, they rode side by side, fingers intertwined. Silent.

Because he was riding ahead of them, Night Thunder hadn't

been aware of the joining until he glanced back at them. The small, hard snowflakes that had been punishing them for so long had been replaced by fat, lazy leaves of white and the wind no longer cut as sharply as it had before—maybe because Wind Maker had decided to smile on Blackfeet today. He had always loved the snow when it was like this, gentle and playful, and might one day love it again.

He'd seen the first Snake attack White Calf, but before he could reach her, his brother had appeared. It had been important, vital, that he reclaim Deep Scar and secure the pack animals carrying the buffalo meat, but that wasn't why he'd turned his attention to the horses. In a way that went beyond his comprehension, he'd known that that battle had been Raven's Cry's, that if White Calf was to live, his brother had to give her the gift.

Raven's Cry had and they were together, moving as one. United while he—

"Night Thunder, where are you going?" Raven's Cry asked, the words startling him.

Blinking, he looked around, but he'd been inside himself too long and didn't know where they were.

"This is not the way to our people," his brother pointed out, his tone gentle.

Not the way home.

28

"Be careful. Please."

"I will."

White Calf gave him a look which said she didn't trust him to concern himself with his safety, but Night Thunder barely acknowledged it. How could he when his body hummed with energy, or maybe desperation when he wanted neither thing?

"Remember this, brother," Raven's Cry said. "You are named for the thunder that rolls across the night sky, but Thunder is a powerful spirit. Never controllable."

"I know." How he knew!

"Do you? I wish I did not have to say this again, but I must. Once you walked with fear in your heart. It lived in your eyes and revealed what you wanted to keep to yourself."

Raven's Cry had let go of White Calf as the three of them stood talking, but his knee nearly touched hers, and she seemed to be leaning toward him. When she stared at her husband, her mouth slackened and softened and her eyes came alive. Night Thunder took in those things, but only briefly, because until he knew whether Little Rain still lived, nothing else mattered.

That need, like Thunder's power, was beyond his control.

"I was unsure of myself, yes," he admitted. "I looked inside myself and found things that no warrior should, but that is in the past."

"I know about your courage; I have seen it, experienced it. Still, I am afraid for you." This came from White Calf. "Never forget, Death walks this land."

"Are you certain?" Raven's Cry asked. "I thought—perhaps it reached for you but because I willed you to live, prayed to the spirits to keep you with me, Death had spent itself."

"I—I know, my husband." White Calf's eyes brimmed with tears. "I felt your strengh keeping me in this world and took some for myself, but Death—I feel it yet. It—"

"But you do not know who it stalks." Night Thunder sucked in cold air and courage.

"No. I wish . . ." Her eyes squeezed shut, and she pulled her hand out from under her blanket and covered her chest with it. "I need Death to speak to me," she admitted, her voice raspy. "I—I order it to do so, but—I tell it that I have seen into it and had it touch me and yet I remain alive—because of my husband."

Swaying slightly, she blinked back tears. "I do not fear it for myself because Raven's Cry is beside me, but Death continues to hide its truth from me." She coughed and rubbed her throat.

"Listen to her," Raven's Cry insisted. He sounded, not full of himself, but accepting of something that defied comprehension. "Her wisdom—"

"I know about her wisdom. Her magic. I will never doubt it." *But I do not dare allow it to guide my steps today. Those things I must do for myself.*

"Perhaps you should," White Calf whispered, as if she knew what he was thinking. "If I cannot hand you what you need to know, how can you trust anything I say?"

"White Calf, do not make everything that is Blackfoot your burden," he told her. "I believe the spirits have set a journey for me. It is not your task to show me the way, or for my brother to travel it with me."

Raven's Cry stared at him.

"Take those things without explanation that exist inside you, both of you," he told them, feeling both wise and old. "Nurture them and listen to their truth. But do not think that you must walk my walk for me."

Raven's Cry started to protest, but White Calf nodded and put a restraining hand on her husband's arm. "Your brother speaks from his heart," she said. Her voice threatened to give out on her, and yet it carried deep strength. "It is time for that heart to guide him."

His heart, Night Thunder pondered once he was alone, once that unknown but compelling force inside him had broken free and taken over. What did his heart have to do with today?

He was heading toward Cree country because if Little Rain had escaped the Snakes and was able to travel, nothing would matter to her except getting back to her people. *Her* people, not the Blackfeet.

She was on foot and probably had nothing to eat with her and maybe not enough to protect her against the weather, but as long as she could move, she'd struggle to return home. He'd seen her strength and courage and knew of her love for her people, even her twisted father. Like him when he'd faced danger, she'd do what she had to.

If he found her, he'd give her the horse he'd brought with him, not so she could accompany him to where the Blackfeet were but so her journey to her people would be easier. She didn't want him and he didn't want her; surely not.

He'd taken her from her people and it was his responsibility to see that she returned to them.

And if she and her baby were dead, maybe he'd take her body to her father.

That was all.

Night had already crept onto the horizon and was making its inexorable way into the sky. Most of the clouds had cleared away and the weather promised to turn bitterly cold. Even Deep Scar plodded with his head swaying, and Night Thunder knew they couldn't go much farther. If he stopped now, the two horses might be able to paw through the snow for something to eat, but if he waited, ice would crust over everything.

He hadn't given enough thought to how he'd stay warm tonight. Raven's Cry had insisted on giving him two extra blankets, and if he could get the horses to lay down close to each other, they'd provide him with needed warmth. He should be looking for shelter now while he could see a little, but with every crunching step, he was reminded that Little Rain—if she was alive—was on foot and ill-equipped to survive another prairie night.

White Calf knew which spirits listened to desperate prayers, and because Bunch of Lodges had been his father as well as the shaman, he'd absorbed some of his father's knowledge. He'd already sent out messages to Thunder and Mother Earth to look after Little Rain and deny Death its victory, but maybe they hadn't heard him, or if they had, they didn't care because they were Blackfeet spirits and Little Rain was a Cree. Weren't they? Knowing Little Rain had changed his beliefs on so many things—confused him and made him question things he'd always accepted.

Faced with these questions, he'd gone deep inside himself for what he knew of the woman. Her thoughts were uncomplicated by the kinds of doubts and questions that had once consumed him. Instead, she saw the prairies and mountains as her home, was as much at peace in them as she was skinning a buffalo or gathering firewood. She knew winter's rhythm and the wisdom and necessity of listening to the wind.

She might not have tried to leave the Blackfeet camp and make her way home after he'd taken her because she'd been treated with kindness, and White Calf had wanted her there, and the distance between the two tribes had been so far to travel, but everything had changed now. She knew which direction the journey to Cree land took and must be on it, if the land she loved and Wind Maker hadn't killed her.

No! he ordered himself again. No, he wouldn't allow himself to be crushed by that thought. Instead, he'd follow the steps he prayed she'd taken. He'd become Cree, walk Cree, think Cree.

Think like Little Rain.

The howl, when it came, was a softly beaten drum, a bone flute, a whistle clenched in the teeth of a warrior during the Sun Dance. He heard it in his mind and muscles, nerves and heart, and stopped.

Already a few stars were working their way out from their day hiding places. The moon, shy and reluctant, would be nearly full when it revealed itself. His grandfather's grandfather had approached buffalo by draping a wolf skin over him and pretending to be one, but what he'd just heard hadn't come from his long dead ancestor.

Neither, he believed, had the sound been made by a living wolf.

"I hear you, Wolf," he announced, unafraid. "Hear and wait for your wisdom."

Both horses were already pawing at the snow when the second howl came. Neither animal stopped what they were doing, but it didn't matter because Wolf had no message for horses.

"What is it?" Night Thunder asked. "Are you—do you speak for Death?"

A low yip followed the question, but he couldn't determine its meaning. Urging Deep Scar on, he turned his head to the side so he could hear more clearly. What little remained of the wind reminded him of a sleeping child, all innocent breath and promise.

Wolf spoke to him again, the low barking-howl floating on the breeze, going on and on until it became as much a part of him as Little Rain had been.

Now the newborn stars illuminated the gray predator, showing its proud carriage and intellect, its courage and agelessness. Death could look like that, hiding its deadly reality behind deep and deceptively gentle eyes. Still, Night Thunder left Deep Scar and the other horse and walked closer, up the slight incline to where a bush the height of a man pulled what it needed for life out of the rocky earth. The bush itself lay nearly buried under a soft mountain of white, part of the land, as much a part of it as Night Thunder felt. When he was only a few feet away, the wolf stopped looking at him and shifted its gaze to the plant's base.

A mound, curled in upon itself.

Crying wordlessly, Night Thunder started running. Although the snow lapped at his legs and hips, he forced himself on until he felt swallowed by Wolf's gaze, and by reality.

Little Rain—he'd already known it would be her—lay half under the bush. If she'd crawled closer to it, she would be like a bear in a cave, but maybe she'd run out of strength before she could do that.

Maybe she was dead.

The next howl was both plaintive and unreal, low and yet strong, mournful. Night Thunder's attention flickered briefly to the watching, waiting wolf but didn't stay on it. Instead, he dropped to his knees, as if by covering Little Rain's body with his, he could keep Death from her.

"Little Rain. Please, you cannot—I am here. Here."

She didn't move, and if she was breathing, he couldn't tell. Something cold clenched his insides, instantly weakening him. He thought he knew the meaning of terror, had faced and defeated and walked beyond it, but nothing had prepared him for this emotion. His heart raged and burned.

"No, please! No!"

A movement, maybe. A sigh, maybe. Or perhaps he only imagined what he needed.

"Little Rain, please."

When his plea went unanswered, he dug at her with frantic fingers, turning her over so he could see her face. She looked so pale he wasn't sure he could bear it, her flesh tinged silver as if from the moon. Her teeth were clamped together, her mouth stretched and white over them. White Calf had been right about Death's presence after all. Death had won and the loneliness and sorrow in him came close to killing him. If he could bring himself to release her, he would have lifted his face and arms to the sky and howled his misery.

"Little Rain?" he sobbed.

A moan, yes! "Little Rain? Please, please be alive."

"N–ight Thunder?"

"Creator Sun, thank you," he moaned as his senses recorded the wonderful fact that what he'd heard was her whisper and not the wind. Pulling her to him, he wrapped himself around her cold body, rocking her the way a mother does a crying child. Emotion made it impossible for him to do more or less than that.

"What . . ." She burrowed herself into him, seeking his warmth. "You are here?"

"Yes." *Thunder spirit, thank you!*

"H–ow?"

The question was so complex that he couldn't begin to answer her. Instead of trying, he lifted her icy hands to his mouth and breathed on them over and over again until he was lightheaded and she'd begun to move her fingers. Throughout his efforts, she remained nestled against him, their warmth blending together.

He didn't know how long they remained like that and he would have been content to hold her until morning if a thought didn't occur to him. Although it was too small and new for it to have made its presence known, he imagined her baby nestled safe— please—within her. But, White Calf had spoken of Death. Just because Little Rain—

"You are all right? You and . . ."

"My baby? Yes." She sobbed. "I had to live for it, had to stay alive so it would be born."

Relief so strong that he had no words for it coursed through him. He continued to hold her, his attention now riveted on her belly, his silent prayer of thanksgiving going out to all spirits.

"What is it?" she demanded with unexpected strength. "You wanted—wanted it gone from me?"

"No! Never."

"Then what—"

"I prayed to the spirits that I would find you alive," he told her. "but Death travels with the storm and I feared . . ."

"Feared? For me?"

"And for your child," he said simply, when it wasn't simple at all. She must have understood the emotion behind his words because for a long time she said nothing, only breathed when he did.

"Wolf has been with me," she whispered at length. "From the moment I fled the Snakes."

He wanted to know what had compelled her to run from them and what she'd done since then and how she'd survived, but those things, like how he'd found her, could wait.

"You are all right," he managed, his throat aching. "All right."

"I—know. You—thank you."

That silenced him. He realized she was no longer crying, and that Wolf was still there, patient, watching and waiting. He could hear the horses as they attacked the freezing snow, chewed, swallowed.

The wind, although a shadow of what it had been during the day, remained with them, whispering of things known only to itself. It occurred to him that he had no idea where they were, but it wouldn't matter until morning.

"You came looking for me?" she asked, her voice shaky. "Why?"

"I didn't want you to die," he said; everything in him felt exposed but even if he'd known how to shield himself, he wouldn't have tried.

"But why?" she demanded. "We came together as enemies. I carry the child of the man who killed your brother."

"The man I killed, yes, but that is behind us, and this baby will not know of those things for a long, long time, and by then I pray it will not matter."

"Can that be? You and I will know."

You and I.

"I brought two horses," he said, because if he spoke of other things, she might know he'd stepped inside her heart or maybe had carried it inside him all the time he'd been traveling and that's how he'd been able to find her. "One is yours."

"Is it?"

"To do with whatever you want."

"Whatever . . ."

"When you are ready to return to your people . . ."

He'd fallen back into silence and darkness. Wolf was there with him and Little Rain's body pressed against his, new life cradled safe between them, but if she wanted nothing to do with him . . .

"No," she said. "No."

"You do not—"

"I tried," she whispered. Then she took a deep breath and continued in a stronger tone. "When I ran from the Snakes, at first all that mattered was that I find my village. But when I was alone and no longer so afraid, I looked at the storm, at the land. I remembered what White Calf had said about Blackfeet and Cree needing to learn the truth of each other and how I might be the one to start that journey. I listened to Wind Maker and knew He belonged to neither Blackfeet or Cree, that he is for all of us."

"Maybe he is."

"Night Thunder," she said, "because Wolf was with me, I thought much about him. He spoke to the Blackfoot woman White Calf and had messages for two Blackfeet brothers, but he also revealed himself to me, a Cree woman."

"Yes, he did."

"Maybe—maybe Wolf does not care which tribe we belong to."

"Maybe he does not," he said, thinking her incredibly wise.

"I tried to make an image of my family in my mind," she continued softly, "but that would not come. Instead—instead I saw you."

"You are certain?" he asked. Her answer meant everything and would give his heart a reason to go on beating.

"Yes. I did not want it, told myself it was impossible. But then I stopped fighting and listened to . . ."

"To what?"

"My heart."

"Your heart?"

She sighed, the sound long and low. "It knows the truth, where I—we—now belong. If you will have us."

Us. Woman and child. Perhaps the howl he heard existed only in his mind, and maybe Wolf was speaking for him, saying things he was incapable of. When he rested his hand on her belly, Little Rain wrapped her arms around his neck, her lips brushing his flesh. She trembled, but maybe not from the cold. Her breath was still ragged and might falter at any moment. If it did, he'd hold her through the next wave of weakness.

And when it was over they'd talk about the journey each of their hearts had taken and how, in the summer, their hearts would be joined by another, but now, tonight, they'd listen to the wind and watch the stars and moon and Wolf would sing for them.

They'd cease to be Blackfoot and Cree and become the same.

That was all he knew. It was enough.

Epilogue

When she first woke, White Calf tried to recapture the nothingness of sleep by snuggling against Raven's Cry's broad back, but before long, the arm she was resting on began to tingle, and she got up. Although she didn't want to disturb Raven's Cry, who'd been with the other members of the Bulls until late, she nevertheless knelt and kissed his exposed shoulder before leaving him.

He'd had no more dreams with meaning, and although he'd asked her if there was anything he could or should do to welcome them back, she'd told him it didn't matter; he was her husband and she loved him—loved the strength and kindness of him, needed him to guide her through her own visions. At first he didn't say anything in reply, but later, while they lay with their bodies tangled together, he'd told her she was right.

Dawn had just begun to show itself, and her first thought upon leaving the tepee was to replenish the coals still glowing in the fire ring the men had sat around for so long last night. However, someone had already tended to that chore. Instead of going in search of wood to add to the small pile near the fire, she first brushed ice crystals off a rock and then sat on it, stretching her legs toward the flames. The nights were still cold and it had recently snowed, but the wind's teeth were no longer as sharp as they'd been at the height of winter, and before much longer, the Blackfeet would leave this home. The thought of setting up at one of the spring-fed creeks filled her with anticipation, but she'd have to be patient, since the move would take place only once the warriors had made that decision.

A smile played at the corners of her mouth as she imagined the endless pipe smoking and lengthy conversations that would have to take place before anything else. She'd have to ask her husband if he ever grew impatient with all that talk, but maybe he would look at her in confusion since men—particularly Bulls—seemed to gain a great deal of pleasure from talk, so much of it boasting. Besides, she was so proud of his newly earned status within the men's most revered society that she would never make fun of its members' ways.

Reaching down, she picked up a long stick and used that to stir the fire. When she drew her gaze off her handiwork, she spotted Little Rain approaching, her arms full of branches. Hurrying over to her, she took half of the load.

"You are up early," she observed as the two women sat down on the rocks that ringed the pit. "I thought you said you could not get enough sleep these days."

Chuckling, Little Rain patted her stomach. "This one needs many naps and when it does, it wants its mother to rest with it. But when it is awake, there is no sleeping for me. What brings you out when the others have not stirred?" She indicated the many tepees settled within the small valley the tribe had selected, her gesture taking in several long frames that sagged under the weight of the buffalo meat strips drying on them.

"Thoughts," White Calf answered vaguely. "Besides, my husband may sleep for a long time yet."

"So may mine. I do not know what keeps the tongues of warriors wagging for so long," Little Rain said, her voice trailing off at the end. After a moment of silence, she went on. "It still seems unreal that I am married again when I believed that would never happen."

"So much of our lives is not for us to know," White Calf observed. "Last winter I was a girl and now I am a woman. And last winter Takes-Knife-at-Night was alive."

"Yes. And so was Bunch of Lodges."

White Calf nodded, and her attention briefly went to Dirty Knee Sits's lodge. Raven's Cry, Night Thunder, Little Rain, and she had barely returned with the meat cache when Dirty Knee Sits announced that she had consulted the spirits and they'd informed her that she was the one they'd chosen to take over for her dead shaman husband.

Because she was all too aware of Dirty Knee Sits's capacity for hatred, White Calf had been skeptical of Dirty Knee Sits's motives as well as her curing powers, but the rest of the tribe now believed that the older woman had been a keen observer as her husband had gone about his work. More than that, she'd made magic, and after a few days, the hunting party with Chief Sleeps Too Long at its head had returned, successful.

Sleeps Too Long, once he'd stopped boasting about his role in the buffalo hunt, had announced to the entire tribe that he, as war chief, should be the first to embrace the new shaman. Dirty Knee Sits had probably expected to remain the center of attention, but her moments of glory hadn't lasted long because by the time the tribe sat down at the feast to celebrate the hunters' success, the chief had turned the conversation on him. How much longer Dirty Knee Sits and Sleeps Too Long would continue to speak well of each other remained to be seen.

"You are quiet," Little Rain said. "What are your thoughts?"

Smiling, White Calf reached out and patted Little Rain's shoulder. "That I am glad you are here and I can call you my sister."

"I am blessed to have you as my sister," Little Rain replied, her smile echoing White Calf's. "And that it does not matter whose blood runs in one's veins. What matters is that there is love between people."

"Hm."

"You do not agree?"

"What? Of course. I was thinking . . ."

"Of what?"

"Our chief," she replied, grasping at the first thing to enter her mind. "He was so full of himself, proclaiming that only he could have guided the other hunters to the herd."

"He never told anyone that without your guidance, they would not have found anything, did he?"

"No." Although she was still distracted, White Calf shook her head. "Sleeps Too Long will live to regret his boasting."

"I think he already does. It is also my belief that the warriors will continue to meet until one and then all of them says what must be said."

Little Rain didn't need to go on because White Calf knew what was on her mind. Unable to listen to any more of Sleeps Too Long's boasting, she'd finally told the assembled tribe that it was her sight that had sent the hunters in the right direction. If anyone had a right to call attention to themselves, she said, it was the two warriors who'd attacked the thieving Snakes and taken back the precious meat the Blackfoot shaman had sacrificed himself for.

"Who do you believe our people will choose as their new chief?" Little Rain asked.

Noting that Little Rain included herself in the question, White Calf turned her full attention to answering her. It didn't take long.

"Our husbands share the same blood, the same courage. Together they will lead."

"Those are my thoughts as well. Our husbands are not so different after all, brothers in all the ways that count," Little Rain said, then stood. "It does not matter that Raven's Cry has not had another telling dream; he is a leader."

"That is what I told him, that his presence helps guide my dreams and we should not ask for more."

"Hm. Sister, I have another question of you."

"You do?"

"Yes. I prayed for the patience for you to come to me on your own but perhaps what has happened to you is too new for that. When my child is born, Night Thunder and I will travel to the Cree so my family can see, so my father can hold his grandchild and perhaps put death and hatred behind him."

"Night Thunder will go with you?"

"Yes, although he will not show himself to my father unless I believe it is safe. White Calf, I tell you that because I want to be with you when your child is born just as I want you at my side when this one comes into the world."

"My—how did you know?" White Calf managed. "You—you have the sight?"

Laughing, Little Rain held out her hands and helped White Calf to her feet. The women embraced.

"I will never be like you, but my heart is a woman's heart and my eyes are a woman's eyes, and I use those things to see the truth of you."

"I—I am glad," White Calf said, meaning it as maybe she'd never meant anything in life.

In Little Rain's arms, she absorbed her surroundings, took in the world of her people, and made a vow to spend her life walking in that world. No longer would she look into the future and fear it. Today, tomorrow, her child in her arms and her husband at her side were enough.

1